"*NEVERWHERE* displays the kind of wit, mythological invention and attention to the odd detail that will be familiar to anyone who has read Gaiman's groundbreaking comic series *The Sandman*."
San Francisco Examiner & Chronicle

"DARKLY WHIMSICAL...
The narrative whips along at a breakneck pace... There are plenty of laughs as geography takes on a mythical dimension and the Underground transforms into a house of mystery and imagination. You'll never look at the tube the same way again."
Wired

"A RICH BLEND OF OBSERVATION AND IMAGINATION—SEEDY, SCARY, CHARMING, ALIVE.
His novel offers droll Douglas Adams-type humor along with colorful characters, including satisfyingly creepy villains, and a protagonist who's neither a hero nor an anti-hero, but a person. It's a well-paced, entertaining read with a bracing core of pain and sweetness."
Minneapolis Star Tribune

"THIS IS [GAIMAN'S] DEBUT AS A SOLO NOVELIST. AND AN AUSPICIOUS DEBUT IT IS."
Rocky Mountain News

"DELIGHTFUL...Inventively horrific...
[It] draws equally from George Lucas, Monty Python,
Doctor Who, and John Milton...The chimerical
stuff of nightmare and daydream."
USA Today

"MORE THAN MERE ENTERTAINMENT...
[A] strange place where fabulous worlds
collide with mundane reality."
Seattle Times/Post Intelligencer

"A DELIRIOUS, DREAMLIKE TRIP,
A WORK OF IMAGINATIVE VIRTUOSITY.
Neverwhere is an eye-popping *Alice in Wonderland*
for the new millennium."
Mark Frost, author of *The List of 7*

"[A] DARKLY ENTERTAINING NOVEL...
Gaiman's fans shouldn't be disappointed, and it's nice
for those who haven't encountered his work before."
Detroit Free Press

"A TERRIFIC SURPRISE...
Consistently witty, suspenseful,
and hair-raisingly imaginative...
Some of the best pure storytelling around."
Kirkus Reviews

"*ALICE IN WONDERLAND* WITH A PUNK EDGE
doesn't begin to do justice to Neil Gaiman's first solo
novel, but it may serve to set the tone. Gaiman is a
master of creating and peopling his own worlds.
In *Neverwhere* he has surpassed himself, creating a
twisting tale to be treasured."
Poppy Z. Brite, author of *Exquisite Corpse*

"POETIC...FASCINATING...
GAIMAN WORKS HIS MAGIC...
[He] can create such a lovely sentence
that you just want to wrap your tongue around it
and say it in your head, over and over."
Memphis Commercial Appeal

"NEIL GAIMAN IS A STAR.
He constructs stories like some demented cook might
make a wedding cake, building layer upon layer,
including all kinds of sweet and sour in the mix."
Clive Barker

"I DIDN'T EVER WANT THIS BOOK TO END...
Hunter, Islington, Door—these characters are part of
my life now...I'm over the moon about this book."
Tori Amos

"CHARM AND WHIMSY...SEASONED WITH A
VERY ADULT-SIZED DOSE OF HORROR...
This book will take you someplace different."
Arizona Daily Star

Books by Neil Gaiman

Novels and Collections
ANANSI BOYS • AMERICAN GODS
STARDUST • SMOKE AND MIRRORS • NEVERWHERE
GOOD OMENS (*with Terry Pratchett*)

For Children
THE DAY I SWAPPED MY DAD FOR TWO GOLDFISH
THE WOLVES IN THE WALLS
(*both illustrated by Dave McKean*)
CORALINE

Graphic Novels (*with Dave McKean*)
VIOLENT CASES • SIGNAL TO NOISE • MR. PUNCH

Other
MIRRORMASK (*with Dave McKean*)

Sandman
PRELUDES & NOCTURNES • THE DOLL'S HOUSE
DREAM COUNTRY • SEASON OF MISTS • A GAME FOR YOU
FABLES AND REFLECTIONS • BRIEF LIVES • WOLDS' END
THE KINDLY ONES • THE WAKE

Death
THE HIGH COST OF LIVING • THE TIME OF YOUR LIFE

Miscellaneous Graphic Novels
THE BOOKS OF MAGIC • MIRACLEMAN: THE GOLDEN AGE
BLACK ORCHID

Nonfiction
DON'T PANIC!
GHASTLY BEYOND BELIEF (*with Kim Newman*)

NEIL GAIMAN

NEVERWHERE

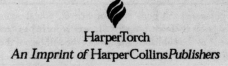

HarperTorch
An Imprint of HarperCollins*Publishers*

"I'm a Believer" written by Neil Diamond © 1996 Stonebridge Music and Colgems-EMI Music. Inc. International copyright secured. All rights reserved. Used by permission.

HARPERTORCH
An Imprint of HarperCollinsPublishers
10 East 53rd Street
New York, New York 10022-5299

Copyright © 1996, 1997 by Neil Gaiman
Excerpt from American Gods copyright © 2001 by Neil Gaiman
Excerpt from Stardust copyright © 1999 by Neil Gaiman
Back cover author photo © 1996 by Kelli Bickman
Library of Congress Catalog Card Number: 96-53681
ISBN: 0-380-78901-9

First HarperTorch paperback printing: October 2001
First Avon Books paperback printing: November 1998
First Avon Books special printing: June 1998
First Avon Books hardcover printing: July 1997

HarperCollins®, HarperTorch™, and ♦™ are trademarks of HarperCollins Publishers Inc.
Avon Trademark Reg. U.S. Pat. Off. and in Other Countries, Marca Registrada, Hecho en U.S.A.

Printed in the United States of America

Visit HarperTorch on the World Wide Web at www.harpercollins.com

30   29   28   27   26

For Lenny Henry, friend and colleague,
who made it happen all the way;
and Merrilee Heifetz, friend and agent,
who makes everything good.

I have never been to St. John's Wood. I dare not.
I should be afraid of the innumerable night of
fir trees, afraid to come upon a blood red cup
and the beating of the wings of the Eagle.

—*The Napoleon of Notting Hill*, G. K. Chesterton

If ever thou gavest hosen or shoon
Then every night and all
Sit thou down and put them on
And Christ receive thy soul

This aye night, this aye night
Every night and all
Fire and fleet and candlelight
And Christ receive they soul

If ever thou gavest meat or drink
Then every night and all
The fire shall never make thee shrink
And Christ receive thy soul

—*The Lyke Wake Dirge* (traditional)

PROLOGUE

THE NIGHT BEFORE HE WENT TO LONDON, Richard Mayhew was not enjoying himself.

He had begun the evening by enjoying himself: he had enjoyed reading the good-bye cards, and receiving the hugs from several not entirely unattractive young ladies of his acquaintance; he had enjoyed the warnings about the evils and dangers of London, and the gift of the white umbrella with the map of the London Underground on it that his friends had chipped in money to buy; he had enjoyed the first few pints of ale; but then, with each successive pint he found that he was enjoying himself significantly less; until now he was sitting and shivering on the sidewalk outside the pub in a small Scottish town, weighing the relative merits of being sick and not being sick, and not enjoying himself at all.

Inside the pub, Richard's friends continued to celebrate his forthcoming departure with an enthusiasm that, to Richard, was beginning to border on the sinister. He sat on the sidewalk and held on tightly to the rolled-up umbrella, and wondered whether going south to London was really a good idea.

"You want to keep a eye out," said a cracked old

1

voice. "They'll be moving you on before you can say Jack Robinson. Or taking you in, I wouldn't be surprised." Two sharp eyes stared out from a beaky, grimy face. "You all right?"

"Yes, thank you," said Richard. He was a fresh-faced, boyish young man, with dark, slightly curly hair and large hazel eyes; he had a rumpled, just-woken-up look to him, which made him more attractive to the opposite sex than he would ever understand or believe.

The grimy face softened. "Here, poor thing," she said, and pushed a fifty-pence piece into Richard's hand. "'Ow long you been on the streets, then?"

"I'm not homeless," explained Richard, embarrassed, attempting to give the old woman her coin back. "Please—take your money. I'm fine. I just came out here to get some air. I go to London tomorrow," he added.

She peered down at him suspiciously, then took back her fifty pence and made it vanish beneath the layers of coats and shawls in which she was enveloped. "I've been to London," she confided. "I was married in London. But he was a bad lot. Me mam told me not to go marrying outside, but I was young and beautiful, although you'd never credit it today, and I followed my heart."

"I'm sure you did," said Richard. The conviction that he was about to be sick was starting, slowly, to fade.

"Fat lot of good it done me. I been homeless, so I know what it's like," said the old woman. "That's why I thought you was. What you going to London for?"

"I've got a job," he told her proudly.

"Doing what?" she asked.

"Um, Securities," said Richard.

"I was a dancer," said the old woman, and she tottered awkwardly around the sidewalk, humming tunelessly to herself. Then she teetered from side to side like a spinning top coming to rest, and finally she stopped, facing Richard. "Hold out your hand," she told him, "and I'll tell yer fortune." He did as he was told. She put her old hand into his, and held it tightly, and then she blinked a few times, like an owl who had swallowed a mouse that was beginning to disagree with it. "You got a long way to go . . ." she said, puzzled.

"London," Richard told her.

"Not just London. . . ." The old woman paused. "Not any London I know." It started to rain then, softly. "I'm sorry," she said. "It starts with doors."

"Doors?"

She nodded. The rain fell harder, pattering on the roofs and on the asphalt of the road. "I'd watch out for doors if I were you."

Richard stood up, a little unsteadily. "All right," he said, a little unsure of how he ought to treat information of this nature. "I will. Thanks."

The pub door was opened, and light and noise spilled out into the street. "Richard? You all right?"

"Yeah, I'm fine. I'll be back in a second." The old lady was already wobbling down the street, into the pelting rain, getting wet. Richard felt he had to do something for her: he couldn't give her money, though. He hurried after her, down the narrow street, the cold rain drenching his face and hair. "Here," said Richard. He fumbled with the handle of the umbrella, trying to find the button that opened it. Then a click, and it blossomed into a huge white map of the London Underground network, each line drawn in a different color, every station marked and named.

The old woman took the umbrella, gratefully, and smiled her thanks. "You've a good heart," she told him. "Sometimes that's enough to see you safe wherever you go." Then she shook her head. "But mostly, it's not." She clutched the umbrella tightly as a gust of wind threatened to tug it away from her or pull it inside out. She wrapped her arms around it and bent almost double against the rain and the wind. Then she walked away into the rain and the night, a round white shape covered with the names of London Tube stations—Earl's Court, Marble Arch, Blackfriars, White City, Victoria, Angel, Oxford Circus . . .

Richard found himself pondering, drunkenly, whether there really was a circus at Oxford Circus: a real circus with clowns, beautiful women, and dangerous beasts. The pub door opened once more: a blast of sound, as if the pub's volume control had just been turned up high. "Richard, you idiot, it's your bloody party, and you're missing all the fun." He walked back in the pub, the urge to be sick lost in all the oddness.

"You look like a drowned rat," said someone.

"You've never seen a drowned rat," said Richard.

Someone else handed him a large whisky. "Here, get that down you. That'll warm you up. You know, you won't be able to get real Scotch in London."

"I'm sure I will," sighed Richard. Water was dripping from his hair into his drink. "They have everything in London." And he downed the Scotch, and after that someone bought him another, and then the evening blurred and broke up into fragments: afterward he remembered only the feeling that he was about to leave somewhere small and rational—a place that made sense—for somewhere huge and old that didn't; and vomiting interminably into a gutter flowing with rainwater, somewhere in the small hours of the morning; and a white shape marked with strange-colored symbols, like a little round beetle, walking away from him in the rain.

The next morning he boarded the train for the six-hour journey south that would bring him to the strange gothic spires and arches of St. Pancras Station. His mother gave him a small walnut cake that she had made for the journey and a thermos filled with tea; and Richard Mayhew went to London feeling like hell.

ONE

She had been running for four days now, a harum-scarum tumbling flight through passages and tunnels. She was hungry, and exhausted, and more tired than a body could stand, and each successive door was proving harder to open. After four days of flight, she had found a hiding place, a tiny stone burrow, under the world, where she would be safe, or so she prayed, and at last she slept.

Mr. Croup had hired Ross at the last Floating Market, which had been held in Westminster Abbey. "Think of him," he told Mr. Vandemar, "as a canary."

"Sings?" asked Mr. Vandemar.

"I doubt it; I sincerely and utterly doubt it." Mr. Croup ran a hand through his lank orange hair. "No, my fine friend, I was thinking metaphorically—more along the lines of the birds they take down mines." Mr. Vandemar nodded, comprehension dawning slowly: yes, a canary. Mr. Ross had no other resemblance to a canary. He was huge—almost as big as Mr. Vandemar—and extremely grubby, and quite hairless, and he said very little, although he had made a point of telling each of them that he liked to kill things, and he was good at it; and this amused Mr. Croup and Mr. Vandemar. But he was a canary, and he never knew it. So Mr. Ross went first, in his filthy T-shirt and his crusted blue-jeans, and Croup and Vandemar walked behind him, in their elegant black suits.

There are four simple ways for the observant to tell Mr. Croup and Mr. Vandemar apart: first, Mr. Vandemar is two and a half heads taller than Mr. Croup; second, Mr. Croup has eyes of a faded china blue, while Mr. Vandemar's eyes are brown; third, while Mr. Vandemar fashioned the rings he wears on his right hand out of the skulls of four ravens, Mr. Croup has no obvious jewelery; fourth, Mr. Croup likes words, while Mr. Vandemar is always hungry. Also, they look nothing at all alike.

A rustle in the tunnel darkness; Mr. Vandemar's knife was in his hand, and then it was no longer in his hand, and it was quivering gently almost thirty feet away. He walked over to his knife and picked it up by the hilt. There was a gray rat impaled on the blade, its mouth opening and closing impotently as the life fled. He crushed its skull between finger and thumb.

"Now, there's one rat that won't be telling any more tales," said Mr. Croup. He chuckled at his own joke. Mr. Vandemar did not respond. "Rat. Tales. Get it?"

Mr. Vandemar pulled the rat from the blade and began to munch on it, thoughtfully, head first. Mr. Croup slapped it out of his hands. "Stop that," he said. Mr. Vandemar put his knife away, a little sullenly. "Buck up," hissed Mr. Croup, encouragingly.

"There will always be another rat. Now: onward. Things to do. People to damage."

Three years in London had not changed Richard, although it had changed the way he perceived the city. Richard had originally imagined London as a gray city, even a black city, from pictures he had seen, and he was surprised to find it filled with color. It was a city of red brick and white stone, red buses and large black taxis, bright red mailboxes and green grassy parks and cemeteries.

It was a city in which the very old and the awkwardly new jostled each other, not uncomfortably, but without respect; a city of shops and offices and restaurants and homes, of parks and churches, of ignored monuments and remarkably unpalatial palaces; a city of hundreds of districts with strange names—Crouch End, Chalk Farm, Earl's Court, Marble Arch—and oddly distinct identities; a noisy, dirty, cheerful, troubled city, which fed on tourists, needed them as it despised them, in which the average speed of transportation through the city had not increased in three hundred years, following five hundred years of fitful road-widening and unskillful compromises between the needs of traffic, whether horse-drawn, or, more recently, motorized, and the needs of pedestrians; a city inhabited by and teeming with people of every color and manner and kind.

When he had first arrived, he had found London huge, odd, fundamentally incomprehensible, with only the Tube map, that elegant multicolored topographical display of underground railway lines and stations, giving it any semblance of order. Gradually he realized that the Tube map was a handy fiction that made life easier but bore no resemblance to the reality of the shape of the city above. It was like belonging to a political party, he thought once, proudly, and then, having tried to explain the resemblance between the Tube map and politics, at a party, to a cluster of bewildered strangers, he had decided in the future to leave political comment to others.

He continued, slowly, by a process of osmosis and white knowledge (which is like white noise, only more useful), to comprehend the city, a process that accelerated when he realized that the actual City of London itself was no bigger than a square mile, stretching from Aldgate in the east to Fleet Street and the law courts of the Old Bailey in the west, a tiny municipality, now home to London's financial institutions, and that that was where it had all begun.

Two thousand years before, London had been a little Celtic village on the north shore of the Thames, which the Romans had encountered, then settled in. London had grown, slowly, until, roughly a thousand years later, it met the tiny Royal City of Westminster immediately to the west, and, once London Bridge had been built, London touched the town of Southwark directly across the river; and it continued to grow, fields and woods and marshland slowly vanishing beneath the flourishing town, and it continued to expand, encountering other little villages and hamlets as it grew, like Whitechapel and Deptford to the east, Hammersmith and Shepherd's Bush to the west, Camden and Islington in the north, Battersea and Lambeth across the Thames to the south, absorbing all of them, just as a pool of mercury encounters and incorporates smaller beads of mercury, leaving only their names behind.

London grew into something huge and contradictory. It was a good place, and a fine city, but there is a price to be paid for all good places, and a price that all good places have to pay.

After a while, Richard found himself taking London for granted; in time, he began to pride himself on having visited none of the sights of London (except for the Tower of London, when his Aunt Maude came down to the city for a weekend, and Richard found himself her reluctant escort).

But Jessica changed all that. Richard found himself, on otherwise sensible weekends, accompanying her to places like the National Gallery and the Tate Gallery, where he learned that walking around museums too long hurts your feet, that the great art treasures of the world all blur into each other after a while, and that it is almost beyond the human capacity for belief to accept how much museum cafeterias will brazenly charge for a slice of cake and a cup of tea.

"Here's your tea and your éclair," he told her. "It would have cost less to buy one of those Tintorettos."

"Don't exaggerate," said Jessica cheerfully. "Anyway, there aren't any Tintorettos at the Tate."

"I should have had that cherry cake," said Richard. "Then they would have been able to afford another Van Gogh."

Richard had met Jessica in France, on a weekend trip to Paris two years earlier; had in fact discovered her in the Louvre, trying to find the group of his office friends who had organized the trip. Staring up at an immense sculpture, he had stepped backwards into Jessica, who was admiring an extremely large and historically important diamond. He tried to apologize to her in French, which he did not speak, gave up, and began to apologize in English, then tried to apologize in French for having to apologize in English, until he noticed that Jessica was about as English as it was possible for any one person to be. By this time she decided he should buy her an expensive French sandwich and some overpriced carbonated apple juice, by way of apology, and, well, that was the start of it all, really. He had never been able to convince Jessica that he wasn't the kind of person who went to art galleries after that.

On weekends when they did not go to art galleries or to museums, Richard would trail behind Jessica as she went shopping, which she did, on the whole, in affluent Knightsbridge, a short walk and an even shorter taxi ride from her apartment in a Kensington mews. Richard would accompany Jessica on her tours of such huge and intimidating emporia as Harrods and Harvey Nichols, stores where Jessica was able to purchase anything, from jewelry, to books, to the week's groceries.

Richard had been awed by Jessica, who was beautiful, and often quite funny, and was certainly going somewhere. And Jessica saw in Richard an enormous amount of potential, which, properly harnessed by the right woman, would have made him the perfect matrimonial accessory. If only he were a little more focused, she would murmur to herself, and so she gave him books with titles like *Dress for Success* and *A Hundred and Twenty-Five Habits of Successful Men*, and books on how to run a business like a military campaign, and Richard always said thank you, and always intended to read them. In Harvey Nichols's men's fashion department she would pick out for him the kinds of clothes she thought that he should wear—and he wore them, during the week, anyway; and, a year to the day after their first encounter, she told him she thought it was time that they went shopping for an engagement ring.

"Why do you go out with her?" asked Gary, in Corporate Accounts, eighteen months later. "She's terrifying."

Richard shook his head. "She's really sweet, once you get to know her."

Gary put down the plastic troll doll he had picked up from Richard's desk. "I'm surprised she still lets you play with these."

"The subject has never come up," said Richard, picking up one of the creatures from his desk. It had a shock of Day-Glo orange hair, and a slightly baffled expression, as if it were lost.

And the subject had indeed come up. Jessica had, however, convinced herself that Richard's troll collection was a mark of endearing eccentricity, comparable to Mr. Stockton's collection of angels. Jessica was in the process of organizing a traveling exhibition of Mr. Stockton's angel collection, and she had come to the conclusion that great men always collected something. In actuality Richard did not really collect trolls. He had found a troll on the sidewalk outside the office, and, in a vain attempt at injecting a little personality into his working world, he had placed it on his computer monitor. The others had followed over the next few months, gifts from colleagues who had noticed that Richard had a penchant for the ugly little creatures. He had taken the gifts and positioned them, strategically, around his desk, beside the telephones and the framed photograph of Jessica.

The photograph had a yellow Post-it note stuck to it.

It was a Friday afternoon. Richard had noticed that events were cowards: they didn't occur singly, but instead they would run in packs and leap out at him all at once. Take this particular Friday, for example. It was, as Jessica had pointed out to him at least a dozen times in the last month, the most important day of his life. So it was unfortunate that, despite the Post-it note Richard had left on his fridge door at home, and the other Post-it note he had placed on the photograph of Jessica on his desk, he had forgotten about it completely and utterly.

Also, there was the Wandsworth report, which was overdue and taking up most of his head. Richard checked another row of figures; then he noticed that page 17 had vanished, and he set it up to print out again; and another page down, and he knew that if he were only left alone to finish it . . . if, miracle of miracles, the phone did not ring. . . . It rang. He thumbed the speakerphone.

"Hello? Richard? The managing director needs to know when he'll have the report."

Richard looked at his watch. "Five minutes, Sylvia. It's almost wrapped up. I just have to attach the P & L projection."

"Thanks, Dick. I'll come down for it." Sylvia was, as she liked to explain, "the MD's PA," and she moved in an atmosphere of crisp efficiency. He thumbed the speakerphone off; it rang again, immediately. "Richard," said the speaker, with Jessica's voice, "it's Jessica. You haven't forgotten, have you?"

"Forgotten?" He tried to remember what he could have forgotten. He looked at Jessica's photograph for inspiration and found all the inspiration he could have needed in the shape of a yellow Post-it note stuck to her forehead.

"Richard? Pick up the telephone."

He picked up the phone, reading the Post-it note as he did so. "Sorry, Jess. No, I hadn't forgotten. Seven P.M., at Ma Maison Italiano. Should I meet you there?"

"Jessica, Richard. Not Jess." She paused for a moment. "After what happened last time? I don't think so. You really could get lost in your own backyard, Richard."

Richard thought about pointing out that *anyone* could have confused the National Gallery with the National Portrait Gallery, and that it wasn't *she* who had spent the whole day standing in the rain (which was, in his opinion, every bit as much fun as walking around either place until his feet hurt), but he thought better of it.

"I'll meet you at your place," said Jessica. "We can walk down together."

"Right, Jess. Jessica—sorry."

"You *have* confirmed our reservation, haven't you, Richard."

"Yes," lied Richard earnestly. The other line on his phone had begun to ring. "Jessica, look, I . . ."

"Good," said Jessica, and she broke the connection. He picked up the other line.

"Hi Dick. It's me, Gary." Gary sat a few desks down from Richard. He waved. "Are we still on for drinks? You said we could go over the Merstham account."

"Get off the bloody phone, Gary. Of course we are." Richard put down the phone. There was a telephone number at the bottom of the Post-it note;

Richard had written the Post-it note to himself, several weeks earlier. And he *had* made the reservation: he was almost certain of that. But he had not confirmed it. He had kept meaning to, but there had been so much to do and Richard had known that there was plenty of time. But events run in packs . . .

Sylvia was now standing next to him. "Dick? The Wandsworth report?"

"Almost ready, Sylvia. Look, just hold on a sec, can you?"

He finished punching in the number, breathed a sigh of relief when somebody answered, "Ma Maison. Can I help you?"

"Yes," said Richard. "A table for three, for tonight. I think I booked it. And if I did I'm confirming the reservation. And if I didn't, I wondered if I could book it. Please." No, they had no record of a table for tonight in the name of Mayhew. Or Stockton. Or Bartram—Jessica's surname. And as for booking a table . . .

It wasn't the words that Richard found so unpleasant: it was the tone of voice in which the information was transmitted. A table for *tonight* should certainly have been booked years before—perhaps, it was implied, by Richard's parents. A table for *tonight* was impossible: if the pope, the prime minister, and the president of France arrived this evening without a confirmed reservation, even they would be turned out into the street with a continental jeer. "But it's for my fiancée's boss. I know I should have phoned before. There are only three of us, can't you *please* . . ."

They had put down the phone.

"Richard?" said Sylvia. "The MD's waiting."

"Do you think," asked Richard, "they'd give me

a table if I phoned back and offered them extra money?"

In her dream they were all together in the house. Her parents, her brother, her baby sister. They were standing together in the ballroom, staring at her. They were all so pale, so grave. Portia, her mother, touched her cheek and told her that she was in danger. In her dream, Door laughed, and said she knew. Her mother shook her head: no, no—*now* she was in danger. *Now.*

Door opened her eyes. The door was opening, quietly, quietly; she held her breath. Footsteps, quiet on the stone. *Perhaps he won't notice me,* she thought. *Perhaps he'll go away.* And then she thought, desperately, *I'm hungry.*

The footsteps hesitated. She was well hidden, she knew, under a pile of newspapers and rags. And it was possible that the intruder meant her no harm. *Can't he hear my heartbeat?* she thought. And then the footsteps came closer, and she knew what she had to do, and it scared her. A hand pulled the covers off her, and she looked up into a blank, utterly hairless face, which creased into a vicious smile. She rolled, then, and twisted, and the knife blade, aimed at her chest, caught her in the upper arm.

Until that moment, she had never thought she could do it. Never thought she would be brave enough, or scared enough, or desperate enough to dare. But she reached up one hand to his chest, and she *opened* . . .

He gasped, and tumbled onto her. It was wet and warm and slippery, and she slithered and staggered out from under the man, and she stumbled out of the room.

She caught her breath in the tunnel outside, narrow and low, as she fell against the wall, breathing in gasps and sobs. That had taken the last of her strength; now she was spent. Her shoulder was beginning to throb. *The knife*, she thought. But she was safe.

"My, oh my," said a voice from the darkness on her right. "She survived Mister Ross. Well I never, Mister Vandemar." The voice oozed. It sounded like gray slime.

"Well I never either, Mister Croup," said a flat voice on her left.

A light was kindled and flickered. "Still," said Mr. Croup, his eyes gleaming in the dark beneath the earth, "she won't survive us."

Door kneed him, hard, in the groin: and then she pushed herself forward, her right hand holding her left shoulder.

And she ran.

"Dick?"

Richard waved away the interruption. Life was almost under his control, now. Just a little more time . . .

Gary said his name again. "Dick? It's six-thirty."

"It's *what*?" Papers and pens and spreadsheets and trolls were tumbled into Richard's briefcase. He snapped it shut and ran.

He pulled his coat on as he went. Gary was following. "Are we going to have that drink, then?"

Richard paused for a moment. If ever, he decided, they made disorganization an Olympic sport, he could be disorganized for Britain. "Gary," he said, "I'm sorry. I blew it. I have to see Jessica tonight. We're taking her boss out to dinner."

"Mister Stockton? Of Stocktons? *The* Stockton?"
Richard nodded. They hurried down the stairs. "I'm
sure you'll have fun," said Gary, insincerely. "And
how is the Creature from the Black Lagoon?"

"Jessica's from Ilford, actually, Gary. And she remains the light and love of my life, thank you very
much for asking." They reached the lobby, and Richard made a dash for the automatic doors, which
spectacularly failed to open.

"It's after six, Mister Mayhew," said Mr. Figgis,
the building's security guard. "You have to sign
out."

"I don't need this," said Richard to no one in particular, "I really don't."

Mr. Figgis smelled vaguely of medicinal liniment
and was widely rumored to have an encyclopedic
collection of soft-core pornography. He guarded the
doors with a diligence that bordered upon madness,
never quite having lived down the evening when an
entire floor's worth of computer equipment upped
and left, along with two potted palms and the managing director's Axminster carpet.

"So our drink's off, then?"

"I'm sorry, Gary. Is Monday okay for you?"

"Sure. Monday's fine. See you Monday."

Mr. Figgis inspected their signatures and satisfied
himself they had no computers, potted palms, or car-
pets about their persons, then he pressed a button
under his desk, and the door slid open.

"Doors," said Richard.

The underway branched and divided; she picked
her way at random, ducking through tunnels, running and stumbling and weaving. Behind her
strolled Mr. Croup and Mr. Vandemar, as calmly

and cheerfully as Victorian dignitaries visiting the Crystal Palace exhibition. When they arrived at a crossroads, Mr. Croup would kneel and find the nearest spot of blood, and they would follow it. They were like hyenas, exhausting their prey. They could wait. They had all the time in the world.

Luck was with Richard, for a change. He caught a black taxi, driven by an elderly man who took Richard home by an unlikely route involving streets Richard had never before seen, while holding forth, as Richard had discovered all London taxi drivers will hold forth—given a living, breathing, English-speaking passenger—on London's inner-city traffic problems, how best to deal with crime, and thorny political issues of the day. Richard jumped out of the cab, left a tip and his briefcase behind, managed to flag down the cab again before it made it into the main road and so got his briefcase back, then he ran up the stairs and into his apartment. He was already shedding clothes as he entered the hall: his briefcase spun across the room and crash-landed on the sofa; he took his keys from his pocket and placed them carefully on the hall table, in order to ensure he did not forget them.

Then he dashed into the bedroom. The buzzer sounded. Richard, three-quarters of the way into his best suit, launched himself at the speaker.

"Richard? It's Jessica. I hope you're ready."

"Oh. Yes. Be right down." He pulled on a coat, and he ran, slamming the door behind him. Jessica was waiting for him at the bottom of the stairs. She always waited for him there. Jessica didn't like Richard's apartment: it made her feel uncomfortably female. There was always the chance of finding a pair of Richard's underwear, well, anywhere, not to mention the wandering lumps of congealed toothpaste on the bathroom sink: no, it was not Jessica's kind of place.

Jessica was very beautiful; so much so Richard would occasionally find himself staring at her, wondering, *how did she end up with me?* And when they made love—which they did at Jessica's apartment in fashionable Kensington, in Jessica's brass bed with the crisp white linen sheets (for Jessica's parents had told her that down comforters were decadent)—in the darkness, afterwards, she would hold him very tightly, and her long brown curls would tumble over his chest, and she would whisper to him how much she loved him, and he would tell her he loved her and always wanted to be with her, and they both believed it to be true.

"Bless me, Mister Vandemar. She's slowing up."

"Slowing up, Mister Croup."

"She must be losing a lot of blood, Mister V."

"Lovely blood, Mister C. Lovely wet blood."

"Not long now."

A click: the sound of a switchblade opening, empty and lonely and dark.

"Richard? What are you doing?" asked Jessica.

"Nothing, Jessica."

"You haven't forgotten your keys again, have you?"

"No, Jessica." Richard stopped patting himself and pushed his hands deep into the pockets of his coat.

"Now, when you meet Mister Stockton tonight," said Jessica, "you have to appreciate that he's not just a very important man. He's also a corporate entity in his own right."

"I can't wait," sighed Richard.

"What was that, Richard?"

"I can't wait," said Richard, rather more enthusiastically.

"Oh, please hurry up," said Jessica, who was beginning to exude an aura of what, in a lesser woman, might almost have been described as nerves. "We mustn't keep Mister Stockton waiting."

"No, Jess."

"Don't call me that, Richard. I loathe pet names. They're so demeaning."

"Spare any change?" The man sat in a doorway. His beard was yellow and gray, and his eyes were sunken and dark. A hand-lettered sign hung from a piece of frayed string around his neck and rested on his chest, telling anyone with the eyes to read it that he was homeless and hungry. It didn't take a sign to tell you that; Richard, hand already in his pocket, fumbled for a coin.

"Richard. We haven't got the time," said Jessica, who gave to charity and invested ethically. "Now, I do want you to make a good impression, fiancé-wise. It is vital that a future spouse makes a good impression." And then her face creased, and she hugged him for a moment, and said, "Oh, Richard. I *do* love you. You do know that, don't you?"

And Richard nodded, and he did.

Jessica checked her watch and increased her pace. Richard discreetly flicked a pound coin back through the air toward the man in the doorway, who caught it in one grimy hand.

"There wasn't any problem with the reservations, was there?" asked Jessica. And Richard, who was not much good at lying when faced with a direct question, said, "Ah."

She had chosen wrongly—the corridor ended in a blank wall. Normally that would hardly have given her pause, but she was so tired, so hungry, in so much pain. . . . She leaned against the wall, feeling the brick's roughness against her face. She was gulping breath, hiccuping and sobbing. Her arm was cold, and her left hand was numb. She could go no farther, and the world was beginning to feel very distant. She wanted to stop, to lie down, and to sleep for a hundred years.

"Oh, bless my little black soul, Mister Vandemar, do you see what I see?" The voice was soft, close: they must have been nearer to her than she had imagined. "I spy, with my little eye, something that's going to be—"

"Dead in a minute, Mister Croup," said the flat voice, from above her.

"Our principal will be delighted."

And the girl pulled whatever she could find deep inside her soul, from all the pain, and the hurt, and the fear. She was spent, burnt out, and utterly exhausted. She had nowhere to go, no power left, no time. "If it's the last door I open," she prayed, silently, to the Temple, to the Arch. "Somewhere . . . anywhere . . . *safe* . . ." and then she thought, wildly, "*Somebody.*"

And, as she began to pass out, she tried to open a door.

As the darkness took her, she heard Mr. Croup's voice, as if from a long way away. It said, "Bugger and blast."

* * *

Jessica and Richard walked down the sidewalk toward the restaurant. She had her arm through his, and was walking as fast as her heels permitted. He hurried to keep up. Streetlights and the fronts of closed stores illuminated their path. They passed a stretch of tall, looming buildings, abandoned and lonely, bounded by a high brick wall.

"You are honestly telling me you had to promise them an extra fifty pounds for our table tonight? You are an idiot, Richard," said Jessica, her dark eyes flashing.

"They had lost my reservation. And they said all the tables were booked." Their steps echoed off the high walls.

"They'll probably have us sitting by the kitchen," said Jessica. "Or the door. Did you tell them it was for Mister Stockton?"

"Yes," replied Richard.

Jessica sighed. She continued to drag him along, as a door opened in the wall, a little way ahead of them. Someone stepped out and stood swaying for one long terrible moment, and then collapsed to the concrete. Richard shivered and stopped in his tracks. Jessica tugged him into motion.

"Now, when you're talking to Mister Stockton, you must make sure you don't interrupt him. Or disagree with him—he doesn't like to be disagreed with. When he makes a joke, laugh. If you're in any doubt as to whether or not he's made a joke, look at me. I'll . . . mm, tap my forefinger."

They had reached the person on the sidewalk. Jessica stepped over the crumpled form. Richard hesitated. "Jessica?"

"You're right. He might think I'm bored," she

mused. "I know," she said brightly, "if he makes a joke, I'll rub my earlobe."

"Jessica?" He could not believe that she was simply ignoring the figure at their feet.

"What?" She was not pleased to be jerked out of her reverie.

"Look."

He pointed to the sidewalk. The person was face down, and enveloped in bulky clothes; Jessica took his arm and tugged him toward her. "Oh. I see. If you pay them any attention, Richard, they'll walk all over you. They all have homes, really. Once she's slept it off, I'm sure she'll be fine." *She*? Richard looked down. It *was* a girl. Jessica continued, "Now, I've told Mister Stockton that we ..." Richard was down on one knee. "Richard? What are you doing?"

"She isn't drunk," said Richard. "She's hurt." He looked at his fingertips. "She's bleeding."

Jessica looked down at him, nervous and puzzled. "We're going to be late," she pointed out.

"She's *hurt*."

Jessica looked back at the girl on the sidewalk. Priorities: Richard had no priorities. "Richard. We're going to be late. Someone else will be along; someone else will help her."

The girl's face was crusted with dirt, and her clothes were wet with blood. "She's hurt," he said, simply. There was an expression on his face that Jessica hadn't seen before.

"Richard," she warned, and then she relented, a little, and offered a compromise. "Dial 999 and call an ambulance then. Quickly, now."

Suddenly the girl's eyes opened, white and wide in a face that was little more than a smudge of dust and blood. "Not a hospital, please. They'll find me.

Take me somewhere safe. Please." Her voice was weak.

"You're bleeding," said Richard. He looked to see where she had come from, but the wall was blank and brick and unbroken. He looked back to her still form, and asked, "Why not a hospital?"

"Help me?" the girl whispered, and her eyes closed.

Again he asked her, "Why don't you want to go to the hospital?" This time there was no answer at all.

"When you call the ambulance," said Jessica, "don't give your name. You might have to make a statement or something, and then we'd be late ... Richard? What are you doing?"

Richard had picked the girl up, cradling her in his arms. She was surprisingly light. "I'm taking her back to my place, Jess. I can't just leave her. Tell Mister Stockton I'm really sorry, but it was an emergency. I'm sure he'll understand."

"Richard Oliver Mayhew," said Jessica, coldly. "You put that girl down and come back here this minute. Or this engagement is at an end as of now. I'm warning you."

Richard felt the sticky warmth of blood soaking into his shirt. Sometimes, he realized, there is nothing you can do. He walked away, leaving behind Jessica, who stood there on the sidewalk, her eyes stung with tears.

Richard did not, at any point on his walk, stop to think. It was not something over which he had any volition. Somewhere in the sensible part of his head, someone—a normal, sensible Richard Mayhew— was telling him how ridiculous he was being: that he should just have called the police, or an ambulance; that it was dangerous to lift an injured person; that he had really, seriously upset Jessica; that he was going to have to sleep on the sofa tonight; that he was ruining his only really good suit; that the girl smelled terrible . . . but Richard found himself placing one foot in front of the other, and, arms cramping and back hurting, ignoring the looks he got from passers-by, he just kept walking. And after a while he was at the ground floor door of his building, and he was stumbling up the staircase, and then he was standing in front of the door to his apartment and realizing that he had left his keys on the hall table, inside . . .

The girl reached out one filthy hand to the door, and it swung open.

Never thought I'd be pleased that the door hadn't latched properly, thought Richard, and he carried the girl in—closing the door behind him with his foot— and put her down on his bed. His shirtfront was soaked in blood.

She seemed semiconscious; her eyes were closed, but fluttering. He peeled off her leather jacket. There was a long cut on her left upper arm and shoulder. Richard caught his breath. "Look, I'm going to call a doctor," he said quietly. "Can you hear me?"

Her eyes opened, wide and scared. "Please, no. It'll be fine. It's not as bad as it looks. I just need sleep. No doctors."

"But your arm—your shoulder—"

"I'll be fine. Tomorrow. Please?" It was little more than a whisper.

"Um, I suppose, all right," and with sanity beginning to assert itself, he said, "Look, can I ask—?"

But she was asleep. Richard took an old scarf from

his closet and wrapped it firmly around her left upper arm and shoulder; he did not want her to bleed to death on his bed before he could get her to a doctor. And then he tiptoed out of his bedroom and shut the door behind him. He sat down on the sofa, in front of the television, and wondered what he had done.

TWO

*HE IS SOMEWHERE DEEP BENEATH THE
ground: in a tunnel, perhaps, or a sewer. Light comes in
flickers, defining the darkness, not dispelling it. He is not
alone. There are other people walking beside him, although
he cannot see their faces. They are running, now, through
the inside of the sewer, splashing through the mud and
filth. Droplets of water fall slowly through the air, crystal
clear in the darkness.*

He turns a corner, and the beast is waiting for him.

*It is huge. It fills the space of the sewer: massive head
down, bristled body and breath steaming in the chill of
the air. Some kind of boar, he thinks at first, and then
realizes that no boar could be so huge. It is the size of a
bull, of a tiger, of an ox.*

*It stares at him, and it pauses for a hundred years,
while he lifts his spear. He glances at his hand, holding
the spear, and observes that it is not his hand: the arm is
furred with dark hair, the nails are almost claws.*

And then the beast charges.

*He throws his spear, but it is already too late, and he
feels the beast slice his side with razor-sharp tusks, feels
his life slip away into the mud: and he realizes he has
fallen face down into the water, which crimsons in thick*

swirls of suffocating blood. And he tries so to scream, he tries to wake up, but he can breathe only mud and blood and water, he can feel only pain . . .

"Bad dream?" asked the girl.

Richard sat up on the couch, gasping for breath. The curtains were still drawn, the lights and the television still on, but he could tell, from the pale light coming in through the cracks, that it was morning. He fumbled on the couch for the remote control, which had wedged itself into the small of his back during the night, and he turned off the television.

"Yes," he said. "Sort of."

He wiped away the sleep from his eyes and took stock of himself, pleased to notice that he had at least taken off his shoes and jacket before he had fallen asleep. His shirtfront was covered with dried blood and with dirt. The homeless girl didn't say anything. She looked bad: pale, beneath the grime and brown dried blood, and small. She was dressed in a variety of clothes thrown over each other: odd clothes, dirty velvets, muddy lace, rips and holes through which other layers and styles could be seen. She looked, Richard thought, as if she'd done a midnight raid on the History of Fashion section of the Victoria and Albert Museum, and was still wearing everything she'd taken. Her short hair was filthy, but looked like it might have been a dark reddish color under the dirt.

"You're awake," said Richard.

"Whose barony is this?" asked the girl. "Whose fiefdom?"

"Um. Sorry?"

She looked around her suspiciously. "Where am I?"

"Newton Mansions, Little Comden Street . . ." He stopped. She had opened the curtains, blinking at the cold daylight. The girl stared out at the rather ordinary view from Richard's window, astonished, peering wide-eyed at the cars and the buses and the tiny sprawl of shops—a bakery, a drugstore and a liquor store—below them.

"I'm in London Above," she said, in a small voice.

"Yes, you're in London," said Richard. *Above what?* he wondered. "I think maybe you were in shock or something last night. That is a nasty cut on your arm." He waited for her to say something, to explain. She glanced at him, and then looked back down at the buses and the shops. Richard continued: "I, um, found you on the pavement. There was a lot of blood."

"Don't worry," she said, seriously. "Most of the blood was someone else's."

She let the curtain fall back. Then she began to unwrap the scarf, now bloodstained and crusted, from her arm. She examined the cut and made a face. "We're going to have to do something about this," she said. "Do you want to give me a hand?"

Richard was beginning to feel a little out of his depth. "I don't really know too much about first aid," he said.

"Well," she said, "if you're really squeamish you only have to hold the bandages and tie the ends where I can't reach. You do have bandages, don't you?"

Richard nodded. "Oh yes," he said. "In the first aid kit. In the bathroom. Under the sink." And then he went into his bedroom and changed his clothes, wondering whether the mess on his shirt (his best shirt, bought for him by, oh God, Jessica, she would have a *fit*) would ever come off.

The bloody water reminded him of something, some kind of dream he had once had, perhaps, but he could no longer, for the life of him, remember exactly what. He pulled the plug, let the water out of the sink, and filled it with clean water again, to which he added a cloudy splash of liquid disinfectant: the sharp antiseptic smell seemed so utterly sensible and medicinal, a remedy for the oddness of his situation, and his visitor. The girl leaned over the sink, and he splashed warm water over her arm and shoulder.

Richard was never as squeamish as he thought he was. Or rather, he was squeamish when it came to blood on screen: a good zombie movie or even an explicit medical drama would leave him huddled in a corner, hyperventilating, with his hands over his eyes, muttering things like "Just tell me when it's over." But when it came to real blood, real pain, he simply did something about it. They cleaned out the cut—which was much less severe than Richard remembered it from the night before—and bandaged it up, and the girl did her very best not to wince in the process. And Richard found himself wondering how old she was, and what she looked like under the grime, and why she was living on the streets and—

"What's your name?" she asked.

"Richard. Richard Mayhew. Dick." She nodded, as if she were committing it to memory. The doorbell rang. Richard looked at the mess in the bathroom, and the girl, and wondered how it would look to an outside observer. Such as, for example ... "Oh Lord," he said, realizing the worst. "I bet it's Jess. She's going to kill me." *Damage control. Damage control.* "Look," he told the girl. "You wait in here."

He shut the door of the bathroom behind him and walked down the hall. He opened the front door, and breathed a huge and quite heartfelt sigh of relief. It wasn't Jessica. It was—what? Mormons? Jehovah's Witnesses? The police? He couldn't tell. There were two of them, at any rate.

They wore black suits, which were slightly greasy, slightly frayed, and even Richard, who counted himself among the sartorially dyslexic, felt there was something odd about the cut of the coats. They were the kind of suits that might have been made by a tailor two hundred years ago who had had a modern suit described to him but had never actually seen one. The lines were wrong, and so were the grace notes.

A fox and a wolf, thought Richard, involuntarily. The man in front, the fox, was a little shorter than Richard. He had lank, greasy hair, of an unlikely orange color, and a pallid complexion; as Richard opened the door, he smiled, widely, and just a fraction too late, with teeth that looked like an accident in a graveyard. "A good morrow to you, good sir," he said, "on this fine and beautiful day."

"Ah. Hello," said Richard.

"We are conducting a personal enquiry of a delicate nature as it were, door to door. Do you mind if we come in?"

"Well, it's not very convenient right now," said Richard. Then he asked, "Are you with the police?" The second of the visitors, a tall man, the one he had thought of as a wolf, his gray and black hair cut bristle-short, stood a little behind his friend, holding a stack of photocopies to his chest. He had said nothing until this moment—just waited, huge and impassive. Now he laughed, once, low and dirtily. There was something unhealthy about that laugh.

"The police? Alas," said the smaller man, "we cannot claim that felicity. A career in law and order, although indubitably enticing, was not inscribed on the cards Dame Fortuna dealt my brother and me. No, we are merely private citizens. Allow me to make introductions. I am Mister Croup, and this gentleman is my brother, Mister Vandemar."

They did not look like brothers. They did not look like anything Richard had seen before. "Your brother?" asked Richard. "Shouldn't you have the same name?"

"I am impressed. What a brain, Mister Vandemar. Keen and incisive isn't the half of it. Some of us are so sharp," he said as he leaned in closer to Richard, went up on tiptoes into Richard's face, "we could just cut ourselves." Richard took an involuntary step backwards. "Can we come inside?" asked Mr. Croup.

"What do you want?"

Mr. Croup sighed, in what he obviously imagined was a rather wistful manner. "We are looking for our sister," he explained. "A wayward child, willful and headstrong, who has close to broken our poor dear widowed mother's heart."

"Ran away," explained Mr. Vandemar, quietly. He thrust a photocopied sheet into Richard's hands. "She's a little . . . funny," he added, and then he twirled one finger next to his temple in the universal gesture to indicate mental incapacity.

Richard looked down at the paper.
It said:

HAVE YOU SEEN THIS GIRL?

Beneath that was a photocopy-gray photograph of
a girl who looked to Richard like a cleaner, longer-
haired version of the young lady he had left in his
bathroom.

Under that it said:

ANSWERS TO THE NAME OF DOREEN.
BITES AND KICKS. RUN AWAY.
TELL US IF YOU SAW HER.
WANT HER BACK. REWARD PAYED.

And below that, a telephone number. Richard
looked back at the photograph. It was definitely the
girl in his bathroom. "No," he said. "I haven't seen
her, I'm afraid. I'm sorry."

Mr. Vandemar, however, was not listening. He
had raised his head and was sniffing the air, like a
man smelling something odd or unpleasant. Richard
reached out to give him back his piece of paper, but
the big man simply pushed past him and walked
into the apartment, a wolf on the prowl. Richard ran
after him. "What do you think you are doing? Will
you stop that? Get out. Look, you can't go in there—
"Mr. Vandemar was headed straight for the bathroom. Richard hoped that the girl—Doreen?—had
had the presence of mind to lock the bathroom door.
But no; it swung open at Mr. Vandemar's push. He
walked in, and Richard, feeling like a small and in-
effectual dog yapping at the heels of a postman, followed him in.

It was not a large bathroom. It contained a bathtub, a toilet, a sink, several bottles of shampoo, a bar of soap, and a towel. When Richard had left it, a couple of minutes before, it had also contained a dirty, bloody girl, a very bloody sink, and an open first aid kit. Now, it was gleamingly clean.

There was nowhere the girl could have been hiding. Mr. Vandemar stepped out of the bathroom and pushed open Richard's bedroom door, walked in, looked around. "I don't know what you think you're doing," said Richard. "But if you two don't get out of my apartment this minute, I'm phoning the police."

Then Mr. Vandemar, who had been in the process of examining Richard's living room, turned back toward Richard, and Richard suddenly realized that he had never been so scared of another human being in his life.

And then foxy Mr. Croup said, "Why yes, whatever can have come over you, Mister Vandemar? It's grief for our dear sweet sibling, I'll wager, has turned his head. Now apologize to the gentleman, Mister Vandemar."

Mr. Vandemar nodded, and pondered for a moment. "Thought I needed to use the toilet," he said. "Didn't. Sorry."

Mr. Croup began to walk down the hall, pushing Mr. Vandemar in front of him. "There. Now, you'll forgive my errant brother his lack of social graces, I trust. Worry over our poor dear widowed mother, and over our sister, whom even as we speak is wandering the streets of London unloved and uncared-for, has nigh unhinged him, I'll be bound. But for all that, he's a good fellow to have at your side. Is't not so, stout fellow?" They were out of Richard's apartment now, into the stairwell. Mr. Vandemar said nothing. He did not look unhinged with grief. Croup turned back to Richard and essayed another foxy smile. "You will tell us if you see her," he said.

"Good-bye," said Richard. Then he closed the door and locked it. And, for the first time since he had lived there, he attached the security chain.

Mr. Croup, who had cut Richard's phone line at the first mention of calling the police, was starting to wonder whether he had cut the right cord or not. Twentieth-century telecommunications technology not being his strongest point. He took one of the photocopies from Vandemar, and positioned it on the wall of the stairwell. "Spit!" he said to Vandemar.

Mr. Vandemar hawked a mouthful of phlegm from the back of his throat and spat it neatly onto the back of the handbill. Mr. Croup slapped the handbill hard onto the wall, next to Richard's door. It stuck immediately and stuck hard.

HAVE YOU SEEN THIS GIRL? it asked.

Mr. Croup turned to Mr. Vandemar. "Do you believe him?"

They turned back down the stairs. "Do I Hell," said Mr. Vandemar. "I could smell her."

Richard waited by his front door until he heard the main door slam, several floors below. He started to walk down the hall, back toward the bathroom, when the phone rang loudly, startling him. He sprinted back down the hall and picked up the receiver. "Hello?" said Richard. "Hello?"

No sound came out of the receiver. Instead, there was a click, and Jessica's voice came out of the answering machine on the table next to the phone. Her voice said, "Richard? This is Jessica. I'm sorry you're not there, because this would have been our last conversation, and I did so want to tell you this to your face." The phone, he realized, was completely dead. The receiver trailed a foot or so of cord, and was then neatly cut off.

"You embarrassed me very deeply last night, Richard," the voice continued. "As far as I'm concerned our engagement is at an end. I have no intention of returning the ring, nor indeed of ever seeing you again. Bye."

The tape stopped turning, there was another click, and the little red light began to flash.

"Bad news?" asked the girl. She was standing just behind him, in the kitchen part of the apartment, with her arm neatly bandaged. She was getting out tea bags, putting them in mugs. The kettle was boiling.

"Yes," said Richard. "Very bad." He walked over to her, handed her the HAVE YOU SEEN THIS GIRL? poster. "That's you, isn't it?"

She raised an eyebrow. "The photograph's me."

"And you are . . . Doreen?"

She shook her head. "I'm Door, Richardrichardmayhewdick. Milk and sugar?"

Richard was feeling utterly out of his league by now. And he said, "Richard. Just Richard. No sugar." Then he said, "Look, if it isn't a personal question, what happened to you?"

Door poured the boiling water into the mugs. "You don't want to know," she said, simply.

"Oh, well, I'm sorry if I—"

"No. Richard. Honestly, you *don't* want to know.

It wouldn't do you any good. You've done more than you should have already."

She removed the tea bags and handed him a mug of tea. He took it from her and realized that he was still carrying around the receiver. "Well. I mean. I couldn't just have left you there."

"You could have," she said. "You didn't." She pressed herself up against the wall and peered out of the window. Richard walked over to the window and looked out. Across the street, Mr. Croup and Mr. Vandemar were coming out of the bakery, and HAVE YOU SEEN THIS GIRL? was stuck in a place of prominence in its window.

"Are they really your brothers?" he asked.

"Please," said Door. "Give me a break."

He sipped his tea and tried to pretend that everything was normal. "So where were you?" he asked. "Just now?"

"I was here," she said. "Look, with those two still around we have to get a message to . . ." She paused. "To someone who can help. I don't dare leave here."

"Well, isn't there somewhere you could go? Someone that we could call?"

She took the dead receiver from his hand, wire trailing, and shook her head. "My friends aren't on the phone," she said. She put it back in its cradle, where it sat, useless and lonely. Then she smiled, fast and wicked. "Breadcrumbs," she said.

"Sorry?" said Richard.

There was a little window in the back of the bedroom that looked out on an area of roof tiles and gutters. Door stood on Richard's bed to reach it, opened the window, and sprinkled the breadcrumbs around. "But I don't understand," said Richard.

"Of course you don't," she agreed. "Now, shush." There was a flutter of wings, and the purple-gray-green sheen of a pigeon. It pecked at the bread-crumbs, and Door reached out her right hand and picked it up. It looked at her curiously but made no complaint.

They sat down on the bed. Door got Richard to hold the pigeon, while she attached a message to its leg, using a vivid blue rubber band that Richard had previously used to keep his electricity bills all in one place. Richard was not an enthusiastic holder of pi-geons, even at the best of times. "I don't see the point in this," he explained. "I mean, it's not a hom-ing pigeon. It's just a normal London pigeon. The kind that craps on Lord Nelson."

"That's right," said Door. Her cheek was grazed, and her dirty reddish hair was tangled; tangled, but not matted. And her eyes . . . Richard realized that he could not tell what color her eyes were. They were not blue, or green, or brown, or gray; they re-minded him of fire opals: there were burning greens and blues, and even reds and yellows that vanished and glinted as she moved. She took the bird from him, gently, held it up, and looked it in the face. It tipped its head on one side and stared back at her with bead-black eyes. "Okay," she said, and then she made a noise that sounded like the liquid bur-bling of pigeons. "Okay *Crrppllrr*, you're looking for the marquis de Carabas. You got that?"

The pigeon burbled liquidly back at her.

"Attagirl. Now, this is important, so you'd better—" The pigeon interrupted her with a rather impatient-sounding burble. "I'm sorry," said Door. "You know what you're doing, of course." She took the bird to the window and let it go.

Richard had watched the whole routine with some amazement. "Do you know, it almost sounded like it understood you?" he said, as the bird shrank in the sky and vanished behind some rooftops.

"How about that," said Door. "Now. We wait."

She went over to the bookshelf in the corner of the bedroom, found a copy of *Mansfield Park* Richard had not previously known that he possessed, and went into the living room. Richard followed her. She settled herself on his sofa and opened the book.

"So is it short for Doreen?" he asked.

"What?"

"Your name."

"No. It's just Door."

"How do you spell it?"

"D-o-o-r. Like something you walk through to go places."

"Oh." He had to say something, so he said, "What kind of a name is Door, then?"

And she looked at him with her odd-colored eyes, and she said, "My name." Then she went back to Jane Austen.

Richard picked up the remote control and turned on the television. Then he changed the channel. Changed it again. Sighed. Changed it again. "So, what are we waiting for?"

Door turned the page. She didn't look up. "A reply."

"What kind of a reply?" Door shrugged. "Oh. Right." It occurred to Richard then that her skin was very white, now that some of the dirt and blood had been removed. He wondered if she were pale from illness, or from loss of blood, or if she simply didn't get out much, or was anemic. Maybe she'd been in prison, although she looked a bit too young for that.

Perhaps the big man had been telling the truth when he had said she was mad. "Listen, when those men came over . . ."

"Men?" A flash of the opal-colored eyes.

"Croup and, um, Vanderbilt."

"Vandemar." She mused for a moment, then nodded. "I suppose you could call them men, yes. Two legs, two arms, a head each."

Richard kept talking. "When they came in here, before. Where *were* you?"

She licked her finger and turned a page. "I was here."

"But—" He stopped talking, out of words. There wasn't anywhere in the apartment that she could have hidden herself. But she hadn't left the apartment. But—

There was a scratching noise, and a dark shape larger than a mouse scurried out from the mess of videotapes beneath the television. "Jesus!" said Richard, and he threw the remote control at it as hard as he could. It crashed into the videos with a bang. Of the dark shape there was no sign.

"Richard!" said Door.

"It's okay," he explained. "I think it was just a rat or something."

She glared at him. "Of course it was a rat. You'll have scared it now, poor thing." She looked around the room, then made a low whistling noise between her front teeth. "Hello?" she called. She knelt on the floor, *Mansfield Park* abandoned. "Hello?"

She flashed a glance back at Richard. "If you've hurt it . . ." she threatened; then, softly, to the room, "I'm sorry, he's an idiot. Hello?"

"I'm not an idiot," said Richard.

"Shh," she said. "Hello?" A pink nose and two

small black eyes peered out from under the sofa. The rest of the head followed, and it scrutinized its surroundings suspiciously. It was indeed much too big to be a mouse, Richard was certain of that. "Hi," said Door, warmly. "Are you okay?" She extended her hand. The animal climbed into it, then ran up her arm, nestling in the crook of it. Door stroked its side with her finger. It was dark brown, with a long pink tail. There was something that looked like a folded piece of paper attached to its side.

"It's a rat," said Richard.

"Yes, it is. Are you going to apologize?"

"What?"

"Apologize."

Maybe he hadn't heard her properly. Maybe he was the one who was going mad. "To a rat?"

Door said nothing, fairly meaningfully. "I'm sorry," said Richard, to the rat, with dignity, "if I startled you."

The rat looked up at Door. "No, he really does mean it," she said. "He's not just saying it. So what have you got for me?" She fumbled at the rat's side, and pulled out a much-folded piece of brown paper, which had been held on with something that looked to Richard like a vivid blue rubber band.

She opened it up: a piece of ragged-edged brown paper, with spidery black handwriting on it. She read it and nodded. "Thank you," she said, to the rat. "I appreciate all you've done." It scampered down onto the couch, glared up at Richard for a moment, and then was gone in the shadows.

The girl called Door passed the paper to Richard. "Here," she said. "Read this."

*　　*　　*

It was late afternoon in Central London, and, with autumn drawing on, it was getting dark. Richard had taken the Tube to Tottenham Court Road and was now walking west down Oxford Street, holding the piece of paper. Oxford Street was the retail hub of London, and even now the sidewalks were packed with shoppers and tourists.

"It's a message," she said, when she gave it to him. "From the marquis de Carabas."

Richard was sure he had heard the name before. "That's nice," he said. "Out of postcards, was he?"

"This is quicker."

He passed the lights and the noise of the Virgin megastore, and the shop that sold souvenir London police helmets and little red London buses, and the place next door that sold individual slices of pizza, and then he turned right.

"You have to follow the directions written on here. Try not to let anyone follow you." Then she sighed, and said, "I really shouldn't involve you this much."

"If I follow these directions . . . will it get you out of here faster?"

"Yes."

He turned into Hanway Street. Although he had taken only a few steps from the well-lit bustle of Oxford Street, he might have been in another city: Hanway Street was empty, forsaken; a narrow, dark road, little more than an alleyway, filled with gloomy record shops and closed restaurants, the only light spilling out from the secretive drinking clubs on the upper floors of buildings. He walked along it, feeling apprehensive.

" ' . . . turn right into Hanway Street, left into Hanway Place, then right again into Orme Passage. Stop at the

first streetlight you come to . . .' Are you sure this is right?''

"Yes."

He did not remember an Orme Passage, although he had been to Hanway Place before: there was an underground Indian restaurant there his friend Gary liked a lot. As far as Richard could remember, Hanway Place was a dead end. The Mandeer, that was the restaurant. He passed the brightly lit front door, the restaurant's steps leading invitingly down into the underground, and then he turned left . . .

He had been wrong. There *was* an Orme Passage. He could see the sign for it, high on the wall.

ORME PASSAGE W1

No wonder he hadn't noticed it before: it was scarcely more than a narrow alleyway between houses, lit by a sputtering gas-jet. You don't see many of those anymore, thought Richard, and he held up his instructions to the gaslight, peering at them.

" 'Then turn around thrice, widdershins'?"

"Widdershins means counterclockwise, Richard."

He turned, three times, feeling stupid. *"Look, why do I have to do all this, just to see your friend. I mean, all this nonsense . . ."*

"It's not nonsense. Really. Just—humor me on this, okay?" And she had smiled at him.

He stopped turning. Then he walked down the alley to the end. Nothing. No one. Just a metal garbage can, and beside it something that might have been a pile of rags. "Hello?" called Richard. "Is anyone here? I'm Door's friend. Hello?"

No. There was no one there. Richard was relieved.

Now he could go home and explain to the girl that nothing had happened. Then he would call in the appropriate authorities, and they would sort it all out. He crumpled the paper into a tight ball, and tossed it toward the bin.

What Richard had taken for a pile of rags unfolded, expanded, stood up in one fluid motion. A hand caught the crumpled paper in midair.

"Mine, I believe," said the marquis de Carabas. He wore a huge dandyish black coat that was not quite a frock coat nor exactly a trench coat, and high black boots, and, beneath his coat, raggedy clothes. His eyes burned white in an extremely dark face. And he grinned white teeth, momentarily, as if at a private joke of his own, and bowed to Richard, and said, "De Carabas, at your service, and you are . . . ?"

"Um," said Richard. "Er. Um."

"You are Richard Mayhew, the young man who rescued our wounded Door. How is she now?"

"Er. She's okay. Her arm's still a bit—"

"Her recovery time will undoubtedly astonish us all. Her family had remarkable recuperative powers. It's a wonder anyone managed to kill them at all, isn't it?" The man who called himself the marquis de Carabas walked restlessly up and down the alley. Richard could already tell that he was the type of person who was always in motion, like a great cat.

"Somebody killed Door's family?" asked Richard.

"We're not going to get very far if you keep repeating everything I say, now, are we?" said the marquis, who was now standing in front of Richard. "Sit down," he ordered. Richard looked around the alley for something to sit on. The marquis put a hand on his shoulder and sent him sprawling to the cobblestones. "She knows I don't come cheap. What exactly is she offering me?"

"Sorry?"

"What's the deal? She sent you here to negotiate, young man. I'm not cheap, and I never give freebies."

Richard shrugged, as well as he could shrug from a supine position. "She said to tell you that she wants you to accompany her home—wherever that is—and to fix her up with a bodyguard."

Even when the marquis was at rest, his eyes never ceased moving. Up, down, around, as if he were looking for something, thinking about something. Adding, subtracting, evaluating. Richard wondered whether the man was quite sane. "And she's offering me?"

"Well. Nothing."

The marquis blew on his fingernails and polished them on the lapel of his remarkable coat. Then he turned away. "She's offering *me*. Nothing." He sounded offended.

Richard scrambled back up to his feet. "Well, she didn't say anything about money. She just said she was going to have to owe you a favor."

The eyes flashed. "Exactly what kind of favor?"

"A really big one," said Richard. "She said she was going to have to owe you a really big favor."

De Carabas grinned to himself, a hungry panther sighting a lost peasant child. Then he turned on Richard. "And you left her alone?" he asked. "With Croup and Vandemar out there? Well, what are you waiting for?" He knelt down and took from his pocket a small metal object, which he pushed into a manhole cover at the edge of the alley and twisted. The manhole cover came up easily; the marquis put

away the metal object and took something out of
another pocket that reminded Richard a little of a
long firework, or a flare. He held it in one hand, ran
his other hand along it, and the far end erupted into
scarlet flame.

"Can I ask a question?" said Richard.

"Certainly not," said the marquis. "You don't ask
any questions. You don't get any answers. You don't
stray from the path. You don't even think about
what's happening to you right now. Got it?"

"But—"

"Most important of all: no buts," said de Carabas.
"And time is of the essence. Move." He pointed into
the depths revealed by the open manhole cover.
Richard moved, clambering down the metal ladder
set into the wall beneath the manhole, feeling so far
out of his depth that it didn't even occur to him to
question any further.

Richard wondered where they were. This didn't
seem to be a sewer. Perhaps it was a tunnel for telephone cables, or for very small trains. Or for . . .
something else. He realized that he did not know
very much about what went on beneath the streets
of London. He walked nervously, worried that he'd
catch his feet in something, that he'd stumble in the
darkness and break his ankle. De Carabas strode on
ahead, nonchalantly, apparently not caring whether
Richard was with him or not. The crimson flame cast
huge shadows on the tunnel walls.

Richard ran to catch up. "Let's see . . ." said de
Carabas. "I'll need to get her to the market. The next
one's in, mm, two days' time, if I recall correctly, as
of course I unfailingly do. I can hide her until then."

"Market?" asked Richard.

"The Floating Market. But you don't want to know about that. No more questions."

Richard looked around. "Well, I was going to ask you where we are now. But I suppose you were going to refuse to tell me."

The marquis grinned once more. "Very good," he said, approvingly. "You are in enough trouble already."

"You can say that again," sighed Richard. "My fiancée's dumped me, and I'll probably have to get a new telephone—"

"Temple and Arch. A telephone is the least of your troubles." De Carabas put the flare down on the ground, resting it against the wall, where it continued to sputter and flame, and he began to climb up some metal rungs set into the wall. Richard hesitated, and then followed him. The rungs were cold and rusted; he could feel them crumbling roughly against his hands as he climbed, fragments of rust getting in his eyes and mouth. The scarlet light from below was flickering, and then it went out. They climbed in total darkness.

"So, are we going back to Door?" Richard asked.

"Eventually. There's a little something I need to organize first. Insurance. And when we get into daylight, don't look down."

"Why not?" asked Richard. And then daylight hit his face, and he looked down.

It was daylight (*how was it daylight? a tiny voice asked, in the back of his head. It had been almost night when he entered the alley, what, an hour ago?*), and he was holding onto a metal ladder that ran up the outside of a very high building (*but a few seconds ago he was climbing up the same ladder, and he had been inside, hadn't he?*), and below him, he could see . . .

London.

Tiny cars. Tiny buses and taxis. Tiny buildings. Trees. Miniature trucks. Tiny, tiny people. They swam in and out of focus beneath him.

To say that Richard Mayhew was not very good at heights would be perfectly accurate, but it would fail to give the full picture. Richard hated clifftops, and high buildings: somewhere not far inside him was the fear—the stark, utter, silently screaming terror—that if he got too close to the edge, then something would take over and he would find himself walking to the edge of a clifftop and stepping off into space. It was as if he could not entirely trust himself, and that scared Richard more than the simple fear of falling ever could. So he called it vertigo, and hated it and himself, and kept away from high places.

Richard froze on the ladder. His hands clamped tightly to the rungs. His eyes hurt, somewhere behind the eyeballs. He started breathing too fast, too deeply. "Somebody," said an amused voice above him, "wasn't listening, was he?"

"I . . ." Richard's throat didn't work. He swallowed, moistening it. "I can't move." His hands were sweating. What if they sweated so much that he simply slipped off into the void . . . ?

"Of course you can move. Or, if you don't you can stay here, hanging onto the side of the wall until your hands freeze and your legs buckle and you tumble to a messy death a thousand feet below." Richard looked up at the marquis. He was looking down at Richard, and still smiling; when he saw that Richard was watching him, he let go of the rungs with both his hands, and waggled his fingers at him.

Richard felt a wave of sympathetic vertigo run through him. "Bastard," he said, under his breath, and he let go of the rung with his right hand and moved it up eight inches, until it found the next rung. Then he moved his right leg up one rung. Then he did it again, with his left hand. After a while he found himself at the edge of a flat roof, and he stepped over it and collapsed.

He was aware that the marquis was striding along the roof, away from him. Richard felt the rooftop with his hands, and felt the solid structure beneath him. His heart was pounding in his chest.

A gruff voice some distance away shouted, "You're not wanted here, de Carabas. Get away. Clear off."

"Old Bailey," he heard de Carabas say. "You're looking wonderfully healthy."

And then footsteps shuffled toward him, and a finger prodded him gently in the ribs. "You all right, laddie? I've got some stew cookin' back there. You want some? It's starling."

Richard opened his eyes. "No thank you," he said.

He saw the feathers, first. He wasn't sure if it was a coat, or a cape, or some kind of strange covering that had no name, but whatever kind of outer garment it was, it was covered thickly and entirely in feathers. A face, kind and creased, with grey muttonchop whiskers, peered out from the top of the feathers. The body beneath the face, where it was not covered with feathers, was wound round and about with ropes. Richard found himself remembering a theatrical performance of *Robinson Crusoe* he had been taken to as a child: this was what Robinson Crusoe might have looked like, if he had been shipwrecked on a rooftop instead of a desert island.

"They call me Old Bailey, lad," said the man. He fumbled at a battered pair of glasses, on a string around his neck, and pulled them on, staring through them at Richard. "I don't recognize ye. What barony do you give fealty to? What's your name?"

Richard pulled himself into a sitting position. They were on the roof of an old building, built of brown stone, with a tower above them. Weathered gargoyles, missing wings and limbs and, in a couple of cases, even heads, jutted sadly from the corners of the tower. From far below he could hear the wail of a police siren, and the muted roar of traffic. Across the rooftop, in the shadow of the tower, was something that looked like a tent; an old brown tent, much mended, spackled white with bird shit. He opened his mouth to tell the old man his name.

"You. Shut up," said the marquis de Carabas. "Don't say another word." Then he turned to Old Bailey. "People who put their noses where they aren't wanted sometimes"—he snapped his fingers, loudly, beneath the old man's nose, making him jump—"lose them. Now. You've owed me a favor for twenty years, Old Bailey. A big favor. And I'm calling it in."

The old man blinked. "I was a fool," he said quietly.

"No fool like an old fool," agreed the marquis. He reached a hand into an inside pocket of his coat and pulled out a silver box, larger than a snuffbox, smaller than a cigar box, and a good deal more ornate than either. "Do you know what this is?"

"I wish I didn't."

"You'll keep it safe for me."

"I don't want it."

"You don't have any choice," said the marquis. The old roof-man took the silver box from him and held it, awkwardly, in both hands, as if it were something that might explode at any moment. The marquis prodded Richard gently with his square-toed black boot. "Right," he said. "We'd better get a move on, hadn't we?" He strode off across the roof, and Richard got to his feet and followed, keeping well away from the side of the building. The marquis opened a door in the side of the tower, beside a high cluster of chimneys, and they went down a poorly lit spiral staircase.

"Who was that man?" asked Richard, peering through the dim light. Their footsteps echoed and reverberated down the metal stairs.

The marquis de Carabas snorted. "You haven't heard a word I've said, have you? You're in trouble already. Everything you do, everything you say, everything you hear, just makes it worse. You had better pray you haven't stepped too far in."

It was now completely dark, and Richard stumbled slightly as he reached the last of the steps and found himself looking for a step that wasn't there. "Mind your head," said the marquis, and he opened a door. Richard banged his forehead into something hard and said "ow," and then he stepped out through a low door, shielding his eyes against the light.

Richard rubbed his forehead, then he rubbed his eyes. The door they had just come through was the door to the broom closet in the stairwell of his apartment building. It was filled with brooms, an elderly mop, and a huge variety of cleaning fluids, powders, and waxes. It had no stairs at the back of it that he could see, just a wall on which a stained old calendar hung, quite uselessly—unless 1979 ever came back around.

The marquis was examining the HAVE YOU SEEN THIS GIRL? poster stuck beside Richard's front door. "Not her best side," he said.

Richard shut the door to the broom closet. He took his keys from his back pocket, unlocked his front door, and he was home. It was, he was rather relieved to see through the kitchen windows, nighttime once more.

"Richard," said Door. "You did it." She had washed herself while he was gone, and her layers of clothes looked like she had at least made an effort to get the worst of the filth and the blood off them. The grime was gone from her face and hands. Her hair, when washed, was a dark shade of auburn, with copper and bronze highlights. Richard wondered how old she was: fifteen? Sixteen? Older? He still couldn't tell.

She had put on the brown leather jacket she had been wearing when he had found her, huge and enveloping, like an old flying jacket, which somehow made her look smaller than she was, and even more vulnerable.

"Well, yes," said Richard.

The marquis de Carabas went down on one knee to the girl and lowered his head. "My lady," he said.

She seemed uncomfortable. "Oh, do get up, de Carabas. I'm pleased you came."

He stood in one smooth movement. "I understand," he said, "that the words *favor*, *really*, and *big* have been used. In conjunction."

"Later." She walked over to Richard and took his hands in hers. "Richard. Thanks. I really appreciate everything you've done. I changed the sheets on the bed. And I wish there was something I could do to pay you back."

"You're leaving?"

She nodded. "I'll be safe now. More or less. I hope. For a little while."

"Where are you going now?"

She smiled gently and shook her head. "Uh-uh. I'm out of your life. And you've been wonderful." She went up on tiptoes then and kissed him on the cheek, as friends kiss friends.

"If I ever need to get in touch with you—?"

"You don't. Ever. And . . ." and then she paused. "Look, I'm sorry, okay?"

Richard inspected his feet, in an awkward sort of way. "There's nothing to be sorry about," he said, and added, doubtfully, "it was fun." Then he looked up again.

But there was nobody there.

THREE

ON SUNDAY MORNING RICHARD TOOK THE
Batmobile-shaped telephone he had been given for
Christmas several years earlier by his Aunt Maude
out of the drawer at the bottom of the closet and
plugged it into the wall. He tried telephoning Jessica,
but without success. Her answering machine was
turned off, as was her cellular phone. He supposed
she had gone back to her parents' house in the country, and he had no desire to phone her there. Richard
found Jessica's parents deeply intimidating, each in
their separate ways. Neither of them had entirely ap-
proved of him as a future son-in-law: in fact, her
mother had, on one occasion, mentioned to him
quite casually how disappointed they were by Richard and Jessica's engagement, and her conviction
that Jessica could, if she wanted to, do so much better.

Richard's own parents were both dead. His father
had died quite suddenly when Richard was still a
small boy, of a heart attack. His mother died very
slowly after that, and once Richard left home she
simply faded away: six months after he moved to
London he took the train back up to Scotland, to

spend her last two days in a small county hospital sitting beside her bed. Sometimes she had known him; at other times she had called him by his father's name.

Richard sat on his couch, and he brooded. The events of the previous two days became less and less real, increasingly less likely. What was real was the message that Jessica had left on his machine, telling him she did not want to see him again. He played it, and replayed it, that Sunday, hoping each time that she would relent, that he'd hear warmth in her voice. He never did.

He thought about going out and buying a Sunday paper but decided not to. Arnold Stockton, Jessica's boss, a many-chinned, self-made caricature of a man, owned all the Sunday papers that Rupert Murdoch had failed to buy. His own papers talked about him, and so did the rest. Reading a Sunday paper would, Richard suspected, probably end up reminding him of the dinner he had failed to attend on Friday night. So instead Richard had a long hot bath and a number of sandwiches, and several cups of tea. He watched a little Sunday afternoon television and constructed conversations with Jessica in his head. At the end of each mental dialogue they would fall into each other's arms, make wild, angry, tear-stained and passionate love; and then everything would be all right.

On Monday morning Richard's alarm failed to go off. He came out onto the street at a run at ten to nine, briefcase swinging, staring up and down the road like a madman, praying for a taxi. Then he sighed with relief, because a big black car was head-

ing down the road toward him, its yellow "taxi"
sign bright. He waved at it and yelled.

The taxi slid gently past him, ignoring him completely; it turned a corner and was gone.

Another taxi. Another yellow light that meant the
taxi was available. This time Richard stepped out
into the middle of the road to flag it down. It
swerved past him and continued on its way. Richard
began to swear under his breath. Then he ran for the
nearest Tube station.

He pulled out a pocketful of coins, stabbed the button of the ticket machine for a single ticket to Charing
Cross, and thumbed his change into the slot. Every
coin he put in went straight through the guts of the
machine and clattered into the tray at the bottom.
No ticket appeared. He tried another ticket machine,
with the same lack of result. And another. The ticket
seller in the office was speaking to someone on the
telephone when Richard went over to complain and
to buy his ticket manually; and despite—or perhaps
because of—Richard's cries of "Hey!" and "Excuse
me!" and his desperate tapping on the plastic barrier
with a coin, the man remained resolutely on the telephone.

"Fuck it," announced Richard, and he vaulted the
barrier. No one stopped him; no one seemed to care.
He ran, breathless and sweating, down the escalator,
and made it onto the crowded platform just as a
train came in.

As a child, Richard had had nightmares in which
he simply wasn't there, in which, no matter how
much noise he made, no matter what he did, nobody
ever noticed him at all. He began to feel like that
now, as people pushed in front of him; he was buffeted by the crowd, pushed this way and that by

commuters getting off, by others getting on.

He persisted, pushing and shoving in his turn, until he was almost on the train—he had one arm inside—when the doors began to hiss closed. He pulled his hand back, but his coat-sleeve was trapped. Richard began to hammer on the door, and to shout, expecting the driver at least to open the door enough for him to free his sleeve. But instead the train began to move off, and Richard was forced to run down the platform, stumbling, faster and faster. He dropped his briefcase onto the platform, pulled desperately at his sleeve with his free hand. The sleeve ripped, and he fell forward, scraping his hand on the platform, ripping his trousers at the knee. Richard climbed, a little unsteadily, to his feet, then walked back down the platform and retrieved his briefcase.

He looked at his ripped sleeve and his grazed hand and his torn trousers. Then he walked up the stone stairs and out of the Underground station. Nobody asked him for a ticket on the way out.

"I'm sorry I'm late," said Richard, to no one in particular in the crowded office. The clock on the office wall said that it was 10:30. He dropped his briefcase on his chair, wiped the sweat from his face with his handkerchief. "You wouldn't believe what it was like getting here," he continued. "It was a nightmare."

He looked down at his desktop. There was something missing. Or, more precisely, there was everything missing. "Where are my things?" he asked the room, a little more loudly. "Where is my telephone? Where are my trolls?"

He checked the desk drawers. They were empty

too: not even a Mars bar wrapper or a twisted paper clip to show that Richard had ever been there. Sylvia was coming toward him, in conversation with two rather hefty gentlemen. Richard walked over to her. "Sylvia? What's going on?"

"I'm sorry?" said Sylvia, politely. She pointed the desk out to the hefty gentlemen, who each took an end of it, and began to carry it out of the office. "Careful now," she told them.

"My desk. Where are they taking it?"

Sylvia stared at him, gently puzzled. "And you are . . . ?"

I don't need this shit, thought Richard. "Richard," he said, sarcastically. "Richard Mayhew."

"Ah," said Sylvia. Then her attention slid off Richard, like water off an oiled duck, and she said, "No, not over there. For heaven's sakes," to the removal men, and hurried after them as they carried off Richard's desk.

Richard watched her go. Then he walked through the office until he got to Gary's workstation. Gary was answering e-mail. Richard looked at the screen: the e-mail Gary seemed to be writing was both sexually explicit and addressed to someone who was not Gary's girlfriend. Embarrassed, Richard moved around to the other side of the desk.

"Gary. What's going on? Is this a joke or something?"

Gary looked around, as if he had heard something. He flicked the keyboard, activating a screensaver of dancing hippopotami, then he shook his head as if to clear it, picked up the telephone, and began to dial. Richard slammed his hand down on the phone, cutting Gary off.

"Look, this isn't funny. I don't know what everyone's playing at." Finally, to his enormous relief, Gary looked up at him. Richard continued, "If I've been fired then just tell me I've been fired, but all this pretending I'm not here . . ."

And then Gary smiled and said, "Hi. Yeah. I'm Gary Perunu. Can I help you?"

"I don't think so," said Richard, coldly, and he walked out of the office, leaving his briefcase behind him.

Richard's offices were on the third floor of a big, old, drafty building, just off the Strand. Jessica worked about halfway up a large crystalline, mirrored structure in the City of London, fifteen minutes' walk up the road.

Richard jogged up that road. He got to the Stockton building in ten minutes, walked straight past the uniformed security guards on duty on the ground floor, stepped into the elevator, and went up. The inside of the elevator was mirrored, and he stared at himself as he went up. His tie was half-undone and askew, his coat was ripped, his pants torn, his hair was a sweaty mess. . . . God, he looked awful.

There was a fluting tone, and the elevator door opened. Jessica's floor was quite opulent, in an underdecorated sort of way. There was a receptionist by the elevator, a poised and elegant creature who looked like her take-home pay beat Richard's hands down. She was reading *Cosmopolitan*. She did not look up as Richard came over.

"I need to talk to Jessica Bartram," said Richard. "It's important. I have to speak with her."

The receptionist ignored him, intent upon examining her nails. Richard walked down the corridor until he got to Jessica's office. He opened the door and went in. She was standing in front of three large posters, each advertising "Angels over England—A Traveling Exhibition," each with a different image of an angel on it. She turned as he came in, and she smiled warmly at him.

"Jessica. Thank God. Listen, I think I'm going mad or something. It started when I couldn't get a taxi this morning, and then the office and the Tube and—" He showed her his ragged sleeve. "It's like I've become some kind of non-person." She smiled at him some more, reassuringly. "Look," said Richard. "I'm sorry about the other night. Well, not about what I did, but about upsetting you, and . . . look, I'm sorry, and it's all crazy, and I don't honestly know what to do."

And Jessica nodded, and continued to smile sympathetically, and then she said, "You're going to think I'm absolutely awful, but I have a really dreadful memory for faces. Give me a second, and I know I'll get it."

And at that point, Richard knew that it was real, and a heavy dread settled in the pit of his stomach. Whatever madness was happening that day was really happening. It was no joke, no trick or prank. "It's okay," he said, dully. "Forget it."

And he walked away, out the door and down the corridor. He was almost at the lift when she called his name.

"Richard!"

He turned. It *had* been a joke. Some kind of petty revenge. Something he could explain. "Richard . . . Maybury?" She seemed proud of herself for remembering that much.

"Mayhew," said Richard, and he got into the elevator, and the doors sang a sad fluting downward trill as they closed behind him.

Richard walked back to his flat, upset and confused and angry. Sometimes he would wave at taxis, but never with any real hope that they would stop, and none of them did. His feet hurt, and his eyes stung, and he knew that soon enough he would wake up from today and a proper Monday, a sensible Monday, a decent, honest Monday would begin.

When he reached the apartment, he filled the bathtub with hot water, abandoned his clothes on the bed, and, naked, walked through the hall and climbed into the relaxing waters. He had almost dozed off when he heard a key turn, a door open and close, and a smooth male voice say, "Of course, you're the first I've shown around today, but I've got a list of people as long as your arm who are interested."

"It's not as large as I imagined, from the details your office sent us," said a woman.

"It's compact, yes. But I like to think of that as a virtue."

Richard had not bothered locking the bathroom door. He was, after all, the only person there.

A gruffer, rougher male voice said, "Thought you said it was an unfurnished apartment. Looks pretty damned furnished to me."

"The previous tenant must have left some of his accoutrements behind. Funny. They never told me anything about that."

Richard stood up in the bathtub. Then, because he was naked, and the people could walk in at any moment, he sat back down. Rather desperately, he looked around the bathroom for a towel. "Oh look, George," said the woman in the hallway. "Someone's left a towel on this chair."

Richard inspected and rejected as poor towel substitutes a loofah, a half-empty bottle of shampoo, and a small yellow rubber duck. "What's the bathroom like?" asked the woman. Richard grabbed a washcloth and draped it in front of his crotch. Then he stood up, with his back to the wall, and prepared to be mortified. The door was pushed open. Three people walked into the bathroom: a young man in a camel-hair coat, and a middle-aged couple. Richard wondered if they were as embarrassed as he was.

"It's a bit small," said the woman.

"Compact," corrected the camel-hair coat, smoothly. "Easy to take care of." The woman ran her finger along the side of the sink and wrinkled her nose. "I think we've seen it all," said the middle-aged man. They walked out of the bathroom.

"It *would* be very convenient for everything," said the woman. A conversation continued in lower tones. Richard climbed out of the bath and edged over to the door. He spotted the towel on the chair in the hall, and he leaned out and grabbed it. "We'll take it," said the woman.

"You will?" said the camel-hair coat.

"It's just what we want," she explained. "Or it will be, once we've made it homey. Could it be ready for Wednesday?"

"Of course. We'll have all of this rubbish cleaned out of here tomorrow, no problem."

Richard, cold and dripping and wrapped in his towel, glared at them from the doorway. "It's not rubbish," he said. "It's my stuff."

"We'll pick up the keys from your office, then."

"Excuse me," said Richard, plaintively. "I live here."

They pushed past Richard on their way to the front door. "Pleasure doing business with you," said the camel-hair coat.

"Can you . . . can any of you hear me? This is my apartment. I live here."

"If you fax contract details to my office—" said the gruff man, then the door slammed behind them and Richard stood in the hallway of what used to be his apartment. He shivered, in the silence, from the cold. "This," announced Richard to the world, in direct defiance of the evidence of his senses, "is not happening." The Batphone shrilled, and its headlights flashed. Richard picked it up, warily. "Hello?"

The line hissed and crackled as if the call were coming from a long way away. The voice at the other end of the phone was unfamiliar. "Mister Mayhew?" it said. "Mister Richard Mayhew?"

"Yes," he said. And then, delighted, "You can hear me. Oh thank God. Who is this?"

"My associate and I met you on Saturday, Mister Mayhew. I was enquiring as to the whereabouts of a certain young lady. Do you remember?" The tones were oily, nasty, foxy.

"Oh. Yes. It's you."

"Mister Mayhew. You said Door wasn't with you. We have reason to believe that you were embroidering the truth more than perhaps a little."

"Well, *you* said you were her brother."

"*All* men are brothers, Mister Mayhew."

"She's not here anymore. And I don't know where she is."

"We know that, Mister Mayhew. We are perfectly

cognizant of both of those facts. And to be magnificently frank, Mister Mayhew—and I'm sure you
want me to be frank, don't you?—were I you, I
would no longer worry about the young lady. Her
days are numbered, and the number in question isn't
even in the double digits."

"Why are you calling me?"

"Mister Mayhew," said Mr. Croup, helpfully, "do
you know what your own liver tastes like?" Richard
was silent. "Because Mister Vandemar has promised
me that he's personally going to cut it out and stuff
it into your mouth before he slits your sad little
throat. So you'll find out, won't you?"

"I'm calling the police. You can't threaten me like
this."

"Mister Mayhew. You can call anyone you wish.
But I'd hate you to think we were making a threat.
Neither myself nor Mister Vandemar make threats,
do we Mister Vandemar?"

"No? Then what the hell *are* you doing?"

"We're making a promise," said Mr. Croup
through the static and the echo and the hiss. "And
we do know where you live." And he hung up.

Richard held the phone tightly, staring at it, then
he stabbed the nine key three times: Fire, Police, and
Ambulance. "Emergency services," said the emergency operator. "What service do you require?"

"Can you put me through to the police, please? A
man just threatened to kill me, and I don't think he
was joking."

There was a pause. He hoped he was being put
through to the police. After a few moments, the
voice said, "Emergency services. Hello? Is there anyone there? Hello?" And then Richard put down the
phone, went into his bedroom, and put his clothes

on, because he was cold and naked and scared, and there wasn't really anything else he could do.

Eventually, and after some deliberation, he took the black sports bag from under the bed and put socks into it. Underpants. Some T-shirts. His passport. His wallet. He was wearing jeans, sneakers, a thick sweater. He remembered the way the girl who called herself Door had said good-bye. The way she had paused, the way she had said she was sorry. . . .

"You knew," he said to the empty apartment. "You knew this would happen." He went into the kitchen, took some fruit from the bowl, put that into the bag. Then he zipped it up and walked out onto the darkened street.

The ATM took his card with a whirr. PLEASE ENTER YOUR PIN NUMBER, it said. Richard typed in his secret pin number (D-I-C-K). The screen went blank. PLEASE WAIT, it said, and the screen went blank. Somewhere in the depths of the machine something grumbled and growled.

THIS CARD IS NOT VALID. PLEASE CONTACT CARD ISSUER. There was a chunking noise, and the card slid out again.

"Spare any change?" said a tired voice from behind him. Richard turned: the man was short and old and balding, his scraggly beard a matted tangle of yellow and gray. The lines of his face were etched deeply in black dirt. He wore a filthy coat over the ruin of a dark gray sweater. His eyes were gray as well, and rheumy.

Richard handed the man his card. "Here," he said. "Keep it. There's about fifteen hundred pounds in there, if you can get to it."

The man took the card in his street-blackened hands, looked at it, turned it over, and said, flatly, "Thanks a bunch. That and sixty pence'll get me a nice cup of coffee." He gave Richard his card back, and began to walk down the street.

Richard picked up his bag. Then he went after the man and said, "Hey. Hang on. You can see me."

"Nothing wrong with *my* eyes," said the man.

"Listen," said Richard, "have you ever heard of a place called 'The Floating Market'? I need to get there. There's a girl called Door . . ." But the man had begun, nervously, to back away from Richard. "Look, I really need help," said Richard. "Please?"

The man stared at him, without pity. Richard sighed. "Okay," he said. "I'm sorry I troubled you." He turned away, and, clenching the handle of his bag in both hands so that they hardly shook at all, he began to walk down the High Street.

"Oy," hissed the man. Richard looked back at him. He was beckoning. "Come on, down here, quickly man." The man hurried down some steps on the derelict houses at the side of the road—garbage-strewn steps, leading down to abandoned basement apartments. Richard stumbled after him. At the bottom of the steps was a door, which the man pushed open. He waited for Richard to go through, and shut the door behind them. Through the door, they were in darkness. There was a scratch, and the noise of a match flaring into life: the man touched the match to the wick of an old railwayman's lamp, which caught, casting slightly less light than the match had, and they walked together through a dark place.

It smelled musty, of damp and old brick, of rot and the dark. "Where are we?" Richard whispered.

His guide shushed him to silence. They reached another door set in a wall. The man rapped on it rhythmically. There was a pause, and then the door swung open.

For a moment, Richard was blinded by the sudden light. He was standing in a huge, vaulted room, an underground hall, filled with firelight and smoke. Small fires burned around the room. Shadowy people stood by the flames, roasting small animals on spits. People scurried from fire to fire. It reminded him of Hell—or rather, the way that he had thought of Hell, as a schoolboy. The smoke irritated his lungs, and he coughed. A hundred eyes turned, then, and stared at him: a hundred eyes, unblinking and unfriendly.

A man scuttled toward them. He had long hair, a patchy brown beard, and his ragged clothes were trimmed with fur—orange-and-white-and-black fur, like the coat of a calico cat. He would have been taller than Richard, but he walked with a pronounced stoop, his hands held up at his chest, fingers pressed together. "What? What is it? What is this?" he asked Richard's guide. "Who've you brought us, Iliaster? Talk-talk-talk."

"He's from the Upside," said the guide. (*Iliaster?* thought Richard.) "Was asking about the Lady Door. And the Floating Market. Brought him to you, Lord Rat-speaker. Figured you'd know what to do with him." There were now more than a dozen of the fur-trimmed people standing around them, women and men, and even a few children. They moved in scurries: moments of stillness, followed by hasty dashes toward Richard.

The Lord Rat-speaker reached inside his fur-trimmed rags and pulled out a wicked-looking sliver of glass, about eight inches long. Some poorly cured fur had been tied around the bottom half of it to form an improvised grip. Firelight glinted from the glass blade. The Lord Rat-speaker put the shard to Richard's throat. "Oh yes. Yes-yes-yes," he chittered, excitedly. "I know *exactly* what to do with him."

FOUR

MR. CROUP AND MR. VANDEMAR HAD SET
up their home in the cellar of a Victorian hospital,
closed down ten years earlier because of National
Health Service budget cutbacks. The property de-
velopers, who had announced their intention of
turning the hospital into an unparalleled block of
unique luxury-living accommodations, had faded
away as soon as the hospital had been closed, and
so it stood there, year after year, gray and empty
and unwanted, its windows boarded up, its doors
padlocked shut. The roof was rotten, and rain
dripped through the empty hospital's interior,
spreading damp and decay through the building.
The hospital was ranged around a central well,
which let in a certain amount of gray and unfriendly
light.

The basement world beneath the empty hospital
wards comprised more than a hundred tiny rooms,
some of them empty, others containing abandoned
hospital supplies. One room held a squat, giant
metal furnace, while the next room housed the
blocked and waterless toilets and showers. Most of
the basement floors were covered with a thin layer

of oily rainwater, which reflected the darkness and the decay back toward the rotting ceilings.

If you were to walk down the hospital steps, as far down as you could go, through the abandoned shower rooms, past the staff toilets, past a room filled with broken glass, where the ceiling had collapsed entirely, leaving it open to the stairwell above, you would reach a small, rusting iron staircase, from which the once-white paint was peeling in long, damp strips. And if you went down the staircase, and traversed the marshy place at the bottom of the steps, and pushed your way through a half-decayed wooden door, you would find yourself in the sub-cellar, a huge room in which a hundred and twenty years of hospital waste had accumulated, been abandoned, and, eventually, forgotten; and it was here that Mr. Croup and Mr. Vandemar had, for the present, made their home. The walls were damp, and water dripped from the ceiling. Odd things moldered in corners: some of them had once been alive.

Mr. Croup and Mr. Vandemar were killing time. Mr. Vandemar had obtained from somewhere a centipede—a reddish orange creature, almost eight inches long, with vicious, poisonous fangs—and was letting it run over his hands, watching it as it twined between his fingers, vanished up one sleeve, appeared a minute later out of the other. Mr. Croup was playing with razor blades. He had found, in a corner, a whole box of fifty-year-old razor blades, wrapped in wax paper, and he had been trying to think of things to do with them.

"If I might have your attention, Mister Vandemar," he said, at length. "Pipe your beady eyes on this."

Mr. Vandemar held the centipede's head delicately between a huge thumb and a massive forefinger to stop it wriggling. He looked at Mr. Croup.

Mr. Croup put his left hand against a wall, fingers spread. He took five razor blades in his right hand, took careful aim, and threw them at the wall. Each blade stuck into the wall, between Mr. Croup's fingers; it was like a top knife-thrower's act in miniature. Mr. Croup took his hand away, leaving the blades in the wall, outlining the place his fingers had been, and he turned to his partner for approval.

Mr. Vandemar was unimpressed. "What's so clever about that, then?" he asked. "You didn't even hit *one* finger."

Mr. Croup sighed. "I didn't?" he said. "Well, slit my gullet, you're right. How could I have been such a ninny?" He pulled the razor blades out of the wall, one by one, and dropped them onto the wooden table. "Why don't you show me how it should have been done?"

Mr. Vandemar nodded. He put his centipede back into its empty marmalade jar. Then he put his left hand against the wall. He raised his right arm: his knife, wicked and sharp and perfectly weighted, was in his right hand. He narrowed his eyes, and he threw. The knife flew through the air and thudded into the damp plaster wall blade-first, the blade having first hit and penetrated the back of Mr. Vandemar's hand on its way.

A telephone began to ring.

Mr. Vandemar looked around at Croup, satisfied, his hand still pinned to the wall. "*That's* how it's done," he said.

There was an old telephone in the corner of the room, an antique, two-part telephone, unused in the hospital since the 1920s, made of wood and Bakelite. Mr. Croup picked up the earpiece, which was on a long, cloth-wrapped cord, and spoke into the mouthpiece, which was attached to the base. "Croup and Vandemar," he said, smoothly, "the Old Firm. Obstacles obliterated, nuisances eradicated, bothersome limbs removed and tutelary dentistry."

The person at the other end of the phone said something. Mr. Croup cringed. Mr. Vandemar tugged at his left hand. It wasn't coming free.

"Oh. Yes, sir. Yes, indeed. And might I say how your telephonic confabulation brightens up and cheers our otherwise dreary and uneventful day?" Another pause. "Of course I'll stop toadying and crawling. Delighted to. An honor, and—what do we know? We know that—" An interruption; he picked his nose, reflectively, patiently, then: "No, we don't know where she is at this precise moment. But we don't have to. She'll be at the market tonight and—" His mouth tightened, and, "We have no intention of violating their market truce. More of waiting till she has left the market and scrobbling her . . ." He was silent then, and listened, nodding from time to time.

Mr. Vandemar tried to pull the knife out of the wall with his free hand, but the knife was stuck quite fast.

"That might be arranged, yes," said Mr. Croup, into the mouthpiece. "I mean it *will* be arranged. Of course. Yes. I realize that. And, sir, perhaps we could talk about—" But the caller had hung up. Mr. Croup stared at the earpiece for a moment, then put it back on its hook. "You think you're so damned clever," he whispered. Then he noticed Mr. Vandemar's predicament and said, "Stop that." He leaned over, pulled the knife out of the wall and out of the back of Mr. Vandemar's hand, and put it down on the table.

Mr. Vandemar shook his left hand and flexed the fingers, then wiped the fragments of damp plaster from his knife-blade. "Who was that?"

"Our employer," said Mr. Croup. "It seems the other one isn't going to work out. Not old enough. It's going to have to be the Door female."

"So we aren't allowed to kill her any more?"

"That, Mister Vandemar, would be about the short and the long of it, yes. Now, it seems that Little Miss Door has announced that she shall be hiring a body-guard. At the market. Tonight."

"So?" Mr. Vandemar spat on the back of his hand, where the knife had gone in, and on the palm of his hand, where the knife had come out. He rubbed at the spit with a massive thumb. The flesh closed, knit-ted, was whole again.

Mr. Croup picked up his old coat, heavy, black, and shiny with age, from the floor. He put it on. "So, Mister Vandemar," he said, "shall we not also hire ourselves a bodyguard?"

Mr. Vandemar slid his knife back into the holster in his sleeve. He put his coat on as well, pushed his hands deep into the pockets, and was pleasantly sur-prised to find an almost untouched mouse in one pocket. Good. He was hungry. Then he pondered Mr. Croup's last statement with the intensity of an anatomist dissecting his one true love, and, realizing the flaw in his partner's logic, Mr. Vandemar said, "We don't need a bodyguard, Mister Croup. We hurt people. We don't get hurt."

Mr. Croup turned out the lights. "Oh, Mister Van-demar," he said, enjoying the sound of the words, as he enjoyed the sound of all words, "if you cut us, do we not bleed?"

Mr. Vandemar pondered this for a moment, in the dark. Then he said, with perfect accuracy, "No."

"A spy from the Upworld," said the Lord Rat-speaker. "Heh? I should slit you from gullet to gizzard and tell fortunes with your guts."

"Look," said Richard, his back against the wall, with the glass dagger pressed against his Adam's apple. "I think you're making a bit of a mistake here. My name is Richard Mayhew. I can prove who I am. I've got my library cards. Credit cards. Things," he added, desperately.

At the opposite end of the hall, Richard noticed, with the dispassionate clarity that comes when a lunatic is about to slit your throat with a piece of broken glass, people were throwing themselves to the ground, bowing low, and remaining on the floor. A small black shape was coming toward them along the ground. "I think a moment's reflection might prove that we're all being very silly," said Richard. He had no idea what the words meant, just that they were coming out of his mouth, and that as long as he was talking, he was not dead. "Now, why don't you put that away, and—excuse me, that's my bag," this last to a thin, bedraggled girl in her late teens who had taken Richard's bag and was roughly tipping his possessions out onto the ground.

The people in the hall continued to bow, and to stay bowed, as the small shape came closer. It reached the group of people around Richard, although not a one of them noticed it. They were all looking at Richard.

It was a rat, which looked up at Richard, curiously. He had the bizarre and momentary impression that it *winked* one of of its little black oildrop eyes at him. Then it chittered, loudly.

The man with the glass dagger threw himself on his knees. So did the people gathered around them. So, too, after a moment's hesitation, and a little more awkwardly, did the homeless man, the one they had called Iliaster. In a moment, Richard was the only one standing. The thin girl tugged at his elbow, and he, too, went down on one knee.

Lord Rat-speaker bowed so low that his long hair brushed the ground, and he chittered back at the rat, wrinkling his nose, showing his teeth, squeaking and hissing, for all the world like an enormous rat himself.

"Look, can anybody tell me . . ." muttered Richard.

"Quiet!" said the thin girl.

The rat stepped—a little disdainfully, it seemed—into the Lord Rat-speaker's grubby hand, and the man held it, respectfully, up in front of Richard's face. It waved its tail languidly as it inspected Richard's features. "This is Master Longtail, of the clan Gray," said the Lord Rat-speaker. "He says you looks exceeding familiar. He wants to know if he's met you afore."

Richard looked at the rat. The rat looked at Richard. "I suppose it's possible," he admitted.

"He says he was discharging an obligation to the marquis de Carabas."

Richard stared at the animal more closely. "It's *that* rat? Yes, we've met. Actually, I threw the TV remote control at it." Some of the people standing around looked shocked. The thin girl actually squeaked. Richard hardly noticed them; at least something was familiar in this madness. "Hello, Ratty," he said. "Good to see you again. Do you know where Door is?"

"Ratty!" said the girl in something between a squeak and a horrified swallow. She had a large, water-stained red button pinned to her ragged clothes, the kind that comes attached to birthday cards. It said, in yellow letters, I AM 11.

Lord Rat-speaker waved his glass dagger admonishingly at Richard. "You must not address Master Longtail, save through me," he said. The rat squeaked an order. The man's face fell. "Him?" he said, looking at Richard disdainfully. "Look, I can't spare a soul. How about if I simply slice his throat and send him down to the Sewer Folk. . . ."

The rat chittered once more, decisively, then leapt from the man's shoulder onto the ground and vanished into one of the many holes that lined the walls.

The Lord Rat-speaker stood up. A hundred eyes were fixed on him. He turned back to the hall and looked at his subjects, crouched beside their greasy fires. "I don't know what you lot are all looking at," he shouted. "Who's turning the spits, eh? You want the grub to burn? There's nothing to see. Go on. Get-get away with the lot of you." Richard stood up, nervously. His left leg had gotten numb, and he rubbed life into it, as it prickled with pins and needles. Lord Rat-speaker looked at Iliaster. "He's got to be taken to the market. Master Longtail's orders."

Iliaster shook his head, and spat onto the ground. "Well, I'm not taking him," he said. "More than my life's worth, that journey. You rat-speakers have always been good to me, but I can't go back there. You know that."

The Lord Rat-speaker nodded. He put his dagger

away, in the furs of his robe. Then he smiled at Richard with yellow teeth. "You don't know how lucky you were, just then," he said.

"Yes I do," said Richard. "I really do."

"No," said the man, "you don't. You really don't." And he shook his head and said to himself, marvelling, " 'Ratty.' "

The Lord Rat-speaker took Iliaster by the arm, and the two of them walked a little way out of earshot and began to talk, darting looks back at Richard as they did so.

The thin girl was gulping down one of Richard's bananas in what was, Richard reflected, the least erotic display of banana-eating he had ever seen. "You know, that was going to be my breakfast," said Richard. She looked up at him guiltily. "My name's Richard. What's yours?"

The girl, who, he realized, had already managed to eat most of the fruit that Richard had brought with him, swallowed the last of the banana and hesitated. Then she half-smiled, and said something that sounded a lot like Anaesthesia. "I was hungry," she said.

"Well, so'm I," he told her.

She glanced at the little fires across the room. Then she looked back at Richard. She smiled again. "Do you like cat?" she said.

"Yes," said Richard. "I quite like cats."

Anaesthesia looked relieved. "Thigh?" she asked. "Or breast?"

The girl called Door walked down the court, followed by the marquis de Carabas. There were a hundred other little courts and mews and alleys in London just like this one, tiny spurs of old-time, unchanged for three hundred years. Even the smell of piss here was the same as it had been in Pepys's time, three hundred years before. There was still an hour until dawn, but the sky was beginning to lighten, turning a stark, leaden color. Strands of mist hung like livid ghosts on the air.

The door was roughly boarded up and covered with stained posters for forgotten bands and long-closed nightclubs. The two of them stopped in front of it, and the marquis eyed it, all boards and nails and posters, and he appeared unimpressed; but then, unimpressed was his default state.

"So this is the entrance?" he said.

She nodded. "One of them."

He folded his arms. "Well? Say 'Open sesame,' or whatever it is that you do."

"I don't want to do this," she said. "I'm really not sure that we're doing the right thing."

"Very well," he unfolded his arms. "I'll be seeing you, then." He turned on his heel and began to walk back the way that they had come. Door seized his arm. "You'd abandon me?" she asked. "Just like that?"

He grinned, without humor. "Certainly. I'm a very busy man. Things to see. People to do."

"Look, hold on." She let go of his sleeve, bit her lower lip. "The last time I was here . . ." she trailed off.

"The last time you were here, you found your family dead. Well, there you are. You don't have to explain it anymore. If we aren't going in, then our business relationship is at an end."

She looked up at him, her elfin face pale in the pre-dawn light. "And that's all?"

"I could wish you the best of luck in your future

career, but I'm afraid I rather doubt you'll live long enough to have one."

"You're a piece of work, aren't you?"

He said nothing. She walked back toward the door. "Well," she said. "Come on. I'll take us in." Door put her left hand on the boarded-up door, and with her right hand she took the marquis's huge brown hand. Her tiny fingers twined into his larger ones. She closed her eyes.

. . . something whispered and shivered and changed . . .

. . . and the door collapsed into darkness.

The memory was fresh, only a few days old: Door moved through the House Without Doors calling "I'm home," and "Hello?" She slipped from the anteroom to the dining room, to the library, to the drawing room; no one answered. She moved to another room.

The swimming pool was an indoor Victorian structure, constructed of marble and of cast iron. Her father had found it when he was younger, abandoned and about to be demolished, and he had woven it into the fabric of the House Without Doors. Perhaps in the world outside, in London Above, the room had long been destroyed and forgotten. Door had no idea where any of the rooms of her house were, physically. Her grandfather had constructed the house, taking a room from here, a room from there, all through London, discrete and doorless; her father had added to it.

She walked along the side of the old swimming pool, pleased to be home, puzzled by the absence of her family. And then she looked down.

There was someone floating in the water, trailing twin clouds of blood behind him, one from the throat, one from the groin. It was her brother, Arch. His eyes were open

wide and sightless. She realized that her mouth was open.
She could hear herself screaming.

"That hurt," said the marquis. He rubbed his forehead, hard, twisted his head around on his neck, as
if he were trying to ease a sudden, painful crick.

"Memories," she explained. "They're imprinted in
the walls."

He raised an eyebrow. "You could have warned
me."

They were in a huge white room. Every wall was
covered with pictures. Each picture was of a different room. The white room contained no doors: no
openings of any kind. "Interesting décor," acknowledged the marquis.

"This is the entrance hall. We can go from here to
any room in the House. They are all linked."

"Where are the other rooms located?"

She shook her head. "I don't know. Miles away,
probably. They're scattered all over the Underside."

The marquis had managed to cover the whole
room in a series of impatient strides. "Quite remarkable. An associative house, every room of which is
located somewhere else. So imaginative. Your
grandfather was a man of vision, Door."

"I never knew him." She swallowed, then continued, talking to herself as much as to him. "We
should have been safe here. Nobody should have
been able to hurt us. Only my family could move
around it."

"Let's hope your father's journal gives us some
clues," he said. "Where do we start looking?" Door
shrugged. "You're certain he kept a journal?" he
pressed.

She nodded. "He used to go into his study, and

private the links until he'd finished dictating."

"We'll start in the study, then."

"But I looked there. I did. I *looked* there. When I was cleaning up the body . . ." And she began to cry, in low, raging sobs, that sounded like they were being tugged from inside her.

"There. There," said the marquis de Carabas, awkwardly, patting her shoulder. And he added, for good measure, "There." He did not comfort well.

Door's odd-colored eyes were filled with tears. "Can you . . . can you just give me a sec? I'll be fine." He nodded and walked to the far end of the room. When he looked back she was still standing there, on her own, silhouetted in the white entrance chamber filled with pictures of rooms, and she was hugging herself, and shuddering, and crying like a little girl.

Richard was still upset about the loss of his bag.

The Lord Rat-speaker remained unmoved. He stated baldly that the rat—Master Longtail—had said nothing at all about returning Richard's things. Just that he was to be taken to market. Then he told Anaesthesia that she was taking the Upworlder to the market, and that, yes, it was an order. And to stop snivelling, and to get a move on. He told Richard that if he, Lord Rat-speaker, ever saw him, Richard, again, then he, Richard, would be in a great deal of trouble. He reiterated that Richard did not know how lucky he was, and, ignoring Richard's requests that he return Richard's stuff—or at least the wallet—he led them to a door and locked it behind them.

Richard and Anaesthesia walked into the darkness side by side.

She carried an improvised lamp made of a candle, a can, some wire, and a wide-mouthed glass lemonade bottle. Richard was surprised at how quickly his eyes became used to the near darkness. They seemed to be walking through a succession of underground vaults and storage cellars. Sometimes he thought he could see movement in far corners of the vaults, but whether human, or rat, or something else altogether, it was always gone by the time they reached the place it had been. When he tried to talk to Anaesthesia about the movements, she hissed him to silence.

He felt a cold draught on his face. The rat-girl squatted without warning, put down her candle-lamp, and tugged and pulled hard at a metal grille set in the wall. It opened suddenly, sending her sprawling. She motioned Richard to come through. He crouched, edged through the hole in the wall; after about a foot, the floor stopped completely. "Excuse me," whispered Richard. "There's a hole here."

"It's not a big drop," she told him. "Go on."

She shut the grille behind her. She was now uncomfortably close to Richard. "Here," she said. She gave him the handle of her little lamp to hold, and she clambered down into the darkness. "There," she said. "That wasn't that bad, was it?" Her face was a few feet below Richard's dangling feet. "Here. Pass me the lamp."

He lowered it down to her. She had to jump to take it from him. "Now," she whispered. "Come on." He edged nervously forward, climbed over the edge, hung for a moment, then let go. He landed on his hands and feet in soft, wet mud. He wiped the mud off his hands onto his sweater. A few feet forward, and Anaesthesia was opening another door.

They went through it, and she pulled it closed behind them. "We can talk now," she said. "Not loud. But we can. If you want to."

"Oh. Thanks," said Richard. He couldn't think of anything to say. "So. Um. You're a rat, are you?" he said.

She giggled, like a Japanese girl, covering her face with her hand as she laughed. Then she shook her head, and said, "I should be so lucky. I wish. No, I'm a rat-speaker. We talk to rats."

"What, just chat to them?"

"Oh no. We do stuff for them. I mean," and her tone of voice implied that this was something that might never have occurred to Richard unassisted, "there *are* some things rats *can't* do, you know. I mean, not having fingers, and thumbs, an' things. Hang on—" She pressed him against the wall, suddenly, and clamped a filthy hand over his mouth. Then she blew out the candle.

Nothing happened.

Then he heard distant voices. They waited, in the darkness and the cold. Richard shivered.

People walked past them, talking in low tones. When all sounds had died away, Anaesthesia took her hand from Richard's mouth, relit the candle, and they walked on. "Who were they?" asked Richard.

She shrugged. "It dun't matter," she said.

"Then what makes you think that they wouldn't have been pleased to see us?"

She looked at him rather sadly, like a mother trying to explain to an infant that, yes *this* flame was hot, too. *All* flames were hot. Trust her, please. "Come on," she said. "I know a shortcut. We can nip through London Above for a bit." They went up some stone steps, and the girl pushed open a door.

They stepped through, and the door shut behind them.

Richard looked around, puzzled. They were standing on the Embankment, the miles-long walkway that the Victorians had built along the the north shore of the Thames, covering the drainage system and the newly created District Line of the Underground, and replacing the stinking mudflats that had festered along the banks of the Thames for the previous five hundred years. It was still night—or perhaps it was night once more. He was unsure how long they had been walking through the underplaces and the dark.

There was no moon, but the night sky was a riot of crisp and glittering autumn stars. There were streetlights too, and lights on buildings and on bridges, which looked like earthbound stars, and they glimmered, repeated, as they were reflected with the city in the night water of the Thames. *It's fairyland*, thought Richard.

Anaesthesia blew out her candle. And Richard said, "Are you sure this is the right way?"

"Yes," she said. "Pretty sure."

They were approaching a wooden bench, and the moment he set eyes on it, it seemed to Richard that that bench was one of the most desirable objects he had ever seen. "Can we sit down?" he asked. "Just for a minute."

She shrugged. They sat down at opposite ends of the bench. "On Friday," said Richard, "I was with one of the finest investment analyst firms in London."

"What's a investment an' a thing?"

"It was my job."

She nodded, satisfied. "Right. And ... ?"

"Just reminding myself, really. Yesterday . . . it was like I didn't exist anymore, to anybody up here."

"That's 'cos you don't," explained Anaesthesia.

A late-night couple, who had been slowly walking along the Embankment toward them, holding hands, sat down in the middle of the bench, between Richard and Anaesthesia, and commenced to kiss each other, passionately. "Excuse me," said Richard to them. The man had his hand inside the woman's sweater and was moving it around enthusiastically, a lone traveler discovering an unexplored continent. "I want my life back," Richard told the couple.

"I love you," said the man to the woman.

"But your wife—" she said, licking the side of his face.

"Fuck her," said the man.

"Don' wanna fuck *her*," said the woman, and she giggled, drunkenly. "Wanna fuck *you* . . ." She put a hand on his crotch and giggled some more.

"Come on," said Richard to Anaesthesia, feeling that the bench had started to become a less desirable neighborhood. They got up and walked away. Anaesthesia peered back, curiously, at the couple on the bench, who were gradually becoming more horizontal.

Richard said nothing. "Something wrong?" asked Anaesthesia.

"Only everything," said Richard. "Have you always lived down there?"

"Nah. I was born up here," she hesitated. "You don't want to hear about me." Richard realized, almost surprised, that he really did.

"I do. Really."

She fingered the rough quartz beads that hung in

a necklace around her neck, and she swallowed. "There was me and my mother and the twins . . ." she said, and then she stopped talking. Her mouth clamped shut.

"Go on," said Richard. "It's all right. Really it is. Honest."

The girl nodded. She took a deep breath, and then she began to talk, without looking at him as she talked, her eyes fixed on the ground ahead of her. "Well, my mother had me an' my sisters, but she got a bit funny in the head. One day I got home from school, and she was crying and crying, and she didn't have any clothes on, and she was breaking stuff. Plates and stuff. But she never hurt us. She never did. The lady from the social services came and took the twins away, an' I had to go and stay with my aunt. She was living with this man. I didn't like him. And when she was out of the house . . ." The girl paused; she was quiet for so long that Richard wondered if she had finished. Then she began once more, "Anyway. He used to hurt me. Do other stuff. In the end, I told my aunt, an' she started hitting me. Said I was lying. Said she'd have the police on me. But I wasn't lying. So I run away. It was my birthday."

They had reached the Albert Bridge, a kitsch monument spanning the Thames, joining Battersea to the south with the Chelsea end of the Embankment, a bridge hung with thousands of tiny white lights.

"I didn't have anywhere to go. And it was so cold," said Anaesthesia, and she stopped again. "I slept on the streets. I'd sleep in the day, when it was a bit warmer, and walk around at night, just to keep moving. I was only eleven. Stealing bread an' milk off people's doorsteps to eat. Hated doing that so I started hanging around the street markets, taking the rotten apples an' oranges an' things people threw away. Then I got really sick. I was living under an overpass in Notting Hill. When I come to, I was in London Below. The rats had found me."

"Have you ever tried to return to all this?" he asked, gesturing. Quiet, warm, inhabited houses. Late-night cars. The real world . . . she shook her head. *All fire burns, little baby. You'll learn.* "You can't. It's one or the other. Nobody ever gets both."

"I'm sorry," said Door, hesitantly. Her eyes were red, and she looked as if she had been vigorously blowing her nose and scrubbing her tears from her eyes and cheeks.

The marquis had been amusing himself while he waited for her to collect herself by playing a game of knucklebones with some old coins and bones he kept in one of the many pockets of his coat. He looked up at her coldly. "Indeed?"

She bit her lower lip. "No. Not really. I'm not sorry. I've been running and hiding and running so hard that . . . this was the first chance I've really had to . . ." she stopped.

The marquis swept up the coins and the bones, and returned them to their pocket. "After you," he said. He followed her back to the wall of pictures. She put one hand on the painting of her father's study and took the marquis's large black hand with the other.

. . . reality twisted . . .

They were in the conservatory, watering the plants. First Portia would water a plant, directing the flow of the water toward the soil at the base of the plant, avoiding

*the leaves and the blossoms. "Water the shoes," she said
to her youngest daughter. "Not the clothes."*

*Ingress had her own little watering can. She was so
proud of it. It was just like her mother's, made of steel,
painted bright green. As her mother finished with each
plant, Ingress would water it with her tiny watering can.
"On the shoes," she told her mother. She began laughing,
then, spontaneous little-girl laughter.*

*And her mother laughed too, until foxy Mr. Croup
pulled her hair back, hard and sudden, and cut her white
throat from ear to ear.*

"Hello, Daddy," said Door, quietly.

She touched the bust of her father with her fingers,
stroking the side of his face. A thin, ascetic man, almost bald. *Caesar as Prospero,* thought the marquis
de Carabas. He felt a little sick. That last image had
hurt. Still: he was in Lord Portico's study. *That* was
a first.

The marquis took in the room, eyes sliding from
detail to detail. The stuffed crocodile hanging from
the ceiling; the leather-bound books, an astrolabe,
convex and concave mirrors, odd scientific instruments; there were maps on the walls, of lands and
cities de Carabas had never heard of; a desk, covered
in handwritten correspondence. The white wall behind the desk was marred by a reddish-brown stain.
There was a small portrait of Door's family on the
desk. The marquis stared at it. "Your mother and
your sister, your father, and your brothers. All dead.
How did *you* escape?" he asked.

She lowered her hand. "I was lucky. I'd gone off
exploring for a few days . . . did you know there are
still some Roman soldiers camped out by the Kil-
burn River?"

The marquis had not known this, which irritated him. "Hmm. How many?"

She shrugged. "A few dozen. They were deserters from the Nineteenth Legion, I think. My Latin's a bit patchy. Anyway, when I got back here . . ." She paused, swallowed, her opal-colored eyes brimming with tears.

"Pull yourself together," said the marquis, shortly. "We need your father's journal. We have to find out who did this."

She frowned at him. "We know who did this. It was Croup and Vandemar—"

He opened a hand, waggled his fingers as he spoke. "They're arms. Hands. Fingers. There's a head that ordered it, that wants you dead, too. Those two don't come cheap." He looked around the cluttered office. "His journal?" said the marquis.

"It's not here," she said. "I told you. I looked."

"I was under the misapprehension that your family was skilled in locating doors, both obvious and otherwise."

She glowered at him. Then she closed her eyes and put her finger and thumb on each side of the bridge of her nose. Meanwhile, the marquis examined the objects on Portico's desk. An inkwell; a chess-piece; a bone die; a gold pocket-watch; several quill-feathers and . . .

Interesting.

It was a small statue of a boar, or a crouching bear, or perhaps a bull. It was hard to tell. It was the size of a large chess-piece, and it had been roughly carved out of black obsidian. It reminded him of something, but of what he could not say. He picked it up casually, turned it over, curled his fingers around it.

Door lowered her hand from her face. She looked puzzled and confused. "What's the matter?" he asked.

"It *is* here," she said, simply. She began to walk through the study, head turning first to one side and then to the other. The marquis slipped the carving discreetly into an inside pocket.

Door stood before a high cabinet. "There," she said. She reached out a hand: there was a click, and a small panel in the side of the cabinet swung open. Door reached into the darkness and removed something roughly the size and shape of a small cannon-ball. She passed it to the marquis. It was a sphere, constructed of old brass and polished wood, inset with polished copper and glass lenses. He took it from her.

"This is it?"

She nodded.

"Well done."

She looked grave. "I don't know how I could have missed it before."

"You were upset," said the marquis. "I was certain it would be here. And I am so rarely wrong. Now . . ." he held the little wooden globe up. The light caught the polished glass and glinted from the brass and copper fittings. It galled him to admit ignorance about anything, but he said it anyway. "How does this work?"

Anaesthesia led Richard into a small park on the south side of the bridge, then down some stone steps, set beside a wall. She relit her candle-in-a-bottle, and then she opened a workman's door and closed it behind them. They went down some steps, with the darkness all around them.

"There's a girl named Door," said Richard. "She's a bit younger than you. Do you know her?"

"The Lady Door. I know who she is."

"So which, um, barony is she part of?"

"No barony. She's of the House of the Arch. Her family used to be very important."

"Used to be? Why did they stop?"

"Somebody killed them."

Yes, he remembered the marquis saying something about that, now. A rat cut across their path. Anaesthesia stopped on the steps and performed a deep curtsey. The rat paused. "Sire," she said, to the rat. "Hi," said Richard. The rat looked at them for a heartbeat, then it darted off down the steps. "So," said Richard. "What is a floating market?"

"It's very big," she said. "But rat-speakers hardly ever need to go to the market. To tell the truth—" She hesitated. "Nah. You'll laugh at me."

"I won't," said Richard, honestly.

"Well," said the thin girl. "I'm a little scared."

"Scared? Of the market?"

They had reached the bottom of the steps. Anaesthesia hesitated and then turned left. "Oh. No. There's a truce in the market. If anyone hurt anyone there, the whole of London Below would be down on them like a ton of sewage."

"So what are you scared of?"

"Getting there. They hold it in a different place every time. It moves around. And to get to the place it'll be tonight . . ." she fingered the quartz beads around her neck, nervously. "We'll have to go through a really nasty neighborhood." She *did* sound scared.

Richard suppressed the urge to put an arm around her. "And where would that be?" he asked. She turned to him, pushed the hair from her eyes, and told him.

"Knightsbridge," repeated Richard, and he began to chuckle, gently.

The girl turned away. "See?" she said. "I said you'd laugh."

The deep tunnels had been dug in the early days of the Second World War. Troops had been quartered there in their thousands, their waste needing to be pumped up by compressed air to the level of the sewers far above. Both sides of the tunnels had been lined with metal bunk beds for the troops to sleep on. There had been plans to assimilate the tunnels into a high speed extension to the underground system, but these plans came to nothing, and when the war ended the bunk beds had stayed in the tunnels, and on their wire bases cardboard boxes were stored, each box filled with letters and files and papers: secrets, of the dullest kind, stored down deep, to be forgotten. Economies had closed the deep tunnels completely in the early 1990s. The boxes of secrets were removed, to be scanned and sorted on computers, or shredded, or burned.

Varney made his home in the deepest of the deep tunnels, far beneath Camden Town Tube. He had piled abandoned metal bunk beds in front of the only entrance. Then he had decorated. Varney liked weapons. He made his own, out of whatever he could find, or take, or steal, parts of cars and rescued bits of machinery, which he turned into hooks and shivs, crossbows and arbalests, small mangonels and trebuchets for breaking walls, cudgels, glaives and knobkerries. They hung on the wall of the deep tunnel, or sat in corners, looking unfriendly.

Varney looked like a bull might look, if the bull

were to be shaved, dehorned, covered in tattoos, and suffered from complete dental breakdown. Also, he snored. The oil lamp next to his head was turned down low. Varney slept on a pile of rags, snoring and snuffling, with the hilt of a homemade two-bladed sword on the ground beside his hand.

A hand turned up the oil lamp.

Varney had the two-bladed sword in his hand, and he was on his feet almost before his eyes were open. He blinked, stared around him. There was no one there: nothing had disturbed the pile of bunk beds blocking the door. He began to lower the sword.

A voice said, "Psst."

"Hh?" said Varney.

"Surprise," said Mr. Croup, stepping into the light.

Varney took a step back: a mistake. There was a knife at his temple, the point of the blade next to his eye. "Further movements are not recommended," said Mr. Croup, helpfully. "Mister Vandemar might have a little accident with his old toad-sticker. Most accidents do occur in the home. Is that not so, Mister Vandemar?"

"I don't trust statistics," said Mr. Vandemar's blank voice. A gloved hand reached down from behind Varney, crushed his sword, and dropped the twisted thing to the floor.

"How are you, Varney?" asked Mr. Croup. "Well, we trust? Yes? In fine form, fetlock and fettle for the market tonight? Do you know who we are?"

Varney did the nearest thing he could to a nod that didn't actually involve moving any muscles. He knew who Croup and Vandemar were. His eyes were searching the walls. Yes, there: the morning-star: a spiked wooden ball, studded with nails, on a chain, in the far corner of the room . . .

"There is talk that a certain young lady will be auditioning bodyguards this evening. Had you thought of trying out for the task?" Mr. Croup picked at his tombstone teeth. "Enunciate clearly."

Varney picked up the morning-star with his mind. It was his Knack. Gentle, now . . . slowly . . . He edged it off the hook and pulled it up toward the top of the tunnel arch. . . . With his mouth, he said, "Varney's the best bravo and guard in the Underside. They say I'm the best since Hunter's day."

Varney mentally positioned the morning-star in the shadows above and behind Mr. Croup's head. *He would crush Croup's skull first, then he'd take Vandemar . . .*

The morning-star plunged toward Mr. Croup's head: Varney flung himself down, away from the knife-blade at his eye. Mr. Croup did not look up. He did not turn. He simply moved his head, obscenely fast, and the morning-star crashed past him, into the floor, where it threw up chips of brick and concrete. Mr. Vandemar picked Varney up with one hand. "Hurt him?" he asked his partner.

Mr. Croup shook his head: *not yet.* To Varney, he said, "Not bad. So, 'best bravo and guard,' we want you to get yourself to the market tonight. We want you to do whatever you have to, to become that certain young lady's personal bodyguard. Then, when you get the job, one thing you don't forget. You may guard her from the rest of the world, but when we want her, we take her. Got it?"

Varney ran his tongue over the wreck of his teeth. "Are you bribing me?" he asked.

Mr. Vandemar had picked up the morning-star.

He was pulling the chain apart, with his free hand, link by link, and dropping the bits of twisted metal onto the floor. *Chink.* "No," said Mr. Vandemar. *Chink.* "We're intimidating you." *Chink.* "And if you don't do what Mister Croup says, we're . . ." *chink* ". . . hurting you . . ." *chink* ". . . very badly, before we're . . ." *chink* ". . . killing you."

"Ah," said Varney. "Then I'm working for you, aren't I?"

"Yes, you are," said Mr. Croup. "I'm afraid we don't have any redeeming features."

"That doesn't bother me," said Varney.

"Good," said Mr. Croup. "Welcome aboard."

It was a large but elegant mechanism, built of polished walnut and oak, of brass and glass, copper and mirrors and carved and inlaid ivory, of quartz prisms and brass gears and springs and cogs. The whole thing was rather larger than a wide-screen television, although the actual screen itself was no more than six inches across. A magnifying lens placed across it increased the size of the picture. There was a large brass horn coming out of the side—the kind you could find on an antique gramophone. The whole mechanism looked rather like a combined television and video player might look, if it had been invented and built three hundred years ago by Sir Isaac Newton. Which was, more or less, exactly what it was.

"Watch," said Door. She placed the wooden ball onto a platform. Lights shone through the machine and into the ball. It began to spin around and around.

A patrician face appeared on the small screen, vividly colored. Slightly out of time, a voice came from the horn, crackling in mid-speech. ". . . that two cities should be so near," said the voice, "and yet in all things so far; the possessors above us, and the dispossessed, we who live below and between, who live in the cracks."

Door stared at the screen, her face unreadable.

". . . still," said her father, "I am of the opinion that what cripples us, who inhabit the Underside, is our petty factionalism. The system of baronies and fiefdoms is both divisive and foolish." The Lord Portico was wearing a threadbare old smoking jacket and a skullcap. His voice seemed to be coming to them across the centuries, not days or weeks. He coughed. "I am not alone in this belief. There are those who wish to see things the way they are. There are others who want the situation to worsen. There are those . . ."

"Can you speed it up?" asked the marquis. "Find the last entry?"

Door nodded. She touched an ivory lever at the side: the image ghosted, fragmented, re-formed.

Now Portico wore a long coat. His skullcap was gone. There was a scarlet gash down one side of his head. He was no longer sitting at his desk. He was talking urgently, quietly. "I do not know who will see this, who will find this. But whoever you are, please take this to my daughter, the Lady Door, if she lives . . ." A static burst wiped across the picture and the sound. Then, "Door? Girl, this is bad. I don't know how long I've got before they find this room. I think my poor Portia and your brother and sister are dead." The sound and picture quality began to degrade.

The marquis glanced at Door. Her face was wet: tears were brimming from her eyes, glistening down her cheeks. She seemed unaware that she was crying, made no attempt to wipe away the tears. She just stared at her father's image, listened to his words. *Crackle. Wipe. Crackle.* "Listen to me, girl," said her dead father. "Go to Islington . . . you can trust Islington. . . . You must believe in Islington . . ." He ghosted. Blood dripped from his forehead into his eyes. He wiped it off. "Door? Avenge us. Avenge your family."

A loud bang came from the gramophone horn. Portico turned his head to look offscreen, puzzled and nervous. "What?" he said, and he stepped out of frame. For a moment, the picture remained unchanged: the desk, the blank white wall behind it. Then an arc of vivid blood splashed across the wall. Door flicked a lever on the side, blanking the screen, and turned away.

"Here." The marquis passed her a handkerchief.

"Thanks." She wiped her face, blew her nose vigorously. Then she stared into space. Eventually, she said, "Islington."

"I've never had any dealings with Islington," said the marquis.

"I thought it was just a legend," she said.

"Not at all." He reached across the desk, picked up the gold pocket-watch, thumbed it open. "Nice workmanship," he observed.

She nodded. "It was my father's."

He closed the cover with a click. "Time to go to market. It starts soon. Mister Time is not our friend."

She blew her nose once more, put her hands deep into the pockets of her leather jacket. Then she turned to him, elfin face frowning, odd-colored eyes bright. "Do you honestly think we can find a bodyguard who will be able to deal with Croup and Vandemar?"

The marquis flashed his white teeth at her. "There's been no one since Hunter who'd even have a chance. No, I'll settle for someone who could give you the time you might need to get away." He fastened the fob of the watch chain to his waistcoat, slid the watch into his vest pocket.

"What are you doing?" asked Door. "That's my father's watch."

"He's not using it anymore, is he?" He adjusted the golden chain. "There. That looks rather elegant." He watched the emotions flicker across her face: quiet anger and, finally, resignation.

"We'd better go," was all she said.

"The Bridge isn't very far now," said Anaesthesia.

Richard hoped that was true. They were now on their third candle. The walls flickered and oozed, the passageway seemed to stretch on forever. He was astonished that they were still under London: he was half-convinced that they had walked most of the way to Wales.

"I'm really scared," she continued. "I've never crossed the bridge before."

"I thought you said you'd been to this market already," he asked, mystified.

"It's the *Floating* Market, silly. I told you already. It moves. Different places. Last one I went to was held in that big clock tower. Big . . . someone. And the next was—"

"Big Ben?" he suggested.

"Maybe. We were inside where all the big wheels went around, and that was where I got this—" She held up her necklace. The candlelight glimmered yellow off the shiny quartz. She smiled, like a child. "Do you like it?" she asked.

"It's great. Was it expensive?"

"I swapped some stuff for it. That's how things work down here. We swap stuff." And then they turned a corner, and saw the bridge. It could have been one of the bridges over the Thames, five hundred years ago, thought Richard; a huge stone bridge spanning out over a vast black chasm, into the night. But there was no sky above it, no water below. It rose into darkness. Richard wondered who had built it, and when. He wondered how something like this could exist, beneath the city of London, without everyone knowing. He felt a sinking feeling in the pit of his stomach. He was, he realized, deeply, pathetically scared of the bridge itself.

"Do we have to go across it?" he asked. "Can't we get to the market some other way?" They paused at the base of the bridge.

Anaesthesia shook her head. "We can get to the place it's in," she said. "But the market wouldn't be there."

"Huh? But that's ridiculous. I mean, something's either there or it's not. Isn't it?"

She shook her head. There was a buzz of voices from behind them, and someone pushed Richard to the ground. He looked up: a huge man, crudely tattooed, dressed in improvised rubber and leather clothes that looked like they had been cut out of the inside of cars, stared back down at him, dispassionately. Behind the huge man were a dozen others, male and female: people who looked like they were on their way to a particularly low-rent costume party. "Somebody," said Varney, who was not in a good mood, "was in my way. Somebody ought to watch where he's going."

Once, as a small boy walking home from school, Richard had encountered a rat in a ditch by the side of the road. When the rat saw Richard it had reared up onto its hind legs and hissed and jumped, terrifying Richard. He backed away marvelling that something so small had been so willing to fight something so much larger than itself. Now Anaesthesia stepped between Richard and Varney. She was less than half his size, but she glared at the big man and bared her teeth, and she hissed like an angry rat at bay. Varney took a step backwards. He spat at Richard's shoes. Then he turned away, and, taking the knot of people with him, he walked across the bridge and into the dark.

"Are you all right?" asked Anaesthesia, helping Richard back to his feet.

"I'm fine," he said. "That was really brave of you."

She looked down, shyly. "I'm not really brave," she said. "I'm still scared of the bridge. Even they were scared. That was why they all went over together. Safety in numbers."

"If you are crossing the bridge, I will go with you," said a female voice, rich as cream and honey, coming from behind them. Richard was not able to place her accent. He turned, and standing there was a tall woman, with long, tawny hair, and skin the color of burnt caramel. She wore dappled leather clothes, mottled in shades of gray and brown. She had a battered leather duffel bag over her shoulder. She was carrying a staff, and she had a knife at her belt and an electric flashlight strapped to her wrist.

She was also, without question, the most beautiful woman that Richard had ever seen.

"Safety in numbers. You're welcome to come with us," he said, after a moment's hesitation. "My name's Richard Mayhew. This is Anaesthesia. She's the one us who knows what she's doing." The rat-girl preened.

The leather woman looked him up and looked him down. "You're from London Above," she told him.

"Yes." As lost as he was in this strange other-world, he was at least learning to play the game. His mind was too numb to make any sense of where he was, or why he was here, but it was capable of following the rules.

"Travelling with a rat-speaker. My word."

"I'm his guardian," said Anaesthesia, truculently.

"Who are you? Who do you owe fealty to?"

The woman smiled. "I owe no man fealty, rat-girl. Have either of you crossed Night's Bridge before?" Anaesthesia shook her head. "Well. Isn't this going to be fun?"

They walked toward the bridge. Anaesthesia handed Richard her candle-lamp. "Here," she said.

"Thanks." Richard looked at the woman in leather. "Is there anything, really, to be scared of?"

"Only the night on the bridge," she said.

"The kind in armor?"

"The kind that comes when day is over."

Anaesthesia's hand sought Richard's. He held it tightly, her tiny hand in his. She smiled at him, squeezed his hand. And then they set foot on Night's Bridge and Richard began to understand darkness: darkness as something solid and real, so much more than a simple absence of light. He felt it touch his skin, questing, moving, exploring: gliding through his mind. It slipped into his lungs, behind his eyes, into his mouth . . .

With each step they took the light of the candle became dimmer. He realized the same thing was happening to the leather woman's flashlight. It felt not so much as if the lights were being turned down but as if the darkness were being turned up. Richard blinked, and opened his eyes on nothing—nothing but darkness, complete and utter. *Sounds.* A rustling, a squirming. Richard blinked, blinded by the night. The sounds were nastier, hungrier. Richard imagined he could hear voices: a horde of huge, misshapen trolls, beneath the bridge. . . .

Something slithered past them in the dark. "What's that?" squeaked Anaesthesia. Her hand was shaking in his.

"Hush," whispered the woman. "Don't attract its attention."

"What's happening?" whispered Richard.

"Darkness is happening," said the leather woman, very quietly. "Night is happening. All the nightmares that have come out when the sun goes down, since the cave times, when we huddled together in fear for safety and for warmth, are happening. Now," she told them, "now is the time to be afraid of the dark." Richard knew that something was about to creep over his face. He closed his eyes: it made no difference to what he saw or felt. The night was complete. It was then that the hallucinations started.

He saw a figure falling toward him through the night, burning, its wings and hair on fire.

He threw up his hands: there was nothing there.

Jessica looked at him, with contempt in her eyes. He wanted to shout to her, tell her he was sorry.

Place one foot after another.

He was a small child, walking home from school, at night, down the one road with no streetlights. No matter how many times he did it, it never got any easier, never got any better.

He was deep in the sewers, lost in a labyrinth. The Beast was waiting for him. He could hear a slow drip of water. He knew the Beast was waiting. He gripped his spear. . . . Then a rumbling bellow, deep in its throat, from behind him. He turned. Slowly, agonizingly slowly, it charged at him, through the dark.

And it charged.

He died.

And kept walking.

Slowly, agonizingly slowly, it charged at him, over and over, through the dark.

There was a sputter, and a flare so bright it hurt, making Richard squint and stagger. It was the candle flame, in its lemonade-bottle holder. He had never known how brightly a single candle could burn. He held it up, gasping and gulping and shaking with relief. His heart was pounding and shuddering in his chest.

"We would appear to have crossed successfully," said the leather woman.

Richard's heart was pounding in his chest so hard that, for a few moments, he was unable to talk. He forced himself to breathe slowly, to calm down. They were in a large anteroom, exactly like the one on the other side. In fact, Richard had the strange feeling that it was the same room they had just left. Yet the shadows were deeper, and there were after-images floating before Richard's eyes, like those one saw after a camera flash. "I suppose," Richard said, haltingly, "we weren't in any real danger. . . . It was like a haunted house. A few noises in the dark . . . and your imagination does the rest. There wasn't really anything to be scared of, was there?"

The woman looked at him, almost pityingly; and Richard realized that there was nobody holding his hand. "Anaesthesia?"

From the darkness at the crown of the bridge came a gentle noise, like a rustle or a sigh. A handful of irregular quartz beads pattered down the curve of the bridge toward them. Richard picked one up. It was from the rat-girls necklace. His mouth opened, but no sound came out. Then he found his voice. "We'd better. We have to go back. She's . . ."

The woman raised her flashlight, shone it across the bridge. Richard could see all the way across the bridge. It was deserted. "Where is she?" he asked.

"Gone," said the woman, flatly. "The darkness took her."

"We've got to do something," said Richard urgently.

"Such as?"

Once again, he opened his mouth. This time, he found no words. He closed it again. He fingered the lump of quartz, looked at the others on the ground.

"She's gone," said the woman. "The bridge takes its toll. Be grateful it didn't take you too. Now if you're going to the market, it's through here, up this way." She gestured toward a narrow passageway that rose up into the dimness in front of them, barely illuminated by the beam of her flashlight.

Richard did not move. He felt numb. He found it hard to believe that the rat girl was gone—lost, or

stolen, or strayed, or . . . —and harder to believe that
the leather woman was able to carry on as if nothing
at all out of the ordinary had happened—as if this
were utterly usual. Anaesthesia could not be
dead . . .

He completed the thought. She could not be dead,
because if she were, then it was his fault. She had
not asked to go with him. He held the quartz bead
so tightly it hurt his hand, thinking of the pride with
which Anaesthesia had shown it to him, of how fond
he had become of her in the handful of hours that
he had known her.

"Are you coming?"

Richard stood there in the darkness for a few
pounding heartbeats, then he placed the quartz bead
gently into the pocket of his jeans. He followed the
woman, who was still some paces ahead of him. As
he followed her, he realized that he still did not
know her name.

FIVE

PEOPLE SLIPPED AND SLID THROUGH THE darkness about them, holding lamps, torches, flashlights, and candles. It made Richard think of documentary films he had seen of schools of fish, glittering and darting through the ocean ... Deep water, inhabited by things that had lost the use of their eyes.

Richard followed the leather woman up some steps. Stone steps, edged with metal. They were in an Underground station. They joined a line of people waiting to slip through a grille, which had been opened a foot or so to uncover the door, which led out onto the pavement.

Immediately in front of them were a couple of young boys, each with a string tied around his wrist. The strings were held by a pallid, bald man, who smelled of formaldehyde. Immediately behind them in the line waited a gray-bearded man with a black-and-white kitten sitting on his shoulder. It washed itself, intently licked the man's ear, then curled up on his shoulder and went to sleep. The line moved slowly, as, one by one, the figures at the end slipped through the space between the grille and the wall and edged into the night. "Why are you going to the market, Richard Mayhew?" asked the leather woman, in a low voice. Richard still could not place her accent: he was beginning to suspect that she was African or Australian—or perhaps she came from somewhere even more exotic and obscure.

"I have friends I'm hoping to meet there. Well, just one friend. I don't actually know many people from this world. I was sort of getting to know Anaesthesia, but . . ." he trailed off. Asked the question he had not dared to voice until this moment. "Is she dead?"

The woman shrugged. "Yes. Or as good as. I trust your visit to the market will make her loss worthwhile."

Richard shivered. "I don't think it could," he said. He felt empty, and utterly alone. They were approaching the front of the line. "What do you do?" he asked.

She smiled. "I sell personal physical services."

"Oh," he said. "What kind of personal physical services?" he asked.

"I rent my body." She did not elaborate.

"Ah." He was too weary to pursue it, to press her to explain just what she meant; he had an idea, though. And then they stepped out into the night. Richard looked back. The sign on the station said KNIGHTSBRIDGE. He didn't know whether to smile or to mourn. It felt like the small hours of the morning. Richard looked down at his watch and was not surprised to notice that the digital face was now completely blank. Perhaps the batteries had died, or, he thought, more likely, time in London Below had only a passing acquaintance with the kind of time he was used to. He did not care. He unstrapped the watch and dropped it into the nearest garbage can.

The odd people were crossing the road in a stream, walking through the double doors facing them. "There?" he said, appalled.

The woman nodded. "There."

The building was large, and it was covered with many thousands of burning lights. Conspicuous coats of arms on the wall facing them proudly proclaimed that it sold all sorts of things by appointment to various members of the British Royal Family. Richard, who had spent many a footsore weekend hour trailing behind Jessica through every prominent shop in London, recognized it immediately, even without the huge sign, proclaiming it to be, "Harrods?"

The woman nodded. "Only for tonight," she said. "The next market could be anywhere."

"But I mean," said Richard. "Harrods." It seemed almost sacrilegious to be sneaking into this place at night.

They walked in through the side door. The room was dark. They passed the *bureau de change* and the gift-wrapping section, through another darkened room selling sunglasses and figurines, and then they stepped into the Egyptian Room. Color and light broke over Richard like a wave hitting the shore. His companion turned to him: she yawned, catlike, shading the vivid pinkness of her mouth with the back of her caramel hand. And then she smiled, and said, "Well. You're here. Safe and, more or less, sound. I have business to attend to. Fare you well." She nodded curtly and slipped away into the crowd.

Richard stood there, alone in the throng, drinking it in. It was pure madness—of that there was no doubt at all. It was loud, and brash, and insane, and it was, in many ways, quite wonderful. People argued, haggled, shouted, sang. They hawked and touted their wares, and loudly declaimed the superiority of their merchandise. Music was playing—a dozen different kinds of music, being played a dozen different ways on a score of different instruments, most of them improvised, improved, improbable. Richard could smell food. All kinds of food—the smells of curries and spices seemed to predominate, with, beneath them, the smells of grilling meats and mushrooms. Stalls had been set up all throughout the shop, next to, or even on, counters that, during the day, had sold perfume, or watches, or amber, or silk scarves. Everybody was buying. Everybody was selling. Richard listened to the market cries as he began to wander through the crowds.

"Lovely fresh dreams. First-class nightmares. We got 'em. Get yer lovely nightmares here."

"Weapons! Arm yourself! Defend your cellar, cave, or hole! You want to hit 'em? We got 'em. Come on darling, come on over here . . ."

"Rubbish!" screamed a fat, elderly woman, in Richard's ear, as he passed her malodorous stall. "Junk!" she continued. "Garbage! Trash! Offal! Debris! Come and get it! Nothing whole or undamaged! Crap, tripe, and useless piles of shit. You know you want it."

A man in armor beat a small drum and chanted, "Lost Property. Roll up, roll up, and see for yourself. Lost property. None of your found things here. Everything guaranteed properly lost."

Richard wandered through the huge rooms of the store, like a man in a trance. He was unable to even guess how many people there were at the night market. A thousand? Two thousand? Five thousand?

One stall was piled high with bottles, full bottles

and empty bottles of every shape and every size, from bottles of booze to one huge glimmering bottle that could have contained nothing but a captive djinn; another sold lamps with candles, made of many kinds of wax and tallow; a man thrust what appeared to be a child's severed hand clutching a candle toward him as he passed, muttering, "Hand of Glory, sir? Send 'em up the wooden hill to Bedfordshire. Guaranteed to work." Richard hurried past, not wishing to find out what a Hand of Glory was, nor how it worked; he passed a stall selling glittering gold and silver jewelry, another selling jewelry made from what looked like the valves and wires of antique radios; there were stalls that sold every manner of book and magazine; others that sold clothes—old clothes patched, and mended, and made strange; several tattooists; something that he was almost certain was a small slave market (he kept well clear of this); a dentist's chair, with a hand-operated manual drill, with a line of miserable people standing beside it, waiting to have their teeth pulled or filled by a young man who seemed to be having altogether too good a time; a bent old man selling unlikely things that might have been hats and might have been modern art; something that looked very much like a portable shower facility; even a blacksmith's . . .

And every few stalls there would be somebody selling food. Some of them had food cooking over open fires: curries, and potatoes, and chestnuts, and huge mushrooms, and exotic breads. Richard found himself wondering why the smoke from the fires didn't set off the building's sprinkler system. Then he found himself wondering why no one was looting the store: why set up their own little stalls? Why not just take things from the shop itself? He knew better, at this point, than to risk asking anyone. . . . He seemed marked as a man from London Above, and thus worthy of great suspicion.

There was something deeply tribal about the people, Richard decided. He tried to pick out distinct groups: there were the ones who looked like they had escaped from a historical reenactment society; the ones who reminded him of hippies; the albino people in gray clothes and dark glasses; the polished, dangerous ones in smart suits and black gloves; the huge, almost identical women who walked together in twos and threes, and nodded when they saw each other; the tangle-haired ones who looked like they probably lived in sewers and who smelled like hell; and a hundred other types and kinds . . .

He wondered how normal London—*his* London— would look to an alien, and that made him bold. He began to ask them, as he went, "Excuse me? I'm looking for a man named de Carabas and a girl called Door. Do you know where I'd find them?" People shook their heads, apologized, averted their eyes, moved away.

Richard took a step back and stepped on someone's foot. Someone was well over seven feet tall, and was covered in tufty ginger-colored hair. Someone's teeth had been sharpened to points. Someone picked Richard up with a hand the size of a sheep's head, and put Richard's head so close to someone's mouth that Richard almost gagged. "I'm really sorry," said Richard. "I—I'm looking for a girl named Door. Do you know—" But someone dropped him onto the floor and moved on.

Another whiff of cooking food wafted across the

floor, and Richard, who had managed to forget how hungry he was ever since he had declined the prime cut of tomcat—he could not think how many hours before—now found his mouth watering, and his thinking processes beginning to grind to a halt.

The iron-haired woman running the next food stall he approached did not reach to Richard's waist. When Richard tried to talk to her, she shook her head, drew a finger across her lips. She could not talk, or did not talk, or did not want to talk. Richard found himself conducting the negotiations for a cottage cheese and lettuce sandwich and a cup of what looked and smelled like home-brewed lemonade, in sign language. His food cost him a ballpoint pen, and a book of matches he had forgotten he had. The little woman must have felt that she had got by far the better of the deal, for, as he took his food, she threw in a couple of small, nutty cookies.

Richard stood in the middle of the throng, listening to the music—someone was, for no reason that Richard could easily discern, singing the lyrics of "Greensleeves" to the tune of "Yakkety-Yak"—watching the bizarre bazaar unfold around him, and eating his sandwiches.

As he finished the last of the sandwiches, he realized that he had no idea how anything he had just eaten had tasted; and he resolved to slow down, and chew the cookies more slowly. He sipped the lemonade, making it last. "You need a bird, sir?" asked a cheery voice, close at hand. "I got rooks and ravens, crows and starlings. Fine, wise birds. Tasty *and* wise. Brilliant."

Richard said, "No, thank you," and turned around.

The hand-painted sign above the stall said:

OLD BAILEY'S BIRDS AND INFORMATION

There were other, smaller, signs scattered about: YOU WANTS IT, WE KNOWS IT, and YOU WON'T FIND A PLUMPER STARLING!!!! and WHEN IT'S TIME FOR A ROOK, IT'S TIME FOR OLD BAILEY!! Richard found himself thinking of the man he had seen when he had first come to London, who used to stand outside Leicester Square Tube station with a huge hand-painted sandwich board that exhorted the world to "Less Lust Through Less Protein, Eggs, Meat, Beans, Cheese and Sitting."

Birds hopped and fluttered about small cages that looked as if they had been woven out of TV antennae. "Information, then?" continued Old Bailey, warming to his own sales-pitch. "Roof-maps? History? Secret and mysterious knowledge? If I don't knows it, it's probbly better forgot. That's what I says." The old man still wore his feathered coat, was still wrapped about with ropes and cords. He blinked at Richard, then pulled on the pair of spectacles tied about his neck with string. He inspected Richard carefully through them. "Hang on—I knows you. You was with the marquis de Carabas. On the rooftops. Remember? Eh? I'm Old Bailey. Remember me?" He thrust out his hand, pumped Richard's hand furiously.

"Actually," said Richard, "I'm looking for the marquis. And for a young lady named Door. I think they're probably together."

The old man did a little jig, causing several feathers to detach themselves from his coat; this provoked a chorus of raucous disapproval from the various birds around them. "Information! Information!" he announced to the crowded room. "See? I told 'em.

Diversify, I said. *Diversify!* You can't sell rooks for the stewpot forever—anyway, they taste like boiled slipper. And they're so stupid. Thick as custard. You ever eaten rook?" Richard shook his head. That was something he could be certain of, at any rate. "What'll you give me?" asked Old Bailey.

"Sorry?" said Richard, awkwardly leaping from ice floe to ice floe in the stream of the old man's consciousness.

"If'n I give ye your information. What'll I get?"

"I don't have any money," said Richard. "And I just gave my pen away."

He began to pull out the contents of Richard's pockets. "There," said Old Bailey. "That!"

"My hankie?" asked Richard. It was not a particularly clean handkerchief; it had been a present from his Aunt Maude, on his last birthday. Old Bailey seized it and waved it above his head, happily.

"Never you fear, laddie," he sang, triumphantly. "Your quest is at an end. Go down there, through that door. You can't miss them. They're auditioning." He was pointing towards Harrods' extensive network of Food Halls. A rook cawed maliciously. "None of your beak," said Old Bailey, to the rook. And, to Richard, he said, "Thank'ee for the little flag." He jigged around his stall, delighted, waving Richard's handkerchief to and fro.

Auditioning? thought Richard. And then he smiled. It didn't matter. His quest, as the mad old roof-man had put it, was at an end. He walked toward the Food Halls.

Fashion, in bodyguards, seemed to be everything. They all had a Knack of one kind or another, and each of them was desperate to demonstrate it to the world. At the moment, Ruislip was facing off against the Fop With No Name.

The Fop With No Name looked somewhat like an early eighteenth-century rake, one who hadn't been able to find real rake clothes and had had to make do with what he could find at the Salvation Army store. His face was powdered to white, his lips painted red. Ruislip, the Fop's opponent, resembled a bad dream one might have if one fell asleep watching sumo wrestling on the television with a Bob Marley record playing in the background. He was a huge Rastafarian who looked like nothing so much as an obese and enormous baby.

They were standing face to face, in the middle of a cleared circle of spectators and other bodyguards and sightseers. Neither man moved a muscle. The Fop was a good head taller than Ruislip. On the other hand, Ruislip looked as if he weighed as much as four fops, each of them carrying a large leather suitcase entirely filled with lard. They stared at each other, without breaking eye contact.

The marquis de Carabas tapped Door on the shoulder and pointed. Something was about to happen.

One moment there were two men standing impassively, just looking at each other, then the Fop's head rocked back, as if he'd just been hit in the face. A small, reddish purple bruise appeared on his cheek. He pursed his lips and fluttered his eyelashes. "La," he said, then stretched his rouged lips wide, in a ghastly parody of a smile.

The Fop gestured. Ruislip staggered, and clutched his stomach.

The Fop With No Name smirked outrageously, waggled his fingers, and blew kisses to several spectators. Ruislip stared angrily at the Fop, redoubling his mental assault. Blood began to drip from the Fop's lips. His left eye started to swell. He staggered. The audience muttered appreciatively.

"It's not as impressive as it looks," whispered the marquis to Door.

The Fop With No Name stumbled, suddenly, going onto his knees, as if someone were forcing him down, and fell, awkwardly, to the floor. Then he jerked, as if someone had just kicked him, hard, in the stomach. Ruislip looked triumphant. The spectators clapped, politely. The Fop writhed and spat blood onto the sawdust on the floor of Harrods' Fish and Meat Hall. He was dragged off into the corner by some friends, and was violently sick.

"Next," said the marquis.

The next would-be bodyguard was again thinner than Ruislip (being about the size of two and a half fops, carrying but a single suitcase filled with lard between them). He was covered in tattoos and dressed in clothes that looked like they had been stitched together from old car seats and rubber mats. He was shaven-headed, and he sneered at the world through rotten teeth. "I'm Varney," he said, and he hawked, and spat green on the sawdust. He walked into the ring.

"When you're ready, gentlemen," said the marquis.

Ruislip stamped his bare feet on the floor, sumo-like, one-two, one-two, and commenced to stare hard at Varney. A small cut opened on Varney's forehead, and blood began to drip from it into one eye. Varney ignored it; and instead appeared to be concentrating on his right arm. He pulled his arm up slowly, like a man fighting a great deal of pressure. Then he slammed his fist into Ruislip's nose, which began to spurt blood. Ruislip drew one long, horrible breath, and hit the ground with the sound of half a ton of wet liver being dropped into a bathtub. Varney giggled.

Ruislip slowly pulled himself back to his feet, blood from his nose soaking his mouth and chest, dripping onto the sawdust. Varney wiped the blood from his forehead and bared his ruined mouth at the world in an appalling grin. "Come on," he said. "Fat bastard. Hit me again."

"That one's promising," muttered the marquis.

Door raised an eyebrow. "He doesn't look very nice."

"*Nice* in a bodyguard," lectured the marquis, "is about as useful as the ability to regurgitate whole lobsters. He looks *dangerous*." There was a murmur of appreciation, then, as Varney did something rather fast and painful to Ruislip, something that involved the sudden connection of Varney's leather-bound foot and Ruislip's testicles. The murmur was the kind of restrained and deeply unenthusiastic applause one normally only hears in England on sleepy sunny Sunday afternoons, at village cricket matches. The marquis clapped politely with the rest of them. "Very good, sir," he said.

Varney looked at Door, and he winked at her, almost proprietorially, before he returned his attention to Ruislip. Door shivered.

Richard heard the clapping and walked toward it. Five almost identically dressed, pale young women walked past him. They wore long dresses made of velvet, each dress as dark as night, one each of dark green, dark chocolate, royal blue, dark blood, and pure black. Each woman had black hair and wore silver jewelry; each was perfectly coiffed, perfectly made up. They moved silently: Richard was aware only of a swish of heavy velvet as they went past, a swish that sounded almost like a sigh. The last of the women, the one dressed in utter black, the palest and the most beautiful, smiled at Richard. He smiled back at her, warily. Then he walked on toward the audition.

It was being held in the Fish and Meat Hall, on the open area of floor beneath Harrods' fish sculpture. The audience had their back to him, were standing two or three people deep. Richard wondered if he would easily be able to find Door and the marquis: and then the crowd parted, and he saw them both, sitting on the glass top of the smoked-salmon counter. He opened his mouth to shout out Door's name; and as he did so, he realized why the crowd had parted, as an enormous dreadlocked man, naked but for a green, yellow, and red cloth wrapped like a diaper around his middle, came catapulting through the crowd, as if tossed by a giant, landing squarely on top of him.

"Richard?" she said.

He opened his eyes. The face swam in and out of focus. Fire opal-colored eyes, peering into his, from a pale, elfin face.

"Door?" he said.

She looked furious; she looked beyond fury. "Temple and Arch, Richard. I don't be*lieve* it. What are you doing here?"

"It's nice to see you, too," said Richard, weakly. He sat up and wondered if he was suffering from a concussion. He wondered how he'd know if he was, and he wondered why he had ever thought that Door would have been pleased to see him. She stared intently at her nails, nostrils flaring, as if she did not trust herself to say anything else.

The big man with the very bad teeth, the man who had knocked Richard over on the bridge, was fighting with a dwarf. They were fighting with crowbars, and the fight was not as unequal as one might have imagined. The dwarf was preternaturally fast: he rolled, he struck, he bounced, he dove; his every movement made Varney appear lumbering and awkward by comparison.

Richard turned to the marquis, who was watching the fight intently. "What is happening?" he asked.

The marquis spared him a glance, and then returned his gaze to the action in front of them. "*You*," he said, "are out of your league, in deep shit, and, I would imagine, a few hours away from an untimely and undoubtedly messy end. *We*, on the other hand, are auditioning bodyguards." Varney connected his crowbar with the dwarf, who instantly stopped bouncing and darting, and instantly began lying insensible. "I think we've seen enough," said the marquis, loudly. "Thank you all. Mister Varney, if you could wait behind?"

"Why did you have to come here?" Door said to Richard, frostily.

"I didn't really have much choice," said Richard.

She sighed. The marquis was walking around the perimeter, dismissing the various bodyguards who had already auditioned, distributing a few words of praise here, of advice there. Varney waited patiently, off to one side. Richard essayed a smile at Door. It was ignored. "How did you get to the market?" she asked.

"There are these rat people—" Richard began.

"Rat-speakers," she said.

"And you see, the rat who brought us the marquis's message—"

"Master Longtail," she said.

"Well, he told them they had to get me here."

She raised an eyebrow, cocked her head slightly on one side. "A rat-speaker brought you here?"

He nodded. "Most of the way. Her name was Anaesthesia. She . . . well, something happened to her. On the bridge. This other lady brought me the rest of the way here. I think she was a . . . you know." He hesitated, then said it. "Hooker."

The marquis had returned. He stood in front of Varney, who looked obscenely pleased with himself. "Weapons expertise?" asked the marquis.

"Whew," said Varney. "Put it like this. If you can cut someone with it, blow someone's head off with it, break a bone with it, or make a nasty hole in someone with it, then Varney's the master of it."

"Previous satisfied employers include?"

"Olympia, the Shepherd Queen, the Crouch Enders. I done security for the May Fair for a bit, as well."

"Well," said the marquis de Carabas. "We're all very impressed with your skill."

"I had heard," said a female voice, "that you had put out a call for bodyguards. Not for enthusiastic amateurs." Her skin was the color of burnt caramel, and her smile would have stopped a revolution. She was dressed entirely in soft mottled gray and brown leathers. Richard recognized her immediately.

"That's her," Richard whispered to Door. "The hooker."

"Varney," said Varney, affronted, "is the best

guard and bravo in the Underside. Everyone knows that."

The woman looked at the marquis. "You've finished the trials?" she asked.

"Yes," said Varney.

"Not necessarily," said the marquis.

"Then," she told him. "I would like to audition."

There was a beat before the marquis de Carabas said, "Very well," and stepped backward.

Varney was undoubtedly dangerous, not to mention a bully, a sadist, and actively harmful to the physical health of those around him. What he was not, though, was particularly quick on the uptake. He stared at the marquis as the penny dropped, and dropped, and kept on dropping. Finally, in disbelief, he asked, "I have to fight *her?*"

"Yes," said the leather woman. "Unless you'd like a little nap, first." Varney began to laugh: a manic giggle. He stopped laughing a moment later, when the woman kicked him, hard, in the solar plexus, and he toppled like a tree.

Near his hand, on the floor, was the crowbar he had used in the fight with the dwarf. He grabbed it, slammed it into the woman's face—or would have, had she not ducked out of the way. She clapped her open hands onto his ears, very fast. The crowbar went flying across the room. Still reeling from the pain in his ears, Varney pulled a knife from his boot. He was not entirely sure what happened after that: only that the world swung out from under him, and then he was lying, face down, on the ground, with blood coming from his ears, and his own knife at his throat, while the marquis de Carabas was saying,

"Enough!"

The woman looked up, still holding Varney's knife to his throat. "Well?" she said.

"Very impressive," said the marquis. Door nodded.

Richard was thunderstruck: it had been like watching Emma Peel, Bruce Lee, and a particularly vicious tornado, all rolled into one and sprinkled with a generous helping of a mongoose killing a king cobra. That was how she had moved. That was how she had fought.

Richard normally found displays of real violence unnerving. But he found watching this woman in action exhilarating, as if she were finding a part of him he had not known existed. It seemed utterly right, in this unreal mirror of the London he had known, that she should be here and that she should be fighting so dangerously and so well.

She was part of London Below. He understood that now. And as he thought that, he thought about London Above, and a world in which no one fought like this—no one needed to fight like this—a world of safety and of sanity and, for a moment, the homesickness engulfed him like a fever.

The woman looked down at Varney. "Thank you, Mister Varney," she said, politely. "I'm afraid we won't be needing your services after all." She got off him, and put his knife away in her belt.

"And you are called?" asked the marquis.

"I'm called Hunter," she said.

Nobody said anything. Then Door spoke, hesitantly, "*The* Hunter?"

"That's right," said Hunter, and she brushed the dust of the floor from her leather leggings. "I'm back."

From somewhere a bell sounded, twice, a deep

bonging noise that made Richard's teeth vibrate. "Five minutes," muttered the marquis. Then he said, to the remains of the crowd, "I think we've found our bodyguard. Thank you all very much. Nothing more to see."

Hunter walked over to Door, and looked her up and down. "Can you stop people from killing me?" asked Door. Hunter inclined her head toward Richard. "I saved *his* life three times today, crossing the bridge, coming to the market."

Varney, who had stumbled to his feet, picked up the crowbar with his mind. The marquis watched him do it; he said nothing.

The ghost of a smile hovered about Door's lips. "That's funny," she said. "Richard thought you were a—"

Hunter never found out what Richard thought she was. The bar came hurtling toward her head. She simply reached out a hand and caught it: it *thwapped*, satisfyingly, into the palm of her hand.

She walked over to Varney. "Is this yours?" she asked. He bared his teeth at her, yellow and black and brown. "Right now," said Hunter, "we're under Market Truce. But if you try something like that again, I'll waive the truce, and I'll break off both your arms and make you carry them home in your teeth. Now," she continued, bending his wrist behind his back, "say sorry, nicely."

"Ow," said Varney.

"Yes?" she said, encouragingly.

He spat it out as if it were choking him. "I'm sorry." She let him go. Varney backed away to a safe distance, plainly scared and furious, watching Hunter. When he reached the door to the Food Halls, he hesitated, and shouted, "You're dead. You're fuck-

ing dead, you are!" in a voice that hovered on the
edge of tears, and then he turned, and he ran from
the room.

"Amateurs," sighed Hunter.

They walked back through the store the way that
Richard had come. The bell he had heard was now
tolling deeply and continually. When they came
upon it, he saw that it was a huge brass bell, suspended on a wooden frame, with a rope suspended
from the clapper. It was being tolled by a large black
man, wearing the black robes of a Dominican monk,
and it had been set up next to Harrods' gourmet jelly
bean stand.

Impressive as the market had been to watch, Richard found the speed at which it was being disman-
tled, broken down, and put away even more
impressive. All evidence that it had ever been there
was vanishing: stalls were being taken apart, loaded
onto people's backs, hauled off into the streets. Richard noticed Old Bailey, his arms filled with his crude
signs and with bird cages, stumbling out of the store.
The old man waved happily at Richard and vanished off into the night.

The crowds thinned, the market vanished, and almost instantly the ground floor of Harrods looked
as usual, as sedate, elegant, and clean as any time
he had walked around it in Jessica's wake on a Saturday afternoon. It was as if the market had never
existed.

"Hunter," said the marquis. "I've heard of you, of
course. Where have you been, all this time?"

"Hunting," she said, simply. Then, to Door. "Can
you take orders?"

Door nodded. "If I have to."

"Good. Then maybe I *can* keep you alive," said Hunter. "If I take the job."

The marquis stopped. His eyes flickered over her, distrustfully. "You said, *if* you take the job . . . ?"

Hunter opened the door, and they stepped out onto the pavement of London at night. It had rained while they had been at the market, and the streetlights now glimmered on the wet tarmac. "I've taken it," said Hunter.

Richard stared at the glistening street. It all seemed so normal, so quiet, so sane. For a moment, he felt that all he needed to get his life back would be to hail a taxi and tell it to take him home. And then he would sleep the night through in his own bed. But a taxi would not see him or stop for him, and he had nowhere to go, even if one did.

"I'm tired," he said.

No one said anything. Door would not meet his eyes, the marquis was cheerfully ignoring him, and Hunter was treating him as an irrelevance. He felt like a small child, unwanted, following the bigger children around, and that made him irritated. "Look," he said, clearing his throat, "I know you are all very busy people. But what about me?"

The marquis turned and stared at him, eyes huge and white in his dark face. "You?" he said. "What about you?"

"Well," said Richard. "How do I get back to normal again? It's like I've walked into a nightmare. Last week everything made sense, and now nothing makes sense . . ." He trailed off. Swallowed. "I want to know how to get my life back," he explained.

"You won't get it back traveling with us, Richard," said Door. "It's going to be hard enough for you anyway. I . . . I really am sorry."

Hunter, in the lead, knelt down on the pavement. She took a small metal rod from her belt and used it to unlock the cover to a sewer. She pulled up the sewer cover, looked into it warily, climbed down, then ushered Door into the sewer. Door did not look at Richard as she went down. The marquis scratched the side of his nose. "Young man," he said, "understand this: there are two Londons. There's London Above—that's where you lived—and then there's London Below—the Underside—inhabited by the people who fell through the cracks in the world. Now you're one of them. Good night."

He began to climb down the sewer ladder. Richard said, "Wait," and caught the sewer cover before it could close. He followed the marquis down. It smelled like drains at the top of the sewer—a dead, soapy, cabbagey smell. He expected it to get worse as he went down, but instead the smell quickly dissipated as he approached the floor of the sewer. Gray water ran, shallow but fast, along the bottom of the brick tunnel. Richard stepped into it. He could see the lights of the others up ahead, and he ran and splashed down the tunnel until he caught up with them.

"Go away," said the marquis.

"No," he said.

Door glanced up at him. "I am really sorry, Richard," she said.

The marquis stepped between Richard and Door. "You can't go back to your old home or your old job or your old life," he said to Richard, almost gently. "None of those things exist. Up there, *you* don't exist." They had reached a junction: a place where three tunnels came together. Door and Hunter set off along one of them, the one that was empty of water, and they did not look back. The marquis lingered.

"You'll just have to make the best of it down here," he said to Richard, "in the sewers and the magic and the dark." And then he smiled, hugely, whitely: a gleaming grin, monumental in its insincerity. "Well—delightful to see you again. Best of luck. If you can survive for the next day or two," he confided, "you might even make it through a whole month." And with that he turned and strode off through the sewer, after Door and Hunter.

Richard leaned against a wall and listened to their footsteps, echoing away, and to the rush of the water running past on its way to the pumping stations of East London, and the sewage works. "Shit," he said. And then, to his surprise, for the first time since his father died, alone in the dark, Richard Mayhew began to cry.

The Underground station was quite empty, and quite dark. Varney walked through it, keeping close to walls, darting nervous looks behind him, and in front of him, and from side to side. He had picked the station at random, had headed for it over the rooftops and through the shadows, making certain that he was not being followed. He was not heading back to his lair in the Camden Town deep tunnels. Too risky. There were other places where Varney had cached weapons and food. He would go to ground for a little while, until this all blew over.

He stopped beside a ticket machine and listened, in the darkness: absolute silence. Reassured that he was alone, he allowed himself to relax. He stopped at the top of the spiral staircase and drew a deep breath.

An oily voice from beside him said conversationally, "Varney's the finest bravo and guard in the Underside. Everyone knows that. Mister Varney told us so himself." A voice from the other side of him responded, dully, "It's not nice to lie, Mister Croup."

In the pitch darkness, Mr. Croup expanded on his theme. "It isn't, Mister Vandemar. I have to say, I regard it as a personal betrayal, and I was deeply wounded by it. And disappointed. When you don't have any redeeming features, you don't take particularly kindly to disappointment, do you, Mister Vandemar?"

"Not kindly at all, Mister Croup."

Varney threw himself forward, and ran, headlong, in the dark, down the spiral staircase. A voice from the top of the stairs, Mr. Croup's: "Really," it said, "we ought to look upon it as a mercy killing."

The sound of Varney's feet clattered off the metal railings, echoed throughout the stairwell. He puffed, and he panted, his shoulders glancing off the walls, tumbling blindly downwards in the dark. He reached the bottom of the steps, next to the sign warning travelers that there were 259 steps up to the top, and only healthy people should even think about attempting it. Everyone else, suggested the sign, should use the elevator.

The elevator?

Something clanked, and the elevator doors opened, magnificently slowly, flooding the passageway with light. Varney fumbled for his knife: cursed, when he realized the Hunter-bitch still had it. He reached for the machete in his shoulder sheath. It was gone.

He heard a polite cough behind him, and he turned.

Mr. Vandemar was sitting on the steps, at the bottom of the spiral staircase. He was picking his fingernails with Varney's machete.

And then Mr. Croup fell upon him, all teeth and talons and little blades; and Varney never had a chance to scream. "Bye," said Mr. Vandemar, impassively, and he continued paring his nails. After that the blood began to flow. Wet, red blood in enormous quantities, for Varney was a big man, and he had been keeping it all inside. When Mr. Croup and Mr. Vandemar were finished, however, one would have been hard put even to notice the slight stain on the floor at the bottom of the spiral staircase.

The next time the floors were washed, it was gone forever.

Hunter was in the lead. Door walked in the middle. The marquis de Carabas took up the rear. None of them had said a word since leaving Richard half an hour earlier.

Door stopped, suddenly. "We can't do this," she said, flatly. "We can't leave him back there."

"Of course we can," said the marquis. "We did."

She shook her head. She had felt guilty and stupid ever since she saw Richard, lying on his back beneath Ruislip, at the audition. She was tired of it.

"Don't be foolish," said the marquis.

"He saved my life," she told him. "He could have left me on the sidewalk. He didn't."

It was her fault. She knew that was true. She had opened a door to someone who could help her, and help her he had. He had taken her somewhere warm, and he had cared for her, and he had brought her help. The action of helping her had tumbled him from his world into hers.

It was foolish to even think about bringing him with them. They could not afford to bring someone with them: she was unsure that the three of them would be able to take care of themselves on the journey that confronted them.

She wondered, briefly, if it were simply the door that she had opened, that had taken her to him, which had allowed him to notice her, or if there were, somehow, more to it than that.

The marquis raised an eyebrow: he was detached, removed, a creature of pure irony. "My dear young lady," he said. "We are not bringing a guest along on this expedition."

"Don't patronize me, de Carabas," said Door. She was so tired. "And I think I can decide who comes with us. You *are* working for me, aren't you? Or is it the other way around?" Her sorrow and exhaustion had drained her of her patience. She needed de Carabas—she couldn't afford to drive him away—but she had reached her limit.

De Carabas stared at her, coldly angry. "He is *not* coming with us," he stated, flatly. "Anyway, he's probably dead by now."

Richard was not dead. He was sitting in the dark, on a ledge, on the side of a storm drain, wondering what to do, wondering how much further out of his league he could possibly get. His life so far, he decided, had prepared him perfectly for a job in Securities, for shopping at the supermarket, for watching soccer on the television on the weekends, for turning up the thermostat if he got cold. It had magnificently failed to prepare him for a life as an un-person on the roofs and in the sewers of London, for a life in the cold and the wet and the dark.

A light glimmered. Footsteps came toward him. If, he decided, it was a bunch of murderers, cannibals, or monsters, he would not even put up a fight. Let them end it all for him; he'd had enough. He stared down into the dark, to the place where his feet should be. The footsteps came closer.

"Richard?" The voice was Door's. He jumped. Then he studiously ignored her. *If it weren't for you,* he thought . . .

"Richard?"

He didn't look up. "What?" he said.

"Look," she said. "You really wouldn't be in this mess if it weren't for me." *You can say that again,* he thought. "And I don't think you'll be any safer with us. But. Well." She stopped. A deep breath. "I'm sorry. I really am. Are you coming?"

He looked at her then: a small creature with huge eyes staring at him urgently from a heart-shaped, pale face. Okay, he said to himself. I guess I'm not quite ready to just give up and die. "Well, I don't have anywhere else to be right now," he said, with a studied unconcern that bordered on hysteria. "Why not?"

Her face changed. She threw her arms around his chest and hugged him, tightly. "And we will try to get you back home again," she said. "Promise. Once we've found what I'm looking for." He wondered if she meant it, suspected, for the first time, that what she was offering might be impossible. But he pushed that thought out of his head. They began to walk down the tunnel. Richard could see Hunter and the marquis waiting for them at the tunnel's mouth. The marquis looked as if he had been forced to swallow a pulped lemon.

"What *are* you looking for, anyway?" asked Richard, cheering up a little.

Door took a deep breath, and answered after a long pause. "It's a long story," she said, solemnly. "Right now we're looking for an angel named Islington." It was then that Richard began to laugh; he couldn't help himself. There was hysteria in there, certainly, but there was also the exhaustion of someone who had managed, somehow, to believe several dozen impossible things in the last twenty-four hours, without ever getting a proper breakfast. His laughter echoed down the tunnels.

"An angel?" he said, giggling helplessly. "Called Islington?"

"We've got a long way to go," said Door.

And Richard shook his head, and felt wrung out, and emptied, and flayed. "An angel," he whispered, hysterically, to the tunnels and the dark. "An angel."

There were candles all over the Great Hall: candles stood by the iron pillars that held the roof up; candles waited by the waterfall that ran down one wall and into the small rock-pool below; candles clustered on the sides of the rock wall; candles huddled on the floor; candles were set into candlesticks by the huge door that stood between two dark iron pillars. The door was built of polished black flint set into a silver base that had tarnished, over the centuries, almost to black. The candles were unlit; but as the tall form walked past, they flickered into flame. No hand touched them; no fires touched their wicks.

The figure's robe was simple, and white; or more than white. A color, or an absence of all colors, so bright as to be startling. Its feet were bare on the cold rock floor of the Great Hall. Its face was pale and wise, and gentle; and, perhaps, a little lonely.

It was very beautiful.

Soon every candle in the Hall was burning. It paused by the rock-pool; knelt beside the water, cupped its hands, lowered them into the clear water, raised them, and drank. The water was cold, but very pure. When it had finished drinking the water it closed its eyes for a moment, as if in benediction. Then it stood up, and walked away, back through the Hall, the way it had come; and the candles went out as it passed, as they had done for tens of thousands of years. It had no wings; but still, it was, unmistakably, an angel.

Islington left the Great Hall; and the last of the candles went out, and the darkness returned.

SIX

RICHARD WROTE A DIARY ENTRY IN HIS head.

Dear Diary, he began. *On Friday I had a job, a fiancée, a home, and a life that made sense. (Well, as much as any life makes sense.) Then I found an injured girl bleeding on the pavement, and I tried to be a Good Samaritan. Now I've got no fiancée, no home, no job, and I'm walking around a couple of hundred feet under the streets of London with the projected life expectancy of a suicidal fruitfly.*

"This way," said the marquis, gesturing elegantly, his filthy lace cuff flowing.

"Don't all these tunnels look the same?" asked Richard, tabling his diary entry for the moment. "How can you tell which is which?"

"You can't," said the marquis, sadly. "We're hopelessly lost. We'll never be seen again. In a couple of days we'll be killing each other for food."

"Really?" He hated himself for rising to the bait, even as he said it.

"No." The marquis's expression said that torturing this poor fool was too easy to even be amusing. Richard found that he cared less and less what these people thought of him, however. Except, perhaps, for Door.

He went back to writing his mental diary. *There are hundreds of people in this other London. Thousands maybe. People who come from here, or people who have fallen through the cracks. I'm wandering around with a girl called Door, her bodyguard, and her psychotic grand vizier. We slept last night in a small tunnel that Door said was once a section of Regency sewer. The bodyguard was awake when I went to sleep, and awake when they woke me up. I don't think she ever sleeps. We had some fruitcake for breakfast; the marquis had a large lump of it in his pocket. Why would anyone have a large lump of fruitcake in his pocket? My shoes dried out mostly while I slept.*

I want to go home. Then he mentally underlined the last sentence three times, rewrote it in huge letters in red ink, and circled it before putting a number of exclamation marks next to it in his mental margin.

At least the tunnel they were now walking down was dry. It was a high-tech tunnel: all silvery pipes and white walls. The marquis and Door walked together, in front. Richard tended to stay a couple of paces behind them. Hunter moved about: sometimes she was behind them, sometimes to one side of them or to the other, often a little way in front, merging with the shadows. She made no sound when she moved, which Richard found rather disconcerting.

There was a crack of light ahead of them. "There we go," said the marquis. "Bank Station. Good place to start looking."

"You're out of your mind," said Richard. He did not mean it to be heard, but the most *sotto* of *voces* carried and echoed in the darkness.

"Indeed?" said the marquis. The ground began to rumble: an Underground train was somewhere close at hand.

"Richard, just leave it," said Door.

But it was coming out of his mouth: "Well," he said. "You're both being silly. There are no such things as angels."

The marquis nodded, said, "Ah. Yes. I understand you now. There are no such things as angels. Just as there is no London Below, no rat-speakers, no shepherds in Shepherd's Bush."

"There are *no* shepherds in Shepherd's Bush. I've been there. It's just houses and stores and roads and the BBC. That's all," pointed out Richard, flatly.

"There are shepherds," said Hunter, from the darkness just next to Richard's ear. "Pray you never meet them." She sounded perfectly serious.

"Well," said Richard, "I still don't believe that there are flocks of angels wandering about down here."

"There aren't," said the marquis. "Just one." They had reached the end of the tunnel. There was a locked door in front of them. The marquis stood back. "My lady?" he said, to Door. She rested a hand on it, for a moment. The door opened, silently.

"Maybe," Richard said, persisting, "we're thinking of different things. The angels I have in mind are all wings, haloes, trumpets, peace-on-earth-goodwill-unto-men."

"That's right," said Door. "You got it. Angels."

They went through the door. Richard shut his eyes, involuntarily, at the sudden flood of light: it stabbed into his head like a migraine. As his eyes became used to the light, Richard found, to his surprise, that he knew where he was: they were in the long pedestrian tunnel that links Monument and Bank Tube stations. There were commuters wandering through the tunnels, none of whom gave the four

of them even a first look. The perky wail of a saxophone echoed along the tunnel: Burt Bacharach and
Hal David's "I'll Never Fall In Love Again," being
played more or less competently. They walked toward Bank Station.

"Who are we looking for again, then?" he asked,
more or less innocently. "The Angel Gabriel? Raph-
ael? Michael?"

They were passing a Tube map. The marquis
tapped Angel Station with one long dark finger: Islington.

Richard had passed through Angel Station hundreds of times. It was in trendy Islington, a district
filled with antique shops and places to eat. He knew
very little about angels, but he was almost certain
that Islington's tube stop was named after a pub, or
a landmark. He changed the subject. "You know,
when I tried to get on a Tube train a couple of days
ago, it wouldn't let me."

"You just have to let them know who's boss, that's
all," said Hunter, softly, from behind him.

Door chewed her lower lip. "This train we're looking for will let us on," she said. "If we can find it."
Her words were almost drowned out by music coming from somewhere nearby. They went down a
handful of steps and turned a corner.

The saxophone player had his coat in front of him,
on the floor of the tunnel. On the coat were a few
coins, which looked as if the man had placed them
there himself to persuade passersby that everyone
was doing it. Nobody was fooled.

The saxophone player was extremely tall; he had
shoulder-length dark hair and a long, forked dark
beard, which framed deep-set eyes and a serious
nose. He wore a ragged T-shirt and oil-stained blue

jeans. As the travelers reached him, he stopped playing, shook the spit from the saxophone mouthpiece,
replaced it, and sounded the first notes of the old
Julie London song, "Cry Me A River."

Now, you say you're sorry . . .

Richard realized, with surprise, that the man
could see them—and also that he was doing his best
to pretend that he couldn't. The marquis stopped in
front of him. The wail of the saxophone trailed off
in a nervous squeak. The marquis flashed a cold
grin. "It's Lear, isn't it?" he asked.

The man nodded, warily. His fingers stroked the
keys of his saxophone. "We're looking for Earl's
Court," continued the marquis. "Would you happen
to have such a thing as a train schedule about your
person?"

Richard was beginning to catch on. He assumed
that the Earl's Court he referred to wasn't the familiar Tube station he had waited in innumerable
times, reading a paper, or just daydreaming. The
man named Lear moistened his lips with the tip of
his tongue. "'S not impossible. What'd be in it for
me, if I did?"

The marquis thrust his hands deep into the pockets of his coat. Then he smiled, like a cat who had
just been entrusted with the keys to a home for wayward but plump canaries. "They say," he said, idly,
as if he were simply passing the time, "that Merlin's
master Blaise once wrote a reel so beguiling that it
would charm the coins from the pockets of anyone
who heard it."

Lear's eyes narrowed. "That'd be worth more than

just a train schedule," he said. "If you actually had it."

The marquis did a perfectly good impression of someone realizing, *my, it would, wouldn't it?* "Well, then," he said, magnanimously, "I suppose you would have to owe me, wouldn't you?"

Lear nodded, reluctantly. He fumbled in his back pocket, pulled out a much-folded scrap of paper, and held it up. The marquis reached for it. Lear moved his hand away. "Let me hear the reel first, you old trickster," he said. "And it had better work."

The marquis raised an eyebrow. He darted a hand into one of the inside pockets of his coat; when he pulled it out again it was holding a pennywhistle and a small crystal ball. He looked at the crystal ball, made the kind of "hmmm" noise that means, "ah, so that's where that went," and he put it away again. Then he flexed his fingers, put the pennywhistle to his lips, and began to play an odd, rollicking tune that leapt and twisted and sang. It made Richard feel as if he were thirteen years old again, listening to the Top Twenty on his best friend's transistor radio at school during lunch hour, back when pop music had mattered as it only can in your early teenage years: the marquis's reel was everything he had ever wanted to hear in a song . . .

A handful of coins chinked onto Lear's coat, thrown by passers-by, who walked on with a smile on their faces and a spring in their step. The marquis lowered his pennywhistle. "I owe you, then, you old rascal," said Lear, nodding.

"Yes. You do." The marquis took the paper—the train schedule—from Lear, and scanned it, and nodded. "But a word to the wise. Don't overuse it. A little goes a very long way."

And the four of them walked away, down the long corridor, surrounded by posters advertising films and underwear, and the occasional official-looking notices warning musicians playing for coins to move away from the station, listening to the sob of the saxophone, and to the sound of money landing on a coat.

The marquis led them to a Central Line platform. Richard walked over to the edge of the platform and looked down. He wondered, as he always did, which one the live rail was; and decided, as he always did, that it was the one farthest from the platform, with the large whitish porcelain insulators between it and the ground; and then he found himself smiling, involuntarily, at a tiny dark gray mouse who was bravely prowling the tracks, three feet below him, in a mousy quest for abandoned sandwiches and dropped potato chips.

A voice came over the loudspeaker, that formal, disembodied male voice that warned "Mind the Gap." It was intended to keep unwary passengers from stepping into the space between the train and the platform. Richard, like most Londoners, barely heard it anymore—it was like aural wallpaper. But suddenly, Hunter's hand was on his arm. "Mind the Gap," she said urgently, to Richard. "Stand back over there. By the wall."

"What?" said Richard.

"I *said*," said Hunter, "mind the—"

And then it erupted over the side of the platform. It was diaphanous, dreamlike, a ghost-thing, the color of black smoke, and it welled up like silk under water, and, moving astonishingly fast while still seeming to drift almost in slow motion, it wrapped itself tightly around Richard's ankle. It stung, even through the fabric of his Levi's. The thing pulled him toward the edge of the platform, and he staggered.

He realized, as if from a distance, that Hunter had pulled out her staff and was smacking the tentacle of smoke with it, hard, repeatedly.

There was a faraway screaming noise, thin and mindless, like an idiot child deprived of its toy. The smoke-tentacle let go of Richard's ankle and slid back over the edge of the platform, and it was gone. Hunter took Richard by the scruff of the neck and pulled him toward the back wall, where Richard slumped against it. He was trembling, and the world seemed suddenly utterly unreal. The color had been sucked from his jeans wherever the thing had touched him, making them look as if they'd been ineptly bleached. He pulled up the trouser leg: tiny purple welts were coming up on the skin of his ankle and calf. "What . . ." he tried to say, but nothing came out. He swallowed, and tried again. "What was that?"

Hunter looked down at him impassively. Her face could have been carved from brown wood. "I don't think it has a name," she said. "They live in the gaps. I did warn you."

"I've . . . never seen one before."

"You weren't part of the Underside before," said Hunter. "Just wait by the wall. It's safer."

The marquis was checking the time on a large gold pocket-watch. He returned it to his waistcoat pocket, consulted the paper Lear had given him, and nodded, satisfied. "We're in luck," he pronounced. "The Earl's Court train should be coming through here in about half an hour."

"Earl's Court Station isn't on the Central Line," pointed out Richard.

The marquis stared at Richard, openly amused. "What a refreshing mind you have, young man," he said. "There really is nothing quite like total ignorance, is there?"

The warm wind began to blow. An Underground train pulled up at the station. People got off and other people got on, going about the business of their lives, and Richard watched them with envy. "Mind the Gap," intoned the recorded voice. "Stand clear of the doors. Mind the Gap." Door took one look at Richard. Then, apparently worried about what she was seeing, she walked over to him, and she took his hand. He was very pale, and his breath was coming shallow and fast. "Mind the Gap," boomed the recorded voice again. "I'm fine," lied Richard bravely, to no one in particular.

The central courtyard of Mr. Croup and Mr. Vandemar's hospital was a dank and cheerless place. Ragged grass grew up through the abandoned desks, rubber tires, and bits of office furniture. The overall impression given by the area was that a decade before (perhaps out of boredom, perhaps out of frustration, perhaps even as a statement, or as performance art) a number of people had thrown the contents of their offices out of their windows, high above, and had left them there on the ground to rot.

There was broken glass there, as well, broken glass in abundance. There were also several mattresses, some of which looked like they had at some point been set on fire. Grass grew up through the springs. An entire ecology had evolved around the ornamental fountain in the center of the well, which had for a long time been neither particularly ornamental nor a fountain. A cracked and leaking water pipe nearby had, with the aid of some rainwater, transformed it into a breeding ground for a number of little frogs who plopped about cheerfully, rejoicing in their freedom from any non-airborne natural predators. Crows and blackbirds and even occasional seagulls, however, regarded the place as a cat-free delicatessen, specializing in frogs.

Slugs sprawled indolently under the springs of the burnt mattresses; snails left slime trails across the broken glass; large black beetles scuttled industriously over smashed gray plastic telephones and mysteriously mutilated Barbie dolls.

Mr. Croup and Mr. Vandemar had come up for a change of air. They were walking slowly around the perimeter of the central yard, broken glass crunching beneath their feet; they looked like shadows in their frayed black suits. Mr. Croup was in a cold fury. He was walking twice as fast as Mr. Vandemar, circling him, and almost dancing in his anger. At times, as if unable to contain the rage inside, Mr. Croup would fling himself at the hospital wall, physically attack it with his fists and feet, as if it were a poor substitute for a real person. Mr. Vandemar, on the other hand, simply walked. It was too consistent, too steady and inexorable a walk to be described as a stroll: Death walked like Mr. Vandemar. Mr. Vandemar watched Mr. Croup, impassively, as Mr. Croup kicked a sheet of glass that had been leaning against a wall. It shattered with a satisfying crash.

"I, Mister Vandemar," said Mr. Croup, surveying the wreckage, "I, for one, have had almost as much as I'm willing to take. Almost. Pussyfooting, trifling, lollygagging, shilly-shallying . . . whey-faced toad—

I could pop out his eyes with my thumbs..."

Mr. Vandemar shook his head. "Not yet," he said. "He's our boss. For this job. After we've been paid, maybe we could have some fun on our own time."

•Mr. Croup spat on the ground. "He's a worthless, conniving dunderhead.... We should butcher the bitch. Annul, cancel, inhume, and amortize her."

A telephone began to ring, loudly. Mr. Croup and Mr. Vandemar looked around, puzzled. Eventually Mr. Vandemar found the telephone, halfway down a pile of rubble on top of a scree of water-stained medical records. Broken wires trailed from the back of it. He picked it up and passed it to Mr. Croup. "For you," he said. Mr. Vandemar did not like telephones.

"Mister Croup here," said Croup. Then, obsequiously, "Oh. It's you, sir..." A pause. "At present, as you requested, she is walking around, free as a daisy. I'm afraid your bodyguard idea went down like a dead baboon...Varney? Yes, he's quite dead." Another pause.

"Sir, I am commencing to have certain conceptual problems with the role of myself and my partner in these shenanigans." There was a third pause, and Mr. Croup went paler than pale. "Unprofessional?" he asked, mildly. "Us?" He curled his hand into a fist, which he slammed, hard, into the side of a brick wall. There was no change, however, in his tone of voice as he said, "Sir. Might I with due respect remind you that Mister Vandemar and myself burned down the City of Troy? We brought the Black Plague to Flanders. We have assassinated a dozen kings, five popes, half a hundred heroes and two accredited gods. Our last commission before this was the torturing to death of an entire monastery in sixteenth-century Tuscany. We are *utterly* professional."

Mr. Vandemar, who had been amusing himself by catching little frogs and seeing how many he could stuff into his mouth at a time, said, with his mouth full, "I liked doing that . . ."

"My point?" asked Mr. Croup, and he flicked some imaginary dust from his threadbare black suit, ignoring the real dust as he did so. "My point is that we are assassins. We are cutthroats. We kill." He listened to something, then said, "Well, what about the Upworlder? Why can't we kill him?" Mr. Croup twitched, spat once more, and kicked the wall, as he stood there holding the rust-stained, half-broken telephone.

"*Scare her?* We're cutthroats, not scarecrows." A pause. He took a deep breath. "Yes, I understand, but I don't like it." The person at the other end of the phone had hung up. Mr. Croup looked down at the telephone. Then he hefted it in one hand and proceeded methodically to smash it into shards of plastic and metal by banging it against the wall.

Mr. Vandemar walked over. He had found a large black slug with a bright orange underbelly, and he was chewing it, like a fat cigar. The slug was trying to crawl away down Mr. Vandemar's chin. "Who was that?" asked Mr. Vandemar.

"Who the hell do you think it was?"

Mr. Vandemar chewed, thoughtfully, then sucked the slug into his mouth. "A scarecrow man?" he ventured.

"Our employer."

"That was going to be my next guess."

"Scarecrows," spat Mr. Croup, disgusted. He was moving from a red rage to an oily gray sulk.

Mr. Vandemar swallowed the contents of his mouth and wiped his lips on his sleeve. "Best way to scare crows," said Mr. Vandemar, "you just creep up behind them and put your hand round their little crow necks and squeeze until they don't move anymore. That scares the stuffing out of them."

And then he was silent; and from far above they heard the sound of crows flying, cawing angrily.

"Crows. Family *Corvidae*. Collective noun," intoned Mr. Croup, relishing the sound of the word, "a murder."

Richard waited against the wall, next to Door. She said very little; she chewed her fingernails, ran her hands through her reddish hair until it was sticking up in all directions, then tried to push it back down again. She was certainly unlike anyone he had ever known. When she noticed him looking at her, she shrugged and shimmied down further into her layers of clothes, deeper into her leather jacket. Her face looked out at the world from inside the jacket. The expression on her face made Richard think of a beautiful homeless child he had seen, the previous winter, behind Covent Garden: he had not been certain whether it was a girl or a boy. Its mother was begging, pleading with the passers-by for coins to feed the child and the infant that she carried in her arms. But the child stared out at the world and said nothing, although it must have been cold and hungry. It just stared.

Hunter stood by Door, looking back and forth down the platform. The marquis had told them where to wait, and then he had slipped away. From somewhere, Richard heard a baby begin to cry. The marquis slipped out of an exit-only door and walked toward them. He was chewing on a piece of candy.

"Having fun?" asked Richard. A train was coming toward them, its approach heralded by a gust of warm wind.

"Just taking care of business," said the marquis. He consulted the piece of paper and his watch. He pointed to a place on the platform. "This should be the Earl's Court train. Stand behind me here, you three." Then, as the Underground train—a rather boring-looking, normal train, Richard was disappointed to observe—rumbled and rattled its way into the station, the marquis leaned across Richard and said to Door, "My lady? There is something that perhaps I should have mentioned earlier."

She turned her odd-colored eyes on him. "Yes?"

"Well," he said, "the earl might not be *entirely* pleased to see me."

The train slowed down and stopped. The car that had pulled up in front of Richard was quite empty: its lights were turned off, it was bleak and empty and dark. From time to time Richard had noticed cars like this one, locked and shadowy, on Tube trains, and he had wondered what purpose they served. The other doors on the train hissed open, and passengers got on and got off. The doors of the darkened car remained closed. The marquis drummed on the door with his fist, an intricate rhythmic rap. Nothing happened. Richard was just wondering if the train would now pull out without them on it, when the door of the dark car was pushed open from the inside. It opened about six inches, and an elderly, bespectacled face peered out at them.

"Who knocks?" he said.

Through the opening, Richard could see flames

burning, and people, and smoke inside the car. Through the glass in the doors, however, he still saw a dark and empty carriage. "The Lady Door," announced the marquis, smoothly, "and her companions."

The door slid open all the way, and they were inside Earl's Court.

SEVEN

THERE WAS STRAW SCATTERED ON THE floor, over a layer of rushes. There was an open log fire, sputtering and blazing in a large fireplace. There were a few chickens, strutting and pecking on the floor. There were seats with hand-embroidered cushions on them, and there were tapestries covering the windows and the doors.

Richard stumbled forward as the train lurched out of the station. He reached out, grabbed hold of the nearest person, and regained his balance. The nearest person happened to be a short, gray, elderly man-at-arms, who would have looked, Richard decided, exactly like a recently retired minor official were it not for the tin hat, the surcoat, the rather clumsily knitted chain mail, and the spear; instead he looked like a recently retired minor official who had, somewhat against his will, been dragooned into his local amateur dramatic society, where he had been forced to play a man-at-arms.

The little gray man blinked shortsightedly at Richard as Richard grabbed him, and then he said, lugubriously, "Sorry about that."

"My fault," said Richard.

"I know," said the man.

An enormous Irish wolfhound padded down the aisle and stopped beside a lute player, who sat on the floor picking at a melody in a desultory fashion. The wolfhound glared at Richard, snorted with disdain, then lay down and went to sleep. At the far end of the carriage an elderly falconer, with a hooded falcon on his wrist, was exchanging pleasantries with a small knot of damsels of a certain age. Some passengers obviously stared at the four travelers; others, just as obviously, ignored them. It was, Richard realized, as if someone had taken a small medieval court and put it, as best they could, in one car of an Underground train.

A herald raised his bugle to his lips and played a tuneless blast, as an immense, elderly man, in a huge fur-lined dressing gown and carpet slippers, staggered through the connecting door from the next compartment, his arm resting on the shoulder of a jester in shabby motley. The old man was larger than life in every way: he wore an eye-patch over his left eye, which had the effect of making him look slightly helpless, and unbalanced, like a one-eyed hawk. There were fragments of food in his red-gray beard, and what appeared to be pajama pants were visible at the bottom of his shabby fur gown.

That, thought Richard, correctly, *must be the earl.*

The earl's jester was an elderly man with a pinched, humorless mouth and a painted face. He led the earl to a thronelike carved wooden seat in which, a trifle unsteadily, the earl sat down. The wolfhound got up, padded down the length of the carriage, and settled itself at the earl's slippered feet.

Earl's Court, thought Richard. *Of course.* And then he began to wonder whether there was a baron in

Barons Court Tube station, or a Raven in Raven-scourt or, . . .

The little old man-at-arms coughed asthmatically and said, "Right then, you lot. State your business." Door stepped forward. She held her head up high, suddenly seeming taller and more at ease than Richard had previously seen her, and she said, "We seek an audience with His Grace the Earl."

The earl called down the carriage. "What did the little girl say, Halvard?" he asked. Richard wondered if he was deaf.

Halvard, the elderly man-at-arms, shuffled around and cupped his hand to his mouth. "They seek an audience, Your Grace," he shouted, over the rattle of the train.

The earl pushed aside his thick fur cap and scratched his head, meditatively. He was balding underneath his cap. "They do? An audience? How splendid. Who are they, Halvard?"

Halvard turned back to them. "He wants to know who you all are. Keep it short, though. Don't go on."

"I am the Lady Door," announced Door. "The Lord Portico was my father."

The earl brightened at this, leaned forward, peered through the smoke with his one good eye. "Did she say she was Portico's oldest girl?" he asked the jester.

"Yus, your grace."

The earl beckoned to Door. "Come here," he said. "Come-come-come. Let me look at you." She walked down the swaying carriage, grabbing the thick rope straps that hung from the ceiling as she went, to keep her balance. When she stood before the earl's wooden chair, she curtseyed. He scratched at his beard and stared at her. "We were all quite devastated to hear of your father's unfortunate—" said the earl, and then he interrupted himself, and said, "Well, all your family, it was a—" and he trailed off, and said, "You know I had warmest regards for him, did a bit of business together . . . good old Portico . . . full of ideas . . ." He stopped. Then he tapped the jester on the shoulder and whispered, in a querulous boom, loud enough that it could be heard easily over the noise of the train, "Go and make jokes at them, Tooley. Earn your keep."

The earl's fool staggered up the aisle with an arthritic step. He stopped in front of Richard. "And who might you be?" he asked.

"Me?" said Richard. "Um. Me? My name? It's Richard. Richard Mayhew."

"*Me*?" squeaked the fool, in an elderly, rather theatrical imitation of Richard's Scottish accent. "*Me? Um. Me?* La, nuncle. 'Tis not a man, but a mooncalf." The courtiers sniggered, dustily.

"And I," de Carabas told the jester, with a blinding smile, "call myself the marquis de Carabas." The fool blinked.

"De Carabas the thief?" asked the jester. "De Carabas the bodysnatcher? De Carabas the traitor?" He turned to the courtiers around them. "But this cannot be de Carabas. For why? Because de Carabas has long since been banished from the earl's presence. Perhaps it is instead a strange new species of *stoat*, who grew particularly large." The courtiers tittered uneasily, and a low buzz of troubled conversation began. The earl said nothing, but his lips were pressed together tightly, and he had begun to tremble.

"I am called Hunter," said Hunter to the jester.

The courtiers were silent then. The jester opened

his mouth, as if he were going to say something, and then he looked at her, and he closed his mouth again. A hint of a smile played at the corner of Hunter's perfect lips. "Go on," she said. "Say something funny."

The jester stared at the trailing toes of his shoes. Then he muttered, "My hound hath no nose."

The earl, who had been staring at the marquis de Carabas with eyes like a slow-burning fuse, now exploded to his feet, a gray-bearded volcano, an elderly berserker. His head brushed the roof of the carriage. He pointed at the marquis and shouted, spittle flying, "I will not stand for it, I will not. Make him come forward."

Halvard waggled a gloomy spear at the marquis, who sauntered to the front of the train, until he stood beside Door in front of the earl's throne. The wolfhound growled in the back of its throat.

"You," said the earl, stabbing the air with a huge, knotted finger. "I know you, de Carabas. I haven't forgotten. I may be old, but I haven't forgotten."

The marquis bowed. "Might I remind Your Grace," he said urbanely, "that we had a deal? I negotiated the peace treaty between your people and the Raven's Court. And in return you agreed to provide a little favor." *So there is a raven's court,* thought Richard. He wondered what it was like.

"A little favor?" said the earl. He turned a deep beet red color. "Is that what you call it? I lost a dozen men to your foolishness in the retreat from White City. I lost an eye."

"And if you don't mind my saying so, Your Grace," said the marquis, graciously, "that is a very fetching patch. It sets off your face perfectly."

"I swore . . ." fulminated the earl, beard bristling,

"I swore . . . that if you ever set foot in my domain I would . . ." he trailed off. Shook his head, confused and forgetful. Then he continued. "It'll come back to me. I do not forget."

"He might not be entirely pleased to see you?" whispered Door to de Carabas.

"Well, he's not," he muttered back.

Door stepped forward once more. "Your Grace," she said, loudly, clearly, "de Carabas is here with me as my guest and my companion. For the fellowship there has ever been between your family and mine, for the friendship between my father and—"

"He abused my hospitality," boomed the earl. "I swore that . . . if he ever again entered my domain I would have him gutted and dried . . . like, like something that had been gutted, first . . . like . . ."

"Perchance—then dried a kipper, my lord?" suggested the jester.

The earl shrugged. "It is of no matter. Guards, seize him." And they did. While neither of the guards would ever see sixty again, each of them was holding a crossbow, pointed at the marquis, and their hands did not tremble, neither with age nor with fear. Richard looked at Hunter. She seemed untroubled by this: she was watching it almost with amusement, like someone attending the theater.

Door folded her arms and stood taller, putting her head back, raising her pointed chin. She looked less like a ragged street pixie; more like someone used to getting her own way. The opal eyes flashed. "Your Grace, the marquis is with me as my companion, on my quest. Our families have been friends for a long time now—"

"Yes. They have," interrupted the earl, helpfully. "Hundreds of years. Hundreds and hundreds. Knew your grandfather, too. Funny old fellow. Bit vague," he confided.

"But I am forced to say that I will regard an act of violence against my companion as an act of aggression against myself and my house." The girl stared up at the old man. He towered over her. They stood for some moments, frozen. He tugged on his red-and-gray beard, agitatedly, then he thrust out his lower lip like a small child. "I will not have him here," he said.

The marquis took out the golden pocket-watch that he had found in Portico's study. He examined it, carelessly. Then he turned to Door and said, as if none of the events around them had occurred. "My lady, I will obviously be of more use to you off this train than on. And I have other avenues to explore."

"No," she said. "If you go, we all go."

"I don't think so," said the marquis. "Hunter will look after you as long as you stay in London Below. I'll meet you at the next market. Don't do anything too stupid in the meantime." The train was coming into a station.

Door fixed the earl with her look: there was something more ancient and powerful in that glance than her young years would have seemed to allow. Richard noticed that the room fell quiet whenever she spoke. "Will you let him go in peace, Your Grace?" she asked.

The earl ran his hands over his face, rubbed his good eye and his eye-patch, then looked back at her. "Just make him go," said the earl. He looked at the marquis. "Next time . . ." he ran a thick old finger across his Adam's apple ". . . kipper."

The marquis bowed low. "I'll see myself out," he said to the guards, and stepped toward the open door. Halvard raised his crossbow and pointed it toward the marquis's back. Hunter reached out her hand and pushed the end of the crossbow back down toward the floor. The marquis stepped onto the platform, turned and waved with an elaborate flourish. The door hissed closed behind him.

The earl sat down on his huge chair at the end of the car. He said nothing. The train rattled and lurched through the dark tunnel. "Where are my manners?" muttered the earl to himself. He looked at them with one staring eye. Then he said it again, in a desperate boom that Richard could feel in his stomach, like a bass drumbeat. *"Where are my manners?"* He motioned one of the elderly men-at-arms to him. "They will be hungry after their journey, Dagvard. Thirsty, too, I shouldn't wonder."

"Yes, Your Grace."

"Stop the train!" called the earl. The doors hissed open, and Dagvard scuttled off onto a platform. Richard watched the people on the platform. No one came into their car. No one seemed to notice that anything was at all unusual.

Dagvard walked over to a vending machine on the side of the platform. He took off his metal helmet. Then he rapped, with one mailed glove, on the side of the machine. "Orders from the earl," he said. "Choc'lits." A ratcheting whirr came from deep in the guts of the machine, and it began to spit out dozens of Cadbury's Fruit and Nut chocolate bars, one after another. Dagvard held his helmet below the opening to catch them. The doors began to close. Halvard put the handle of his pike between the doors, and they opened again and began bumping open and shut on the pike handle. *"Please stand clear*

of the doors," said a loudspeaker voice. *"The train cannot leave until the doors are all closed."*

The earl was staring at Door lopsidedly, with his
one good eye. "So. What brings you here to me?"
he asked.

She licked her lips. "Well, indirectly, Your Grace,
my father's death."

He nodded, slowly. "Yes. You seek vengeance.
Quite right, too." He coughed, then recited, in a
basso profundo, *"Brave the battling blade, flashes the
furious fire, steel sword sheathed in hated heart, crimsons
the . . . the . . .* something. Yes."

"Vengeance?" Door thought for a moment. "Yes.
That was what my father said. But I mostly just want
to understand what happened, and to protect myself. My family had no enemies." Dagvard staggered
back onto the train then, his helmet filled with chocolate bars and cans of Coke; the doors were permitted to close, and the train moved off once more.

Lear's coat, still on the floor of the tunnel, was
covered in coins and bills, now, but it was also covered with shoes—kicking the coins, smearing and
tearing the bills, ripping the fabric of the coat. Lear
had begun to cry. "Please. Why won't you leave me
alone?" he begged. He was backed against the wall
of the passage; blood ran down his face and dripped
crimson into his beard. His saxophone hung limply,
awkwardly, on his chest, dented and scraped.

He was surrounded by a small crowd of people—
more than twenty, less than fifty—every one of them
shoving and pushing, in a mindless mob, their eyes
blank and staring, each man and woman desperately
fighting and clawing in order to give Lear their
money. There was blood on the tiled wall, where

Lear had knocked his head. Lear flailed out at one middle-aged woman, her purse wide open, a fistful of five-pound notes thrust out at him. She clawed at his face in her eagerness to give him her money. He twisted to avoid her fingernails and fell to the tunnel floor.

Someone stepped on his hand. His face was pushed into a slurry of coins. He began to sob, and to curse. "I told you not to overuse that tune," said an elegant voice, nearby. "Naughty."

"Help me," gasped Lear.

"Well, there *is* a counter-charm," admitted the voice, almost reluctantly.

The crowd was pressing closer now. A flung fifty-pence coin opened Lear's cheek. He curled into a fetal ball, hugging himself, burying his face in his knees. "Play it, damn you," sobbed Lear. "Whatever you want . . . just make them stop . . ."

A pennywhistle piping began softly, and echoed down the passage. A simple phrase, repeated over and over, slightly different every time: the de Carabas variations. The footsteps were moving away. Shuffling, at first, then picking up pace: moving away from him. Lear opened his eyes. The marquis de Carabas was leaning against the wall, playing the pennywhistle. When he saw Lear looking at him he took the whistle from his lips and replaced it in an inside pocket of his coat. He tossed Lear a lace-edged handkerchief of patched linen. Lear wiped the blood from his forehead and face. "They would have killed me," he said, accusingly.

"I *did* warn you," said de Carabas. "Just count yourself lucky that I was coming back this way." He helped Lear into a sitting position. "Now," he said. "I think you owe me another favor."

Lear picked up his coat—torn and muddy and imprinted with the marks of many feet—from the passage floor. He suddenly felt very cold, and he
wrapped the shredded coat around his shoulders.
Coins fell, and bills fluttered to the floor. He let them
lie. "Was I really lucky? Or did you set me up?"

The marquis looked almost offended. "I don't
know how you could even bring yourself to think
such a thing."

"'Cos I know you. That's how. So what is it that
you want me to do this time? Theft? Arson?" Lear
sounded resigned, and a little sad. And then, "Murder?"

De Carabas reached down and took back his
handkerchief. "Theft, I'm afraid. You were right the
first time," he said, with a smile. "I find myself in
rather urgent need of a piece of T'ang dynasty sculpture." Lear shivered. Then, slowly, he nodded.

Richard was handed a bar of Cadbury's Fruit and
Nut chocolate and a large silver goblet, ornamented
around the rim with what appeared to Richard to be
sapphires. The goblet was filled with Coca-Cola. The
jester, whose name seemed to be Tooley, cleared his
throat loudly. "I would like to propose a toast to our
guests," he said. "A child, a bravo, a fool. May they
each get what they deserve."

"Which one am I?" whispered Richard to Hunter.

"The fool, of course," she said.

"In the old days," said Halvard dismally, after
sipping his Coke, "we had wine. I prefer wine. It's
not as sticky."

"Do all the machines just give you things like
that?" asked Richard.

"Oh yes," said the old man. "They listen to the

earl, y'see. He rules the Underground. The bit with the trains. He's lord of the Central, the Circle, the Jubilee, the Victorious, the Bakerloo—well, all of them except the Underside Line."

"What's the Underside Line?" asked Richard.

Halvard shook his head and pursed his lips. Hunter brushed Richard's shoulder with her fingers. "Remember what I told you about the shepherds of Shepherd's Bush?"

"You said I didn't want to meet them, and there were some things I was probably better off not knowing."

"Good," she said. "So now you can add the Underside Line to the list of those things."

Door came back down the carriage toward them. She was smiling. "The earl's agreed to help us," she said. "Come on. He's meeting us in the library." Richard began to follow, as he realized that the question What library? had not risen to his lips. The longer he was here, the more he took at face value. Instead, he followed Door toward the earl's empty throne, and round the back of it, and through the connecting door behind it, and into the library. It was a huge stone room, with a high wooden ceiling. Each wall was covered with shelves. Each shelf was laden with objects: there were books, yes. But the shelves were filled with a host of other things: tennis rackets, hockey sticks, umbrellas, a spade, a notebook computer, a wooden leg, several mugs, dozens of shoes, pairs of binoculars, a small log, six glove puppets, a lava lamp, various CDs, records (LPs, 45s, and 78s), cassette tapes and eight-tracks, dice, toy cars, assorted pairs of dentures, watches, flashlights, four garden gnomes of assorted sizes (two fishing, one of them mooning, the last smoking a cigar), piles of newspapers, magazines, grimoires, three-legged stools, a box of cigars, a plastic nodding-head Alsatian, socks . . . the room was a tiny empire of lost property.

"This is his real domain," muttered Hunter. "Things lost. Things forgotten."

There were windows set in the stone wall. Through them, Richard could see the rattling darkness and the passing lights of the Underground tunnels. The earl was sitting on the floor with his legs splayed, patting the wolfhound and scratching it underneath the chin. The jester stood beside him, looking embarrassed. The earl clambered to his feet when he saw them. His forehead creased. "Ah. There you are. Now, there was a reason I asked you here, it'll come to me . . ." He tugged at his red-gray beard, a tiny gesture from such a huge man.

"The Angel Islington, Your Grace," said Door politely.

"Oh yes. Your father had a lot of ideas for changes, you know. Asked me about them. I don't trust change. I sent him to Islington." He stopped. Blinked his one eye. "Did I tell you this already?"

"Yes, Your Grace. And how can *we* get to Islington?"

The earl nodded as if Door had said something profound. "Only once by the quick way. After that you have to go the long way down. Dangerous."

Door said, patiently, "And the quick way is . . . ?"

"No, no. Need to be an opener to use it. Only good for Portico's family." He rested a huge hand on her shoulder. Then his hand slid up to her cheek. "Better off staying here with me. Keep an old man warm at night, eh?" He leered at her and touched her tangle of hair with his old fingers. Hunter took a step toward Door. Door gestured with her hand: *No. Not yet.*

Door looked up at the earl, and said, "Your Grace, I *am* Portico's oldest daughter. How do I get to the Angel Islington?" Richard found himself amazed that Door was able to keep her temper in the face of the earl's losing battle with temporal drift.

The earl winked his single eye in a solemn blink: an old hawk, his head tipped on one side. Then he took his hand from her hair. "So you are. So you are. Portico's daughter. How is your dear father? Keeping well, I hope? Fine man. Good man."

"How do we get to the Angel Islington?" said Door, but now there was a tremble in her voice.

"Hmm? Use the Angelus, of course."

Richard found himself imagining the earl sixty, eighty, five hundred years ago: a mighty warrior, a cunning strategist, a great lover of women, a fine friend, a terrifying foe. There was still the wreckage of that man in there somewhere. That was what made him so terrible, and so sad. The earl fumbled on the shelves, moving pens and pipes and pea-shooters, little gargoyles and dead leaves. Then, like an aged cat stumbling on a mouse, he seized a small, rolled-up scroll, and handed it to the girl. "Here y'go, lassie," said the earl. "All in here. And I suppose we'd better drop you off where you need to go."

"You'll drop us off?" asked Richard. "In a train?"

The earl looked around for the source of the sound, focused on Richard, and smiled enormously. "Oh, think nothing of it," he boomed. "Anything for Portico's daughter." Door clutched the scroll tightly, triumphantly.

Richard could feel the train beginning to slow, and

he, and Door, and Hunter were led out of the stone room and back into the car. Richard peered out at the platform, as they slowed down.

"Excuse me. What station is this?" he asked. The train had stopped, facing one of the station signs: BRITISH MUSEUM, it said. Somehow, this was one oddity too many. He could accept "Mind the Gap" and the Earl's Court, and even the strange library. But damn it, like all Londoners, he knew his Tube map, and this was going too far. "There isn't a British Museum Station," said Richard, firmly.

"There isn't?" boomed the earl. "Then, mm, then you must be very careful as you get off the train." And he guffawed, delightedly, and tapped his jester on the shoulder. "Hear that, Tooley? I am as funny as you are."

The jester smiled as bleak a smile as ever was seen. "My sides are splitting, my ribs are cracking, and my mirth is positively uncontainable, Your Grace," he said.

The doors hissed open. Door smiled up at the earl. "Thank you," she said. "Off, off," said the vast old man, shooing Door and Richard and Hunter out of the warm, smoky carriage onto the empty platform. And then the doors closed, and the train moved away, and Richard found himself staring at a sign which, no matter how many times he blinked—nor even if he looked away from it and looked back suddenly to take it by surprise—still obstinately persisted in saying:

BRITISH MUSEUM

EIGHT

I<small>T WAS EARLY EVENING, AND THE CLOUD</small>-less sky was transmuting from royal blue to a deep violet, with a smudge of fire orange and lime green over Paddington, four miles to the west, where, from Old Bailey's perspective anyway, the sun had recently set.

Skies, thought Old Bailey, in a satisfied sort of a way. Never a two of them alike. Not by day nor not by night, neither. He was a bit of a connoisseur of skies, was Old Bailey, and this was a good 'un. The old man had pitched his tent for the night on a roof opposite St. Paul's Cathedral, in the center of the City of London.

He was fond of St. Paul's, and it, at least, had changed little in the last three hundred years. It had been built in white Portland stone, which had, before it was even completed, begun to turn black from the soot and the filth in the smoky London air and now, following the cleaning of London in the 1970s, was more or less white again; but it was still St. Paul's. He was not sure that the same could be said for the rest of the City of London: he peered over the roof, stared away from his beloved sky, down to the

165

sodium-lit pavement below. He could see security cameras affixed to a wall, and a few cars, and one late office worker, locking a door and then walking toward the Tube. *Brrr.* Even the thought of going underground made Old Bailey shudder. He was a roof-man and proud of it; had fled the world at ground level so long ago. . . .

Old Bailey remembered when people had actually *lived* here in the City, not just worked; when they had lived and lusted and laughed, built ramshackle houses one leaning against the next, each house filled with noisy people. Why, the noise and the mess and the stinks and the songs from the alley across the way (then known, at least colloquially, as Shitten Alley) had been legendary in their time, but no one lived in the City now. It was a cold and cheerless place of offices, of people who worked in the day and went home to somewhere else at night. It was not a place for living anymore. He even missed the stinks.

The last smudge of orange sun faded into nocturnal purple. The old man covered the cages, so the birds could get their beauty sleep. They grumbled, then slept. Old Bailey scratched his nose, after which he went into his tent and fetched a blackened stew-pot, some water, some carrots and potatoes, salt, and a well-hanged pair of dead, plucked starlings. He walked out onto the roof, lit a small fire in a soot-blackened coffee can, and was putting his stew on to cook when he became aware that someone was watching him from the shadows by a chimney stack.

He picked up his toasting fork and waved it threateningly at the chimney stack. "Who's there?"

The marquis de Carabas stepped out of the shadows, bowed perfunctorily, and smiled gloriously.

Old Bailey lowered his toasting fork. "Oh," he said. "It's you. Well, what do you want? Knowledge? Or birds?"

The marquis walked over, picked a slice of raw carrot from Old Bailey's stew, and munched it. "Information, actually," he said.

Old Bailey chortled. "Hah," he said. "There's a first. Ehh?" Then he leaned toward the marquis. "What'll you trade for it?"

"What do you need?"

"Maybe I should do what you do. I should ask for another favor. An investment for one day down the road." Old Bailey grinned.

"Much too expensive, in the long run," said the marquis, without humor.

Old Bailey nodded. Now the sun had gone down, it was getting very cold, very fast. "Shoes, then," he said. "And a balaclava hat." He inspected his fingerless gloves: they were more hole than glove. "And new gloveses. It's going to be a bastard winter."

"Very well. I'll bring them to you." The marquis de Carabas put his hand into an inside pocket and produced, like a magician producing a rose from thin air, the black animal figure he had taken from Portico's study. "Now. What can you tell me about this?"

Old Bailey pulled on his glasses. He took the object from de Carabas. It was cold to the touch. He sat down on an air-conditioning unit, then, turning the black obsidian statue over and over in his hand, he announced: "It's the Great Beast of London." The marquis said nothing. His eyes flickered from the statue to Old Bailey, impatiently.

Old Bailey, enjoying the marquis's minor discomfort, continued at his own pace. "Now, they say that back in first King Charlie's day—him 'as got his head all chopped off, silly bugger—before the fire and the plague, this was, there was a butcher lived down by the Fleet Ditch, had some poor creature he was going to fatten up for Christmas. Some says it was a piglet, and some says it wusn't, and there's some—and I list meself as one of them—that wusn't never properly certain. One night in December the beast runned away, ran into the Fleet Ditch, and vanished into the sewers. And it fed on the sewage, and it grew, and it grew. And it got meaner, and nastier. They'd send in hunting parties after it, from time to time."

The marquis pursed his lips. "It must have died three hundred years ago."

Old Bailey shook his head. "Things like that, they're too vicious to die. Too old and big and nasty."

The marquis sighed. "I thought it was just a legend," he said. "Like the alligators in the sewers of New York City."

Old Bailey nodded, sagely. "What, the big white buggers? They're down there. I had a friend lost a head to one of them." A moment of silence. Old Bailey handed the statue back to the marquis. Then he raised his hand and snapped it, like a crocodile head, at de Carabas. "It was okay," gurned Old Bailey with a grin that was most terrible to behold. "He had another."

The marquis sniffed, uncertain whether or not Old Bailey was pulling his leg. He made the statue of the Beast vanish inside his coat once more.

"Hang on," said Old Bailey. He went back inside his brown tent and returned holding the ornate silver box the marquis had given him on their previous meeting. He held it out to the marquis. "How about this then?" he asked. "Are you ready to take it back? It fair gives me the creepy shivers, having it around."

The marquis walked to the edge of the roof, dropped the eight feet to the next building. "I'll take it back, when all this is over," he called. "Let us hope that you don't have to use it."

Old Bailey leaned over. 'How will I know if I do?"

"You'll know," called the marquis. "And the rats will tell you what to do with it." And with that he was over the side of the building, slipping down, using drainpipes and ledges as handholds.

"Hope I never finds out, that's all I can say," said Old Bailey to himself. Then a thought struck him. "Hoy," he called out to the night and the City. "Don't forget the shoeses and the gloveses!"

The advertisements on the walls were for refreshing and health-giving malted drinks, for two-shilling day excursions by train to the seaside, for kippered herrings, moustache wax and bootblack. They were smoke-blackened relics of the late twenties or the early thirties. Richard stared at them in disbelief. It seemed completely abandoned: a forgotten place. "It *is* British Museum Station," admitted Richard. "But . . . but there never *was* a British Museum Station. This is all wrong."

"It was closed down in about 1933, and sealed off," said Door.

"How bizarre," said Richard. It was like walking through history. He could hear trains echoing through tunnels nearby, felt the push of air as they passed. "Are there many stations like this?"

"About fifty," said Hunter. "They aren't all accessible, though. Not even to us."

There was a movement in the shadows at the edge of the platform. "Hello," said Door. "How are you?" She went down into a crouch. A brown rat stepped out into the light. It sniffed at Door's hand.

"Thank you," said Door, cheerfully. "I'm glad *you* aren't dead, too."

Richard edged over. "Um, Door. Could you tell the rat something for me?"

The rat turned its head toward him. "Miss Whiskers says that if there's anything you've got to say to her, you can tell it to her yourself," said Door.

"Miss Whiskers?"

Door shrugged. "It's a literal translation," she said. "It sounds better in rat."

Richard did not doubt it. "Um. Hello . . . Miss Whiskers . . . Look, there was one of your rat-speaker people, a girl named Anaesthesia. She was taking me to the market. We were crossing this bridge in the dark, and she just never made it across."

The rat interrupted him, with a sharp *squee*. Door began to talk, hesitantly, like a simultaneous translator. "She says . . . that the rats do not blame you for the loss. Your guide was . . . mm . . . taken by the night . . . as tribute."

"But—"

The rat squeaked again. "Sometimes they come back . . ." said Door. "She has taken note of your concern . . . and thanks you for it." The rat nodded to Richard, blinked her bead-black eyes, then leapt to the floor and scurried back into the dark. "Nice rat," said Door. Her disposition seemed to have improved remarkably, now that she had the scroll. "Up there," she said, indicating an archway effectively blocked by an iron door.

They walked over to it. Richard pushed against the metal, but it was locked from the other side. "Looks like it's been sealed up," said Richard. "We'll need special tools."

Door smiled, suddenly; her face seemed to be illuminated. For a moment, her elfin face became beautiful. "Richard," she said. "My family. We're openers. It's our Talent. Look . . ." She reached out a grubby hand, touched the door. For a long moment nothing happened, then there was a loud crash from the other side of the door, and a *chunk* from their side. Door pushed against the door and, with a fierce squeal from the rusted hinges, it opened. Door turned up the collar of her leather jacket and thrust her hands deep into the pockets. Hunter shone her flashlight into the blackness beyond the doorway: a flight of stone steps, going up, into the dark. "Hunter. Can you take the rear?" asked Door. "I'll go on in front. Richard can take the middle."

She walked up a couple of steps. Hunter stayed where she was. "Lady?" said Hunter. "You are going to London Above?"

"That's right," said Door. "We're going to the British Museum."

Hunter bit her lower lip. Then she shook her head. "I must stay in London Below," she said. There was a tremble in her voice. Richard realized that this was the first time he had ever seen Hunter display any emotion other than effortless competence or, occasionally, tolerant amusement.

"Hunter," said Door, bewildered. "You're my bodyguard."

Hunter looked ill at ease. "I am your bodyguard in London Below," she said. "I cannot go with you to London Above."

"But you have to."

"My lady. I cannot. I thought you understood. The marquis knows." *Hunter will look after you as long as you stay in London Below,* thought Richard. *Yes.*

"No," said Door, her pointed chin pushed out and up, her odd-colored eyes narrowed. "I don't understand. What is it?" she added, scornfully. "Some kind of curse or something?" Hunter hesitated, licked her lips, then nodded. It was as if she were admitting to having some socially embarrassing disease.

"Look, Hunter," Richard heard his own voice saying, "don't be silly." For a moment he thought she was about to hit him, which would have been bad, or even to start crying, which would have been much, much worse. Then she took a deep breath, and said, in measured tones, "I will walk by your side when you are in London Below, my lady, and I shall guard your body from all harm that might befall you. But do not ask me to follow you to London Above. I cannot." She folded her arms beneath her breasts, planted her legs a little apart, and looked for all the underworld like a statue of a woman not going anywhere, cast in brass and in bronze and in burnt caramel.

"Right," said Door. "Come on, Richard." And she set off up the steps.

"Look," said Richard. "Why don't we stay down here? We can find the marquis, and then all set off together, and—" Door was disappearing into the darkness above him. Hunter was planted at the foot of the stairs.

"I shall wait here until she returns," Hunter told him. "You may go, or stay, as you will."

Richard chased up the steps, as fast as he could, in the dark. Soon he saw Door's lamp-light above him. "Wait," he panted. "Please." She stopped, and waited for him to catch up. And then, when he had caught up, and was standing next to her on a claustrophobically small landing, she waited for him to catch his breath. "You can't just go running off like that," said Richard. Door said nothing; the line of her lips became slightly more compressed; the angle of her chin was ever-so-slightly raised. "She's your bodyguard," he pointed out.

Door began to walk up the next flight of steps. Richard followed her. "Well, we'll be back soon enough," said Door. "She can start guarding me again then."

The air was close, dank and oppressive. Richard wondered how you could tell if the air was bad, in the absence of a canary, and he contented himself with hoping that it wasn't. "I think the marquis probably did know. About her curse, or whatever it is," he said.

"Yes," she said. "I expect he did."

"He . . ." Richard began. "The marquis. Well, you know, to be honest, he seems a little bit dodgy to me."

Door stopped. The steps dead-ended in a rough brick wall. "Mm," she agreed. "He's a little bit dodgy in the same way that rats are a little bit covered in fur."

"Then why go to him for help? Wasn't there someone else who could have helped you?"

"We'll talk about it later." She opened the scroll the earl had given her, glanced over the spidery handwriting, then rolled it back up. "We'll be fine," she said, decisively. "It's all in here. We've just got to get into the British Museum. We find the Angelus, we get out. Easy. Nothing to it. Close your eyes."

Richard closed his eyes, obediently. "Nothing to it," he repeated. "When people say that on films, it always means that something awful is going to happen."

He felt a breeze against his face. Something in the quality of the darkness beyond his closed eyelids changed. "So what's your point?" asked Door. The acoustics had altered as well: they were in a bigger room. "You can open your eyes now."

He opened his eyes. They were on the other side of the wall, he assumed, in what appeared to be a junk room. Not just any old junk room, though: there was something rather strange and special about the quality of this junk. It was the kind of magnificent, rare, strange, and expensive junk one would only expect to see somewhere like . . .

"Are we in the British Museum?" he asked.

She frowned, and seemed to be thinking, or listening. "Not exactly. We're very near. I think this must be some kind of storage space or something." She reached up to touch the fabric of a suit of antique clothing, displayed on a wax dummy.

"I wish we'd stayed back with the bodyguard," said Richard.

Door tipped her head on one side and looked at him gravely. "And what do you need guarding from, Richard Mayhew?"

"Nothing," he admitted. And then they turned the corner, and he said, "Well . . . maybe them," and, at the same time, Door said, "Shit." Mr. Croup and Mr.

Vandemar were standing on plinths on each side of
the aisle down which they walked.

They reminded Richard horridly of an exhibition
of contemporary art Jessica had once taken him to:
an exciting young artist had announced that he
would break down all the Taboos of Art, and to this
end, had embarked on a campaign of systematic
grave robbery, displaying the thirty most interesting
results of his depredations in glass cases. The exhibit
was closed after the artist sold *Stolen Cadaver Number
25* to an advertising agency for a six-figure sum, and
the relatives of Stolen Cadaver Number 25, seeing a
photo of the sculpture in the *Sun,* had sued both for
a share of the proceeds and to change the name of
the art piece to *Edgar Fospring, 1919–1987 Loving
Husband, Father and Uncle. Rest in Peace, Daddy.* Richard had stared at the glass-bound corpses in their
stained suits and damaged dresses with horror: he
hated himself for looking, but he had not been able
to turn away.

Mr. Croup smiled like a snake with a crescent
moon stuck in its mouth, and his resemblance to Stolen Cadavers Numbers 1 to 30 was, if anything, increased by this. "What?" said the smiling Mr.
Croup. "No Mister 'I'm So Clever and Know Everything' Marquis? No 'Oh, didn't I tell you? Whoops!
I can't go upstairs?' Hunter?" He paused, for dramatic effect. "So paint me gray and call me a dire
wolf if it isn't two little lost lambs, out on their own,
after dark."

"You could call me a wolf, too, Mister Croup,"
said Mr. Vandemar, helpfully.

Mr. Croup clambered down from his plinth. "A
gentle word in your woolly ears, little lambkins," he
said. Richard looked around them. There had to be

somewhere they could run. He reached down, clasped Door's hand, and looked around, desperately.

"No, please. Stay just where you are," said Mr. Croup. "We like you like that. And we don't want to have to hurt you."

"We do," said Mr. Vandemar.

"Well, yes, Mister Vandemar, once you put it like that. We want to hurt you both. We want to hurt you a lot. But that's not why we're here right now. We're here to make things more interesting. You see, when things get dull, my partner and I become restive and, hard as you may find this to believe, we lose our sunny and delightful dispositions."

Mr. Vandemar showed them his teeth, demonstrating his sunny and delightful disposition. It was unquestionably the most horrible thing that Richard had ever seen.

"Leave us alone," said Door. Her voice was clear and steady. Richard squeezed her hand. If she could be brave, so could he. "If you want to hurt her," he said, "you'll have to kill me first."

Mr. Vandemar seemed genuinely pleased by this. "All right," he said. "Thanks."

"And we'll hurt you, too," said Mr. Croup.

"Not yet, though," said Mr. Vandemar.

"You see," explained Mr. Croup, in a voice like rancid butter, "right now, we're just here to worry you."

Mr. Vandemar's voice was a night wind blowing over a desert of bones. "Make you suffer," he said. "Spoil your day."

Mr. Croup sat down at the base of Mr. Vandemar's plinth. "You visited Earl's Court today," he said, in what Richard suspected he fondly imagined were light and conversational tones.

"So?" said Door. She was edging away from them, now.

Mr. Croup smiled. "How did we know that? How did we know where to find you now?"

"Can get to you any time at all," said Mr. Vandemar, almost in a whisper. "You've been sold out, little ladybird," said Mr. Croup to Door—and, Richard realized, to Door alone. "There's a traitor in your nest. A cuckoo."

"Come on," she said, and she ran. Richard ran with her, through the hall filled with junk, toward a door. At Door's touch, it opened.

"Bid them farewell, Mister Vandemar," said Mr. Croup's voice, from behind them.

"Bye bye," said Mr. Vandemar.

"No-no," corrected Mr. Croup. "*Au revoir.*" He made a noise then—the *cuck-koo cuck-koo* that a cuckoo might make, if it were five and a half feet high and had a weakness for human flesh—while Mr. Vandemar, truer to his nature, threw back his bullet head and howled like a wolf, ghostly and feral and mad.

They were outside, in the open air, at night, running down a pavement in Bloomsbury's Russell Street. Richard thought his heart would pound its way through his chest. A large black car went by. The British Museum was on the other side of some high, black-painted railings. Discreet concealed lights illuminated the outside of the high white Victorian building, the huge pillars of the façade, the steps up to the front door. This was the repository of so many of the world's treasures, looted and found and rescued and donated over hundreds of years.

They reached a gate in the railings. Door grabbed it with both hands and pushed against it. Nothing happened. "Can't you make it open?" asked Richard.

"What does it look like I'm trying to do?" she snapped back, an unfamiliar edge to her voice. A few hundred feet down the pavement, at the main gate, large cars were drawing up, couples in smart clothes were climbing out, walking along the drive toward the museum.

"Down there," said Richard. "The main gate."

Door nodded. She looked behind them. "Those two don't seem to be following us," she said. They hurried toward the main gate.

"Are you all right?" asked Richard. "What happened just then?"

Door hunched deep into her leather jacket. She was looking paler than usual, which was extremely pale indeed, and there were dark semicircles beneath her eyes. "I'm tired," she said, flatly. "Opened too many doors today. Takes a lot out of me, each time. I need a little time to recover. Something to eat, and I'll be fine."

There was a guard on the gate, minutely examining the engraved invitations that each of the well-shaven men in dinner jackets and the fragrant women in evening dresses needed to present, then ticking their names off on a list, before allowing them through. A uniformed policeman beside him surveyed the guests implacably. Richard and Door walked through the gate, and no one glanced at them twice. There was a line of people standing on the stone steps that led up to the museum doors, and

Richard and Door joined the line. A white-haired man, accompanied by a woman bravely wearing a mink coat, joined the line immediately and neatly behind them. A thought struck Richard. "Can they see us?" he asked.

Door turned to the gentleman behind them in the line. She stared up at him. "Hello," she said.

The man looked around, a puzzled expression on his face, as if he was unsure what had attracted his attention. Then he caught sight of Door, standing just in front of him. "Hello . . . ?" he said.

"I'm Door," she told him. "This is Richard."

"Oh . . ." said the man. Then he fumbled in an inner pocket, pulled out a cigar case, and forgot all about them. "There. See?" said Door.

"I think so," he replied. They said nothing for some time, as the line moved slowly toward the single open glass door at the museum's main entrance. Door looked at the writing on her scroll, as if she needed to reassure herself of something. Then Richard said, "A traitor?"

"They were just winding us up," said Door. "Trying to upset us."

"Doing a bloody good job of it, too," said Richard. And they walked through the open door, and then they were in the British Museum.

Mr. Vandemar was hungry, so they walked back through Trafalgar Square.

"Scare her," muttered Mr. Croup, disgustedly. *"Scare her.* That we should be brought to this."

Mr. Vandemar had found half a shrimp and lettuce sandwich in a garbage can, and was gently tearing it into small pieces, which he was tossing down onto the flagstones in front of him, attracting a small flock of hungry late-night pigeons. "Should have followed my idea," said Mr. Vandemar. "Would have scared her lots more if I'd pulled his head off while she wasn't looking, then put my hand up through his throat and wiggled my fingers about. They always scream," he confided, "when the eyeballs fall out." He demonstrated with his right hand.

Mr. Croup was having none of it. "Why get so squeamish at this stage in the game?" he asked.

"I'm not squeamish, Mister Croup," said Mr. Vandemar. "I like it when the eyeballs fall out. Peepers and tarriwags." More gray pigeons strutted over to peck at the fragments of bread and shrimp, and to disregard the lettuce.

"Not you," said Mr. Croup. "The boss. Kill her, kidnap her, scare her. Why doesn't he make up his mind?"

Mr. Vandemar ran out of the sandwich he had been using as bait, and now he made a dash into the crowd of pigeons, who took to the wing with some clacking noises and the occasional grumbling coo. "Well caught, Mister Vandemar," said Mr. Croup, approvingly. Mr. Vandemar was holding a surprised and upset pigeon, which grumbled and fidgeted in his grasp and pecked ineffectively at his fingers.

Mr. Croup sighed, dramatically. "Well, anyway. We've certainly put the cat amongst the pigeons now," he said, with relish. Mr. Vandemar held the pigeon up to his face. There was a crunching noise, as he bit off its head and commenced to chew.

The security guards were directing the museum's guests to a hallway that seemed to be functioning as some kind of holding area. Door ignored the guards entirely and set off into the museum halls with Richard trailing along behind her. They went through the Egyptian rooms, up several flights of back stairs, and into a room marked Early English.

"According to this scroll," she said, "the Angelus is in this room somewhere." Then Door looked down at her scroll some more and looked around the hall, more carefully. She made a face. "Tch," she explained, and took off back down the stairs, the way they had come. Richard had an intense feeling of *déjà vu*, before realizing that, yes, of course this felt familiar: it was how he had spent his weekends in the Jessica days. Which were starting to seem, already, like things that had happened to someone else a long, long time ago.

"The Angelus wasn't in that room, then?" asked Richard.

"No, it wasn't there," said Door, a little more fiercely than Richard felt the question had actually warranted.

"Oh," he said. "I only wondered." They went into another room. Richard wondered if he were starting to hallucinate. "I can hear music," he said. It sounded like a string quartet.

"The party," said Door.

Right. The people in the dinner jackets they had lined up with. No, the Angelus didn't seem to be here either. Door walked into the next hall, and Richard trailed in her wake. He wished he could be of more use. "This Angelus," he said. "What does it look like?"

For a moment he thought she was going to reprimand him simply for asking. But she stopped, rubbed her forehead. "This just says it's got a picture of an angel on it. But it can't be that hard to find. After all," she added, hopefully, "how many things with angels on them are there here?"

NINE

JESSICA WAS UNDER A LITTLE PRESSURE. She was worried, and nervous, and jittery. She had catalogued the collection, arranged with the British Museum to host the exhibition, organized the restoration of the prime exhibit, assisted in hanging and exhibiting the collection, and put together the list of invitees to the fabulous launch. It was just as well she didn't have a boyfriend, she would tell her friends. There'd be no time for one even if she had one. Still, it *would* be nice, she thought, when she got a moment: someone to go to galleries with on the weekends. Someone to . . .

No. She did not go to that place in her head. She could no more pin it down than she could put her finger on a bead of mercury, and she refocused on the exhibition. Even now, at the last minute, there were so many things that could go wrong. Many a horse had fallen at the final hurdle. Many an overconfident general had seen certain victory turn to defeat in the closing minutes of a battle. Jessica was simply going to ensure that nothing went wrong. She was wearing a green silk dress, an off-the-shoulder general marshalling her troops and stoically pretending that Mr. Stockton was not half an hour late.

Her troops consisted of a head waiter, a dozen serving staff, three women from the caterers, a string quartet, and her assistant, a young man named Clarence.

She inspected the drinks table. "We're fine for champagne? Yes?" The head waiter pointed to the crate of champagne beneath the table. "And sparkling mineral water?" Another nod. Another crate. Jessica pursed her lips. "What about *plain* mineral water? Bubbles aren't everybody's cup of tea, you know." They had plenty of plain mineral water. Good.

The string quartet was warming up. They were not quite loud enough to drown the noise coming from the hallway outside. It was the noise of a small but affluent crowd: the grumbling of ladies in mink coats, and men, who, were it not for the NO SMOKING signs on the walls—and perhaps the advice of their doctors—would be smoking cigars; the grumbling of journalists and celebrities who could smell the canapés, vol-au-vents, sundry nibbles, and free champagne.

Clarence was talking to someone on his portable phone, a slimline piece of fold-out engineering that made the *Star Trek* communicators look bulky and old-fashioned. He turned it off, pushed down the antenna, put it into the Armani pocket of his Armani suit, where it did not even make a bulge. He smiled, reassuringly. "Jessica, Mister Stockton's driver's phoned from the car. They're still running a couple of minutes late. Nothing to worry about."

"Nothing to worry about," echoed Jessica. Doomed. *Doomed*. The whole thing was going to be a disaster. *Her* disaster. She picked up a glass of champagne from the table, emptied it, and handed the empty glass to the wine waiter.

Clarence tipped his head on one side, listening to the grumbling reverberation from the hallway outside. The crowd wanted *in*. He looked at his watch, then looked at Jessica questioningly, a captain querying his general. *Into the Valley of Death, then, boss*?

"Mister Stockton is on his way, Clarence," Jessica said, calmly. "He has requested a private viewing before the event begins."

"Shall I go out and see how they're doing?"

"No," she said, decisively. Then, just as decisively, "Yes." Food and drink dealt with, Jessica turned to the string quartet and asked them, for the third time that evening, exactly what they planned to play.

Clarence opened the double doors to check on the crowd. It was worse than he had thought: there had to be more than a hundred people in the hall. And they weren't just people. They were People. Some of them were even Personalities.

"Excuse me," said the chairman of the Arts Council. "The invitations said eight o'clock sharp. It's twenty past eight already."

"We'll just be a few more minutes," reassured Clarence, smoothly. "Security arrangements."

A woman in a hat bore down on him. Her voice was stentorian, bullying, and decidedly parliamentary. "Young man," she announced. "Do you know who I am?"

"Not really, no," lied Clarence, who knew exactly who all of them were. "Hold on—I'll see if anyone in here does." He shut the door behind him. "Jessica? They're going to riot."

"Don't exaggerate, Clarence." She was moving

around the room like a green silk whirlwind, positioning her serving staff, with their trays of canapés or drinks, in strategic corners of the hall; checking the public-address system, the podium, the curtain, and the pull-rope. "I can see the headlines now," said Clarence, unfolding an imaginary newspaper. " 'Geritol Billionaires Crush Marketing Babe in Museum Canapé Dash Horror.' "

Somebody began knocking at the door. The volume in the hallway began to increase. Somebody was saying, very loudly, "Excuse me. Um. Excuse me." Someone else was informing the crowd that it was a disgrace, quite simply a disgrace, no other word for it. "Executive decision," said Clarence, suddenly. "I'm letting them in."

Jessica shouted, "No! If you—"

But it was too late. The doors were open, and the horde was pushing its way into the hall. The expression on Jessica's face morphed from one of horror to one of charmed delight. She shimmered toward the door. "Baroness," she said, with a happy smile. "I can't tell you how delighted we are that you were able to come to our little exhibition this evening. Mister Stockton's been unavoidably delayed, but he'll be here momentarily. Please, have some canapés . . ." Over the baroness's mink-draped shoulder, Clarence winked at her, cheerfully. Jessica ran through all the bad words she knew in her head. As soon as the baroness had headed for the vol-au-vents, Jessica walked over to Clarence and, in a whisper, and still smiling, called him several of them.

Richard froze. A security guard was coming straight toward them, the beam of his flashlight flashing from side to side. Richard looked around for somewhere to hide.

Too late. Another guard was walking their way, past the huge statues of dead Greek gods, flashlight beam swinging. "All right?" called the first guard. The other guard kept coming, and stopped just beside Richard and Door.

"I suppose," she said. "I've already had to stop a couple of idiots in suits from carving their initials on the Rosetta stone. I hate these functions."

The first guard shone his flashlight straight into Richard's eyes, then let the beam slide off, skittering over shadows. "I keep telling you," he said, with the satisfied relish of any true prophet, "it's *The Masque of the Red Death* all over again. A decadent elite party, while civilization crumbles about their ears." He picked his nose, wiped it on the leather sole of his well-polished black boot.

The second guard sighed. "Thank you, Gerald. Right, back on patrol."

The guards walked out of the hall together. "Last one of these events we found someone had puked in a sarcophagus," said one of the guards, and then the door closed behind them.

"If you're part of London Below," said Door to Richard, in a conversational voice, as they walked, side by side, into the next hall, "they normally don't even notice you exist unless you stop and talk to them. And even then, they forget you pretty quickly."

"But *I* saw you," said Richard. It had been bothering him for a while.

"I know," said Door. "Isn't that odd?"

"Everything's odd," said Richard, with feeling. The string music was getting louder. The surges of anxiety were somehow worse up here in London Above, where he was forced to reconcile these two universes. At least below, he could just proceed dreamlike, putting one foot in front of the other like a sleepwalker.

"The Angelus is through there," announced Door, interrupting his reverie, pointing to the direction from which the music was coming.

"How do you know?"

"I know," she said, with utter certainty. "Come on." They stepped out of the darkness into a lighted corridor. There was a huge sign hanging across the corridor. It said:

ANGELS OVER ENGLAND
AN EXHIBITION AT THE BRITISH MUSEUM
Sponsored by Stocktons PLC

They crossed the corridor and walked through an open door, into a large room in which a party was going on.

There was a string quartet playing, and a number of serving staff were providing a roomful of well-dressed people with food and drink. There was a small stage in one corner of the room, with a podium on it, beside a high curtain.

The room was completely filled with angels.

There were statues of angels on tiny plinths. There were paintings of angels on the walls. There were angel frescoes. There were huge angels and tiny angels, stiff angels and amiable angels, angels with wings and haloes and angels with neither, warlike angels and peaceable angels. There were modern angels and classical angels. Hundreds upon hundreds

of angels of every size and shape. Western angels,
Middle Eastern angels, Eastern angels. Michelangelo
angels. Joel Peter Witkin angels, Picasso angels, War-
hol angels. Mr. Stockton's angel collection was "in-
discriminate to the point of trashiness, but certainly
impressive in its eclecticism" (*Time Out*).

"Would you think," Richard asked, "that I was
being picky if I pointed out that trying to find something with an angel on it in here is going to be like
trying to find a needle in an oh my God it's Jessica."
Richard felt the blood drain from his face. Until now
he had thought that that was simply a figure of
speech. He hadn't thought it actually happened in
real life.

"Someone you knew?" asked Door.

Richard nodded. "She was my. Well. We were going to be married. We've been together for a couple
of years. She was with me when I found you. She
was the one on the. She left that message. On the
answering machine." He pointed across the room:
Jessica was making animated conversation with Sir
Andrew Lloyd Webber, Bob Geldof, and a bespectacled gentleman who looked suspiciously like a
Saatchi. Every few minutes she checked her watch
and glanced toward the door.

"Her?" said Door, recognizing the woman. Then,
obviously feeling that she should say something nice
about someone Richard had cared for, she said,
"Well, she's very . . ." and she paused, and thought,
and then said, ". . . clean."

Richard stared across the room. "Will she . . . is
she going to be upset that we're here?"

"I doubt it," said Door. "Frankly, unless you do
something stupid, like talk to her, she probably
won't even notice you." And then, with more enthu-

siasm, she said, "Food!" She descended on the canapés like a small, smut-nosed girl in a too-large
leather jacket who had not eaten properly for some-
time. Enormous quantities of food were immediately
crammed into her mouth, masticated and swallowed, while, at the same time, the more substantial
sandwiches were wrapped in paper napkins and
placed into her pockets. Then, with a paper plate
heaped high with chicken legs, melon slices, mushroom vol-au-vents, caviar puffs, and small venison
sausages, she began to circle the room, staring intently at each and every angelic artefact.

Richard trailed along behind her, with a Brie and
fennel sandwich and a glass of freshly squeezed orange juice.

Jessica was deeply puzzled. She had noticed Richard, and having noticed him, she had noticed Door.
There was something familiar about them both: it
was like a tickle at the back of her throat, impossible
to get rid of, utterly irritating.

It reminded Jessica of something her mother had
once told her about, of how Jessica's mother had,
one evening, encountered a woman she had known
all her life—had been to school with, had served on
the parish council with—and how her mother, encountering the woman at a party, had suddenly realized that she was unable to recall the woman's
name, although she knew the woman had a husband
in publishing named Eric and a golden retriever
named Major. It had left Jessica's mother quite dis-
gruntled.

It was driving Jessica to distraction. "Who are
those people?" she asked Clarence.

"Them? Well, *he's* the new editor of *Vogue*, she's

the arts correspondent of the *New York Times*. The one between them is Kate Moss, I think . . ."

"No, not them," said Jessica. "*Them*. There."

Clarence looked in the place that she was pointing. Hm? Oh. *Them*. He couldn't understand how he had failed to see them before. Old age, he thought; he would soon be twenty-three. "Journalists?" he said, without much conviction. "They do look rather trendoid. Grunge chic? Please. I know I invited *The Face* . . ."

"I *know* him," said Jessica, frustrated. Then Mr. Stockton's chauffeur phoned from Holborn to say that he was almost at the British Museum, and Richard slid out of her head, like mercury trickling through her fingers.

"See anything?" asked Richard.

Door shook her head and swallowed a mouthful of hastily chewed chicken leg. "It's like playing 'Spot the Pigeon' in Trafalgar Square," she said. "There's nothing that *feels* like the Angelus. The paper said I'd know it if I saw it." And she wandered off, inspecting angels, pushing her way past a Captain of Industry, the Deputy Leader of the Opposition, and the Highest-Paid Call Girl in the South of England.

Richard turned away and found himself face-to-face with Jessica. Her hair was piled on her head, and it framed her face perfectly in corkscrews of chestnut curls. She was very beautiful. She was smiling at him; it was the smile that did it. "Hello Jessica," he said. "How are you?"

"Hello. You won't believe this," she said, "but my assistant failed to make a note of your newspaper, Mister uh."

"Paper?" said Richard.

"Did I say newspaper?" said Jessica, with a tin-

kling, sweet, and self-deprecating laugh. "Magazine
. . . television station. You *are* with the media?"

"You're looking very fine, Jessica," said Richard.

"You have the advantage of me," she said, smiling
roguishly.

"You're Jessica Bartram. You're a marketing executive at Stocktons. You're twenty-six. Your birthday is April the twenty-third, and in the throes of
extreme passion you have a tendency to hum the
Monkees song 'I'm a Believer' . . ."

Jessica was no longer smiling. "Is this some kind
of joke?" she asked, coldly.

"Oh, and we've been engaged for the last eighteen
months," said Richard.

Jessica smiled nervously. Perhaps this really was
some kind of joke: one of those jokes that everyone
else seemed to get and she never did. "I rather think
I'd know if I'd been engaged to someone for eighteen months, Mister um," said Jessica.

"Mayhew," said Richard helpfully. "Richard
Mayhew. You dumped me, and I don't exist anymore."

Jessica waved, urgently, at no one in particular all
the way across the room. "Be right there," she called,
desperately, and she began to back away.

"*I'm a believer,*" sang Richard, cheerfully, "*I
couldn't leave her if I tried . . .*"

Jessica snatched a glass of champagne from a passing tray, downed it in a gulp. At the far end of the
room she could see Mr. Stockton's chauffeur, and
where Mr. Stockton's chauffeur was. . . .

She headed toward the doors. "So who was he?"
asked Clarence, edging alongside her.

"Who?"

"Your mystery man."

"I don't know," she admitted. Then she said, "Look, maybe you ought to call security."

"Okay. Why?"

"Just . . . just get me security," and then Mr. Arnold Stockton entered the hall, and everything else went out of her head.

Expansive, he was, and expensive, a Hogarth cartoon of a man, enormous of girth, many-chinned and broad-stomached. He was over sixty; his hair was gray and silver, and it was cut too long in the back, because it made people uncomfortable that his hair was too long, and Mr. Stockton liked making people uncomfortable. Compared to Arnold Stockton, Rupert Murdoch was a shady little pipsqueak, and the late Robert Maxwell was a beached whale. Arnold Stockton was a pit bull, which was how caricaturists often chose to draw him. Stocktons owned a little bit of everything: satellites, newspapers, record companies, amusement parks, books, magazines, comics, television stations, film companies.

"I'll make the speech now," said Mr. Stockton, to Jessica, by way of introduction. "Then I'll bugger off. Come back some other time, when there aren't all these stuffed shirts about."

"Right," said Jessica. "Yes. The speech now. Of course."

And she led him up onto the little stage, up to the podium. She tinked her fingernail against a glass, for silence. Nobody heard her, so she said, "Excuse me," into the microphone. This time the conversation quieted. "Ladies and gentlemen. Honored guests. I'd like to welcome all of you to the British Museum," she said, "to the Stockton-sponsored exhibition 'Angels over England,' and to the man behind it all, our chief executive and chairman of the board, Mister Arnold Stockton." The guests applauded, none of them in any doubt as to who had assembled the collection of angels, or, for that matter, paid for their champagne.

Mr. Stockton cleared his throat. "Okay," he said. "This won't take long. When I was a small boy, I used to come to the British Museum on Saturdays, because it was free, and we didn't have much money. But I'd come up the big steps to the museum, and I'd come down to this room round the back and look up at this angel. It was like it knew what I was thinking."

Just at that moment, Clarence came back in, a couple of security guards beside him. He pointed to Richard, who had stopped to listen to Mr. Stockton's speech. Door was still examining exhibits. "No, *him*," Clarence kept saying to the guards, in an undertone. "No, look, there. Yes? *Him.*"

"Anyway. Like anything that's not cared for," continued Mr. Stockton, "it decayed, fell apart under the stresses and strains of modern times. Went rotten. Went bad. Well, it's taken a shitload of money," he paused, to let it sink in—if he, Arnold Stockton, thought it was a shitload, then a shitload it certainly was—"and a dozen craftsmen have spent a great deal of time restoring it and fixing it up. After this the exhibition'll be going to America, and then around the world, so it maybe can inspire some other little penniless brat to start his own communications empire."

He looked around. Turning to Jessica, he muttered, "What do I do now?" She pointed to the pull-rope, at the side of the curtain. Mr. Stockton pulled the rope. The curtain billowed and opened, revealing an old door behind it.

Again, there was a small flurry of activity in Clarence's corner of the room. "No. *Him*," said Clarence. "For heaven's sake. Are you blind?"

It looked like it had once been the door to a cathedral. It was the height of two men, and wide enough for a pony to walk through. Carved into the wood of the door, and painted with red and white and gold leaf, was an extraordinary angel. It stared out at the world with blank medieval eyes. There was an impressed gasp from the guests, then they began to applaud.

"*The Angelus*." Door tugged at Richard's sleeve. "That's it! Richard, come on." She ran for the stage.

"Excuse me, sir," said a guard to Richard. "Might we see your invitation?" said another, taking Richard firmly but discreetly by the arm. "And do you have any identification?"

"No," said Richard.

Door was up on the stage. Richard tried to yank free and follow her, hoping that the guards would forget about him. They didn't: now that he had been brought to their attention they were going to proceed to treat him as they might any other shabby, unwashed, somewhat unshaven gate-crasher. The guard who was holding Richard increased his grip on his arm, muttering, "None of that."

Door paused on the stage, wondering how to make the guards let Richard go. Then she did the only thing she could think of. She went over to the microphone, went up on tiptoes, and she screamed, as loudly as she possibly could, into the public-address system. She had a remarkable scream: it could, with no artificial assistance, go through your head like a new power drill with a bone-saw attachment. And amplified . . . It was simply unearthly.

A waitress dropped her tray of drinks. Heads turned. Hands covered ears. All conversation stopped. People stared at the stage in puzzlement and horror. And Richard made a break for it. "Sorry," he said to the stunned guard, as he yanked his arm out of the man's grip, and fled. "Wrong London." He reached the stage, grabbed Door's outstretched left hand. Her right hand touched the Angelus, the enormous cathedral door. Touched it, and *opened* it.

This time no one dropped any drinks. They were frozen, staring, utterly overwhelmed—and, momentarily, blinded. The Angelus had opened, and light, from behind the door, had flooded the room with radiance. People covered their eyes then, hesitantly, opened them again, and simply stared. It was as if fireworks had been let off in the room. Not indoor fireworks, strange crawling things that sputter and smell bad; nor even the kind of fireworks that you set off in your back yard; but the kind of industrial-strength fireworks that get fired up high enough to cause a potential menace to the airways: the kind of fireworks that end a day at Disney World, or that give the fire marshals headaches at Pink Floyd concerts. It was a moment of pure magic.

The audience stared, entranced and amazed. The only noise to be heard was the gentle, gasping almost-groan of wonderment that people make when they watch fireworks: the sound of awe. Then a grubby young man and a dirty-faced girl in a huge leather jacket walked into the light show and vanished. The door closed, behind them. The light show was over.

And everything was normal again. The guests, and guards, and serving staff, blinked, shook their respective heads, and, having dealt with something entirely outside of their experience, agreed, somehow, without a word, that it had simply never happened. The string quartet began to play once more.

Mr. Stockton walked off, nodding brusquely to various acquaintances as he did so. Jessica walked over to Clarence. "What," she asked, quietly, "are those security guards doing in here?"

The guards in question were standing among the guests, looking around as if they were themselves unsure what they were doing there. Clarence began to explain just what the guards were doing there; and then he realized he had absolutely no idea. "I'll deal with it," said Clarence, efficiently.

Jessica nodded. She looked out over her party and smiled benignly. It was all going rather well.

Richard and Door walked into the light. And then it was dark, and chill, and Richard was blinking at the retinal afterimage of the light, which left him almost blinded: a ghostly series of orange-green splotches that slowly faded, as his eyes accustomed themselves to the darkness that surrounded them.

They were in a huge hall, carved from rock. Iron pillars, black and rust-dusted, held up the roof, went off into the distant dark, perhaps for miles. From somewhere he could hear the gentle splash of water: a fountain, perhaps, or a spring. Door was still holding his hand, tightly. In the distance, a tiny flame flickered and flared. And another, and then another: it was a host of candles, flickering into flame, Richard realized. And walking toward them, through the candles, was a tall figure, dressed in a simple white robe.

The figure seemed to be moving slowly, but it must have been walking very fast, as it was only seconds before it was standing beside them. It had golden hair and a pale face. It was not much taller than Richard, but it made him feel like a little child. It was not a man; it was not a woman. It was very beautiful. Its voice was quiet. It said, "The Lady Door, yes?"

Door said, "Yes."

A gentle smile. It nodded its head to her, almost humbly. "It is an honor finally to meet you and your companion. I am the Angel Islington." Its eyes were clear and wide. Its robes were not white, as Richard had initially thought: they seemed to have been woven from *light*.

Richard did not believe in angels, he never had. He was damned if he was going to start now. Still, it was much easier not to believe in something when it was not actually looking directly at you and saying your name. "Richard Mayhew," it said. "You, too, are welcome here, in my halls." It turned away. "Please," it said. "Follow me."

Richard and Door followed the angel through the caverns. The candles extinguished themselves behind them.

The marquis de Carabas strode through the empty hospital, broken glass and old syringes crunching beneath his square-toed black motorcycle boots. He stepped through a double door that led into a back staircase. He went down the stairs, to the cellars beneath the hospital.

He walked through the rooms beneath the building, stepping fastidiously around the heaps of moldering rubbish. He walked through the showers and the toilets, down an old iron staircase, through a wet, swampy place; and then pulled open a half-rotted wooden door, and went inside. He looked around the room in which he found himself; he inspected, with magnificent disdain, the half-eaten kitten and the heap of razor blades. Then he cleared the debris off a chair, sat down, comfortably, luxuriantly, in the dankness of the cellar, and closed his eyes.

Eventually the door to the cellar was opened and people came in.

The marquis de Carabas opened his eyes and yawned. Then he flashed Mr. Croup and Mr. Vandemar a huge smile. "Hello boys," said de Carabas. "I thought it high time I came down here to talk to you in person."

TEN

"DO YOU DRINK WINE?" IT ASKED.

Richard nodded.

"I had a little wine once," said Door, hesitantly. "My father. He. At dinner. Would let us taste it."

The Angel Islington lifted the bottle: it looked like some kind of decanter. Richard wondered if the bottle was made of glass; it refracted and reflected the candlelight so strangely. Perhaps it was some kind of crystal, or one huge diamond. It even made it seem that the wine inside was glowing, as if it were made of light.

The angel took the top off the crystal and poured an inch of the liquid inside it into a wine glass. It was a white wine, but a wine unlike any Richard had ever seen. It threw light around the caverns, like sunlight on a swimming pool.

Door and Richard sat around an age-blackened wooden table, on huge wooden chairs, and said nothing. "This wine," said Islington, "is the last bottle of its kind. I was given a dozen bottles by one of your ancestors."

It handed the glass to Door, and began to pour another inch of the glowing wine from the decanter into another glass. It did this reverently, almost lovingly, like a priest performing a ritual. "It was a welcome gift. This was, oh, thirty, forty thousand years ago. Quite a while ago, at any rate." It passed the wine glass to Richard. "I suppose that you could accuse me of squandering something I should treasure," it told them. "But I receive guests so rarely. And the way here is hard."

"The Angelus . . ." murmured Door.

"You traveled here using the Angelus, yes. But that way works only once for each traveler." The angel raised its glass high, staring at the light. "Drink it carefully," it advised them. "It is most potent." It sat down at the table, between Richard and Door. "When one tastes it," it said, wistfully, "I like to imagine that one is actually tasting the sunlight of bygone days." It held up its glass. "A toast: to former glories."

"Former glories," chorused Richard and Door. And then, a little warily, they tasted the wine, sipping it, not drinking.

"It's amazing," said Door.

"It really is," said Richard. "I thought old wines turned to vinegar when they were exposed to air."

The angel shook its head. "Not this one. It is all a matter of the type of grape and the place it was grown. This kind of grape, alas, perished when the vineyard vanished beneath the waves."

"It's magical," said Door, sipping the liquid light. "I've never tasted anything like it."

"And you never will again," said Islington. "There is no more wine from Atlantis."

Somewhere inside Richard a small, reasonable voice pointed out that there never was an Atlantis, and, thus emboldened, went on to state that there were no such things as angels, and that, furthermore, most of his experiences of the last few days had been impossible. Richard ignored it. He was learning, awkwardly, to trust his instincts, and to realize that the simplest and most likely explanations for what he had seen and experienced recently were the ones that had been offered to him—no matter how unlikely they might seem. He opened his mouth and tasted the wine once more. It made him feel *happy*. It made him think of skies bigger and bluer than any he had ever seen, a golden sun hanging huge in the sky; everything simpler, everything *younger* than the world he knew.

There was a waterfall to the left of them; clear water ran down the rock and collected in the rock-pool. To the right of them was a door, set between two iron pillars: the door was made of polished flint set in a metal that was almost black.

"You really claim to be an angel?" Richard asked. "I mean, you've actually met God and everything?"

Islington smiled. "I claim nothing, Richard," it said. "But I am an angel."

"You honor us," said Door.

"No. You do me much honor by coming here. Your father was a good man, Door, and a friend to me. I was deeply saddened by his death."

"He said . . . in his journal . . . he said I should come to you. He said I could trust you."

"I only hope that I can be worthy of that trust." The angel sipped its wine. "London Below is the second city that I have cared for. The first sank beneath the waves, and there was nothing I could do to prevent it. I know what pain is, and loss. You have my sympathies. What would you like to know?"

Door paused. "My family . . . they were killed by

Croup and Vandemar. But—who ordered it? I want
. . . I want to know *why*."

The angel nodded. "Many secrets find their way
down to me," it said. "Many rumors, and half-
truths, and echoes." Then it turned to Richard. "And
you? What do you want, Richard Mayhew?"

Richard shrugged. "I want my life back. And my
apartment. And my job."

"That can happen," said the angel.

"Yeah. Right," said Richard, flatly.

"Do you doubt me, Richard Mayhew?" asked the
Angel Islington.

Richard looked into its eyes. They were a lumi-
nescent gray, eyes as old as the universe, eyes that
had seen galaxies congeal from stardust ten million,
million years ago; Richard shook his head. Islington
smiled at him, kindly. "It will not be easy, and you
and your companions will face some very real dif-
ficulties, both in the task, and in the return. But there
could be a way that we can learn: a key to all of our
problems."

It got up, and walked over to a small rock shelf,
where it picked up a figurine, one of several on the
shelf. It was a small black statuette depicting some
kind of animal, made of volcanic glass. The angel
handed it to Door. "This will bring you safely
through the last stage of your journey back to me,"
it said. "The rest is up to you."

"What do you want us to do?" asked Richard.

"The Black Friars are custodians of a key," it said.
"Bring it to me."

"And you can use it to find out who killed my
family?" asked Door.

"I hope so," said the angel. Richard finished his
glass of wine. He felt it warming him, running

through him. He had the strange feeling that if he looked down at his fingers he would be able to see the wine glowing through them. As if he were made of light . . .

"Good luck," whispered the Angel Islington. There was a rushing sound, like a wind soughing across a lost forest, or the beating of mighty wings.

Richard and Door were sitting on the floor in a room in the British Museum, staring up at a carved painting of an angel on a cathedral door. The room was dark and empty. The party had been over for a long time. The sky outside was beginning to lighten. Richard stood up, then leaned down, and helped Door up.

"Black Friars?" he asked.

Door nodded.

He had crossed Blackfriars Bridge, in the City of London, many times, and he had often passed through Blackfriars station, but he had learned by now not to assume anything.

"People."

Richard walked over to the Angelus. He ran a finger down its painted robe. "Do you think he can really do it? Get me my life back?"

"I've never heard of such a thing. But I don't think he would have lied to us. He is an angel."

Door opened her hand, looked at the statue of the Beast. "My father had one of these," she said, sadly. She put it deep in one of the pockets of her brown leather jacket.

"Well," said Richard. "We're not going to get the key back by lollygagging around here, are we?" They walked through the empty museum corridors.

"So what do you know about this key then?" asked Richard.

"Nothing," said Door. They had reached the main doors of the museum. "I've heard of the Black Friars, but I've never actually had anything to do with them." She pressed her fingers against a seriously locked glass door, which swung open at her touch.

"A bunch of monks . . ." said Richard, thoughtfully. "I bet if we just tell them it's for an angel, a real one, they'll give us the sacred key, and—and throw in the magic can-opener and the amazing whistling corkscrew, as a surprise bonus." He began to laugh. He wondered if the wine was still affecting him.

"You're in good spirits," said Door.

He nodded, enthusiastically. "I'm going to go home. Everything is going to be normal again. Boring again. Wonderful again." Richard looked at the stone steps that lead up the British Museum, and decided that they were made to be danced down by Fred Astaire and Ginger Rogers. And seeing that neither of them happened to be available, he began to dance down the steps, doing a Fred Astaire impersonation, while humming something approximately halfway between "Puttin' on the Ritz" and "Top Hat, White Tie, and Tails." "Ya-ta-ta-da-da-ta-ta-ya," he sang, soft-shoeing down the steps and up again.

Door stood at the top of the steps, staring at him in horror. Then she began to giggle, helplessly. He looked up at her and doffed his imaginary white silk top hat to her, mimed tossing it high in the air, catching it, and putting it back on his head.

"Twit," said Door, and smiled at him. In response, Richard grabbed her hand and continued dancing up and down the steps. Door hesitated for a moment, then she, too, began to dance. She danced much better than Richard did. At the bottom of the steps they tumbled, breathless and exhausted and giggling, into each other's arms.

Richard felt his world spin.

He felt her heart beating against his chest. The moment began to transmute, and he wondered if there was something he should do. He wondered if he should kiss her. He wondered if he wanted to kiss her, and he realized that he truly did not know. He looked into her amazing eyes. Door put her head on one side, and pulled free. She pulled up the collar on her brown leather jacket, pulled it around her: armor and protection.

"Let's go and find our bodyguard," said Door. And they walked away together, down the sidewalk, toward British Museum Station, stumbling only a little from time to time.

"What," asked Mr. Croup, "do you want?"

"What," asked the marquis de Carabas, a little more rhetorically, "does anyone want?"

"Dead things," suggested Mr. Vandemar. "Extra teeth."

"I thought perhaps we could make a deal," said the marquis.

Mr. Croup began to laugh. It sounded like a piece of blackboard being dragged over the nails of a wall of severed fingers. "Oh, Messire Marquis. I think I can confidently state, with no risk of contradiction from any parties here present, that you have taken leave of whatever senses you are reputed to have had. You are," he confided, "if you will permit the vulgarism, completely off your head."

"Say the word," said Mr. Vandemar, who was now standing behind the marquis's chair, "and it'll be off his neck before you can say Jack Ketch."

The marquis breathed heavily on his fingernails and polished them on the lapel of his coat. "I have always felt," he said, "that violence was the last refuge of the incompetent, and empty threats the final sanctuary of the terminally inept."

Mr. Croup glared. "What are you doing here?" he hissed.

The marquis de Carabas stretched, like a big cat: a lynx, perhaps, or a huge black panther; and at the end of the stretch he was standing up, with his hands thrust deep in the pockets of his magnificent coat. "You are," he said, idly and conversationally, "I understand, Mister Croup, a collector of T'ang dynasty figurines."

"How did you know that?"

"People tell me things. I'm approachable." The marquis's smile was pure, untroubled, guileless: the smile of a man selling you a used Bible.

"Even if I were . . ." began Mr. Croup.

"If you were," said the marquis de Carabas, "you might be interested in this." He took one hand out of his pocket and displayed it to Mr. Croup. Until earlier that evening it had sat in a glass case in the vaults of one of London's leading merchant banks. It was listed in certain catalogues as *The Spirit of Autumn (Grave Figure)*. It was roughly eight inches high: a piece of glazed pottery that had been shaped and painted and fired while Europe was in the Dark Ages, six hundred years before Columbus's first voyage.

Mr. Croup hissed, involuntarily, and reached for it. The marquis pulled it out of reach, cradled it to his chest. "No no," said the marquis. "It's not as simple as that."

"No?" asked Mr. Croup. "But what's to stop us taking it, and leaving pieces of you all over the Underside? We've never dismembered a marquis before."

"Have," said Mr. Vandemar. "In York. In the fourteenth century. In the rain."

"He wasn't a marquis," said Mr. Croup. "He was the earl of Exeter."

"And marquis of Westmorland." Mr. Vandemar looked rather pleased with himself.

Mr. Croup sniffed. "What's to stop us hacking you into as many pieces as we hacked the marquis of Westmorland?" he asked.

De Carabas took his other hand out of his pocket. It held a small hammer. He tossed the hammer in the air and caught it by the handle, ending with the hammer poised over the china figurine. "Oh, please," he said. "No more silly threats. I think I'd feel better if you were both standing back over there."

Mr. Vandemar shot a look at Mr. Croup, who nodded, almost imperceptibly. There was a tremble in the air, and Mr. Vandemar was standing beside Mr. Croup, who smiled like a skull. "I have indeed been known to purchase the occasional T'ang piece," he admitted. "Is that for sale?"

"We don't go in so much for buying and selling here in the Underside, Mister Croup. Barter. Exchange. That's what we look for. But yes, indeed, this desirable little piece is certainly up for grabs."

Mr. Croup pursed his lips. He folded his arms. He unfolded them. He ran one hand through his greasy hair. Then, "Name your price," said Mr. Croup. The marquis let himself breathe a deep, relieved, and almost audible sigh. It was possible that he was going to be able to pull this whole grandiose ruse off, after all. "First, three answers to three questions," he said.

Croup nodded. "Each way. We get three answers too."

"Fair enough," said the marquis. "Secondly, I get safe conduct out of here. And you agree to give me at least an hour's head start."

Croup nodded violently. "Agreed. Ask your first question." His gaze was fixed on the statue.

"First question. Who are you working for?"

"Oh, that's an easy one," said Mr. Croup. "That's a simple answer. We are working for our employer, who wishes to remain nameless."

"Hmph. Why did you kill Door's family?"

"Orders from our employer," said Mr. Croup, his smile becoming more foxy by the moment.

"Why didn't you kill Door, when you had a chance?"

Before Mr. Croup could answer, Mr. Vandemar said, "Got to keep her alive. She's the only one that can open the door."

Mr. Croup glared up at his associate. "That's it," he said. "Tell him everything, why don't you?"

"I wanted a turn," muttered Mr. Vandemar.

"Right," said Mr. Croup. "So you've got three answers, for all the good that will do you. My first question: why are you protecting her?"

"Her father saved my life," said the marquis, honestly. "I never paid off my debt to him. I prefer debts to be in my favor."

"I've got a question," said Mr. Vandemar.

"As have I, Mr. Vandemar. The Upworlder, Richard Mayhew. Why is he traveling with her? Why does she permit it?"

"Sentimentality on her part," said the marquis de Carabas. He wondered, as he said it, if that was the whole truth. He had begun to wonder whether there might, perhaps, be more to the upworlder than met the eye.

"Now me," said Mr. Vandemar. "What number am I thinking of?"

"I beg your pardon?"

"What number am I thinking of?" repeated Mr. Vandemar. "It's between one and a lot," he added, helpfully.

"Seven," said the marquis. Mr. Vandemar nodded, impressed. Mr. Croup began, "Where is the—" but the marquis shook his head. "Uh-uh," he said. "Now we're getting greedy."

There was a moment of utter silence, in that dank cellar. Then once more water dripped, and maggots rustled; and the marquis said, "An hour's head start, remember."

"Of course," said Mr. Croup.

The marquis de Carabas tossed the figurine to Mr. Croup, who caught it eagerly, like an addict catching a plastic baggie filled with white powder of dubious legality. And then, without a backward glance, the marquis left the cellar.

Mr. Croup examined the figurine minutely, turning it over and over in his hands, a Dickensian curator of the Museum of the Damned contemplating a prize exhibit. His tongue flicked out, from time to time, like a snake's. A perceptible flush appeared on his pallid cheeks. "Oh, fine, fine," he whispered. "T'ang dynasty indeed. Twelve hundred years old, the finest pottery figurines ever made on this earth.

This was created by Kai Lung, finest of potters: there is not a twin to it in existence. Examine the color of the glaze; the sense of proportion; the life ..." He was smiling now, like a baby; the innocent smile looked lost and confused on the shady terrain of Mr. Croup's face. "It adds a little wonder and beauty to the world."

And then he grinned, too widely, and lowered his face to the figurine, and crushed its head in his teeth, chomping and chewing wildly, swallowing in lumps. His teeth ground the china to a fine powder, which dusted the lower part of his face.

He gloried in its destruction, throwing himself into it with the strange madness and uncontrolled blood lust of a fox in a henhouse. And then, when the statue was nothing but dust, he turned to Mr. Vandemar. He seemed strangely mellow, almost languid. "How long did we say we'd give him?"

"An hour."

"Mmm. And how long has it been?"

"Six minutes."

Mr. Croup lowered his head. He ran a finger across his chin, licked the powdered clay from his fingertip. "You follow him, Mister Vandemar," said Mr. Croup. "I need a little more time in which to savor the occasion."

Hunter could hear them walking down the steps. She was standing in the shadows, with her arms folded, in the same position she had been in when they left her. Richard was humming loudly. Door was giggling helplessly; then she would stop, and tell Richard to be quiet. Then she would start giggling again. They walked past Hunter without noticing her.

She stepped out of the shadows, and said, "You have been gone for eight hours." It was a statement of fact, without reproach or curiosity.

Door blinked at her. "It didn't *seem* that long." Hunter said nothing.

Richard grinned blearily at her. "Don't you want to know what happened? Well, we got ambushed by Mister Croup and Mister Vandemar. Unfortunately we didn't have a bodyguard around. Still, I gave them a good run for their money."

Hunter raised a perfect eyebrow. "I am in awe of your pugilistic talents," she said coolly.

Door giggled. "He's kidding. Actually—they killed us."

"As an expert in the termination of bodily functions," Hunter said, "I must beg to differ. You are neither of you dead. At a guess, you are both very drunk."

Door stuck her tongue out at her bodyguard. "Nonsense. Touched hardly a drop. *That* much." She held out two fingers to show how tiny an amount "that much" was.

"Just went to a party," said Richard, "and saw Jessica and saw a real angel and got a little black pig and came back here."

"Just a little drink," continued Door, intently. "Old, old drink. Tiiiiny little drink. Very small. Almost not there." She began to hiccup. Then she giggled again. A hiccup interrupted her, and she sat down suddenly on the platform. "I think maybe we are a bit smashed," she said, soberly. Then she closed her eyes, and began, solemnly, to snore.

The marquis de Carabas was running through the underways as if all the hounds of Hell had his scent and were on his trail. He was splashing through six gray inches of the Tyburn, the hangman's river, kept safe in the darkness in a brick sewer beneath Park Lane on its way south to Buckingham Palace. He had been running for seventeen minutes.

Thirty feet below Marble Arch, he paused. The sewer divided into two branches. The marquis de Carabas ran down the left-hand branch.

Several minutes later, Mr. Vandemar walked through the sewer. And when he reached the junction he, too, paused for a few moments, sniffing the air. And then he, too, walked down the left-hand branch.

Hunter dropped Richard Mayhew's unconscious body into a pile of straw, with a grunt. He rolled in the straw, said something that sounded like "Forthril bjugly mobble wug," and went back to sleep. She put Door down in the straw next to him, more gently. Then she stood beside Door, in the dark stables under the ground, on guard still.

The marquis de Carabas was exhausted. He leaned against the tunnel wall and stared at the steps that went up ahead of him. Then he pulled out the golden pocket-watch and looked at the time. Thirty-five minutes had passed since he had fled the hospital cellar.

"Is it an hour yet?" asked Mr. Vandemar. He was sitting on the steps ahead of the marquis, picking his nails with a knife.

"Not even close," gasped the marquis.

"Felt like an hour," said Mr. Vandemar, helpfully.

There was a shiver in the world, and Mr. Croup stood behind the marquis de Carabas. He still had

powder on his chin. De Carabas stared at Mr. Croup.
He turned back to look at Mr. Vandemar. And then,
spontaneously, the marquis de Carabas began to
laugh. Mr. Croup smiled. "You find us funny, Messire Marquis, do you not? A source of amusement.
Is that not so? With our pretty clothes, and our con-
voluted circumlocutions—"

Mr. Vandemar murmured, "I haven't got a cir-
cumlo . . ."

"—and our little sillinesses of manner and behav-
ior. And perhaps we *are* funny."

Mr. Croup raised one finger then, and waggled it
at de Carabas. "But you must never imagine," he
continued, "that just because something is funny,
Messire Marquis, it is not also dangerous."

And Mr. Vandemar threw his knife at the marquis, hard and accurately. It hit him, hilt first, on the
temple. His eyes rolled up in his head, and his knees
buckled. "Circumlocution," said Mr. Croup to Mr.
Vandemar. "It's a way of speaking around something. A digression. Verbosity."

Mr. Vandemar picked up the marquis de Carabas
by his waistband and dragged him up the stairs, his
head bump-bump-bumping on each step as they
went, and Mr. Vandemar nodded. "I wondered," he
said.

Watching their dreams, now, as they sleep.

Hunter sleeps standing up.

In her dream, Hunter is in the undercity beneath
Bangkok. It is partly a maze, and partly a forest, for
the wilderness of Thailand has retreated deep beneath the ground, under the airport and the hotels
and the streets. The world smells of spice and dried
mango, and it also smells, not unpleasantly, of sex.

It is humid, and she is sweating. It is dark, broken by phosphorescent patches on the wall, greenish grey fungi that give light enough to fool the eye, light enough to walk by.

In her dream Hunter moves silent as a ghost through the wet tunnels, pushing her way through vegetation. She holds a weighted throwing stick in her right hand; a leather shield covers her left forearm.

She smells it, in her dream, acrid and animal, and she pauses beside a wall of ruined masonry, and she waits, part of the shadows, one with the darkness. Hunting, like life, Hunter believes, consists chiefly of waiting. In Hunter's dream, however, she does not wait. Upon her arrival, it comes through the underbrush, a fury of brown and of white, undulating gently, like a wet-furred snake, its red eyes bright and peering through the darkness, its teeth like needles, a carnivore and a killer. The creature is extinct in the world above. It weighs almost three hundred pounds, and is a little over fifteen feet long, from the tip of its nose to the tip of its tail.

As it passes her, she hisses like a snake, and, momentarily, old instincts kicking in, it freezes. And then it leaps at her, nothing but hate and sharp teeth. She remembers, then, in her dream, that this had happened before, and that when it had happened, that time in the past, she had pushed the leather arm-shield into its mouth and crushed its skull with the leaden throwing stick taking care not to damage the pelt. She had given the Great Weasel's pelt to a girl who had caught her eye, and the girl had been appropriately grateful.

But now, in her dream, that is not happening. Instead, the weasel is reaching out a forepaw toward her, and she is dropping her throwing stick and taking its paw. And then and there, in the undercity beneath Bangkok, they are dancing together, in one intricate unending dance: and Hunter is watching them from outside herself, and she is admiring the elaborate movements they make as they move, tail and legs and arms and fingers and eyes and hair all tumbling and twisting powerfully and strangely into the underneath and out across forever.

There is a tiny noise in the waking world, a dreaming whimper from the child Door, and Hunter moves from sleeping to waking fluidly and instantly; she is alert once more, and on guard. She forgets her dream entirely upon waking.

Door is dreaming of her father.

In her dream, he is showing her how to open things. He picks up an orange, and gestures: in one smooth movement it inverts, and twists: the orange flesh is on the outside, now, and the skin is in the center, on the inside. *One must always maintain parity*, her father tells her, peeling off an inside-out orange segment for her. *Parity, symmetry, topology: these will be our subjects for the months to come, Door. But the most important thing for you to understand is this: all things want to open. You must feel that need, and use it.* Her father's hair is brown and thick, as it was a decade before his death, and he has an easy smile, which she remembers but which time had diminished as the years went on.

In her dream, he passes her a padlock. She takes it from him. Her hands are the size and shape of her hands today, although she knows that, in truth, this occurred when she was a tiny child, that she is taking moments and conversations and lessons from

over a dozen years and is compressing them into one
lesson. *Open it*, he tells her.

She holds it in her hand, feeling the cold metal,
feeling the weight of the lock in her hands. Something is bothering her. There is something she has to
know. Door learned to open some time after she
learned to walk. She remembers her mother holding
her tightly, opening a door from Door's bedroom to
the playroom, remembers watching her brother Arch
separating linked silver rings, joining them back together.

She tries to open the padlock. She fumbles at it
with her fingers, and with her mind. Nothing happens. She throws the padlock down onto the floor
and begins to cry. Her father reaches down and
picks up the padlock, puts it back into her hand. His
long finger brushes away a tear from her cheek.

Remember, he tells her, *the padlock wants to open. All
you have to do is let it do what it wants.*

It sits there in her hand, cold and inert and heavy.
And then, suddenly, she understands, and, somewhere in her heart, she lets it be what it wants to be.
There is a loud click, and the padlock opens. Her
father is smiling.

There, she says.

Good girl, says her father. *That's all there is to opening. Everything else is just technique.*

She realizes what it is that is bothering her. *Father?*
she asks. *Your journal. Who put it away? Who could
have hidden it?* But he is receding from her, and already she is forgetting. She calls to him, but he cannot hear her, and although she can hear his voice in
the distance, she can no longer make out what he is
saying.

In the waking world, Door whimpers softly. Then

she rolls over, cradles her arm around her face, snorts once, twice, then sleeps once more, sleeps without dreaming.

Richard knows it waits for them. Each tunnel he goes down, each turning, each branch he walks, the feeling grows in urgency and weight. He knows it is there, waiting, and the sense of impending catastrophe increases with every step. He knows that it should have been a relief when he turns the final corner, and sees it standing there, framed in the tunnel, waiting for him. Instead he feels only dread. In his dream it is the size of the world: there is nothing left in the world but the Beast, its flanks steaming, broken spars and juts of old weapons prickling from its hide. There is dried blood on its horns and on its tusks. It is gross, and vast, and evil. And then it charges.

He raises his hand (but it isn't his hand) and he throws the spear at the creature.

He sees its eyes, wet and vicious and gloating, as they float toward him, all in a fraction of a second that becomes a tiny forever. And then it is upon him . . .

The water was cold, and it hit Richard's face like a slap. His eyes jerked open, and he caught his breath. Hunter was looking down at him. She was holding a large wooden bucket. It was empty. He reached up one hand. His hair was soaked, and his face was wet. He wiped the water from his eyes and shivered with cold.

"You didn't have to do that," said Richard. His mouth tasted like several small animals had been using it as a rest room. He tried to stand, and then he sat down again, suddenly. "Ooh," he explained.

"How's your head?" asked Hunter, professionally.

"It's been better," said Richard.

Hunter picked up another wooden bucket, this one filled with water, and hauled it across the stable floor. "I don't know what you drank," she said. "But it must have been potent." Hunter dipped her hand into the bucket and flicked it at Door's face, spraying her with water. Door's eyes flickered.

"No wonder Atlantis sank," muttered Richard. "If they all felt like this in the morning it was probably a relief. Where are we?"

Hunter flicked another handful of water at Door's face. "In the stables of a friend," she said. Richard looked around. The place did look a little like a stable. He wondered if it were for horses—and if so, what kind of horses would live beneath the ground? There was a device painted on the wall: the letter S (or was it a snake? Richard could not tell) circled by seven stars.

Door reached a tentative hand up to her head and touched it, experimentally, as if she were unsure just what she might find. "Ooh," she said, in a near-whisper. "Temple and Arch. Am I dead?"

"No," said Hunter.

"Pity."

Hunter helped her to a standing position. "Well," said Door, sleepily, "he did warn us it was strong." And then Door woke up completely, very hard, very fast. She grabbed Richard's shoulder, pointed to the device on the wall, the snaky S with the stars surrounding it. She gasped. "Serpentine," she said to Richard, to Hunter. "That's Serpentine's crest. Richard, get up! We have to run—before she finds out we're here . . ."

"And do you think," asked a dry voice from the doorway, "that you could enter Serpentine's house without Serpentine knowing, child?"

Door pushed herself back against the wood of the stable wall. She was trembling. Richard realized, through the pounding in his head, that he had never seen Door so actually and obviously scared before.

Serpentine stood in the doorway. She was wearing a white leather corset and high white leather boots, and the remains of what looked like it had once, long ago, been a silk-and-lace confection of a white wedding dress, now shredded and dirt-stained and torn. She towered above them all: her shock of graying hair brushed the door lintel. Her eyes were sharp, and her mouth was a cruel slash in an imperious face. She looked at Door as if she took terror as her due; as if she had become so used to fear that she now expected it, even liked it.

"Calm yourself," said Hunter.

"But she's Serpentine," wailed Door. "Of the Seven Sisters."

Serpentine inclined her head, cordially. Then she stepped out of the doorway and walked toward them. Behind her was a thin woman with a severe face and long dark hair, wearing a black dress pinched wasp-thin at the waist. The woman said nothing. Serpentine walked over to Hunter. "Hunter worked for me long ago," said Serpentine. She reached out a white finger and gently stroked Hunter's brown cheek with it, a gesture of affection and possession. And then, "You've kept your looks better than I, Hunter." Hunter looked down. "Her friends are my friends, child," said Serpentine. "You are Door?"

"Yes," said Door, dry-mouthed.

Serpentine turned on Richard. "And what are you?" she asked, unimpressed.

"Richard," said Richard.

"I am Serpentine," she told him, graciously.

"So I gathered," said Richard.

"There is food waiting for all of you," said Serpentine, "should you wish to break your fast."

"Oh God no," whimpered Richard politely. Door said nothing. She was still backed against the wall, still trembling gently, like a leaf in an autumn breeze. The fact that Hunter had clearly brought them here as a safe haven was doing nothing to assuage her fear.

"What is there to eat?" asked Hunter.

Serpentine looked at the wasp-waisted woman in the doorway. "Well?" she asked. The woman smiled the chilliest smile Richard had ever seen cross a human face, then she said, "Fried eggs poached eggs pickled eggs curried venison pickled onions pickled herrings smoked herrings salted herrings mushroom stew salted bacon stuffed cabbage calves-foot jelly—"

Richard opened his mouth to plead with her to stop, but it was too late. He was suddenly, violently, awfully sick.

He wanted someone to hold him, to tell him that everything would be all right, that he'd soon be feeling better; someone to give him an aspirin and a glass of water, and show him back to his bed. But nobody did; and his bed was another life away. He washed the sick from his face and hands with water from the bucket. Then he washed out his mouth. Then, swaying gently, he followed the four women to breakfast.

"Pass the calves-foot jelly," said Hunter, with her mouth full.

Serpentine's dining room was on what appeared

to be the smallest Underground platform that Richard had ever seen. It was about twelve feet long, and much of that space was taken up with a dinner table. A white damask cloth was laid on the table, and a formal silver dinner-service on that. The table was piled high with evil-smelling foodstuffs. The pickled quails' eggs, thought Richard, smelled the worst.

His skin felt clammy, and his eyes felt like they had been put in their sockets wrong, while his skull gave him the general impression that someone had removed it while he had slept and swapped it for another two or three sizes too small. An Underground train went past a few feet from them; the wind of its passage whipped at the table. The noise of its passage went through Richard's head like a hot knife through brains. Richard groaned.

"Your hero is unable to hold his wine, I see," observed Serpentine, dispassionately.

"He's not my hero," said Door.

"I'm afraid he is. You learn to recognize the type. Something in the eyes, perhaps." She turned to the woman in black, who appeared to be some kind of majordomo. "A restorative for the gentleman." The woman smiled thinly and glided away.

Door picked at a mushroom dish. "We are very grateful for all this, Lady Serpentine," she said.

Serpentine sniffed. "Just Serpentine, child. I have no time for silly honorifics and imaginary titles. So. You're Portico's oldest girl."

"Yes."

Serpentine dipped her finger in the briny sauce that held what appeared to be several small eels. She licked her finger, nodded approvingly. "I had little time for your father. All that foolishness about uniting the Underside. Stuff and nonsense. Silly man.

Just asking for trouble. The last time I saw your father, I told him that if he ever came back here, I'd turn him into a blindworm." She turned to Door. "How is your father, by the way?"

"He's dead," said Door.

Serpentine looked perfectly satisfied. "See?" she said. "My point exactly." Door said nothing. Serpentine picked at something that was moving in her gray hair. She examined it closely, crushed it between finger and thumb, and dropped it onto the platform. Then she turned to Hunter, who was demolishing a small hill of pickled herrings. "You're Beast-hunting then?" she said. Hunter nodded, her mouth full. "You'll need the spear, of course," said Serpentine.

The wasp-waisted woman was now standing next to Richard, holding a small tray. On the tray was a small glass, containing an aggressively emerald-colored liquid. Richard stared at it, then looked at Door.

"What are you giving him?" asked Door.

"Nothing that will hurt him," said Serpentine, with a frosty smile. "You are guests."

Richard knocked back the green liquid, which tasted of thyme and peppermint and winter mornings. He felt it go down and prepared himself to try to keep it from coming back up again. Instead he took a deep breath and realized, with a little surprise, that his head no longer hurt, and that he was starving.

Old Bailey was not, intrinsically, one of those people put in the world to tell jokes. Despite this handicap, he persisted in trying. He loved to tell shaggy-dog stories of inordinate length, which would end in a sad pun although, often as not, Old Bailey would be unable to remember it by the time he got there. The only public for Old Bailey's jokes consisted of a small captive audience of birds, who, particularly the rooks, viewed his jokes as deep and philosophical parables containing profound and penetrating insights into what it meant to be human, and who would actually ask him, from time to time, to tell them another of his amusing stories.

"All right, all right, all right," Old Bailey was saying. "Stop me if you've heard this one before. There was a man walked into a bar. No, he wasn't a man. That's the joke. Sorry. He was a horse. A horse . . . no . . . a piece of string. Three pieces of string. Right. Three pieces of string walk into a bar."

A huge old rook croaked a question. Old Bailey rubbed his chin, then shrugged. "They just do. It's a joke. They can walk in the joke. He asks for a drink for himself and one for each of his friends. And the barman says, 'We don't serve pieces of string here.' To one of the pieces of string. So. It goes back to its friends and says, 'They don't serve strings here.' And it's a joke, so the middle one does it too, three of them, you see, then the last one, he ties himself around the middle and he pulls the end of him all out. And he orders a drink." The rook croaked again, sagely. "Three drinks. Right. And the barman says, 'here, aren't you one of those pieces of string?' And he says, the piece of string, he says, 'No. I'm a frayed knot.' *Afraid not*, y'see, *a frayed knot*. Pun. Very, very funny."

The starlings made polite noises. The rooks nodded their heads, put their heads on one side. Then the oldest rook cawed at Old Bailey. "Another? I'm not made of hilarity, y'know. Let me think . . ."

There was a noise from the tent, a deep, pulsing noise, like the beating of a distant heart. Old Bailey hurried into his tent. The noise was coming from an old wooden chest in which Old Bailey kept those things he most prized. He opened the chest. The throbbing noise became much louder. The small silver box was sitting on the top of Old Bailey's treasures. He reached down one gnarly hand and picked it up. A red light rhythmically pulsed and glowed inside it, like a heartbeat, and shone out through the silver filigree, and through the cracks and fastenings. "He's in trouble," said Old Bailey.

The oldest rook cawed a question. "No. It's not a joke. It's the marquis," said Old Bailey. "He's in deep trouble."

Richard was halfway through his second plate of breakfast when Serpentine pushed her chair back from the table.

"I think I have had my fill of hospitality," she said. "Child, young man, good day. Hunter . . ." she paused. Then she ran one clawlike finger along the line of Hunter's jaw. "Hunter, you are always welcome here." She nodded to them, imperiously, and stood up and walked away, followed by her wasp-waisted butler.

"We should leave now," said Hunter. She stood up from the table, and Door and Richard, more reluctantly, followed her.

They walked along a corridor that was too thin to allow more than one of them to pass at a time. They went up some stone steps. They crossed an iron bridge in the darkness, while Underground trains echoed by beneath them. Then they entered what seemed like an endless network of underground vaults that smelled of damp and decay, of brick and stone and time. "That was your old boss, eh? She seemed nice enough," said Richard to Hunter. Hunter said nothing.

Door, who had been somewhat subdued, said, "When they want to make children behave themselves in the Underside, they tell them, 'Behave, or Serpentine will take you.' "

"Oh," said Richard. "And you worked for her, Hunter?"

"I worked for all the Seven Sisters."

"I thought that they hadn't spoken to each other for, oh, at least thirty years," said Door.

"Quite possibly. But they were still talking then."

"How old *are* you?" asked Door. Richard was pleased she had asked; he would never have dared.

"As old as my tongue," said Hunter, primly, "and a little older than my teeth."

"Anyway," said Richard, in the untroubled tone of voice of one whose hangover had left him and who knew that, somewhere far above them, someone was having a beautiful day, "that was okay. Nice food. And no one was trying to kill us."

"I'm sure that will remedy itself as the day goes on," said Hunter, accurately. "Which way to the Black Friars, my lady?"

Door paused and concentrated. "We'll go the river way," she said. "Over here."

"Is he coming round yet?" asked Mr. Croup.

Mr. Vandemar prodded the marquis's prone body with one long finger. The breathing was shallow. "Not yet, Mister Croup. I think I broke him."

"You must be more careful with your toys, Mister Vandemar," said Mr. Croup.

ELEVEN

"SO WHAT ARE YOU AFTER?" RICHARD asked Hunter. The three of them were walking, with extreme care, along the bank of an underground river. The bank was slippery, a narrow path along dark rock and sharp masonry. Richard watched with respect as the gray water rushed and tumbled, within arm's reach. This was not the kind of river you fell into and got out of again; it was the other kind.

"After?"

"Well," he said. "Personally, I'm trying to get back to the real London, and my old life. Door wants to find out who killed her family. What are you after?" They edged along the bank, a step at a time, Hunter in the lead. She said nothing in reply. The river slowed and fed into a small underground lake. They walked beside the water, their lamps reflecting in the black surface, their reflections smudged by the river mist. "So what is it?" asked Richard. He did not expect any kind of answer.

Hunter's voice was quiet and intense. She did not break her step as she spoke. "I fought in the sewers beneath New York with the great blind white alligator-king. He was thirty feet long, fat from sewage and fierce in battle. And I bested him, and I killed him. His eyes were like huge pearls in the darkness." Her strangely accented voice echoed in the underground, twined in the mist, in the night beneath the Earth.

"I fought the bear that stalked the city beneath Berlin. He had killed a thousand men, and his claws were stained brown and black from the dried blood of a hundred years, but he fell to me. He whispered words in a human tongue as he died." The mist hung low on the lake. Richard fancied that he could see the creatures she spoke of, white shapes writhing in the vapor.

"There was a black tiger in the undercity of Calcutta. A man-eater, brilliant and bitter, the size of a small elephant. A tiger is a worthy adversary. I took him with my bare hands." Richard glanced at Door. She was listening to Hunter intently: this was news to her too, then. "And I shall slay the Beast of London. They say his hide bristles with swords and spears and knives stuck in him by those who have tried and failed. His tusks are razors, and his hooves are thunderbolts. I will kill him, or I will die in the attempt."

Her eyes shone as she spoke of her prey. The river mist had become a thick yellow fog.

A bell was struck, a little way away, three times, the sound carrying across the water. The world began to lighten. Richard thought he could see the squat shapes of buildings around them. The yellow-green fog became thicker: it tasted of ash, and soot, and the grime of a thousand urban years. It clung to their lamps, muffling the light.

"What is this?" he asked.

"London fog," said Hunter.

"But they stopped years ago, didn't they? Clean Air Act, smokeless fuels, all that?" Richard found himself remembering the Sherlock Holmes books of his childhood. "What did they call them again?"

"Pea-soupers," said Door. "London Particulars. Thick yellow river fogs, mixed with coal-smoke and whatever rubbish was going into the air for the last five centuries. Hasn't been one in the Upworld for, oh, forty years now. We get the ghosts of them down here. Mm. Not ghosts. More like echoes." Richard breathed in a strand of the yellow-green fog and began to cough. "That doesn't sound good," said Door.

"Fog in my throat," said Richard. The ground was becoming stickier, muddier: it sucked at Richard's feet as he walked. "Still," he said, to reassure himself, "a little fog never hurt anyone."

Door looked up at him with big pixie eyes. "There was one in 1952 that they reckon killed four thousand people."

"People from here?" he asked. "Under London?"

"Your people," said Hunter. Richard was willing to believe it. He thought about holding his breath, but the fog was getting thicker. The ground was becoming mushier. "I don't understand," he asked. "Why do you have fogs down here, when we don't have them up there anymore?"

Door scratched her nose. "There are little pockets of old time in London, where things and places stay the same, like bubbles in amber," she explained. "There's a lot of time in London, and it has to go somewhere—it doesn't all get used up at once."

"I may still be hung over," sighed Richard. "That almost made sense."

* * *

The abbot had known that this day would bring pilgrims. The knowledge was a part of his dreams; it surrounded him, like the darkness. So the day became one of waiting, which was, he knew, a sin: moments were to be experienced; waiting was a sin against both the time that was still to come and the moments one was currently disregarding. Still, he was waiting. Through each of the day's services, through their scant meals, the abbot was listening intently, waiting for the bell to sound, waiting to know who and how many.

He found himself hoping for a clean death. The last pilgrim had lasted for almost a year, a gibbering, screaming thing. The abbot regarded his own blindness as neither a blessing nor a curse: it simply *was*; but even so, he had been grateful he had never been able to see the poor creature's face. Brother Jet, who had cared for the creature, still woke in the night, screaming, with its twisted face before him.

The bell tolled late in the afternoon, three times. The abbot was in the shrine, on his knees, contemplating their charge. He pulled himself to his feet and made his way to the corridor, where he waited. "Father?" The voice was that of Brother Fuliginous.

"Who guards the bridge?" the abbot asked him. His voice was surprisingly deep and melodious for such an old man.

"Sable," came the reply from the darkness. The abbot reached out a hand, grasped the young man's elbow, and walked beside him, slowly, through the corridors of the abbey.

There was no solid ground; there was no lake. Their feet were splashing through some kind of marsh, in the yellow fog. "This," announced Richard, "is disgusting." It was seeping through his shoes, invading his socks, and making a much closer acquaintance with his toes than Richard was entirely happy with.

There was a bridge ahead of them, rising up out of the marsh. A figure, dressed in black, waited at the foot of the bridge. He wore the black robes of a Dominican monk. His skin was the dark brown of old mahogany. He was a tall man, and he held a wooden staff as tall as he was. "Hold fast," he called. "Tell me your names, and your stations."

"I am the Lady Door," said Door. "I am Portico's daughter, of the House of the Arch."

"I am Hunter. I am her bodyguard."

"Richard Mayhew," said Richard. "Wet."

"And you wish to pass?"

Richard stepped forward. "Yes, we do actually. We're here for a key." The monk said nothing. He lifted his staff and pushed Richard gently in the chest with it. Richard's feet slid out from under him, and he landed in the muddy water. The monk waited a few moments, to see if Richard would swing up and begin to fight. Richard didn't.

Hunter did.

Richard pulled himself up from the mud, and watched, mouth open, as the monk and Hunter fought with quarter-staves. The monk was good. He was bigger than Hunter, and, Richard suspected, stronger. Hunter, on the other hand, was faster than the monk. The wooden staves clacked and whapped in the mist.

The monk's staff made sudden contact with Hunter's midriff. She stumbled in the mud. He came in close—too close—as he discovered that her stumble had been a feint and her staff slammed into him, hard and precisely, on the backs of his knees, and his legs no longer held his weight. The man tumbled into the wet mud, and Hunter rested the tip of her staff on the back of his neck.

"Enough," called a voice from the bridge.

Hunter took a step back. She stood beside Richard and Door once more. She had not even broken a sweat. The big monk got up from the mud. His lip was bleeding. He bowed low to Hunter, then walked to the foot of the bridge.

"Who are they, Brother Sable?" called the voice.

"The Lady Door, Lord Portico's daughter, of the House of the Arch; Hunter, her bodyguard, and Richard Mayhew, their companion," said Brother Sable, through bruised lips. "She bested me in fair fight, Brother Fuliginous."

"Let them come up," said the voice.

Hunter led the way up the bridge. At the apex of the bridge, another monk was waiting for them: Brother Fuliginous. He was younger and smaller than the first monk they had met, but he was dressed the same way. His skin was a deep, rich brown. There were other black-clad figures, just barely visible, further into the yellow fog. These were the Black Friars, then, Richard realized. The second monk stared at the three of them for a second, and then recited:

"I turn my head, and you may go where you want.
I turn it again, you will stay till you rot.
I have no face, but I live or die
by my crooked teeth—who am I?"

Door took a step forward. She licked her lips and half closed her eyes. "I turn my head . . ." she said, puzzling to herself. "Crooked teeth . . . go where you . . ." Then a smile spread over her face. She stared up at Brother Fuliginous. "A key," she said. "The answer is, you're a key."

"A wise one," acknowledged Brother Fuliginous. "That's two steps taken. One more to take."

A very old man stepped out of the yellow fog and walked cautiously toward them, his gnarled hand holding onto the stone side of the bridge. He stopped when he reached Brother Fuliginous. His eyes were a glaucous blue-white, thick with cataracts. Richard liked him on sight. "How many of them are there?" he asked the younger man, in a deep and reassuring voice.

"Three, Father Abbot."

"And has one of them bested the first gate-keeper?"

"Yes, Father Abbot."

"And did one of them answer the second gate-keeper correctly?"

"Yes, Father Abbot."

There was regret in the old man's voice. "So, one of them is left to face the Ordeal of the Key. Let him or her stand forward now."

Door said, "Oh no."

Hunter said, "Let me take his place. I will face the ordeal."

Brother Fuliginous shook his head. "We cannot permit that."

When Richard was a small boy he had been taken, as part of a school trip, to a local castle. With his class he had climbed the many steps to the highest point in the castle, a partly ruined tower. They had clustered together at the top, while the teacher pointed out to them the whole of the countryside, spread out below. Even at that age, Richard had not been very good at heights. He had clutched the safety rail, and closed his eyes, and tried not to look down. The teacher had told them that the drop from the top of the old tower to the bottom of the hill it overlooked was three hundred feet; then she told them that a penny, dropped from the top of the tower, would have enough force to penetrate the skull of a man at the bottom of the hill, that it would crack a skull like a bullet. That night Richard lay in bed, unable to sleep for imagining the penny falling with the power of a thunderbolt. Still looking like a penny, but such a murderous penny, when it dropped . . .

An ordeal.

The penny dropped for Richard. It was a thunderbolt sort of a penny.

"Hang on a sec," he said. "Back up. Mm-mm: ordeal. Someone's got an ordeal waiting for them. Somebody who didn't have a little fight down in the mud, and didn't get to answer the riddle . . ." He was babbling. He could hear himself babbling, and he just didn't care.

"This ordeal of yours," Richard asked the abbot. "How much of an ordeal is it?"

"This way now," said the abbot.

"You don't want him," said Door. "Take one of us."

"Three of you come. There are three tests. Each of you faces one test: that is fair," said the abbot. "If he passes the ordeal, he will return to you."

A light breeze eased the fog. The other dark figures were holding crossbows. Each crossbow was pointed at Richard, or Hunter, or Door. The friars closed ranks, cutting Richard off from Hunter and from Door. "We're looking for a key—" said Richard to the abbot, in a low voice.

"Yes," said the abbot, placidly.

"It's for an angel," explained Richard.

"Yes," said the abbot. He reached out a hand, found the crook of Brother Fuliginous's arm.

Richard lowered his voice. "Look, you can't say no to an angel, especially a man of the cloth like yourself . . . why don't we just skip the ordeal? You could just hand it over."

The abbot began to walk down the curve of the bridge. There was a door, open at the bottom. Richard followed him. Sometimes there is nothing you can do. "When our order was founded," said the abbot, "we were entrusted with the key. It is one of the holiest, and the most powerful, of all sacred relics. We must pass it on, but only to the one who passes the ordeal and proves worthy."

They walked through winding narrow corridors, Richard leaving a trail of wet mud behind him. "If I fail the ordeal, then we don't get the key, do we?"

"No, my son."

Richard thought about this for a moment. "Could I come back later for a second try?"

Brother Fuliginous coughed. "Not really, my son," said the abbot. "If that should happen, you will in all probability be . . ." he paused, and then said, "beyond caring. But do not fret, perhaps you will be the one to win the key, eh?" There was a ghastly attempt at reassurance in his voice, more terrifying than any attempt to scare him could have been.

"You would kill me?"

The abbot stared ahead with blue-milk eyes. There

was a touch of reproof in his voice. "We are holy men," he said. "No, it is the ordeal that kills you."

They walked down a flight of steps, into a low, cryptlike room with oddly decorated walls. "Now," said the abbot. "Smile!"

There was the electric fizz of a camera flash going off, blinding Richard for a moment. When he could see again, Brother Fuliginous was lowering a battered old Polaroid camera and was yanking out the photograph. The friar waited until it had developed, and then he pinned it to the wall. "This is our wall of those who failed," sighed the abbot, "to ensure that they are none of them forgotten. That is our burden also: memorial."

Richard stared at the faces. A few Polaroids; twenty or thirty other photographic snapshots, some sepia prints and daguerreotypes; and, after that, pencil sketches, and watercolors, and miniatures. They went all the way along one wall. The friars had been at this a very long time.

Door shivered. "I'm so stupid," she muttered. "I should have known. Three of us. I should never have come straight here."

Hunter's head was moving from side to side. She had noted the position of each of the friars and each of the crossbows; she had calculated the odds of getting Door over the side of the bridge first unharmed, then with only minor injuries, and lastly with major injury to herself, but only minor injury to Door. She was now recalculating. "And what would you have done differently if you *had* known?" she asked.

"I wouldn't have brought *him* here, for a start," said Door. "I'd have found the marquis."

Hunter put her head on one side. "You trust

him?" she asked, directly, and Door knew she was talking of de Carabas, not Richard.

"Yes," said Door. "I more or less trust him."

Door had been five years old for just two days. The market was being held in the Gardens at Kew on that day, and her father had taken her with him, as a birthday treat. It was her first market. They were in the butterfly house, surrounded by brightly colored wings, iridescent weightless things that entranced and fascinated her, when her father crouched down beside her. "Door?" he said. "Turn around slowly, and look over there."

She turned, and looked. A dark-skinned man wearing a big coat, his black hair tied behind him in a long ponytail, was standing by the door, talking to two golden-skinned twins, a young man and a young woman. The young woman was crying, in the way that grown-ups cry, keeping it inside as much as they can, and hating it when it still pushes out at the edges, making them ugly and funny-looking on the way. Door turned back to the butterflies. "You saw him?" asked her father. She nodded. "He calls himself the marquis de Carabas," he said. "He's a fraud and a cheat and possibly even something of a monster. If you're ever in trouble, go to him. He will protect you, girl. He has to."

Door looked back at the man. He had a hand on the shoulder of each of the twins and was leading them from the room; but he glanced back over his shoulder, as he left, and he looked straight at her, and smiled an enormous smile; and then he winked at her.

The friars who surrounded them were dark ghosts in the fog. Door raised her voice. "Excuse me, brother," she called to Brother Sable. "But our friend, who's gone to get the key. If he fails, what happens to us?"

He took a step toward them, hesitated, and then

said, "We escort you away from here, and we let you go."

"What about Richard?" she asked. Beneath his cowl, she could see him shaking his head, sadly, finally. "I should have brought the marquis," said Door; and she wondered where he was, and what he was doing.

The marquis de Carabas was being crucified on a large X-shaped wooden construction Mr. Vandemar had knocked together from several old pallets, part of a chair and a wooden gate. He had also used most of a large box of rusting nails.

It had been a very long time since they had crucified anybody.

The marquis de Carabas's arms and legs were spread into a wide X shape. Rusty nails went into his hands and feet. He was also roped around the waist. After experiencing terrible pain, he was now, more or less, unconscious. The whole construction dangled in the air, from several ropes, in a room that had once been the hospital staff cafeteria. On the ground below, Mr. Croup had assembled a large mound of sharp objects, ranging from razors and kitchen knives to abandoned scalpels and lancets. There was even a poker, from the furnace room.

"Why don't you see how he's doing, Mister Vandemar?" asked Mr. Croup.

Mr. Vandemar reached out his hammer, and prodded the marquis experimentally with it.

The marquis de Carabas was not a good man, and he knew himself well enough to be perfectly certain that he was not a brave man. He had long since decided that the world, Above or Below, was a place that wished to be deceived, and, to this end, he had named himself from a lie in a fairy tale, and created himself—his clothes, his manner, his carriage—as a grand joke.

There was a dull pain at his wrists and his feet, and he was finding it harder and harder to breathe. There was nothing more to be gained by feigning unconsciousness, and he raised his head, as best he could, and spat a gob of scarlet blood into Mr. Vandemar's face.

It was a brave thing to do, he thought. And a stupid one. Perhaps they would have let him die quietly, if he had not done that. Now, he had no doubt, they would hurt him more.

And perhaps his death would come the quicker for it.

The open kettle was boiling fiercely. Richard watched the bubbling water, and the thick steam, and wondered what they were going to do with it. His imagination was able to provide any number of answers, most of which would have been unimaginably painful, none of which turned out to be correct.

The boiling water was poured into a pot, to which Brother Fuliginous added three spoons of dried, shredded leaves. The resultant liquid was poured from the pot through a tea strainer, into three china cups. The abbot raised his blind head, sniffed the air, and smiled. "The first part of the Ordeal of the Key," he said, "is the nice cup of tea. Do you take sugar?"

"No, thank you," said Richard, warily.

Brother Fuliginous added a little milk to the tea, and passed a cup and saucer to Richard. "Is it poisoned?" he asked.

The abbot looked almost offended. "Good gracious, no."

Richard sipped the tea, which tasted more or less exactly like tea always tasted. "But this *is* part of the ordeal?"

Brother Fuliginous took the abbot's hands and placed a cup of tea in them. "In a manner of speaking," said the abbot. "We always like to give the seekers a cup of tea before they start. Part of the ordeal for us. Not for you." He sipped his own tea, and a beatific smile spread across his ancient face. "Rather nice tea, all things considered."

Richard put down his teacup, almost untouched. "Would you mind," he asked, "if we just began the ordeal?"

"Not at all," said the abbot. "Not at all." He stood up, and the three of them walked toward a door, at the far end of the room.

"Is there . . ." Richard paused, trying to decide what he was trying to ask. Then he said, "Is there anything you can tell me about the ordeal?"

The abbot shook his head. There really was nothing to say: he led the seekers to the door. And then he would wait, for an hour, or two, in the corridor outside. Then he would go back in, and remove the remains of the seeker from the shrine, and inter it in the vaults. And sometimes, which was worse, they would not be dead, although you could not call what was left of them *alive*, and those unfortunates the Black Friars cared for as best they could.

"Right," said Richard. And he smiled, unconvincingly, and added, "Well, lead on, Macduff."

Brother Fuliginous pulled back the bolts on the door. They opened with a crash, like twin gunshots. He pulled the door open. Richard stepped through it. Brother Fuliginous pushed the door closed behind him, and swung the bolts back into place. He led the abbot back to his chair and placed the cup of tea back in the old man's hand. The abbot sipped his tea, in silence. And then he said, with honest regret in his voice, "It's 'lay on, Macduff,' actually. But I hadn't the heart to correct him. He sounded like such a nice young man."

TWELVE

RICHARD MAYHEW WALKED DOWN THE UN-
derground platform. It was a District Line station:
the sign said BLACKFRIARS. The platform was empty.
Somewhere in the distance an Underground train
roared and rattled, driving a ghost-wind along the
platform, which scattered a copy of the tabloid *Sun*
into its component pages, four-color breasts and
black-and-white invective scurrying and tumbling
off the platform and down onto the rails.

Richard walked the length of the platform. Then
he sat down on a bench and waited for something
to happen.

Nothing happened.

He rubbed his head and felt slightly sick. There
were footsteps on the platform, near him, and he
looked up to see a prim little girl walking past him,
hand in hand with a woman who looked like a
larger, older version of the girl. They glanced at him
and then, rather obviously, looked away. "Don't get
too near to him, Melanie," advised the woman, in a
very audible whisper.

Melanie looked at Richard, staring in the way children stare, without embarrassment or self-

consciousness. Then she looked back at her mother. "Why do people like that stay alive?" she asked, curiously.

"Not enough guts to end it all," explained her mother.

Melanie risked another glance at Richard. "Pathetic," she said. Their feet pattered away down the platform, and soon they were gone. He wondered if he had imagined it. He tried to remember why he was standing on this platform. Was he waiting for a Tube train? Where was he going? He knew the answer was somewhere in his head, somewhere close at hand, but he could not touch it, could not bring it back from the lost places. He sat there, alone and wondering. Was he dreaming? With his hands he felt the hard red plastic seat beneath him, stamped the platform with mud-encrusted shoes (where had the mud come from?), touched his face . . . No. This was no dream. Wherever he was, was real. He felt odd: detached, and depressed, and horribly, strangely saddened. Someone sat down next to him. Richard did not look up, did not turn his head.

"Hello," said a familiar voice. "How are you, Dick? You all right?"

Richard looked up. He felt his face creasing into a smile, hope hitting him like a blow to the chest. "Gary?" he asked, scared. Then, "You can see me?"

Gary grinned. "You always were a kidder," he said. "Funny man, funny."

Gary was wearing a suit and tie. He was cleanshaven, and had not a hair out of place. Richard realized what he must look like: muddy, unshaven, rumpled. . . . "Gary? I . . . listen, I know what I must look like. I can explain." He thought for a moment. "No . . . I can't. Not really."

"It's okay," said Gary reassuringly. His voice was soothing, sane. "Not sure how to tell you this. Bit awkward." He paused. "Look," he explained. "I'm not really here."

"Yes, you are," said Richard.

Gary shook his head, sympathetically. "No," he said. "I'm not. I'm you. Talking to yourself."

Richard wondered vaguely if this was one of Gary's jokes. "Maybe this will help," said Gary. He raised his hands to his face, pushed at it, molded, shaped. His face oozed like warm Silly Putty.

"Is that better?" said the person who had been Gary, in a voice that was jarringly familiar. Richard knew the new face: he had shaved it most weekday mornings since he had left school; he had brushed its teeth, combed its hair, and, on occasion, wished it looked more like Tom Cruise's, or John Lennon's, or anyone else's, really. It was, of course, his face. "You're sitting on Blackfriars Station at rush hour," said the other Richard, casually. "You're talking to yourself. And you know what they say about people who talk to themselves. It's just that you're starting to edge a little closer to sanity, now."

The damp, muddy Richard stared into the face of the clean, well-dressed Richard, and he said, "I don't know who you are or what you're trying to do. But you aren't even very convincing: you don't really look like me." He was lying, and he knew it.

His other self smiled encouragingly, and shook his head. "I'm you, Richard," he said. "I'm whatever's left of your sanity . . ."

It was not the embarassing echo of his voice he heard on answering machines, on tapes and home videos, that horrid parody of a voice that passed for his: the man spoke with Richard's true voice, the voice he heard in his head when he spoke, resonant and real.

"Concentrate!" shouted the man with Richard's face. "Look at this place, try to see the people, try to see the truth . . . you're already the closest to reality that you've been in a week . . ."

"This is bullshit," said Richard, flatly, desperately. He shook his head, denying everything his other self was saying, but, still, he looked at the platform, wondering what it was he was meant to be seeing. Then something flickered, at the corner of his vision; he followed it with his head, but it was gone.

"Look," whispered his double. "See."

"See what?" He was standing on an empty, dimly lit station platform, a lonely mausoleum of a place. And then . . .

The noise and the light struck him like a bottle across the face: he was standing on Blackfriars Station, in the middle of the rush hour. People bustled by him: a riot of noise and light, of shoving, moving humanity. There was an Underground train waiting at the platform, and, reflected in its window, Richard could see himself. He looked crazy; he had a week's growth of beard; food was crusted around his mouth; one eye had recently been blackened, and a boil, an angry red carbuncle, was coming up on the side of his nose; he was filthy, covered in a black, encrusted dirt which filled his pores and lived under his fingernails; his eyes were red and bleary, his hair was matted and snarled. He was a crazy homeless person, standing on a platform of a busy Underground station, in the heart of the rush hour.

Richard buried his face deep in his hands.

When he raised his face, the other people were gone. The platform was dark again, and he was

alone. He sat down on a bench and closed his eyes.
A hand found his hand, held it for some moments,
and then squeezed it. A woman's hand: he could
smell a familiar perfume.

The other Richard sat on his left, and now Jessica
sat on his right, holding his hand in hers, looking at
him compassionately. He had never seen that expression on her face before.

"Jess?" he said.

Jessica shook her head. She let go of his hand. "I'm
afraid not," she said. "I'm still you. But you have to
listen, darling. You're the closest to reality you've
been—"

"You people keep saying, the closest to reality, the
closest to sanity, I don't know what you . . ." He
paused. Something came back to him, then. He
looked at the other version of himself, at the woman
he had loved. "Is this part of the ordeal?" he demanded.

"Ordeal?" asked Jessica. She exchanged a concerned glance with the-other-Richard-who-wasn't-
him.

"Yes. Ordeal. With the Black Friars who live under London," Richard said. As he said it, it became
more real. "There's a key I have to get for this angel
called Islington. If I get him the key, he'll send me
home again . . ." His mouth dried up, and he could
talk no longer.

"Listen to yourself," said the other Richard, gently. "Can't you tell how ridiculous all this sounds?"

Jessica looked as if she were trying not to cry. Her
eyes glistened. "You're not going through an ordeal,
Richard. You—you had some kind of nervous breakdown. A couple of weeks ago. I think you just
cracked up. I broke off our engagement—you'd been

acting so strangely, it was like you were a different person, I—I couldn't cope. . . . Then you vanished . . ." The tears began to run down her cheeks, and she stopped talking to blow her nose on a tissue.

The other Richard began to speak. "I wandered, alone and crazy, through the streets of London, sleeping under bridges, eating food from garbage cans. Shivering and lost and alone. Muttering to myself, talking to people who weren't there . . ."

"I'm so sorry, Richard," said Jessica. She was crying, now, her face contorted and unattractive. Her mascara was beginning to run, and her nose was red. He had never seen her hurting before, and he realized how much he wanted to take her pain away. Richard reached out for her, to try to hold her, to comfort and reassure her, but the world slid and twisted and changed . . .

Someone stumbled into him, cursed and walked away. Richard was lying prone on the platform, in the rush-hour glare. The side of his face was sticky and cold. He pulled his head up off the ground. He had been lying in a pool of his own vomit. At least, he hoped it was his own. Passersby stared at him with revulsion, or, after one flick of the eyes, did not look at him again.

He wiped at his face with his hands and tried to get up, but he could no longer remember how. Richard began to whimper. He shut his eyes tightly, and he kept them shut. When he opened them, thirty seconds, or an hour, or a day later, the platform was in semidarkness. He climbed to his feet. There was nobody there. "Hello?" he called. "Help me. Please."

Gary was sitting on the bench, watching him. "What, you still need someone to tell you what to do?" Gary got up and walked over to where Richard was standing. "Richard," he said, urgently. "I'm you. The only advice I can give you is what you're telling yourself. Only, maybe you're too scared to listen."

"You aren't me," said Richard, but he no longer believed it.

"Touch me," said Gary.

Richard reached a hand out: his hand pushed into Gary's face, squashing and distorting it, as if it were pushing into warm bubble gum. Richard felt nothing in the air around his hand. He pulled his fingers out of Gary's face.

"See?" said Gary. "I'm not here. All there is, is you, walking up and down the platform, talking to yourself, trying to get up the courage to . . ."

Richard had not meant to say anything; but his mouth moved and he heard his voice saying, "Trying to get up the courage to do what?"

A deep voice came over the loudspeaker, and echoed, distorted, down the platform. *"London Transport would like to apologize for the delay. This is due to an incident at Blackfriars Station."* "To do that," said Gary, inclining his head. "Become an incident at Blackfriars Station. To end it all. Your life's a joyless, loveless, empty sham. You've got no friends—"

"I've got you," whispered Richard.

Gary appraised Richard with frank eyes. "I think you're an asshole," he said, honestly. "A complete joke."

"I've got Door, and Hunter, and Anaesthesia."

Gary smiled. There was real pity in the smile, and it hurt Richard more than hatred or enmity could ever have done. "More imaginary friends? We all used to laugh at you round the office for those trolls. Remember them? On your desk." He laughed. Richard started to laugh, too. It was all too horrible: there was nothing else to do but laugh. After some time he stopped laughing. Gary put his hand into his pocket and produced a small plastic troll. It had frizzy purple hair, and it had once sat on the top of Richard's computer screen. "Here," said Gary. He tossed the troll to Richard. Richard tried to catch it; he reached out his hands, but it fell through them as if they were not there. He went down onto his hands and knees on the empty platform, fumbling for the troll. It seemed to him, then, as if it were the only fragment he had of his real life: that if he could only get the troll back, perhaps he could get everything back . . .

Flash.

It was rush hour again. A train disgorged hundreds of people onto the platform, and hundreds of others tried to get on, and Richard was down on his hands and knees, being kicked and buffeted by the commuters. Somebody stepped on his fingers, hard. He screamed shrilly, and stuck his fingers into his mouth, instinctively, like a burned child; they tasted disgusting. He did not care: he could see the troll at the platform's edge, now only ten feet away, and he crawled, slowly, on all fours, through the crowd, across the platform. People swore at him; they got in his way; they buffeted him. He had never imagined that ten feet could be such a long distance to travel.

Richard heard a high-pitched voice giggling, as he crawled, and he wondered who it could belong to. It was a disturbing giggle, nasty and strange. He wondered what manner of crazy person could giggle like that. He swallowed, and the giggling stopped, and then he knew.

He was almost at the edge of the platform. An elderly woman stepped onto the train, and as she did so, her foot knocked the purple-haired troll down into the darkness, down into the gap between the train and the platform. "No," said Richard. He was still laughing, an awkward, wheezing laugh, but tears stung his eyes and spilled down his cheeks. He rubbed his eyes with his hands, making them sting even more.

Flash.

The platform was deserted and dark again. He climbed to his feet and walked, unsteadily, the last few feet, to the edge of the platform. He could see it there, down on the tracks, by the third rail: a small splash of purple, his troll. He looked ahead of him: there were enormous posters stuck to the wall on the other side of the tracks. The posters advertised credit cards and sports shoes and holidays in Cyprus. As he looked the words on the posters twisted and mutated.

New messages:

END IT ALL was one of them.

PUT YOURSELF OUT OF YOUR MISERY.

BE A MAN—DO YOURSELF IN.

HAVE A FATAL ACCIDENT TODAY.

He nodded. He was talking to himself. The posters did not really say that. Yes, he was talking to himself; and it was time that he listened. He could hear the rattling of a train, not far away, coming toward the station. Richard clenched his teeth, and swayed back and forth, as if he were still being buffeted by commuters, although he was alone on the platform.

The train was coming toward him, its headlights shining out from the tunnel like the eyes of a monstrous dragon in a childhood nightmare. And he understood then just how little effort it would take to make the pain stop—to take all the pain he ever had had, all the pain he ever would have, and make it all go away for ever and ever. He pushed his hands deep into his pockets, and took a deep breath. It would be so easy. A moment of pain, and then it would all be over and done . . .

There was something in his pocket. He felt it with his fingers: something smooth and hard and roughly spherical. He pulled it out of his pocket, and examined it: a quartz bead. He remembered picking it up, then. He had been on the far side of Night's Bridge. The bead had been part of Anaesthesia's necklace.

And from somewhere, in his head or out of it, he thought he heard the rat-girl say, "Richard. Hold on." He did not know if there was anyone helping him at that moment. He suspected that he was, truly, talking to himself. That this was the real him speaking, and he was, finally, listening.

He nodded and put the bead back into his pocket. And he stood on the platform and waited for the train to come in. It arrived at the platform, slowed, came to a full stop.

The train doors hissed open. The carriage was filled with every manner and kind of people, all of whom were, unmistakably, quite dead. There were fresh corpses, with ragged cuts in their throats or bullet holes in their temples. There were old, desiccated bodies. There were strap-hanging cadavers, covered with cobwebs, and cancerous things lolling in their seats. Each corpse seemed, as much as one could tell, to have died by its own hand. Some were male, and some were female. Richard thought he had seen some of those faces, pinned to a long wall; but he could no longer remember where he had seen them, could not remember when. The carriage smelled like a morgue might at the end of a long, hot summer during the course of which the refrigeration equipment had failed for good.

Richard had no idea who he was, anymore; no idea what was or what was not true; nor whether he was brave or cowardly, mad or sane, but he knew the next thing he had to do. He stepped onto the train, and all the lights went out.

The bolts were drawn back. Two loud bangs echoed through the room. The door to the tiny shrine was pushed open, letting in lamplight from the hall outside.

It was a small room with a high arched ceiling. A silver key hung from a thread, attached to the highest point of the ceiling. The wind caused by the opening of the door made the key swing back and forth, and then spin slowly, first one way, and then the other. The abbot held Brother Fuliginous's arm, and the two men walked into the shrine, side by side. Then the abbot let go of the brother's arm, and said, "Take the body, Brother Fuliginous."

"But. But Father . . ."

"What is it?"

Brother Fuliginous went down on one knee. The abbot could hear fingers against cloth and skin. "He's not dead."

The abbot sighed. It was an evil thing to think, he knew, but he honestly felt it was so much kinder if they died outright. This was so much worse. "One of those, eh?" he said. "Ah well, we will look after the poor creature until it passes on to its ultimate reward. Lead it to the infirmary."

And a weak voice said, quietly, but firmly, "I am

not a poor creature." The abbot heard someone stand up; heard Brother Fuliginous's sharp intake of breath. "I . . . I think I got through it," said Richard Mayhew's voice, suddenly uncertain. "Unless this is more of the ordeal."

"No, my son," said the abbot. There was something in his voice that might have been awe, and might have been regret.

There was silence. "I . . . I think I will have that cup of tea now, if you don't mind," said Richard.

"Of course," said the abbot. "This way." Richard stared at the old man. The glaucous eyes gazed out at nothing at all. He seemed pleased that Richard was alive, but . . .

"Excuse me?" said Brother Fuliginous, respectfully, to Richard, breaking his train of thought. "Don't forget your key."

"Oh. Yes. Thanks." He had forgotten about the key. He reached out and closed his hand upon the cold silver key, rotating slowly on its thread. He tugged, and the thread snapped easily.

Richard opened his hand, and the key stared up at him from his palm. "By my crooked teeth," asked Richard, remembering, "who am I?"

He put it into his pocket, next to the small quartz bead, and together they left that place.

The fog had begun to thin. Hunter was pleased. She was confident now that, should it become necessary, she could get the Lady Door away from the friars entirely unharmed and get herself away with only minor flesh wounds.

There was a flurry of movement on the far side of the bridge. "Something's happening," said Hunter to Door, under her breath. "Get ready to make a run for it."

The friars drew back. Richard Mayhew, the Upworlder, came toward them through the fog, walking beside the abbot. Richard looked different, somehow.... Hunter scrutinized him, trying to work out what had changed. His center of balance had moved lower, become more centered. No ... it was more than that. He looked less boyish. He looked as if he had begun to grow up.

"Still alive then?" said Hunter. He nodded; put his hand into his pocket, and pulled out a silver key. He tossed it to Door, who caught it, then flung herself at him, wrapping her arms around him, squeezing him as tightly as she could.

Then Door let go of Richard and ran to the abbot. "I can't tell you how much this means to us," she said to him.

He smiled, weakly but graciously. "May the Temple and the Arch be with you all, on your journey through the Underside," he said.

Door curtseyed, and then, clutching the key tightly in her hand, she went back to Richard, and to Hunter. The three travelers walked down the bridge, and away. The friars stood on the bridge until they were out of sight, lost in the old fog of the world beneath the world.

"We have lost the key," said the abbot to himself, as much as to any of them. "God help us all."

THIRTEEN

THE ANGEL ISLINGTON WAS DREAMING A dark and rushing dream.

Huge waves were rising and crashing over the city; the night sky was rent with forks of white lightning from horizon to horizon; the rain fell in sheets, the city trembled; fires started near the great amphitheater and spread, quickly, through the city, defying the storm. Islington was looking down on everything from far above, hovering in the air, as one hovers in dreams, as it had hovered in those long-ago times. There were buildings in that city that were many hundreds of feet high, but they were dwarfed by the gray-green Atlantic waves. And then it heard the people scream. There were four million people in Atlantis, and, in its dream, Islington heard each and every one of their voices, clearly and distinctly, as, one by one, they screamed, and choked, and burned, and drowned, and died. The waves swallowed the city, and, at length, the storm subsided.

When dawn broke, there was nothing to indicate there had ever been a city there at all, let alone an island twice the size of Greece. Nothing of Atlantis remained but the water-bloated bodies of children, of women and of men, floating on the cold morning waves; bodies the seagulls, gray and white, were already beginning to pick with their cruel beaks.

And Islington woke. It was standing in the octagon of iron pillars, beside the great black door, made of flint and tarnished silver. It touched the cold smoothness of the flint, the chill of the metal. It touched the table. It ran its finger lightly along the walls. Then it walked through chambers of its hall, one after another, touching things, as if to reassure itself of their existence, to convince itself it was here, and now. It followed patterns, as it walked, smooth channels its bare feet had worn, over the centuries, in the rock. It stopped when it reached the rock-pool, kneeling down and letting its fingers touch the cold water.

There was a ripple in the water, which began with its fingertips and echoed out to the edges. The reflections in the pool, of the angel itself and the candle flames that framed it, shimmered and transformed. It was looking into a cellar. The angel concentrated for a moment; it could hear a telephone ring, somewhere in the distance.

Mr. Croup walked over to the telephone and picked up the receiver. He looked rather pleased with himself. "Croup and Vandemar," he barked. "Eyes gouged, noses twisted, tongues pierced, chins cleft, throats slit."

"Mister Croup," said the angel. "They now have the key. I want the girl called Door kept safe on her journey back to me."

"Safe," repeated Mr. Croup, unimpressed. "Right. We'll keep her safe. What a marvelous idea—such originality. Positively astounding. Most people would be content with hiring assassins for executions, sly killings, vile murders even. Only you, sir, would hire the two finest cutthroats in the whole of space and time, and then ask them to ensure a little girl remains unharmed."

"See that she is, Mister Croup. Nothing is to hurt her. Permit her to be harmed in any way and you will displease me deeply. Do you understand?"

"Yes." Croup shifted uncomfortably.

"Is there anything else?" asked Islington.

"Yes, sir." Croup coughed into his hand. "Do you remember the marquis de Carabas?"

"Of course."

"I take it that there is no such similar prohibition on extirpating the marquis . . . ?"

"Not any longer," said the angel. "Just protect the girl."

It removed its hand from the water. The reflection was now merely candle flames and an angel of astonishing, perfectly androgynous, beauty. The Angel Islington stood up and returned to its inner chambers to await its eventual visitors.

"What did he say?" asked Mr. Vandemar.

"He said, Mister Vandemar, that we should feel free to do whatsoever we wished to the marquis."

Vandemar nodded. "Did that include killing him painfully?" he asked, a little pedantically.

"Yes, Mister Vandemar, I would say, on reflection, it did."

"That's good, Mister Croup. Wouldn't like another telling-off." He looked up at the bloody thing hanging above them. "Better get rid of the body, then."

*   *   *

One of the front wheels on the supermarket shopping cart squeaked, and it had a pronounced tendency to pull to the left. Mr. Vandemar had found the metal cart on a grassed-in traffic island, near the hospital. It was, he had realized on seeing it, just the right size for moving a body. He could have carried the body, of course; but then it could have bled on him, or dripped other fluids. And he only had the one suit. So he pushed the shopping cart with the body of the marquis de Carabas in it through the storm drain, and the cart went *squee, squee* and pulled to the left. He wished that Mr. Croup would push the shopping cart, for a change. But Mr. Croup was talking. "You know, Mister Vandemar," he was saying, "I am currently too overjoyed, too delighted, not to mention too utterly and illimitably ecstatic, to grouse, gripe or grumble—having finally been permitted to do what we do best—"

Mr. Vandemar negotiated a particularly awkward corner. "Kill someone, you mean?" he asked.

Mr. Croup beamed. "Kill someone I mean indeed, Mister Vandemar, brave soul, glittering, noble fellow. However, by now you must have sensed a lurking 'but' skulking beneath my happy, blithe, and chipper exterior. A minuscule vexation, like the teeniest lump of raw liver sticking to the inside of my boot. You must, I have no doubt, be saying to yourself, 'All is not well in Mister Croup's breast. I shall induce him to unburden himself to me.'"

Mr. Vandemar pondered this while he forced open the round iron door between the storm drain and the sewer and clambered through. Then he manhandled the wire cart with the marquis de Carabas's body through the doorway. And then, more or less certain that he had been thinking nothing of the sort, he said, "No."

Mr. Croup ignored this, and continued, ". . . And, were I then, in response to your pleadings, to divulge to you what vexes me, I would confess that my soul is irked by the necessity to hide our light under a bushel. We should be hanging the former marquis's sad remains from the highest gibbet in London Below. Not tossing it away, like a used . . ." He paused, searching for the exact simile.

"Rat?" suggested Mr. Vandemar. "Thumbscrew? Spleen?" *Squee, squee* went the wheels of the shopping cart.

"Ah well," said Mr. Croup. In front of them was a deep channel of brown water. Drifting on the water's surface were off-white suds of foam, used condoms, and occasional fragments of toilet paper. Mr. Vandemar stopped the shopping cart. Mr. Croup leaned down and picked up the marquis's head by the hair, hissing into its dead ear, "The sooner this business is over and done with, the happier I'll be. There's other times and other places that would properly appreciate two pair of dab hands with the garrotting wire and the boning knife."

Then he stood up. "Goodnight, good marquis. Don't forget to write."

Mr. Vandemar tipped over the cart, and the marquis's corpse tumbled out and splashed into the brown water below them. And then, because he had come to dislike it intensely, Mr. Vandemar pushed the shopping cart into the sewer as well, and watched the current carry it away.

Then Mr. Croup held his lamp up high, and he stared out at the place in which they stood. "It is saddening to reflect," said Mr. Croup, "that there are folk walking the streets above who will never know the beauty of these sewers, Mister Vandemar. These red-brick cathedrals beneath their feet."

"Craftsmanship," agreed Mr. Vandemar.

They turned their backs on the brown water and made their way back into the tunnels. "With cities, as with people, Mister Vandemar," said Mr. Croup, fastidiously, "the condition of the bowels is all-important."

Door tied the key around her neck with a piece of string that she found in one of the pockets of her leather jacket. "That's not going to be safe," said Richard. The girl made a face at him. "Well," he said. "It's not."

She shrugged. "Okay," she said. "I'll get a chain for it when we get to the market." They were walking through a maze of caves, deep tunnels hacked from the limestone that seemed almost prehistoric.

Richard chuckled. "What's so funny?" Door asked.

He grinned. "I was just thinking of the expression on the marquis's face when we tell him we got the key from the friars without his help."

"I'm sure he'll have something sardonic to say about it," she said. "And then, back to the angel. By the 'long and dangerous way.' Whatever that is."

Richard admired the paintings on the cave walls. Russets and ochres and siennas outlined charging boars and fleeing gazelles, woolly mastodons and giant sloths: he imagined that the paintings had to be thousands of years old, but then they turned a corner, and he noticed that, in the same style, there were lorries, house cats, cars, and—markedly inferior to the other images, as if only glimpsed infrequently, and from a long way away—airplanes.

None of the paintings were very high off the ground. He wondered if the painters were a race of subterranean Neanderthal pygmies. It was as likely as anything else in this strange world. "So where is the next market?" he asked.

"No idea," said Door. "Hunter?"

Hunter slipped out of the shadows. "I don't know."

A small figure dashed past them, going back the way they had come. A few moments later another couple of tiny figures came toward them in fell pursuit. Hunter whipped out a hand as they passed, snagging a small boy by the ear. "Ow," he said, in the manner of small boys. "Let me go! She stole my paintbrush."

"That's right," said a piping voice from further down the corridor. "She did."

"I didn't," came an even higher and more piping voice, from even further down the corridor.

Hunter pointed to the paintings on the cave wall. "You did these?" she asked.

The boy had the towering arrogance only seen in the greatest of artists and all nine-year-old boys. "Yeah," he said, truculently. "Some of them."

"Not bad," said Hunter. The boy glared at her.

"Where's the next Floating Market?" asked Door.

"Belfast," said the boy. "Tonight."

"Thanks," said Door. "Hope you get your paintbrush back. Let him go, Hunter."

Hunter let go of the boy's ear. He did not move. He looked her up and down, then made a face, to indicate that he was, without any question at all, unimpressed. "*You're* Hunter?" he asked. She smiled down at him, modestly. He sniffed. "*You're* the best bodyguard in the Underside?"

"So they tell me."

The boy reached one hand back and forward again, in one smooth movement. He stopped, puzzled, and opened his hand, examined his palm. Then he looked up at Hunter, confused. Hunter opened her hand to reveal a small switchblade with a wicked edge. She held it up, out of the boy's reach. He wrinkled his nose. "How'd you do that?"

"Scram," said Hunter. She closed the knife and tossed it back to the boy, who took off down the corridor without a backward glance, in pursuit of his paintbrush.

The body of the marquis de Carabas drifted east, through the deep sewer, face down.

London's sewers had begun their lives as rivers and streams, flowing north to south (and, south of the Thames, south to north) carrying garbage, animal carcasses, and the contents of chamber pots into the Thames, which would, for the most part, carry the offending substances out to sea. This system had more or less worked for many years, until, in 1858, the enormous volume of effluent produced by the people and industries of London, combined with a rather hot summer, produced a phenomenon known at the time as the Great Stink: the Thames itself had become an open sewer. People who could leave London, left it; the ones who stayed wrapped cloths doused in carbolic around their faces and tried not to breathe through their noses. Parliament was forced to recess early in 1858, and the following year it ordered that a programme of sewer-building begin. The thousands of miles of sewers that were built were constructed with a gentle slope from the west to the east, and, somewhere beyond Greenwich, they were pumped into the Thames Estuary, and the sewage was swept off into the North Sea. It was this journey that the body of the late marquis de Carabas was making, traveling west to east, toward the sunrise and the sewage works.

Rats on a high brick ledge, doing the things that rats do when no people are watching, saw the body go by. The largest of them, a big black male, chittered. A smaller brown female chittered back, then she leapt down from the ledge onto the marquis's back and rode it down the sewer a little way, sniffing at the hair and the coat, tasting the blood, and then, precariously, leaning over, and scrutinizing what could be seen of the face.

She hopped off the head into the filthy water and swam industriously to the side, where she clambered up the slippery brickwork. She hurried back along a beam, and rejoined her companions.

"Belfast?" asked Richard.

Door smiled, impishly, and would say nothing more than, "You'll see," when he pressed her about it.

He changed his tack. "How do you know that kid was telling you the truth about the market?" he asked.

"It's not something anyone down here ever lies about. I . . . don't think we *can* lie about it." She paused. "The market's special."

"How did that kid know where it was?"

"Someone told him," said Hunter.

Richard brooded on this for a moment. "How did they know?"

"Someone told them," explained Door.

"But . . ." He wondered who chose the locations in the first place, how the knowledge was spread, trying to frame the question in such a way that he did not sound stupid.

A rich female voice asked from the darkness, "Hss. Any idea when the next market is?"

She stepped into the light. She wore silver jewelry, and her dark hair was perfectly coiffed. She was very pale, and her long dress was jet black velvet. Richard knew immediately that he had seen her before, but it took him a few moments to place her: the first Floating Market, that was it—in Harrods. She had smiled at him.

"Tonight," said Hunter. "Belfast."

"Thank you," said the woman. She had the most amazing eyes, thought Richard. They were the color of foxgloves.

"I'll see you there," she said, and she looked at Richard as she said it. Then she looked away, a little shyly; she stepped into the shadows, and she was gone.

"Who was that?" asked Richard.

"They call themselves Velvets," said Door. "They sleep down here during the day, and walk the Upworld at night."

"Are they dangerous?" asked Richard.

"Everybody's dangerous," said Hunter.

"Look," said Richard. "Going back to the market. Who decides where it gets held, and when? And how do the first people find out where it's being held?" Hunter shrugged. "Door?" he asked.

"I've never thought about it." They turned a corner. Door held up her lamp. "Not bad at all," said Door.

"And fast, too," said Hunter. She touched the painting on the rock wall with her fingertip. The paint was still wet. It was a painting of Hunter and Door and Richard. It was not flattering.

The black rat entered the lair of the Golden deferentially, his head lowered, ears back. He crawled forward, squeeing and chittering.

The Golden had made their lair in a pile of bones. This pile of bones had once belonged to a woolly mammoth, back in the cold times when the great hairy beasts walked across the snowy tundra of the south of England as if, in the opinion of the Golden, they owned the place. This particular mammoth, at least, had been disabused of that idea rather thoroughly and quite terminally by the Golden.

The black rat made its obeisance at the base of the bone pile. Then he lay on his back with his throat exposed, closed his eyes, and waited. After a while a chittering from above told him that he could roll over.

One of the Golden crawled out of the mammoth skull, on top of the heap of bones. It crawled along the old ivory tusk, a golden-furred rat with copper-colored eyes, the size of a large house cat.

The black rat spoke. The Golden thought, briefly, and chattered an order. The black rat rolled on his back, exposing his throat again, for a moment. Then a twist and a wriggle, and he was on his way.

There had been Sewer Folk before the Great Stink, of course, living in the Elizabethan sewers, or the Restoration sewers, or the Regency sewers, as more and more of London's waterways were forced into pipes and covered passages, as the expanding pop-

ulation produced more filth, more rubbish, more effluent; but after the Great Stink, after the great plan
of Victorian sewer-building, that was when the
Sewer Folk came into their own. They could be
found anywhere in the length and breadth of the
sewers, but they made their permanent homes in
some of the churchlike red-brick vaults toward the
east, at the confluence of many of the churning
foamy waters. There they would sit, rods and nets
and improvised hooks beside them, and watch the
surface of the brown water.

They wore clothes—brown and green clothes, covered in a thick layer of something that might have
been mold and might have been a petrochemical
ooze, and might, conceivably, have been something
much worse. They wore their hair long and matted.
They smelled more or less as one would imagine.
Old storm lanterns were hung about the tunnel. Nobody knew what the Sewer Folk used for fuel, but
their lanterns burned with a rather noxious blue-
and-green flame.

It was not known how the Sewer Folk communi-
cated among themselves. In their few dealings with
the outside world, they used a kind of sign language. They lived in a world of gurgles and drips,
the men, the women, and the silent little sewer children.

Dunnikin spotted something in the water. He was
the chief of the Sewer Folk, the wisest and the oldest.
He knew the sewers better than their original build-
ers did. Dunnikin reached for a long shrimping net;
one practiced hand movement and he was fishing
out a rather bedraggled mobile telephone from the
water. He walked over to a small heap of rubbish in
the corner and put the telephone down with the rest

of their haul. The day's catch so far consisted of two odd gloves, a shoe, a cat skull, a sodden packet of cigarettes, an artificial leg, a dead cocker spaniel, a pair of antlers (mounted), and the bottom half of a baby carriage.

It had not been a good day. And tonight was a market night, in the open air. So Dunnikin kept his eyes on the water. You never knew what would turn up.

Old Bailey was hanging his wash out to dry. Blankets and sheets fluttered and blew in the wind on the top of Centre Point, the ugly and distinctive sixties skyscraper that marks the eastern end of Oxford Street, far above Tottenham Court Road Station. Old Bailey did not care very much for Centre Point itself, but, as he'd often tell the birds, the view from the top was without compare, and, furthermore, the top of Centre Point was one of the few places in the West End of London where you did not have to look at Centre Point itself.

The wind ripped feathers from Old Bailey's coat and blew them away, off over London. He did not mind. As he also often told his birds, there were more where those came from.

A large black rat crawled out through a ripped air-vent cover, looked around, then came over to Old Bailey's bird-spattered tent. It ran up the side of the tent, then along the top of Old Bailey's washing line. It squealed at him, urgently.

"Slower, slower," said Old Bailey. The rat repeated itself, at a lower pitch, but just as urgently. "Bless me," said Old Bailey. He ran into his tent and returned with weapons—his toasting fork and a coal shovel. Then he hurried back into the tent again and came out with some bargaining tools. And then he walked back into the tent for the last time, and opened his wooden chest, and pocketed the silver box. "I really don't have time for this tomfoolery," he told the rat, on his final exit from the tent. "I'm a very busy man. Birds don't catch themselves, y'know."

The rat squeaked at him. Old Bailey was unfastening the coil of rope around his middle. "Well," he told the rat, "there's others could get the body. I'm not as young as I was. I don't like the underplaces. I'm a roof-man, I am, born and bred."

The rat made a rude noise.

"More haste, less speed," replied Old Bailey. "I'm goin'. Young whippersnapper. I knew your great-great-grandfather, young feller-me-rat, so don't you try putting on airs. . . . Now, where's the market going to be?" The rat told him. Then Old Bailey put the rat in his pocket and climbed over the side of the building.

Sitting on the ledge beside the sewer, in his plastic lawn chair, Dunnikin was overcome by a presentiment of wealth and prosperity. He could feel it drifting from west to east, toward them.

He clapped his hands, loudly. Other men ran to him, and the women, and the children, seizing hooks and nets and lines as they did so. They assembled along the slippery sewer ledge, in the sputtering green light of their lanterns. Dunnikin pointed, and they waited, in silence, which is how the Sewer Folk wait.

The body of the marquis de Carabas came floating facedown along the sewer, the current carrying him as slow and stately as a funeral barge. They pulled

it in with their hooks and their nets, in silence, and
soon had it up on the ledge. They removed the coat,
the boots, the gold pocket-watch, and the contents
of the coat pockets, although they left the rest of the
clothes on the corpse.

Dunnikin beamed at the loot. He clapped again,
and the Sewer Folk began to ready themselves for
the market. Now they truly had something of value
to sell.

"Are you sure the marquis will be at the market?"
Richard asked Door, as the path began, slowly, to
climb.

"He won't let us down," she said, as confidently
as she could. "I'm sure he'll be there."

FOURTEEN

HMS *BELFAST* IS A GUNSHIP OF 11,000 tons, commissioned in 1939, which saw active service in the Second World War. Since then it has been moored on the south bank of the Thames, in postcard-land, between Tower Bridge and London Bridge, opposite the Tower of London. From its deck one can see St. Paul's Cathedral and the gilt top of the columnlike Monument to the Great Fire of London erected, as so much of London was erected, by Christopher Wren. The ship serves as a floating museum, as a memorial, as a training ground.

There is a walkway onto the ship from the shore, and they came down the walkway in their twos and threes, and in their dozens. They set up their stalls as early as they could, all the tribes of London Below, united both by the Market Truce and by a mutual desire to pitch their own stalls as far as possible from the Sewer Folk's stall.

It had been agreed well over a century before that the Sewer Folk could only set up a stall at those markets held in the open air. Dunnikin and his folk dumped their booty in a large pile on a rubber sheet, beneath a large gun tower. Nobody ever came to the

Sewer Folk's stall immediately: but toward the end of the market they would come, the bargain hunters, the curious, and those few fortunate individuals blessed with no sense of smell.

Richard and Hunter and Door pushed their way through the crowds on the deck. Richard realized that he had somehow lost the need to stop and stare. The people here were no less strange than at the last Floating Market, but, he supposed, he was every bit as strange to them, wasn't he? He looked around, scanning the faces in the crowd as they walked, hunting for the marquis's ironic smile. "I don't see him," he said.

They were approaching a smith's stall, where a man who could easily have passed for a small mountain, if one were to overlook the shaggy brown beard, tossed a lump of red-molten metal from a brazier onto an anvil. Richard had never seen a real anvil before. He could feel the heat from the molten metal and the brazier from a dozen feet away.

"Keep looking. De Carabas'll turn up," said Door, looking behind them. "Like a bad penny." She thought for a moment, and added, "What exactly is a bad penny anyway?" And then, before Richard could answer, she squealed, "Hammersmith!"

The bearded mountain-man looked up, stopped hitting the molten metal, and roared, "By the Temple and the Arch. Lady Door!" Then he picked her up, as if she weighed no more than a mouse.

"Hello, Hammersmith," said Door. "I hoped you'd be here."

"Never miss a market, lady," he thundered, cheerfully. Then he confided, like an explosion with a secret, "This's where the business is, y'see. Now," he said, recollecting the cooling lump of metal on his anvil, "just you wait here a moment." He put Door down at eye level, on the top of his booth, seven feet above the deck.

He banged the lump of metal with his hammer, twisting it as he did so with implements Richard assumed, correctly, were tongs. Under the hammer blows it changed from a shapeless blob of orange metal into a perfect black rose. It was a work of astonishing delicacy, each petal perfect and distinct. Hammersmith dipped the rose into a bucket of cold water beside the anvil: it hissed and steamed. Then he pulled it out of the bucket, wiped it, and handed it to a fat man in chain mail who was standing, patiently, to one side; the fat man professed himself well satisfied and gave Hammersmith, in return, a green plastic Marks and Spencer shopping bag, filled with various kinds of cheese.

"Hammersmith?" said Door, from her perch. "These are my friends."

Hammersmith enveloped Richard's hand in one several sizes up. His handshake was enthusiastic, but very gentle, as if he had, in the past, had a number of accidents shaking hands and had practiced it until he got it right. "Charmed," he boomed.

"Richard," said Richard.

Hammersmith looked delighted. "Richard! Fine name! I had a horse called Richard." He let go of Richard's hand, turned to Hunter, and said, "And you are . . . Hunter? Hunter! As I live, breathe, and defecate! It is!" Hammersmith blushed like a schoolboy. He spat on his hand and attempted, awkwardly, to plaster his hair back. Then he stuck his hand out and realized that he had just spat on it, and he wiped it on his leather apron, and shifted his weight from foot to foot.

"Hammersmith," said Hunter, with a perfect caramel smile.

"Hammersmith?" asked Door. "Will you help me down?"

He looked shamefaced. "Beg pardon, lady," he said, and lifted her down. It came to Richard then that Hammersmith had known Door as a small child, and he found himself feeling unaccountably jealous of the huge man. "Now," Hammersmith was saying to Door. "What can I do for you?"

"Couple of things," she said. "But first of all—" She turned to Richard. "Richard? I've got a job for you."

Hunter raised an eyebrow. "For him?"

Door nodded. "For both of you. Will you go and find us some food? Please?"

Richard felt oddly proud. He had proved himself in the ordeal. He was One of Them. He would Go, and he would Bring Back Food. He puffed out his chest.

"I am your bodyguard. I stay by your side," said Hunter.

Door grinned. Her eyes flashed. "In the market? It's okay, Hunter. Market Truce holds. No one's going to touch me here. And Richard needs looking after more than I do." Richard deflated, but no one was watching.

"And what if someone violates the Truce?" asked Hunter.

Hammersmith shivered, despite the heat of his brazier. "Violate the Market Truce? Brrrr."

"It's not going to happen. Go on. Both of you. Curry, please. And get me some papadums, please. Spicy ones."

Hunter ran her hand through her hair. Then she

turned and walked off into the crowd, and Richard went with her. "So what would happen if someone violated Market Truce?" asked Richard, as they pushed through the crowds.

Hunter thought about this for a moment. "The last time it happened was about three hundred years ago. A couple of friends got into an argument over a woman, in the market. A knife was pulled and one of them died. The other fled."

"What happened to him? Was he killed?"

Hunter shook her head. "Quite the opposite. He still wishes he had been the one to have died."

"He's still alive?"

Hunter pursed her lips. "Ish," she said, after a while. "Alive-ish."

A moment passed, then *"Phew,"* Richard thought he was going to be ill. "What's that—that stink?"

"Sewer Folk."

Richard averted his head and tried not to breathe through his nose until they were well away from the Sewer Folk's stall.

"Any sign of the marquis yet?" he asked. Hunter shook her head. She could have reached out her hand and touched him. They went up a gangplank, toward the food stalls, and more welcoming aromas.

Old Bailey found the Sewer Folk with little difficulty, following his nose.

He knew what he had to do, and he took a certain pleasure in making a bit of a performance of it, ostentatiously examining the dead cocker spaniel, the artificial leg, and the damp and moldy portable telephone, and shaking his head dolorously at each of them. Then he made a point of noticing the marquis's body. He scratched his nose. He put on his spectacles and peered at it. He nodded to himself, glumly, hoping to give the vague impression of being a man in need of a corpse who was disappointed by the selection but was going to have to make do with what they had. Then he beckoned to Dunnikin, and pointed to the corpse.

Dunnikin opened his hands wide, smiled beatifically, and gazed up toward the heavens, conveying the bliss with which the marquis's remains had entered their life. He put a hand to his forehead, lowered it, and looked devastated, in order to convey the tragedy that losing such a remarkable corpse would be.

Old Bailey put a hand in his pocket and produced a half-used stick of deodorant. He handed it to Dunnikin, who squinted at it, licked it, and handed it back, unimpressed. Old Bailey pocketed it. He looked back at the corpse of the marquis de Carabas, half-dressed, barefoot, still damp from its journey through the sewers. The body was ashen, drained of blood from many cuts, small and large, and the skin was wrinkled and prunelike from its time in the water.

Then he pulled out a bottle, three-quarters filled with a yellow liquid, and passed it to Dunnikin. Dunnikin looked at it suspiciously. The Sewer Folk know what a bottle of Chanel No. 5 looks like, and they gathered around Dunnikin, staring. Carefully, self-importantly, he unscrewed the top of the bottle and dabbed the tiniest amount on his wrist. Then, with a gravity the finest Parisian *parfumier* would have envied, Dunnikin sniffed. Then he nodded his head, enthusiastically, and approached Old Bailey to embrace him and conclude the deal. The old man averted his face and held his breath until the embrace was concluded.

Old Bailey held up one finger and tried his best to mime that he was not so young as once he was and that, dead or not, the marquis de Carabas was a bit on the heavy side. Dunnikin picked his nose thoughtfully, and then, with a hand gesture indicating not only magnanimity but also a foolish and misplaced generosity that would, obviously, send him, Dunnikin, and the rest of the Sewer Folk, to the poorhouse, he had one of the younger Sewer Folk tie the corpse to the bottom half of the old baby carriage.

The old roof-man covered the body with a cloth, and he pulled it away from the Sewer Folk, across the crowded deck.

"One portion of vegetable curry, please," said Richard, to the woman at the curry stall. "And, um, I was wondering. The meat curry. What kind of meat is it, then?" The woman told him. "Oh," said Richard. "Right. Um. Better just make that vegetable curries all round."

"Hello again," said a rich voice beside him. It was the pale woman they had met in the caves, with the black dress and the foxglove eyes.

"Hullo," said Richard, with a smile. "—Oh, and some papadums, please. You, um. Here for curry?"

She fixed him with her violet gaze and said, in mock Bela Lugosi, "I do not eat . . . curry." And then she laughed, a lavish, delighted laugh, and Richard found himself realizing how long it had been since he had shared a joke with a woman.

"Oh. Um. Richard. Richard Mayhew." He stuck out his hand. She touched it with her own hand, in something a little like a handshake. Her fingers were very cold, but then, late at night, at the end of autumn, on a ship out on the Thames, everything is very cold.

"Lamia," she said. "I'm a Velvet."

"Ah," he said. "Right. Are there a lot of you?"

"A few," she said.

Richard collected the containers with the curry. "What do you do?" he asked.

"When I'm not looking for food," she said, with a smile, "I'm a guide. I know every inch of the Underside."

Hunter, who Richard could have sworn had been over on the other side of the stall, was standing next to Lamia. She said, "He's not yours."

Lamia smiled sweetly. "I'll be the judge of that," she said.

Richard said, "Hunter, this is Lamia. She's a Velcro."

"Vel-vet," corrected Lamia, sweetly.

"She's a guide."

"I'll take you wherever you want to go."

Hunter took the bag with the food in it from Richard. "Time to go back," she said.

"Well," said Richard. "If we're off to see the you-know-what, maybe she could help."

Hunter said nothing; instead, she looked at Richard. Had she looked at him that way the day before, he would have dropped the subject. But that was then. "Let's see what Door thinks," said Richard. "Any sign of the marquis?"

"Not yet," said Hunter.

Old Bailey had dragged the corpse down the gangplank tied to its baby carriage-base, like a

ghastly Guy Fawkes, one of the effigies that, not so
very long ago, the children of London had wheeled
and dragged around in early November, displaying
to passersby before tossing them to their flaming de-
mise on the bonfires of the fifth of November, Bon-
fire Night. He pulled the corpse over Tower Bridge,
and, muttering and complaining, he hauled it up the
hill past the Tower of London. He made his way
west toward Tower Hill Station and stopped a little
before the station, beside a large gray jut of wall. It
wasn't a roof, thought Old Bailey, but it would do.

It was one of the last remnants of the London
Wall. The London Wall, according to tradition, was
built on the orders of the Roman Emperor Constantine the Great, in the third century A.D., at the request of his mother Helena. At that point, London
was one of the few great cities of the Empire that
did not yet have a magnificent wall. When it was
finished it enclosed the small city completely; it was
thirty feet high, and eight feet wide, and was, un-
arguably, the London Wall.

It was no longer thirty feet high, the ground level
having risen since Constantine's mother's day (most
of the original London Wall is fifteen feet below
street level today), and it no longer enclosed the city.
But it was still an imposing lump of wall. Old Bailey
nodded vigorously to himself. He fastened a length
of rope to the baby carriage, and he scrambled up
the wall; then, grunting and 'bless-me'-ing, he
hauled the marquis up to the top of the wall. He
untied the body from the carriage wheels and laid it
gently out on its back, arms at its side. There were
wounds on the body that were still oozing. It was
very dead.

"You stupid bugger," whispered Old Bailey,

sadly. "What did you want to get yourself killed for, anyway?"

The moon was bright and small and high in the cold night, and autumn constellations speckled the blue-black sky like the dust of crushed diamonds. A nightingale fluttered onto the wall, examined the corpse of the marquis de Carabas, and chirruped sweetly. "None of your beak," said Old Bailey, gruffly. "You birds don't smell like flipping roses, neither." The bird chirped a melodious nightingale obscenity at him, and flew off into the night.

Old Bailey reached into his pocket and pulled out the black rat, who had gone to sleep. It stared about it sleepily, then yawned, displaying a vast and ratty expanse of piebald tongue. "Personally," said Old Bailey to the black rat, "I'll be happy if I never smell anything ever again." He put it down by his feet on the stones of London Wall, and it chittered at him, and gestured with its front paws. Old Bailey sighed. Carefully, he took the silver box out of his pocket, and, from an inner pocket, he pulled the toasting fork.

He placed the silver box on de Carabas's chest, then, nervously, he reached out the toasting fork, and flipped open the lid of the box. Inside the silver box, on a nest of red velvet, was a large duck's egg, pale blue green in the moonlight. Old Bailey raised the toasting fork, closed his eyes, and brought it down on the egg.

There was a *whup* as it imploded.

There was a great stillness for several seconds after that; then the wind began. It had no direction, but seemed somehow to be coming from everywhere, a swirling sudden gale. Fallen leaves, newspaper pages, all the city's detritus blew up from the ground and was driven through the air. The wind touched the surface of the Thames and carried the cold water into the sky in a fine and driving spray. It was a dangerous, crazy wind. The stall holders on the deck of the *Belfast* cursed it and clutched their possessions to keep them from blowing away.

And then, when it seemed that the wind would become so strong that it would blow the world away and blow the stars away and send the people tumbling through the air like so many desiccated autumn leaves—

Just then—

—it was over, and the leaves, and the papers, and the plastic shopping bags, tumbled to the earth, and the road, and the water.

High on the remnant of the London Wall, the silence that followed the wind was, in its way, as loud as the wind had been. It was broken by a cough; a horrid, wet coughing. This was followed by the sound of someone awkwardly rolling over; and then the sound of someone being sick.

The marquis de Carabas vomited sewer water over the side of the London Wall, staining the gray stones with brown foulness. It took a long time to purge the water from his body. And then he said, in a hoarse voice that was little more than a grinding whisper, "I think my throat's been cut. Have you anything to bind it with?"

Old Bailey fumbled in his pockets and pulled out a grubby length of cloth. He passed it to the marquis, who wrapped it around his throat a few times and then tied it tight. Old Bailey found himself reminded, incongruously, of the high-wrapped Beau Brummel collars of the Regency dandies.

"Anything to drink?" croaked the marquis.

Old Bailey pulled out his hip-flask and unscrewed the top, and passed it to the marquis, who swigged back a mouthful, then winced with pain, and coughed weakly. The black rat, who had watched all this with interest, now began to climb down the fragment of wall and away. It would tell the Golden: all favors had been repaid, all debts were done.

The marquis gave Old Bailey back his hip-flask. Old Bailey put it away. "How are ye feeling?" he asked.

"I've felt better." The marquis sat up, shivering. His nose was running, and his eyes flickered about: he was staring at the world as if he had never seen it before.

"What did you have to go and get yourself killed for, anyway, that's what I want to know," asked Old Bailey.

"Information," whispered the marquis. "People tell you so much more when they know you're just about to be dead. And then they talk around you, when you are."

"Then you found out what you wanted to know?"

The marquis fingered the wounds in his arms and his legs. "Oh yes. Most of it. I have more than an inkling of what this affair is actually about." Then he closed his eyes once more, and wrapped his arms about himself, and swayed, slowly, back and forth.

"What's it like then?" asked Old Bailey. "Being dead?"

The marquis sighed. And then he twisted his lips up into a smile, and with a glitter of his old self, he replied, "Live long enough, Old Bailey, and you can find out for yourself."

Old Bailey looked disappointed. "Bastard. After all I done to bring you back from that dread bourne from which there is no returning. Well, usually no returning."

The marquis de Carabas looked up at him. His eyes were very white in the moonlight. And he whispered, "What's it like being dead? It's very cold, my friend. Very dark, and very cold."

Door held up the chain. The silver key hung from it, red and orange in the light of Hammersmith's brazier. She smiled. "Fine work, Hammersmith."

"Thank you, lady."

She hung the chain around her neck and hid the key away inside her layers of clothes. "What would you like in return?"

The smith looked abashed. "I hardly want to presume upon your good nature ..." he mumbled.

Door made her "get on with it" face. He bent down and produced a black box from beneath a pile of metalworking tools. It was made of dark wood, inlaid with ivory and mother-of-pearl, and was the size of a large dictionary. He turned it over and over in his hands. "It's a puzzle-box," he explained. "I took it in return for some smithing a handful of years back. I can't get it to open, though I've tried so hard."

Door took the box and ran her fingers over the smooth surface. "I'm not surprised you haven't been able to open it. The mechanism's all jammed. It's completely fused shut."

Hammersmith looked glum. "So I'll never find out what's in it."

Door made an amused face. Her fingers explored the surface of the box. A rod slid out of the side of the box. She half-pushed the rod back into the box, then twisted. There was a *clunk* from deep inside it, and a door opened in the side. "Here," said Door.

"My lady," said Hammersmith. He took the box from her and pulled the door open all the way. There was a drawer inside the box, which he pulled open. The small toad, in the drawer, croaked and looked about itself with copper eyes, incuriously. Hammersmith's face fell. "I was hoping it would be diamonds and pearls," he said.

Door reached out a hand and stroked the toad's head. "He's got pretty eyes," she said. "Keep him, Hammersmith. He'll bring you luck. And thank you again. I know I can rely on your discretion."

"You can rely on me, lady," said Hammersmith, earnestly.

They sat together on the top of the London Wall, not speaking. Old Bailey slowly lowered the baby carriage wheels to the ground below them.

"Where's the market?" asked the marquis.

Old Bailey pointed to the gunship. "Over there."

"Door and the others. They'll be expecting me."

"You aren't in any condition to go anywhere."

The marquis coughed, painfully. It sounded, to Old Bailey, like there was still plenty of sewer in his lungs. "I've made a long enough journey today," de Carabas whispered. "A little farther won't hurt." He examined his hands, flexed the fingers slowly, as if to see whether or not they would do as he wished. And then he twisted his body around, and began, awkwardly, to climb down the side of the wall. But before he did so, he said, hoarsely and perhaps a little sadly, "It would seem, Old Bailey, that I owe you a favor."

* * *

When Richard returned with the curries, Door ran to him and threw her arms around him. She hugged him tightly, and even patted his bottom, before seizing the paper bag from him and pulling it open with enthusiasm. She took a container of vegetable curry and began, happily, to eat.

"Thanks," said Door, with her mouth full. "Any sign of the marquis yet?"

"None," said Hunter.

"Croup and Vandemar?"

"No."

"Yummy curry. This is really good."

"Got the chain all right?" asked Richard. Door pulled the chain up from around her neck, enough to show it was there, and she let it fall again, the weight of the key pulling it back down.

"Door," said Richard, "this is Lamia. She's a guide. She says she can take us anywhere in the Underside."

"Anywhere?" Door munched a papadum.

"Anywhere," said Lamia.

Door put her head on one side. "Do you know where the Angel Islington is?"

Lamia blinked, slowly, long lashes covering and revealing her foxglove-colored eyes. "Islington?" she said. "You can't go there . . ."

"Do you know?"

"Down Street," said Lamia. "The end of Down Street. But it's not safe."

Hunter had been watching this conversation, arms folded and unimpressed. Now she said, "We don't need a guide."

"Well," said Richard, "I think we do. The marquis isn't around anywhere. We know it's going to be a dangerous journey. We have to get the . . . the thing

I got . . . to the Angel. And then he'll tell Door about her family, and he'll tell me how to get home."

Lamia looked up at Hunter with delight. "And he can give you brains," she said, cheerfully, "and me a heart."

Door wiped the last of the curry from her bowl with her fingers, and licked them. "We'll be fine, just the three of us, Richard. We cannot afford a guide."

Lamia bridled. "I'll take my payment from him, not you."

"And what payment would your kind demand?" asked Hunter.

"That," said Lamia with a sweet smile, "is for me to know and him to wonder."

Door shook her head. "I really don't think so."

Richard snorted. "You just don't like it that I'm figuring everything out for once, instead of following blindly behind you, going where I'm told."

"That's not it at all."

Richard turned to Hunter. "Well, Hunter. Do *you* know the way to Islington?" Hunter shook her head.

Door sighed. "We should get a move on. Down Street, you say?"

Lamia smiled with plum-colored lips. "Yes, lady."

By the time the marquis reached the market they were gone.

FIFTEEN

THEY WALKED OFF THE SHIP, DOWN THE long gangplank, and onto the shore, where they went down some steps, through a long, unlit underpass, and up again. Lamia strode confidently ahead of them. She brought them out in a small, cobbled alley. Gaslights burned and sputtered on the walls.

"Third door along," she said.

They stopped in front of the door. There was a brass plate on it, which said:

THE ROYAL SOCIETY
FOR THE PREVENTION OF CRUELTY
TO HOUSES

And beneath that, in smaller letters:

DOWN STREET. PLEASE KNOCK.

"You get to the street through the house?" asked Richard.

"No," said Lamia. "The street is in the house."

Richard knocked on the door. Nothing happened. They waited, and they shivered from the early morning cold. Richard knocked again. Finally, he rang the doorbell. The door was opened by a sleepy-looking footman, wearing a powdered, crooked wig and scarlet livery. He looked at the motley rabble on his doorstep with an expression that indicated that they had not been worth getting out of bed for.

"Can I help you?" said the footman. Richard had been told to fuck off and die with more warmth and good humor.

"Down Street," said Lamia, imperiously.

"This way," sighed the footman. "If you'll wipe your feet."

They walked through an impressive lobby. Then they waited while the footman lit each of the candles on a candelabra. They went down some impressive, richly carpeted stairs. They went down a flight of less impressive, less richly carpeted stairs. They went down a flight of entirely unimpressive stairs carpeted in a threadbare brown sacking, and, finally, they went down a flight of drab wooden stairs with no carpet on them at all.

At the bottom of those stairs was an antique service elevator, with a sign on it. The sign said:

OUT OF ORDER

The footman ignored the sign and pulled open the wire outer door with a metallic thud. Lamia thanked him, politely, and stepped into the elevator. The others followed. The footman turned his back on them. Richard watched him through the wire mesh, clutching his candelabra, going back up the wooden stairs.

There was a short row of black buttons on the wall of the elevator. Lamia pressed the bottom-most button. The metal lattice door closed automatically,

with a bang. A motor engaged, and the elevator began, slowly, creakily, to descend. The four of them
stood packed in the elevator. Richard realized that
he could smell each of the women in the elevator
with him: Door smelled mostly of curry; Hunter
smelled, not unpleasantly, of sweat, in a way that
made him think of great cats in cages at zoos; while
Lamia smelled, intoxicatingly, of honeysuckle and
lily of the valley and musk.

The elevator continued to descend. Richard was
sweating, in a clammy cold sweat, and digging his
fingernails deep into his palms. In the most conversational tones he could muster, he said, "Now
would be a very bad time to discover that one was
claustrophobic, wouldn't it?"

"Yes," said Door.

"Then I won't," said Richard.

And they went down.

Finally, there was a jerk, and a clunk, and a ratcheting noise, and the elevator stopped. Hunter pulled
open the door, looked about, and then stepped out
onto a narrow ledge.

Richard looked out of the open elevator door.
They were hanging in the air, at the top of something that reminded Richard of a painting he had
once seen of the Tower of Babel, or rather of how
the Tower of Babel might have looked were it inside
out. It was an enormous and ornate spiral path,
carved out of rock, which went down and down
around a central well. Lights flickered dimly, here
and there in the walls, beside the paths, and, far, far
below them, tiny fires were burning. It was at the
top of the central well, a few thousand feet above
solid ground, that the elevator was hanging. It
swayed a little.

Richard took a deep breath and followed the others onto the wooden ledge. Then, although he knew it was a bad idea, he looked down. There was nothing but a wooden board between him and the rock floor, thousands of feet below. There was a long plank stretched between the ledge on which they stood and the top of the rocky path, twenty feet away. "And I suppose," he said, with a great deal less insouciance than he imagined, "this wouldn't be a good time to point out that I'm really bad at heights."

"It's safe," said Lamia. "Or it was the last time I was here. Watch." She walked across the board, a rustle of black velvet. She could have balanced a dozen books on her head and never dropped one. When she reached the stone path at the side, she stopped, and turned, and smiled at them encouragingly. Hunter followed her across, then turned, and waited beside her on the edge.

"See?" said Door. She reached out a hand, squeezed Richard's arm. "It's fine."

Richard nodded, and swallowed. *Fine.*

Door walked across. She did not seem to be enjoying herself; but she crossed, nonetheless. The three women waited for Richard, who stood there. Richard noticed after a while that he did not seem to be starting to walk across the wooden plank, despite the "walk!" commands he was sending to his legs.

Far above them, a button was pressed: Richard heard the *thunk* and the distant grinding of an elderly electric motor. The door of the elevator slammed closed behind him, leaving Richard standing, precariously, on a narrow wooden platform, no wider than a plank itself.

"Richard!" shouted Door. "Move!"

The elevator began to ascend. Richard stepped off the shaking platform, and onto the wooden board; then his legs turned to jelly beneath him, and he found himself on all fours on the plank, holding on for dear life. There was a tiny, rational part of his mind that wondered about the elevator: who had called it back up, and why? The rest of his mind, however, was engaged in telling all his limbs to clutch the plank rigidly, and in screaming, at the top of its mental voice, "I don't want to die." Richard closed his eyes as tightly as he could, certain that if he opened them, and saw the rock wall below him, he would simply let go of the plank, and fall, and fall, and—

"I'm not scared of falling," he told himself. "The part I'm scared of is where you finish falling." But he knew he was lying to himself. It *was* the fall he was scared of—afraid of flailing and tumbling helplessly through the air, down to the rock floor far below, knowing there was nothing he could do to save himself, no miracle that would save him . . .

He slowly became aware that someone was talking to him.

"Just climb along the plank, Richard," someone was saying.

"I . . . can't," he whispered.

"You went through worse than this to get the key, Richard," someone said. It was Door talking.

"I'm really not very good at heights," he said, obstinately, his face pressed against the wooden board, his teeth chattering. Then, "I want to go home." He felt the wood of the plank pressing against his face. And then the plank began to shake. Hunter's voice said, "I'm really not sure how much weight the board will bear. You two put your weight here." The plank vibrated as someone moved along it, toward him. He clung to it, with his eyes closed. Then Hunter said, quietly, confidently, in his ear, "Richard?"

"Mm."

"Just edge forward, Richard. A bit at a time. Come on . . ." Her caramel fingers stroked his white-knuckled hand, clasping the plank. "Come on."

He took a deep breath, and inched forward. And froze again. "You're doing fine," said Hunter. "That's good. Come on." And, inch by inch, creep by crawl, she talked Richard along the plank, and then, at the end of the plank, she simply picked him up, her hands beneath his arms, and placed him on solid ground.

"Thank you," he said. He could not think of anything else to say to Hunter that would be big enough to cover what she had just done for him. He said it again. "Thank you." And then he said, to all of them, "I'm sorry."

Door looked up at him. "It's okay," she said. "You're safe now." Richard looked at the winding spiral road beneath the world, going down, and down; and he looked at Hunter and Door and Lamia; and he laughed until he wept.

"What," Door demanded, when, at length, he had stopped laughing, "is so funny?"

"*Safe,*" he said, simply. Door stared at him, and then she, too, smiled. "So where do we go now?" Richard asked.

"Down," said Lamia. They began to walk down Down Street. Hunter was in the lead, with Door beside her. Richard walked next to Lamia, breathing in the lily-of-the-valley-honeysuckle scent of her, and enjoying her company.

"I really appreciate you coming with us," he told her. "Being a guide. I hope it's not going to be bad luck for you or anything."

She fixed him with her foxglove-colored eyes. "Why should it be bad luck?"

"Do you know who the rat-speakers are?"

"Of course."

"There was a rat-speaker girl named Anaesthesia. She. Well, we got to be sort of friends, and she was guiding me somewhere. And then she got stolen. On Night's Bridge. I keep wondering what happened to her."

She smiled at him sympathetically. "My people have stories about that. Some of them may even be true."

"You'll have to tell me about them," he said. It was cold. His breath was steaming in the chilly air.

"One day," she said. Her breath did not steam. "It's very good of you, taking me with you."

"Least we could do."

Door and Hunter went around the curve in front of them, and were out of sight. "You know," said Richard, "the other two are getting a bit ahead of us. We might want to hurry."

"Let them go," she said, gently. "We'll catch up."

It was, thought Richard, peculiarly like going to a movie with a girl as a teenager. Or rather, like walking home afterwards: stopping at bus shelters, or beside walls, to snatch a kiss, a hasty fumble of skin and a tangle of tongues, then hurrying on to catch up with your friends . . .

Lamia ran a cold finger down his cheek. "You're so warm," she said, admiringly. "It must be wonderful to have so much warmth."

Richard tried to look modest. "It's not something

I think about much, really," he admitted. He heard, distantly, from above, the metallic slam of the elevator door.

Lamia looked up at him, pleadingly, sweetly. "Would you give me some of your heat, Richard?" she asked. "I'm so cold."

Richard wondered if he should kiss her. "What? I . . ."

She looked disappointed. "Don't you like me?" she asked. He hoped, desperately, that he had not hurt her feelings.

"Of course I like you," he heard his voice saying. "You're very nice."

"And you aren't using all your heat, are you?" she pointed out, reasonably.

"I suppose not . . ."

"And you said you'd pay me for being your guide. And it's what I want, as my payment. Warmth. Can I have some?"

Anything she wanted. Anything. The honeysuckle and the lily of the valley wrapped around him, and his eyes saw nothing but her pale skin and her dark plum-bloom lips, and her jet black hair. He nodded. Somewhere inside him something was screaming; but whatever it was, it could wait. She reached up her hands to his face and pulled it gently down toward her. Then she kissed him, long and languorously. There was a moment of initial shock at the chill of her lips, and the cold of her tongue, and then he succumbed to her kiss entirely.

After some time, she pulled back.

He could feel the ice on his lips. He stumbled back against the wall. He tried to blink, but his eyes felt as if they were frozen open. She looked up at him and smiled delightedly, her skin flushed and pink and her lips, scarlet; her breath steamed in the cold air. She licked her red lips with a warm crimson tongue. His world began to go dark. He thought he saw a black shape at the edge of his vision.

"More," she said. And she reached out to him.

He watched the Velvet pull Richard to her for the first kiss, watched the rime and the frost spread over Richard's skin. He watched her pull back, happily. And then he walked up behind her, and, as she moved in to finish what she had begun, he reached out and seized her, hard, by the neck, and lifted her off the ground.

"Give it back," he rasped in her ear. "Give him back his life." The Velvet reacted like a kitten who had just been dropped into a bathtub, wriggling and hissing and spitting and scratching. It did her no good: she was held tight by the throat.

"You can't make me," she said, in decidedly unmusical tones.

He increased the pressure. "Give him his life back," he told her, hoarsely and honestly, "or I'll break your neck." She winced. He pushed her toward Richard, frozen and crumpled against the rock wall.

She took Richard's hand, and breathed into his nose and mouth. Vapor came from her mouth, and trickled into his. The ice on his skin began to thaw, the rime on his hair to vanish.

He squeezed her neck again. "All of it, Lamia."

She hissed, then, extremely grudgingly, and opened her mouth once more. A final puff of steam drifted from her mouth to his, and vanished inside him. Richard blinked. The ice on his eyes had melted to tears, and they were running down his cheeks. "What did you do to me?" he asked.

"She was drinking your life," said the marquis de Carabas, in a hoarse whisper. "Taking your warmth. Turning you into a cold thing like her."

Lamia's face twisted, like a tiny child deprived of a favorite toy. Her foxglove eyes flashed. "I need it more than he does," she wailed.

"I thought you liked me," said Richard, stupidly.

The marquis picked Lamia up, one-handed, and brought her face close to his. "Go near him again, you or any of the Velvet Children, and I'll come by day to your cavern, while you sleep, and I'll burn it to the ground. Understand?"

Lamia nodded. He let go of her, and she dropped to the floor. Then she pulled herself up to her full size, which was not terribly tall, threw back her head, and spat, hard, into the marquis's face. She picked up the front of her black velvet dress and ran up the slope, and away, her footsteps echoing through the winding rock path of Down Street, while her ice-cold spittle ran down the marquis's cheek. He wiped it away with the back of his hand.

"She was going to kill me," stammered Richard.

"Not immediately," said the marquis, dismissively. "You would have died eventually, though, when she finished eating your life."

Richard stared at the marquis. His skin was filthy, and he seemed ashen beneath the dark of his skin. His coat was gone: instead, he wore an old blanket wrapped about his shoulders, like a poncho, with something bulky—Richard could not tell what—strapped beneath it. He was barefoot, and, in what Richard took to be some kind of bizarre fashion af-

fectation, there was a discolored cloth wrapped all
the way around his throat.

"We were looking for you," said Richard.

"And now you've found me," croaked the marquis, drily.

"We were expecting to see you at the market."

"Yes. Well. Some people thought I was dead. I
was forced to keep a low profile."

"Why . . . why did some people think you were
dead?"

The marquis looked at Richard with eyes that had
seen too much and gone too far. "Because they killed
me," he said. "Come on, the others can't be too far
ahead."

Richard looked over the side of the path, across
the central well. He could see Door and Hunter,
across the well, on the level below. They were looking around—for him, he assumed. He called to
them, shouted and waved, but the sound did not
carry. The marquis laid a hand upon Richard's arm.
"Look," he said. He pointed to the level beneath
Door and Hunter. Something moved. Richard
squinted: he could make out two figures, standing
in the shadows. "Croup and Vandemar," said the
marquis. "It's a trap."

"What do we do?"

"Run!" said the marquis. "Warn them. I can't run
yet . . . go, damn you!"

And Richard ran. He ran as fast as he could, as
hard as he could, down the sloping stone road under
the world. He felt a sudden stabbing pain in his
chest: a stitch. And he pushed himself on, and still
he ran.

He turned a corner, and he saw them all. "Hunter!
Door!" he gasped, breathless. "Stop! Watch out!"

Door turned. Mr. Croup and Mr. Vandemar stepped out from behind a pillar. Mr. Vandemar yanked Door's hands behind her back and bound them in one movement with a nylon strip. Mr. Croup was holding something long and thin in a brown cloth cover, like the kind Richard's father had used to carry his fishing poles in. Hunter stood there, her mouth open. Richard shouted, "Hunter. Quickly."

She nodded, spun around, and kicked out one foot, in a smooth, almost balletic, motion.

Her foot caught Richard squarely in the stomach. He fell to the floor several feet away, winded and breathless and hurt. "Hunter?" he gasped.

"I'm afraid so," said Hunter, and she turned away. Richard felt sick, and saddened. The betrayal hurt him as much as the blow.

Mr. Croup and Mr. Vandemar ignored Richard and Hunter entirely. Mr. Vandemar was trussing Door's arms, while Mr. Croup stood and watched. "Don't think of us as murderers and cutthroats, miss," Mr. Croup was saying, conversationally. "Think of us as an escort service."

Hunter stood beside the rock face, looking at none of them, and Richard lay on the rock floor and writhed and tried, somehow, to suck air back into his lungs. Mr. Croup turned back to Door and smiled, showing many teeth. "You see, Lady Door. We are going to make sure you get safely to your destination."

Door ignored him. "Hunter," she called, "what's happening?" Hunter did not move, nor did she answer.

Mr. Croup beamed, proudly. "Before Hunter

agreed to work for you, she agreed to work for our principal. Taking care of you."

"We told you," crowed Mr. Vandemar. "We told you one of you was a traitor." He threw back his head, and howled like a wolf.

"I thought you were talking about the marquis," said Door.

Mr. Croup scratched his head of orange hair, theatrically. "Talking of the marquis, I wonder where he is. He's a bit *late*, isn't he, Mister Vandemar?"

"Very *late* indeed, Mister Croup. As *late* as he possibly could be."

Mr. Croup coughed sententiously and delivered his punch line. "Then from now on, we'll have to call him the *late* marquis de Carabas. I'm afraid he's ever-so-slightly—"

"Dead as a doornail," finished Mr. Vandemar.

Richard finally managed to get enough air into his lungs to gasp, "You traitorous bitch."

Hunter glanced at the ground. "No hard feelings," she whispered.

"The key you obtained from the Black Friars," said Mr. Croup to Door. "Who has it?"

"I do," gasped Richard. "You can search me, if you like. Look." He fumbled in his pockets—noticing something hard and unfamiliar in his back pocket, but there was no time to investigate that now—and he pulled out the front-door key of his old flat. He dragged himself to his feet and staggered over to Mr. Croup and Mr. Vandemar. "Here."

Mr. Croup reached over and took the key from him. "Good gracious me," he said, scarcely glancing at it. "I find myself utterly taken in by his cunning ploy, Mister Vandemar."   He passed the key to Mr.

Vandemar, who held it up between finger and thumb, and crushed it like brass foil. "Fooled again, Mister Croup," he said.

"Hurt him, Mister Vandemar," said Mr. Croup.

"With pleasure, Mister Croup," said Mr. Vandemar, and he kicked Richard in the kneecap. Richard fell to the ground, in agony. As if from a long way away, he could hear Mr. Vandemar's voice; it appeared to be lecturing him. "People think it's how hard you kick that hurts," Mr. Vandemar's voice was saying. "But it's not how hard you kick. It's where. I mean, this's really a very gentle kick . . ."—something slammed into Richard's left shoulder. His left arm went numb, and a purple-white blossom of pain opened up in his shoulder. It felt like his whole arm was on fire, and freezing, as if someone had jabbed an electrical prod deep into his flesh, and turned up the current as high as it would go. He whimpered. And Mr. Vandemar was saying, ". . . but it hurts just as much as *this*—which is much harder . . ." and the boot rammed into Richard's side like a cannonball. He could hear himself screaming.

"I've got the key," he heard Door say.

"If only you had a Swiss army knife," Mr. Vandemar told Richard, helpfully, "I could show you what I do with all the different bits. Even the bottle-opener, and the thing for getting stones out of horses' hooves."

"Leave him, Mister Vandemar. There will be time enough for Swiss army knives. Does she have the token?" Mr. Croup fumbled in Door's pockets, and took out the carved obsidian figure: the tiny Beast the angel had given her.

Hunter's voice was low and resonant. "What about me? Where's my payment?"

Mr. Croup sniffed. He tossed her the fishing pole case. She caught it one-handed. "Good hunting," said Mr. Croup. Then he and Mr. Vandemar turned and walked off down the twisting slope of Down Street, with Door between them. Richard lay on the floor and watched them go, with a terrible feeling of despair spreading outward from his heart.

Hunter knelt on the ground and began to undo the straps on the case. Her eyes were wide and shining. Richard ached. "What is it?" he asked. "Thirty pieces of silver?" She pulled it, slowly, from its fabric cover, her fingers caressing it, stroking it, loving it. "A spear," she said, simply.

It was made of a bronze-colored metal; the blade was long, and it curved like a *kris*, sharp on one side, serrated on the other; there were faces carved into the side of the haft, which was green with verdigris, and decorated with strange designs and odd curlicues. It was about five feet long, from the tip of the blade to the end of the haft. Hunter touched it, almost fearfully, as if it was the most beautiful thing she had ever seen.

"You sold Door out for a spear," said Richard. Hunter said nothing. She wetted a fingertip with her pink tongue, then gently ran it across the side of the head of the spear, testing the edge on the blade; and then she smiled, as if she were satisfied with what she felt. "Are you going to kill me?" Richard asked. He was suprised to find himself no longer scared of death—or at least, he realized, he was not scared of that death.

She turned her head, then, and looked at him. She looked more alive than he had ever seen her; more beautiful, and more dangerous. "And what kind of challenge would I have hunting you, Richard Mayhew?'' she asked, with a vivid smile. "I have bigger game to kill."

"This is your Great-Beast-of-London-hunting spear, isn't it?" he said.

She looked at the spear in a way that no woman had ever looked at Richard. "They say that nothing can stand against it."

"But Door trusted you. *I* trusted you."

She was no longer smiling. "Enough."

Slowly, the pain was beginning to abate, dwindling to a dull ache in his shoulder and his side and his knee. "So who are you working for? Where are they taking her? Who's behind all this?"

"Tell him, Hunter," rasped the marquis de Carabas. He was holding a crossbow pointed at Hunter. His bare feet were planted on the ground; his face was implacable.

"I wondered whether you were as dead as Croup and Vandemar claimed you were," said Hunter, barely turning her head. "You struck me as a hard man to kill."

He inclined his head, in an ironic bow, but his eyes did not move, and his hands remained steady. "And you strike me that way too, dear lady. But a crossbow bolt to the throat, and a fall of several thousand feet may prove me wrong, eh? Put the spear down and step back." She placed the spear on the floor, gently, lovingly; then she stood up and stepped back from it. "You may as well tell him, Hunter," said the marquis. "I know; I found out the hard way. Tell him who's behind all this."

"Islington," she said.

Richard shook his head, as if he were trying to brush away a fly. "It can't be," he said. "I mean, I've

met Islington. He's an angel." And then, almost desperately, he asked, "Why?"

The marquis's eyes had not left Hunter, nor had
the point of the crossbow wavered. "I wish I knew.
But Islington is at the bottom of Down Street, and
at the bottom of this mess. And between us and Islington is the labyrinth and the Beast. Richard, take
the spear. Hunter, walk in front of me, please."

Richard picked up the spear, and then, awkwardly, using the spear to lean on, he pulled himself
up to a standing position. "You want her to come
with us?" he asked, puzzled.

"Would you prefer her behind us?" asked the
marquis, drily.

"You could kill her," said Richard.

"I will, if there are no other alternatives," said the
marquis, "but I would hate to remove an option,
before it was entirely necessary. Anyway, death is
so final, isn't it?"

"Is it?" asked Richard.

"Sometimes," said the marquis de Carabas. And
they went down.

SIXTEEN

THEY WALKED FOR HOURS IN SILENCE, FOL-
lowing the winding stone road downwards. Richard
was still in pain; he was limping, and experiencing
a strange mental and physical turmoil: feelings of
defeat and betrayal roiled within him, which, combined with the near loss of his life to Lamia, the
damage inflicted by Mr. Vandemar, and his experiences on the plank far above, left him utterly
wrecked. Yet, he was certain that his experiences of
the last day paled into something small and insig-
nificant when placed beside whatever the marquis
had experienced. So he said nothing.

The marquis kept silent, as every word he uttered
hurt his throat. He was content to let it heal, and to
concentrate on Hunter. He knew that, should he let
his attention flag for even a moment, she would
know it, and she would be away, or she would turn
on them. So he said nothing.

Hunter walked a little ahead of them. She, also,
said nothing.

After some hours, they reached the bottom of
Down Street. The street ended in a vast Cyclopean
gateway—built of enormous rough stone blocks.

Giants built that gate, thought Richard, half-remembered tales of long-dead kings of mythical London churning in his head, tales of King Bran and of the giants Gog and Magog, with hands the size of oak trees, and severed heads as big as hills. The portal itself had long since rusted and crumbled away. Fragments of it could be seen in the mud beneath their feet, dangling uselessly from a rusted hinge on the side of the gate. The hinge was taller than Richard.

The marquis gestured for Hunter to stop. He moistened his lips, and said, "This gate marks the end of Down Street, and the beginning of the labyrinth. And beyond the labyrinth waits the Angel Islington. And in the labyrinth is the Beast."

"I still don't understand," said Richard. "Islington. I actually met him. It. Him. He's an angel. I mean, a real angel."

The marquis smiled, without humor. "When angels go bad, Richard, they go worse than anyone. Remember, Lucifer used to be an angel."

Hunter watched Richard with nut brown eyes. "The place you visited is Islington's citadel, and also its prison," she said. It was the first thing she had said in hours. "It cannot leave."

The marquis addressed her directly. "I assume that the labyrinth and the Beast are there to discourage visitors."

She inclined her head. "So I would assume also."

Richard turned on the marquis, all his anger and impotence and frustration spewing out of him in one angry blast. "Why are you even talking to her? Why is she still with us? She was a traitor—she tried to make us think that you were the traitor."

"And I saved your life, Richard Mayhew," said

Hunter, quietly. "Many times. On the bridge. At the gap. On the board up there." She looked into his eyes, and it was Richard who looked away.

Something echoed through the tunnels: a bellow, or a roar. The hairs on the back of Richard's neck prickled. It was far away, but that was the only thing about it in which he could take any comfort. He knew that sound: he had heard it in his dreams, but now it sounded neither like a bull nor like a boar; it sounded like a lion; it sounded like a dragon.

"The labyrinth is one of the oldest places in London Below," said the marquis. "Before King Lud founded the village on the Thames marshes, there was a labyrinth here."

"No Beast, though," said Richard.

"Not then."

Richard hesitated. The distant roaring began again. "I ... I think I've had dreams about the Beast," he said.

The marquis raised an eyebrow. "What kind of dreams?"

"Bad ones," said Richard.

The marquis thought about this, eyes flickering. And then he said, "Look, Richard. I'm taking Hunter. But if you want to wait here, well, no one could accuse you of cowardice."

Richard shook his head. Sometimes there is nothing you can do. "I'm not turning back. Not now. They've got Door."

"Right," said the marquis. "Well then. Shall we go?"

Hunter's perfect caramel lips twisted into a sneer. "You'd have to be mad to go in there," she said. "Without the angel's token you could never find your way. Never get past the boar."

The marquis reached his hand under his poncho blanket and produced the little obsidian statue he had taken from Door's father's study. "One of these, you mean?" he asked. The marquis felt, then, that much of what he had gone through in the previous week was made up for by the expression on Hunter's face. They went through the gate, into the labyrinth.

Door's arms were bound behind her back, and Mr. Vandemar walked behind her, one huge beringed hand resting on her shoulder, pushing her along. Mr. Croup scuttled on ahead of them, holding the talisman he had taken from her on high, and peering edgily from side to side, like a particularly pompous weasel on its way to raid the henhouse.

The labyrinth itself was a place of pure madness. It was built of lost fragments of London Above: alleys and roads and corridors and sewers that had fallen through the cracks over the millennia, and entered the world of the lost and the forgotten. The two men and the girl walked over cobbles, and through mud, and through dung of various kinds, and over rotting wooden boards. They walked through daylight and night, through gaslit streets, and sodium-lit streets, and streets lit with burning rushes and links. It was an ever-changing place: and each path divided and circled and doubled back on itself.

Mr. Croup felt the tug of the talisman, and let it take him where it wanted to go. They walked down a tiny alleyway, which had once been part of a Victorian "rookery"—a slum comprised in equal parts of theft and penny gin, of twopenny-halfpenny squalor and threepenny sex—and they heard it, snuffling and snorting somewhere nearby. And then it bellowed, deep and dark. Mr. Croup hesitated, before hurrying forward, up a short wooden staircase; and then, at the end of the alley, he stopped, squinting about him, before he led them down some steps into a long stone tunnel that had once run across the Fleet Marshes, in the Templars' time.

Door said, "You're afraid, aren't you?"

Croup glared at her. "Hush your tongue."

She smiled, although she did not feel like smiling. "You're scared that your safe-conduct token won't get you past the Beast. What are you planning now? To kidnap Islington? Sell both of us to the highest bidder?"

"Quiet," said Mr. Vandemar. But Mr. Croup simply chuckled; and Door knew then that the Angel Islington was not her friend.

She began to shout. "Hey! Beast! Here!" Mr. Vandemar cuffed her head and knocked her against the wall. "Said to be quiet," he told her, calmly. She tasted blood in her mouth and spat scarlet on the mud. Then she parted her lips to begin shouting once more. Mr. Vandemar, anticipating this, had taken a handkerchief from his pocket, and he forced it into her mouth. She tried to bite his thumb as he did so, but it made no appreciable impression on him.

"Now you'll be quiet," he told her.

Mr. Vandemar was very proud of his handkerchief, which was spattered with green and brown and black and had originally belonged to an overweight snuff dealer in the 1820s, who had died of apoplexy and been buried with his handkerchief in his pocket. Mr. Vandemar still occasionally found fragments of snuff merchant in it, but it was, he felt, a fine handkerchief for all that.

They continued in silence.

Richard made another entry in his mental diary. *Today*, he thought, *I've survived walking the plank, the kiss of death, and a lecture on inflicting pain. Right now, I'm on my way through a labyrinth with a mad bastard who came back from the dead and a bodyguard who turned out to be a . . . whatever the opposite of a bodyguard is. I am so far out of my depth that . . .* Metaphors failed him, then. He had gone beyond the world of metaphor and simile into the place of things that *are*, and it was changing him.

They were wading through a narrow passage of wet, marshy ground, between dark stone walls. The marquis held both the token and the crossbow, and he took care to walk, at all times, about ten feet behind Hunter. Richard, in the lead, was carrying Hunter's Beast spear and a yellow flare the marquis had produced from beneath his blanket, which illuminated the stone walls and the mud, and he walked well in front of Hunter. The marshland stank, and huge mosquitoes had begun to settle upon Richard's arms and legs and face, biting him painfully and raising huge, itching welts. Neither Hunter nor the marquis so much as mentioned the mosquitoes.

Richard was beginning to suspect that they were quite lost. It did not help his mood any that there were a large number of dead people in the marsh: leathery preserved bodies, discolored skeletal bones, and pallid, water-swollen corpses. He wondered how long the corpses had been there, and whether they had been killed by the Beast or by the mosquitoes. He said nothing as they walked on for another five minutes and eleven mosquito bites, and then he called out, "I think we're lost. We've been through this way before."

The marquis held up the token. "No. We're fine," he said. "The token is leading us straight. Clever little thing."

"Yeah," said Richard, who was not impressed. "Very clever."

It was then that the marquis stepped, barefoot, on the shattered rib cage of a half-buried corpse, puncturing his heel, and causing him to stumble. The little black statue went flying through the air and tumbled into the black marsh with the satisfied plop of a leaping fish returning to the water. The marquis righted himself and pointed the crossbow at Hunter's back.

"Richard," he called. "I dropped it. Can you come back here?" Richard walked back, holding the flare high, hoping for the glint of flame on obsidian, seeing nothing but wet mud. "Get down into the mud and look," said the marquis.

Richard groaned.

"You've dreamed of the Beast, Richard," said the marquis. "Do you really want to encounter it?"

Richard thought about this for not very long, then he pushed the haft of the bronze spear into the surface of the marsh and stood the flare up into the mud beside it, illuminating the surface of the marsh with a fitful amber light. He got down on his hands and knees in the bog, searching for the statue. He ran his hands over the surface of the marsh, hoping not to encounter any dead faces or hands. "It's hopeless. It could be anywhere."

"Keep looking," said the marquis.

Richard tried to remember how he usually found

things. First he let his mind go as blank as he could, then he let his gaze wander over the surface of the marsh, purposelessly, idly. Something glittered on the boggy surface, five feet to his left. It was the Beast statue. "I can see it," called Richard.

He floundered toward it through the mud. The little glassy beast was head-down in a puddle of dark water. Perhaps the mud was disturbed by Richard's approach; more likely, as Richard was convinced forever after, it was just the sheer cussedness of the material world. Whatever the cause, he was almost next to the little statue when the marsh made a noise that sounded like a giant stomach rumbling, and a large bubble of gas floated up and popped noxiously and obscenely beside the talisman, which vanished beneath the water.

Richard reached the place where the talisman had been and pushed his arms deep into the mud, searching for it wildly, not caring what else his fingers might encounter. It was no use. It was gone forever. "What do we do now?" asked Richard.

The marquis sighed. "Get back over here, and we'll figure out something."

Richard said, quietly, "Too late."

It was coming toward them so slowly, so ponderously that he thought for a fragment of a second that it was old, sick, even dying. That was his first thought. And then he realized how much ground it was covering as it approached, mud and foul water splashing up from its hooves as it ran, and he realized how wrong he had been in thinking it slow. Thirty feet away from them the Beast slowed, and stopped, with a grunt. Its flanks were steaming. It bellowed, in triumph, and in challenge. There were broken spears, and shattered swords, and rusted

knives, bristling from its sides and back. The yellow
flare light glinted in its red eyes, and on its tusks,
and its hooves.

It lowered its massive head. It was some kind of
boar, thought Richard, and then realized that that
had to be nonsense: no boar could be so huge. It was
the size of an ox, of a bull elephant, of a lifetime. It
stared at them, and it paused for a hundred years,
which transpired in a dozen heartbeats.

Hunter knelt, in one fluid motion, and pulled up
the spear from the Fleet Marsh, which released it
with a sucking noise. And, in a voice that was pure
joy, she said, "Yes. At last."

She had forgotten them all; forgotten Richard
down in the mud, and the marquis and his foolish
crossbow, and the world. She was delighted and
transported, in a perfect place, the world she lived
for. Her world contained two things: Hunter, and
the Beast. The Beast knew that too. It was the perfect
match, the hunter, and the hunted. And who was
who, and which was which, only time would reveal;
time and the dance.

The Beast charged.

Hunter waited until she could see the white spittle
dripping from its mouth, and as it lowered its head
she stabbed up with the spear; but, as she tried to
sink the spear into its side, she understood that she
had moved just a fraction of a second too late, and
the spear went tumbling out of her numbed hands,
and a tusk sharper than the sharpest razor blade
opened her side. And as she fell beneath its monstrous weight, she felt its sharp hooves crushing
down on her arm, and her hip, and her ribs. And
then it was gone, vanished back into the darkness,
and the dance was done.

* * *

Mr. Croup was more relieved than he would have admitted to be through the labyrinth. But he and Mr. Vandemar were through it, unharmed, as was their prey. There was a rock face in front of them, an oaken double door set in the rock face, and an oval mirror set in the right-hand door.

Mr. Croup touched the mirror with one grimy hand. The surface of the mirror clouded at his touch, seethed for a moment, bubbling and roiling like a vat of boiling quicksilver, and then was still. The Angel Islington looked out at them. Mr. Croup cleared his throat. "Good morning, sir. It is us, and we have the young lady you sent us to fetch for you."

"And the key?" The angel's gentle voice seemed to come from all around them.

"Hanging around her swanlike neck," said Mr. Croup, a little more anxiously than he intended to.

"Then enter," said the angel. The oak doors swung open at his words, and they went in.

It had all happened so fast. The Beast had come out of the darkness, Hunter had snatched the spear, and it had charged her and disappeared back into the darkness.

Richard strained to hear the Beast. He could hear nothing but, somewhere close to him, the slow *drip, drip* of water, and the high, maddening whine of mosquitoes. Hunter lay on her back in the mud. One arm was twisted at a peculiar angle. He crawled toward her, through the mire. "Hunter?" he whispered. "Can you hear me?"

There was a pause. And then, a whisper so faint he thought for a moment he had imagined it, "Yes."

The marquis was still some yards away, standing stock-still beside a wall. Now he called out, "Richard—stay where you are. The creature's just biding its time. It'll be back."

Richard ignored him. He spoke to Hunter. "Are you . . ." he paused. It seemed such a stupid thing to say. He said it anyway. "Are you going to be all right?" She laughed, then, with blood-flecked lips, and shook her head. "Are there any medical people down here?" he asked the marquis.

"Not in the sense you're thinking of. We have some healers, a handful of leeches and chirurgeons . . ."

Hunter coughed, then, and winced. Bright red, arterial blood trickled from the corner of her mouth. The marquis edged a little closer. "Do you keep your life hidden anywhere, Hunter?" he asked.

"I'm a hunter," she whispered, disdainfully. "We don't go in for that kind of thing . . ." She pulled air into her lungs with an effort, then exhaled, as if the simple effort of breathing were becoming too much for her. "Richard, have you ever used a spear?"

"No."

"Take it," she whispered.

"But . . ."

"Do it." Her voice was low and urgent. "Pick it up. Hold it at the blunt end."

Richard picked up the fallen spear. He held it at the blunt end. "I knew that part," he told her.

A glimmer of a smile breathed across her face. "I know."

"Look," said Richard, feeling, not for the first time, like the only sane person in a madhouse. "Why don't we just stay very quiet. Maybe it'll go away. We'll try to get you some help." And, not for the

first time, the person he was talking to ignored him
utterly.

"I did a bad thing, Richard Mayhew," she whispered, sadly. "I did a very bad thing. Because I
wanted to be the one to kill the Beast. Because I
needed the spear." And then, impossibly, she began
to haul herself to her feet. Richard had not realized
how badly she had been injured; nor could he now
imagine what pain she must be in: he could see her
right arm hanging uselessly, a white shard of bone
protruding horribly from the skin. Blood ran from a
cut in her side. Her rib cage looked *wrong*.

"Stop it," he hissed, futilely. "Get down."

With her left hand she pulled a knife from her belt,
put it into her right hand, closed the nerveless fingers around the hilt. "I did a bad thing," she repeated. "And now I make amends."

She began humming, then. Humming high and
humming low, until she found the note that made
the walls and the pipes and the room reverberate,
and she hummed that note until it felt like the entire
labyrinth must be echoing to her hum. And then,
sucking the air into her shattered rib cage, she
shouted, "Hey. Big boy? Where are you?" There
came no reply. No noise but the low drip of water.
Even the mosquitoes were quiet.

"Maybe it's . . . gone away," said Richard, grip-
ping the spear so tightly that it hurt his hands.

"I doubt it," muttered the marquis.

"Come on, you bastard," Hunter screamed. "Are
you scared?"

There was a deep bellow from in front of them,
and the Beast came out of the dark, and it charged
once more. This time there could be no room for

mistakes. "The dance," whispered Hunter. "The
dance is not yet over."

As the Beast came toward her, its horns lowered,
she shouted, "Now—Richard. Strike! Under and up!
Now!" before the Beast hit her and her words turned
into a wordless scream.

Richard saw the Beast come out from the darkness, into the light of the flare. It all happened very
slowly. It was like a dream. It was like all his
dreams. The Beast was so close he could smell the
shit-and-blood animal stench of it, so close he could
feel its warmth. And Richard stabbed with the spear,
as hard as he could, pushing up into its side and
letting it sink in.

A bellow, then, or a roar, of anguish, and hatred,
and pain. And then silence.

He could hear his heart, thudding in his ears, and
he could hear water dripping. The mosquitoes began
to whine once more. He realized he was still holding
tight to the haft of the spear, although the blade of
it was buried deep within the body of the immobile
Beast. He let go of it, and staggered around the
beast, looking for Hunter. She was trapped beneath
the Beast. It occurred to him that if he moved her,
pulling her out from under it, he might cause her
death, so instead he pushed, as hard as he could,
against the warm dead flanks of the Beast, trying to
move it. It was like trying to push-start a Sherman
tank, but eventually, awkwardly, he tumbled it half-
off her.

Hunter lay on her back, staring up at the darkness
above them. Her eyes were open, and unfocussed,
and Richard knew, somehow, that they saw nothing
at all. "Hunter?" he said.

"I'm still here, Richard Mayhew." Her voice

sounded almost detached. She made no effort to find him with her eyes, no effort to focus. "Is it dead?"

"I think so. It's not moving."

And then she laughed; it was a strange sort of laugh, as if she had just heard the funniest joke that ever the world told a hunter. And, between her spasms of laughter, and the wet, racking coughs that interrupted them, she shared the joke with him. "You killed the Beast," she said. "So now you're the greatest hunter in London Below. The Warrior . . ." And then she stopped laughing. "I can't feel my hands. Take my right hand." Richard fumbled under the Beast's body, and wrapped his hand around Hunter's chill fingers. They felt so small, suddenly. "Is there still a knife in my hand?" she whispered.

"Yes." He could feel it, cold and sticky.

"Take the knife. She's yours."

"I don't want your . . ."

"Take her." He pried the knife free from her fingers. "She's yours now," whispered Hunter. Nothing was moving, save her lips; and her eyes were clouding. "She's always looked after me. Clean my blood off her, though . . . mustn't rust the blade . . . a hunter always looks after her weapons." She gulped air. "Now . . . touch the Beast's blood . . . to your eyes and tongue . . ."

Richard was not sure that he had heard her correctly, nor that he believed what he had heard. "What?"

Richard had not noticed the marquis approach, but now he spoke intently into Richard's ear. "Do it, Richard. She's right. It'll get you through the labyrinth. Do it."

Richard put his hand down to the spear, ran it up the haft until he felt the Beast's hide and the warm

stickiness of the Beast's blood. Feeling slightly foolish, he touched his hand to his tongue, tasting the
salt of the creature's blood: it did not, to his surprise,
revolt him. It tasted utterly natural, like tasting an
ocean. He touched his bloody fingers to his eyes,
where the blood stang like sweat.

Then, "I did it," he told her.

"That's good," whispered Hunter. She said nothing more.

The marquis de Carabas reached out his hand and
closed her eyes. Richard wiped Hunter's knife on his
shirt. It was what she had told him to do. It saved
having to think.

"Better get a move on," said the marquis, standing
up.

"We can't just leave her here."

"We can. We can come back for the body later."

Richard polished the blade as hard as he could on
his shirt. He was crying, now, but he had not noticed. "And if there isn't any later?"

"Then we'll just have to hope that someone dis-
poses of all our remains. Including the Lady Door's.
And she must be getting tired of waiting for us."
Richard looked down. He wiped the last of Hunter's
blood off her knife, and put it through his belt. Then
he nodded. "You go," said de Carabas. "I'll follow
as fast as I can."

Richard hesitated; and then, as best he could, he
ran.

Perhaps it was the Beast's blood that did it; he
certainly had no other explanation. Whatever the
reason, he ran straight and true through the labyrinth, which no longer held any mysteries for him.
He felt that he knew every twist, every path, every

alley and lane and tunnel of it. He ran, stumbling and falling, and still running, exhausted, through the labyrinth, his blood pounding in his temples. A rhyme coursed through his head, as he ran, pounding and echoing to the rhythm of his feet. It was something he had heard as a child.

> *This aye night, this aye night*
> *Every night and all*
> *Fire and fleet and candlelight*
> *And Christ receive thy soul.*

The words went around and around, dirgelike, in his head. *Fire and fleet and candlelight . . .*

At the end of the labyrinth was a sheer granite cliff, and set in the cliff were high wooden double doors. There was an oval mirror hanging on one of the doors. The doors were closed. He touched the wood, and the door opened, silently, to his touch.

Richard went inside.

SEVENTEEN

RICHARD FOLLOWED THE PATH BETWEEN the burning candles, which led him through the angel's vault to the Great Hall. He recognized his surroundings: this was where they had drunk Islington's wine: an octagon of iron pillars supporting the stone roof above them, the huge black stone and metal door, the old wooden table, the candles.

Door was chained up, spread-eagled between two pillars beside the flint and silver door. She stared at him as he came in, her odd-colored pixie eyes wide and scared. The Angel Islington, standing beside her, turned and smiled at Richard as he entered. That was the most chilling thing of all: the gentle compassion, the sweetness of that smile.

"Come in, Richard Mayhew. Come in," said the Angel Islington. "Dear me. You do look a mess." There was honest concern in its voice. Richard hesitated. "Please." The angel gestured, curling a white forefinger, urging him further in. "I think we all know each other. You know the Lady Door, of course, and my associates, Mister Croup, Mister Vandemar." Richard turned. Croup and Vandemar were standing on each side of him. Mr. Vandemar smiled at him. Mr. Croup did not. "I was hoping you would show up," continued the angel. It tipped its head on one side, and asked, "By the bye, where is Hunter?"

"She's dead," said Richard. He heard Door gasp.

"Oh. The poor dear," said Islington. It shook its head sadly, obviously regretting the senseless loss of human life, the frailty of all mortals born to suffer and to die.

"Still," said Mr. Croup chirpily. "Can't make an omelette without killing a few people."

Richard ignored them, as best he could. "Door? Are you all right?"

"More or less, thanks. So far." Her lower lip was swollen, and there was a bruise on her cheek.

"I am afraid," said Islington, "that Miss Door was proving a little intransigent. I was just discussing having Mister Croup and Mister Vandemar . . ." It paused. There were obviously some things it found distasteful actually to say.

"Torture her," suggested Mr. Vandemar, helpfully.

"We are," said Mr. Croup, "after all, famed across the entirety of creation for our skill in the excruciatory arts."

"Good at hurting people," clarified Mr. Vandemar.

The angel continued, staring intently at Richard as it spoke, as if it had heard neither of them. "But then, Miss Door does not strike me as someone who will easily change her mind."

"Give us time enough," said Mr. Croup. "We'd break her."

"Into little wet pieces," said Mr. Vandemar.

Islington shook his head and smiled indulgently

at this display of enthusiasm. "No time," it said to
Richard, "no time. However, she does strike me as
someone who would indeed act to end the pain and
suffering of a friend, a fellow mortal, such as yourself, Richard . . ." Mr. Croup hit Richard in the stomach, then: a vicious rabbit punch to the gut, and
Richard doubled up. He felt Mr. Vandemar's fingers
on the back of his neck, pulling him back to a standing position.

"But it's wrong," said Door.

Islington looked thoughtful. "Wrong?" it said,
puzzled and amused.

Mr. Croup pulled Richard's head close to his, and
smiled his graveyard smile. "He's traveled so far beyond right and wrong he couldn't see them with a
telescope on a nice clear night," he confided. "Now
Mister Vandemar, if you'll do the honors?"

Mr. Vandemar took Richard's left hand in his. He
took Richard's little finger between his huge fingers
and bent it back until it broke. Richard cried out.

The angel turned, slowly. It seemed distracted by
something. It blinked its pearl gray eyes. "There's
someone else out there. Mister Croup?" There was
a dark shimmer where Mr. Croup had been, and he
was there no longer.

The marquis de Carabas was flattened against the
side of the red granite cliff, staring at the oak doors
that led into Islington's dwelling.

Plans and plots whirled through his head, each
scheme fizzling out uselessly as he imagined it. He
had thought he would have known what to do when
he got to this point, and he was discovering, to his
disgust, that he had absolutely no idea. There were
no more favors to call in, no levers to press or but-

tons to push, so he scrutinized the doors and wondered whether they were guarded, whether the angel would know if they were opened. There had to be an obvious solution he was missing, if only he thought hard enough: perhaps something would occur to him. At least, he thought, slightly cheered, he had surprise on his side.

That was until he felt the cold point of a sharp knife placed against his throat, and he heard Mr. Croup's oily voice whispering in his ear. "I already killed you once today," it was saying. "What does it take to teach some people?"

Richard was manacled and chained between a pair of iron pillars when Mr. Croup returned, prodding the marquis de Carabas with his knife. The angel looked at the marquis, with disappointment on its face, then, gently, it shook its beautiful head. "You told me he was dead," it said.

"He is," said Mr. Vandemar.

"He was," corrected Mr. Croup.

The angel's voice was a fraction less gentle and less caring. "I will not be lied to," it said.

"We don't lie," said Mr. Croup, affronted.

"Do," said Mr. Vandemar.

Mr. Croup ran a grimy hand through his filthy orange hair, in exasperation. "Indeed we do. But not this time."

The pain in Richard's hand showed no indication of subsiding. "How can you behave like this?" he asked, angrily. "You're an angel."

"What did I tell you, Richard?" asked the marquis, drily.

Richard thought. "You said, Lucifer was an angel."

Islington smiled superciliously. "Lucifer?" it said. "Lucifer was an idiot. It wound up lord and master of nothing at all."

The marquis grinned. "And you wound up lord and master of two thugs and a roomful of candles?"

The angel licked its lips. "They told me it was my punishment for Atlantis. I told them there was nothing more I could have done. The whole affair was . . ." it paused, as if it were hunting for the correct word. And then it said, with regret, "Unfortunate."

"But millions of people were killed," said Door.

Islington clasped its hands in front of its chest, as if it were posing for a Christmas card. "These things happen," it explained, reasonably.

"Of course they do," said the marquis, mildly, the irony implicit in his words, not in his voice. "Cities sink every day. And you had nothing to do with it?"

It was as if the lid had been pulled off something dark and writhing: a place of derangement and fury and utter viciousness; and, in a time of scary things, it was the most frightening thing Richard had seen. The angel's serene beauty cracked; its eyes flashed; and it screamed at them, crazy-scary and uncontrolled, utterly certain in its righteousness, *"They deserved it."*

There was a moment of silence. And then the angel lowered its head, and sighed, and raised its head, and said, very quietly and with deep regret, "Just one of those things." Then it pointed to the marquis. "Chain him up," it said.

Croup and Vandemar fastened manacles around the marquis's wrists, and chained the manacles securely to the pillars beside Richard. The angel had turned its attention back to Door. It walked over to her, reached out its hand, placed it beneath her pointed chin, and raised her head, to stare into her eyes. "Your family," it said, gently. "You come from a very unusual family. Quite remarkable."

"Then why did you have us killed?"

"Not all of you," it said. Richard thought it was talking about Door, but then it said, "There was always the possibility that you might not have . . . worked out as well as you did." It released her chin and stroked her face with long, white fingers, and it said, "Your family can open doors. They can create doors where there were no doors. They can unlock doors that are locked. Open doors that were never meant to be opened." It ran its fingers down her neck, gently, as if it were caressing her, then closed its hand on the key about her neck. "When I was sentenced here, they gave me the door to my prison. And they took the key to the door, and put it down here too. An exquisite form of torture." It tugged, gently, on the chain, pulling it out from under Door's layers of silk and cotton and lace, revealing the silver key; and then it ran its fingers over the key, as if it were exploring her secret places.

Richard knew, then. "The Black Friars were keeping the key safe from you," he said.

Islington let go of the key. Door was chained up beside the door made of black flint and tarnished silver. The angel walked to it, and placed a hand on it, white against the blackness of the door. "From me," agreed Islington. "A key. A door. An opener of the door. There must be the three, you see: a particularly refined sort of joke. The idea being that when they decided I had earned forgiveness and my freedom, they would send me an opener, and give me the key. I just decided to take matters into my own hands, and will be leaving a little early."

It turned back to Door. Once more it caressed the key. Then it closed its hand about the key and tugged, hard. The chain snapped. Door winced. "I spoke first to your father, Door," the angel continued. "He worried about the Underside. He wanted to unite London Below, to unite the baronies and fiefdoms—perhaps even to forge some kind of bond with London Above. I told him I would help him, if he would help me. Then I told him the nature of the help I needed, and he laughed at me." It repeated the words, as if it still found them impossible to believe. "He laughed. At me."

Door shook her head. "You killed him because he turned you down?"

"I didn't kill him," Islington corrected her, gently. "I had him killed."

"But he told me I could trust you. He told me to come here. In his journal."

Mr. Croup began to giggle. "He didn't," he said. "He never did. That was us. What was it he actually said, Mister Vandemar?"

"Door, child, fear Islington," said Mr. Vandemar, with her father's voice. The voice was exact. "Islington's got to be behind all this. It's dangerous, Door—keep away from it—"

Islington caressed her cheek, with the key. "I thought my version would get you here a little faster."

"We took the journal," said Mr. Croup. "We fixed it, and we returned it."

"Where does the door lead to?" called Richard.

"Home," said the angel.

"Heaven?"

And Islington said nothing, but it smiled.

"So, you figure they won't notice you're back?" sneered the marquis. "Just, 'Oh look, there's another angel, here, grab a harp and on with the hosannas'?"

Islington's gray eyes were bright. "Not for me the smooth agonies of adulation, of hymns and halos and self-satisfied prayers," it said. "I have . . . my own agenda."

"Well, now you've got the key," said Door.

"And I have you," said the angel. "You're the opener. Without you the key is useless. Open the door for me."

"You killed her family," said Richard. "You've had her hunted through London Below. Now you want her to open a door for you so you can single-handedly invade Heaven? You're not much of a judge of character, are you? She'll never do it."

The angel looked at him then, with eyes older than the Milky Way. Then it said, "Ah me," and turned its back, as if it were ill-prepared to watch the unpleasantness that was about to occur.

"Hurt him some more, Mister Vandemar," said Mr. Croup. "Cut off his ear."

Mr. Vandemar raised his hand. It was empty. He jerked his arm, almost imperceptibly, and now he was holding a knife. "Told you one day you'd find out what your own liver tastes like," he said to Richard. "Today's going to be your lucky day." He slid the knife blade gently beneath Richard's earlobe. Richard felt no pain—perhaps, he thought, he had felt too much pain already that day, perhaps the blade was too sharp to hurt. But he felt the warm blood drip, wetly, from his ear down his neck. Door was watching him, and her elfin face and huge opal-colored eyes filled his vision. He tried to send her mental messages. *Hold out. Don't let them make you do this. I'll be fine.* Then Mr. Vandemar put a little pressure on the knife, and Richard bit back a scream. He tried to stop his face from grimacing, but another jab from the blade jerked a grimace and a moan from him.

"Stop them," said Door. "I'll open your door."

Islington gestured, curtly, and Mr. Vandemar sighed piteously and put his knife away. The warm blood dripped down Richard's neck and pooled and puddled in the hollow of his clavicle. Mr. Croup walked over to Door and unlocked the right-hand manacle. She stood there, rubbing her wrist, framed by the pillars. She was still chained to the pillar on the left, but she now had a certain amount of freedom of movement. She put her hand out for the key. "Remember," said Islington. "I have your friends."

Door looked at him with utter contempt, every inch Lord Portico's oldest daughter. "Give me the key," she said. The angel passed her the silver key.

"Door," called Richard. "Don't do it. Don't set it free. We don't matter."

"Actually," said the marquis, "I matter very much. But I have to agree. Don't do it."

She looked from Richard to the marquis, her eyes lingering on their manacled hands, on the heavy chains that bound them to the black iron pillars. She looked very vulnerable; and then she turned away, and walked to the limit of her own chain, until she stood in front of the black door made of flint and tarnished silver. There was no keyhole. She put the palm of her right hand on the door, and closed her eyes, let the door tell her where it opened, what it could do, finding those places inside herself that corresponded with the door. When she pulled her hand away, there was a keyhole that had not been there before. A white light lanced out from behind the keyhole, sharp and bright as a laser in the candlelit darkness of the hall.

The girl pushed the silver key into the keyhole. There was a pause, and then she turned it in the lock. Something went click, and there was a chiming noise, and suddenly the door was framed in light. "When I am gone," said the angel, very quietly, to Mr. Croup and Mr. Vandemar, with charm, and with kindness, and with compassion, "kill them all, howsoever you wish." It turned back to the door, which Door was pulling open: it was opening slowly, as if there was great resistance. She was sweating.

"So your employer's leaving," said the marquis to Mr. Croup. "I hope you've both been paid in full."

Croup peered at the marquis, and said, "What?"

"Well," said Richard, wondering what the marquis was trying to do, but willing to play along, "you don't think you're ever going to see him again, do you?"

Mr. Vandemar blinked, slowly, like an antique camera, and said, "What?"

Mr. Croup scratched his chin. "The corpses-to-be have a point," he said to Mr. Vandemar. He walked toward the angel, who stood, arms folded, in front of the door. "Sir? It might be wise for you to settle up, before you commence the next stage of your travels."

The angel turned, and looked down at him as if he were less important than the least speck of dirt. Then it turned away. Richard wondered what it was contemplating. "It is of no matter now," said the angel. "Soon, all the rewards your revolting little minds can conceive of will be yours. When I have my throne."

"Jam tomorrow, eh?" said Richard.

"Don't like jam," said Mr. Vandemar. "Makes me belch."

Mr. Croup waggled a finger at Mr. Vandemar. "He's welching out on us," he said. "You don't welch on Mister Croup and Mister Vandemar, me bucko. We collect our debts."

Mr. Vandemar walked over to where Mr. Croup was standing. "In full," he said.

"With interest," barked Mr. Croup.

"And meat hooks," said Mr. Vandemar.

"From Heaven?" called Richard, from behind them. Mr. Croup and Mr. Vandemar walked toward the contemplative angel. "Hey!" said Mr. Croup.

The door had opened, only a crack, but it was open. Light flooded through the crack in the door. The angel took a step forward. It was as if it were dreaming with its eyes wide open. The light from the crack in the door bathed its face, and it drank it in like wine. "Have no fear," it said. "For when the vastness of creation is mine, and they gather about my throne to sing hosannas to my name, I shall reward the worthy and cast down those who are hateful in my sight."

With an effort, Door wrenched the black door fully open. The view through the door was blinding in its intensity: a swirling maelstrom of color and light. Richard squinted his eyes, and turned his head away from the glare, all vicious orange and retinal purple. *Is that what Heaven looks like? It seems more like Hell.*

And then he felt the wind.

A candle flew past his head, and vanished

through the door. And then another. And then the
air was filled with candles, all spinning and tumbling through the air, heading for the light. It was
as if the whole room were being sucked through the
door. It was more than a wind, though. Richard
knew that. His wrists began to hurt where they were
manacled—it was as if, suddenly, he weighed twice
as much as he ever had before. And then his perspective changed. The view through the doorway—
it was looking *down*: it was not merely the wind that
was pulling everything toward the door. It was
gravity. The wind was only the air in the hall being
sucked into the place on the other side of the door.
He wondered what was on the other side of the
door—the surface of a star, perhaps, or the event
horizon of a black hole, or something he could not
even imagine.

Islington grabbed hold of the pillar beside the
door, and held on desperately. "That's not Heaven,"
it shouted, gray eyes flashing, spittle on its perfect
lips. "You mad little witch. What have you done?"

Door was clutching the chains that held her to the
black pillar, white-knuckled. There was triumph in
her eyes. Mr. Vandemar had caught hold of a table
leg, while Mr. Croup, in his turn, had caught hold
of Mr. Vandemar. "It wasn't the real key," said
Door, triumphantly, over the roar of the wind. "That
was just a copy of the key I had Hammersmith make
in the market."

"But it opened the door," screamed the angel.

"No," said the girl with the opal eyes, distantly.
"I opened a door. As far and hard away as I could,
I opened a door."

There was no longer any trace of kindness or compassion on the angel's face; only hatred, pure and

honest and cold. "I will kill you," it told her.

"Like you killed my family? I don't think you're going to kill anyone anymore."

The angel was hanging onto the pillar with pale fingers, but its body was at a ninety-degree angle to the room, and was most of the way through the door. It looked both comical and dreadful. It licked its lips. "Stop it," it pleaded. "Close the door. I'll tell you where your sister is . . . She's still alive . . ."

Door flinched.

And Islington was sucked through the door, a tiny, plummeting figure, shrinking as it tumbled into the blinding gulf beyond. The pull was getting stronger. Richard prayed that his chains and manacles would hold: he could feel himself being sucked toward the opening, and, from the corner of his eye, he could see the marquis dangling from his chains, like a string-puppet being sucked up by a vacuum cleaner.

The table, the leg of which Mr. Vandemar was holding tightly, flew through the air and jammed in the open doorway. Mr. Croup and Mr. Vandemar were dangling out of the door. Mr. Croup, who was clinging, quite literally, to Mr. Vandemar's coattails, took a deep breath and began slowly to clamber, hand over hand, up Mr. Vandemar's back. The table creaked. Mr. Croup looked at Door, and he smiled like a fox. "*I* killed your family," said Mr. Croup. "Not him. And now I'm—finally—going to finish the . . ."

It was at that moment that the fabric of Mr. Vandemar's dark suit gave way. Mr. Croup tumbled, screaming, into the void, clutching a long strip of black material. Mr. Vandemar looked down at the flailing figure of Mr. Croup as it fell away from them. He, too, looked over at Door, but there was no menace in his gaze. He shrugged, as best as one can shrug while holding on to a table leg for dear life, and then he said, mildly, "Bye-bye," and let go of the table leg.

Silently he plunged through the door, into the light, shrinking as he fell, heading for the tiny figure of Mr. Croup. Soon the two shapes merged into one little blob of blackness in a sea of churning purple and white and orange light, and then the black dot, too, was gone. It made some sort of sense, Richard thought: they were a team, after all.

It was getting harder to breathe. Richard felt giddy and light-headed. The table in the doorway splintered and was sucked away through the door. One of Richard's manacles popped open, and his right arm whipped free. He grabbed the chain holding the left hand, and gripped it as tightly as he could, grateful that the broken finger was on the hand that was still in the manacle; even so, red and blue flashes of pain were shooting up his left arm. He could hear himself, distantly, shouting in pain.

He could not breathe. White blotches of light exploded behind his eyes. He could feel the chain beginning to give way . . .

The sound of the black door slamming closed filled his whole world. Richard fell violently back against the cold iron pillar, and slumped to the floor. There was silence, then, in the hall—silence, and utter darkness, in the Great Hall under the earth. Richard closed his eyes: it made no difference to the darkness, and he opened his eyes once more.

The hush was broken by the marquis's voice, asking, drily, "So where did you send them?"

And then Richard heard a girl's voice talking. He

knew it had to be Door's, but it sounded so young, like the voice of a tiny child at bedtime, at the end of a long and exhausting day. "I don't know . . . a long way away. I'm . . . very tired now. I . . ."

"Door," said the marquis. "Snap out of it." It was good that he was saying it, thought Richard, somebody had to, and Richard could no longer remember how to talk. There was a click, then, in the darkness: the sound of a manacle opening, followed by the sound of chains falling against a metal pillar. Then the sound of a match being struck. A candle was lit: it burned weakly, and flickered in the thin air. *Fire and fleet and candlelight*, thought Richard, and he could not remember why.

Door walked, unsteadily, to the marquis, holding her candle. She reached out a hand, touched his chains, and his manacles clicked open. He rubbed his wrists. Then she walked over to Richard, and touched his single remaining manacle. It fell open. Door sighed, then, and sat down beside him. He reached out his good arm and cradled her head, holding her close to him. He rocked her slowly back and forth, crooning a wordless lullaby. It was cold, cold, there in the angel's empty hall; but soon the warmth of unconsciousness reached out and enveloped them both.

The marquis de Carabas watched the sleeping children. The idea of sleep—of returning, even for a short time, to a state so horribly close to death—scared him more than he would have ever believed. But, eventually, even he put his head down on his arm, and closed his eyes.

And then there were none.

EIGHTEEN

THE LADY SERPENTINE, WHO WAS, BUT for Olympia, the oldest of the Seven Sisters, walked through the labyrinth beyond Down Street, her head held high, her white leather boots squashing through the dank mud. This was, after all, the furthest she had been from her house in over a hundred years. Her wasp-waisted majordomo, dressed from head to foot all in black leather, walked ahead of her, holding a large carriage-lamp. Two of Serpentine's other women, similarly dressed, walked behind her at a respectful distance.

The ripped lace train of Serpentine's dress dragged in the mire behind her, but she paid it no mind. She saw something glinting in the lamplight ahead of them, and, beside it, a dark and bulky shape.

"There it is," she said.

The two women who had been walking behind her hurried forward, splashing through the marsh, and as Serpentine's butler approached, bringing with her a swinging circle of warm light, the shape resolved into objects. The light had been glinting from a long bronze spear. Hunter's body, twisted and bloody and wretched, lay on its back, half-buried in the mud, in a large pool of scarlet gore, its legs trapped beneath the body of an enormous boar-like creature. Her eyes were closed.

Serpentine's women hauled the body out from under the Beast, and lay it in the mud. Serpentine knelt in the wet mire and ran one finger down Hunter's cold cheek, until it reached her blood-blackened lips, where she let it linger for some moments. Then she stood up. "Bring the spear," said Serpentine.

One of the women picked up Hunter's body; the other pulled the spear from the carcass of the Beast and put it over her shoulder. And then the four figures turned, and went back the way they had come; a silent procession deep beneath the world. The lamplight flickered on Serpentine's ravaged face as she walked; but it revealed no emotion of any kind, neither happy nor sad.

NINETEEN

FOR A MOMENT, UPON WAKING, HE HAD NO idea at all who he was. It was a tremendously lib-erating feeling, as if he were free to be whatever he wanted to be: he could be anyone at all—able to try on any identity; he could be a man or a woman, a rat or a bird, a monster or a god. And then someone made a rustling noise, and he woke up the rest of the way, and in waking he found that he was Rich-ard Mayhew, whoever that was, whatever that meant. He was Richard Mayhew, and he did not know where he was.

There was crisp linen pressed against his face. He hurt all over; in some places—the little finger on his left hand, for example—more than others.

Someone was nearby. Richard could hear breathing, and the hesitant rustling noises of a per-son in the same room he was in, trying to be discreet. Richard raised his head, and discovered, in the rais-ing, more places that hurt. Some of them hurt very badly. Far away—rooms and rooms away—people were singing. The song was so distant and quiet he knew he would lose it if he opened his eyes: a deep, melodious chanting . . .

He opened his eyes. The room was small, and
dimly lit. He was on a low bed, and the rustling
sound he had heard was made by a cowled figure
in a black robe, with his back to Richard. The black
figure was dusting the room, with an incongruously
brightly colored feather duster. "Where am I?"
asked Richard.

The black figure nearly dropped its feather duster,
then it turned, revealing a very nervous, thin, dark
brown face. "Would you like some water?" the
Black Friar asked, in the manner of one who has
been told that if the patient wakes up, he is to be
asked if he would like some water, and has been
repeating it to himself over and over for the last
forty minutes to make sure that he didn't forget.

"I . . ." and Richard realized that he was most
dreadfully thirsty. He sat up in the bed. "Yes, I
would. Thank you very much." The friar poured
some water from a battered metal jug into a battered
metal cup and passed it to Richard. Richard sipped
the water slowly, restraining the impulse to gulp it
down. It was crystal cold and clear and tasted like
diamonds and ice.

Richard looked down at himself. His clothes were
gone. He had been dressed in a long robe, like one
of the Black Friars' habits, but gray. His broken finger had been splinted and neatly bandaged. He
raised a finger to his ear; there was a bandage on it,
and what felt like stitches beneath the bandage.
"You're one of the Black Friars," said Richard.

"Yes, sir."

"How did I get here? Where are my friends?"

The friar pointed to the corridor, wordlessly and
nervously. Richard got out of the bed. He checked
under his gray robe: he was naked. His torso and

legs were covered in a variety of deep indigo and
purple bruises, all of which seemed to have been
rubbed with some kind of ointment: it smelt like
cough syrup and buttered toast. His right knee was
bandaged. He wondered where his clothes were.
There were sandals beside the bed, and he put them
on, then he walked out into the corridor. The abbot
was coming down the passage toward him, holding
onto the arm of Brother Fuliginous, his blind eyes
pearlescent in the darkness beneath his cowl.

"You are awake, then, Richard Mayhew," said the
abbot. "How do you feel?"

Richard made a face. "My hand . . ."

"We set your finger. It had been broken. We
tended your bruises and your cuts. And you needed
rest, which we gave you."

"Where's Door? And the marquis? How did we
get here?"

"I had you brought here," said the abbot. The two
friars began to walk down the corridor, and Richard
walked with them.

"Hunter," said Richard. "Did you bring back her
body?"

The abbot shook his head. "There was no body.
Only the Beast."

"Ah, um. My clothes . . ." They came to the door
of a cell, much like the one Richard had woken in.
Door was sitting on the edge of her bed, reading a
copy of *Mansfield Park* that Richard was certain the
friars had not previously known that they had. She,
too, wore a gray monk's robe, which was much,
much too big for her, almost comically so. She
looked up as they entered. "Hello," she said.
"You've been asleep for ages. How are you feeling?"

"Fine, I think. How are you?"

She smiled. It was not a very convincing smile. "A bit shaky," she admitted. There was a loud rattling in the corridor, and Richard turned to see the marquis de Carabas being wheeled toward them in a rickety and antique wheelchair. The wheelchair was being pushed by a large Black Friar. Richard wondered how the marquis managed to make being pushed around in a wheelchair look like a romantic and swashbuckling thing to do. The marquis honored them with an enormous smile. "Good evening, friends," he said.

"Now," said the abbot, "that you are all here, we must talk."

He led them to a large room, warmed by a roaring scrap wood fire. They arranged themselves around a table. The abbot gestured for them all to sit down. He felt for his chair and sat down in it. Then he sent Brother Fuliginous and Brother Tenebrae (who had been pushing the marquis's wheelchair) out of the room.

"So," said the abbot. "To business. Where is Islington?"

Door shrugged. "As far away as I could send him. Halfway across space and time."

"I see," said the abbot. And then he said, "Good."

"Why didn't you warn us about him?" asked Richard.

"That was not our responsibility."

Richard snorted. "What happens now?" he asked them all.

The abbot said nothing.

"Happens? In what way?" asked Door.

"Well, you wanted to avenge your family. And you have. And you've sent everyone involved off to some distant corner of nowhere. I mean, no one's going to try and kill you anymore, are they?"

"Not for right now," said Door, seriously.

"And you?" Richard asked the marquis de Carabas. "Have you got what you wanted?"

The marquis nodded. "I believe so. My debt to Lord Portico has been paid in full, and the Lady Door owes me a significant favor."

Richard looked to Door. She nodded. "So what about me?" he asked.

"Well," said Door. "We couldn't have done it without you."

"That's not what I meant. What about getting me back home?"

The marquis raised an eyebrow. "Who do you think she is—the Wizard of Oz? We can't send you home. This is your home."

Door said, "I tried to tell you that before, Richard."

"There has to be a way," said Richard, and he slammed his left hand down on the table, hard, for emphasis. It hurt his finger, but he kept his face composed. And then he said, "Ow," but he said it very quietly, because he had gone through much worse.

"Where is the key?" asked the abbot.

Richard inclined his head. "Door," he said.

She shook her pixy head. "I don't have it," she told him. "I slipped it back into your pocket at the last market. When you brought the curry."

Richard opened his mouth, and then he closed it again. Then he opened it and said, "You mean, when I told Croup and Vandemar that I had it, and they were welcome to search me ... I had it?" She nodded. He remembered the hard object in his back pocket, on Down Street; remembered her hugging him on the ship ...

The abbot reached out. His wrinkled brown fingers picked up a small bell from the table, which he shook, summoning Brother Fuliginous. "Bring me the Warrior's trousers," he said. Fuliginous nodded and left.

"I'm no warrior," said Richard.

The Abbot smiled gently. "You killed the Beast," he explained, almost regretfully. "You are the Warrior."

Richard folded his arms, exasperated. "So, after all this, I still don't get to go home, but as a consolation prize I've made it onto some kind of archaic underground honors list?"

The marquis looked unsympathetic. "You can't go back to London Above. A few individuals manage a kind of half-life—you've met Iliaster and Lear. But that's the best you could hope for, and it isn't a good life."

Door reached out a hand, and touched Richard's arm. "I'm sorry," she told him. "But look at all the good you've done. You got the key for us."

"Well," he asked, "what was the point of that? You just forged a new key—" Brother Fuliginous reappeared, carrying Richard's jeans; they were ripped, and covered in mud, and splashed with dried blood, and they stank. The friar handed the trousers to the abbot, who commenced to go through the pockets. Door smiled, sweetly. "I couldn't have had Hammersmith copy it without the original," she reminded him.

The abbot cleared his throat. "You are all very stupid people," he told them, graciously, "and you do not know anything at all." He held up the silver key. It glinted in the firelight. "Richard passed the Ordeal of the Key. He is its master, until he returns it to our keeping. The key has power."

"It's the key to Heaven . . ." said Richard, unsure of what the abbot was getting at, of what point he was trying to make.

The old man's voice was deep and melodious. "The key is the key to all reality. If Richard wants to return to London Above, then the key will take him back to London Above."

"It's that simple?" asked Richard. The old man nodded his blind head, beneath the shadows of his cowl. "Then when could we do this?"

"As soon as you are ready," said the abbot.

The friars had washed and repaired his clothes and returned them to him. Brother Fuliginous led him through the abbey, up a vertiginous series of ladders and steps, up into the bell tower. There was a heavy wooden trapdoor in the top of the tower. Brother Fuliginous unlocked it, and the two men pushed through it and found themselves in a narrow tunnel, thickly cobwebbed, with metal rungs set in the side of one wall. They climbed the rungs, going up for what seemed like thousands of feet, and came out on a dusty Underground station platform.

NIGHTINGALE LANE

said the old signs on the wall. Brother Fuliginous wished Richard well and told him to wait there and he would be collected, and then he clambered down the side of the wall, and he was gone.

Richard sat on the platform for twenty minutes. He wondered what kind of station this was: it seemed neither abandoned, like British Museum, nor real, like Blackfriars: instead it was a ghost-station, an imaginary place, forgotten and strange. He wondered why the marquis had not said good-bye. When Richard had asked Door, she had said that she didn't know, but that maybe good-byes were something else, like comforting people, at which the marquis wasn't much good. Then she told him that she had something in her eye, and she gave him a paper with his instructions on, and she went away.

Something waved from the darkness of the tunnel: something white. It was a handkerchief on a stick. "Hello?" called Richard.

The feather-wrapped roundness of Old Bailey stepped out of the gloom, looking self-conscious and ill at ease. He was waving Richard's handkerchief, and he was sweating. "It's me little flag," he said, pointing to the handkerchief.

"I'm glad it's come in useful."

Old Bailey grinned uneasily. "Right. Just wanted to say. Something I got for you. Here you go." He thrust a hand into a coat pocket and pulled out a long black feather with a blue-purple-green sheen to it; red thread had been wound around the quill end of the feather.

"Um. Well, thanks," said Richard, unsure of what he ought to do with it.

"It's a feather," explained Old Bailey. "And a good one. Memento. Souvenir. Keepsake. And it's free. A gift. Me to you. Bit of a thank-you."

"Yes. Well. Very kind of you."

Richard put it in his pocket. A warm wind blew through the tunnel: a train was coming. "This'll be your train now," said Old Bailey. "I don't take trains, me. Give me a good roof any day." He shook Richard's hand, and fled.

The train pulled in at the station. Its headlights were turned off, and there was nobody standing in the driver's compartment in the front. It came to a full stop: all the carriages were dark, and no doors opened. Richard knocked on the door in front of him, hoping that it was the correct one. The door gaped open, flooding the imaginary station with warm yellow light. Two small, elderly gentlemen holding long, copper-colored bugles stepped off the train and onto the platform. Richard recognized them: Dagvard and Halvard, from Earl's Court; although he could no longer recall, if he had ever known, which gentleman was which. They put their bugles to their lips and performed a ragged, but sincere, fanfare. Richard got onto the train, and they walked in behind him.

The earl was sitting at the end of the carriage, petting the enormous Irish wolfhound. The jester—Tooley, thought Richard, that was his name—stood beside him. Other than that, and the two men-at-arms, the carriage was deserted. "Who is it?" asked the earl.

"It's him, sire," said his jester. "Richard Mayhew. The one who killed the Beast."

"The Warrior?" The Earl scratched his red-gray beard thoughtfully. "Bring him here."

Richard walked down to the earl's chair. The earl eyed him up and down pensively and gave no indication that he remembered ever meeting Richard before. "Thought you'd be taller," said the earl, at length.

"Sorry."

"Well, better get on with it." The old man stood up and addressed the empty car. "Good evening. Here to honor young Mayflower. What was it the bard said?" And then he recited, in a rhythmic alliterative boom, *"Crimson the cuts in the carcass, Fast falls the foe, Dauntless devout defender, Bravest of boys* . . . Not really a boy anymore, though, is he, Tooley?"

"Not particularly, Your Grace."

The earl reached out his hand. "Give me your sword, boy."

Richard put his hand to his belt and pulled out the knife that Hunter had given him. "Will this do?" he asked.

"Yes-yes," said the old man, taking the knife from him.

"Kneel," said Tooley, in a stage whisper, pointing to the train floor. Richard went down on one knee; the earl tapped him gently on each shoulder with the knife. "Arise," he bellowed, "Sir Richard of Maybury. With this knife I do give to you the freedom of the Underside. May you be allowed to walk freely, without let or hindrance . . . and so on and so forth . . . et cetera . . . blah blah blah," he trailed off, vaguely.

"Thanks," said Richard. "It's Mayhew, actually." But the train was coming to a stop.

"This is where you get off," said the earl. He gave Richard his knife—Hunter's knife—once more, patted him on the back, and pointed toward the door.

The place that Richard got off was not an Underground station. It was above ground, and it reminded Richard a little of St. Pancras Station—there was something similarly oversized and mock-Gothic about the architecture. But there was also a *wrongness* that somehow marked it as part of London Below. The light was that strange, strained gray one only sees shortly before dawn and for a few moments after sunset, the times when the world washes out into gloom, and color and distance become impossible to judge.

There was a man sitting on a wooden bench, watching him; and Richard approached him, cautiously, unable to tell, in the gloaming, who the man was, whether it was someone he had met before. Richard was still holding Hunter's knife—his knife—and now he gripped the hilt more tightly, for reassurance. The man looked up as Richard approached, and he sprang to his feet. He tugged at his forelock, something Richard had previously only seen done on television adaptations of classic novels. He looked both comical and unpleasant. Richard recognised the man as the Lord Rat-speaker.

"Well-well. Yes-yes," said the rat-speaker, agitatedly, beginning in mid-sentence. "Just to say, the girl Anaesthesia. No hard feelings. The rats are your friends, still. And the rat-speakers. You come to us. We'll do you all right."

"Thanks," said Richard. *Anaesthesia will take him,* he thought. *She's expendable.*

The Lord Rat-speaker fumbled on the bench, and presented Richard with a black vinyl zip-up sports bag. It was extremely familiar. "It's all there. Everything. Take a look." Richard opened the bag. All his possessions were in there, including, on top of some neatly folded jeans, his wallet. He zipped the bag up, threw it over his shoulder, and walked away from the man, without a thank-you or a backward glance.

Richard walked out of the station and down some gray stone steps.

All was silent. All was empty. Dead autumn

leaves blew across an open court, a flurry of yellow and ochre and brown, a sudden burst of muted color in the dim light. Richard crossed the court and walked down some steps into an underpass. There was a fluttering in the half-dark, and, warily, he turned. There were about a dozen of them, in the corridor behind him, and they slipped toward him almost silently, just a rustle of dark velvet, and, here and there, the clink of silver jewelery. The rustle of the leaves had been so much louder than these pale women. They watched him with hungry eyes.

He was scared, then. He had the knife, true, but he could no more fight with it than he could jump across the Thames. He hoped that, if they attacked, he might be able to scare them away with it. He could smell honeysuckle, and lily of the valley, and musk.

Lamia edged her way to the front of the Velvets, and stepped forward. Richard raised the knife, nervously, remembering the chilly passion of her embrace, how pleasant it was and how cold. She smiled at him, and inclined her head, sweetly. Then she kissed her fingertips, and blew the kiss toward Richard.

He shivered. Something fluttered in the darkness of the underpass; and when he looked again, there was nothing but shadows.

Through the underpass, and Richard walked up some steps, and found himself at the top of a small grassy hill. It was dawn, and he could just make out details of the countryside around him: almost leafless oak, and ash, and beech trees, readily identifiable by the shapes of their trunks. A wide, clean river meandered gently through the green countryside. As

he looked around, he realized that he was on an island of some kind—two smaller rivers ran into the
larger one, cutting him off on his little hill, from the
mainland. He knew then, without knowing how, but
with total certainty, that he was still in London, but
London as it had been perhaps three thousand years
ago, or more, before ever the first stone of the first
human habitation was laid upon a stone.

He unzipped his bag and put the knife away in it,
beside his wallet. Then he zipped it up again. The sky
was starting to lighten, but the light was odd. It was
younger, somehow, than the sunlight he was familiar
with—purer, perhaps. An orange-red sun rose in the
east, where Docklands would one day be, and Richard watched the dawn breaking over forests and
marshes that he kept thinking of as Greenwich and
Kent and the sea.

"Hello," said Door. He had not seen her approach.
She was wearing different clothes beneath her battered brown leather jacket: they were still layered
and ripped and patched, though, in taffeta and lace
and silk and brocade. Her short red hair shone in
the dawn like burnished copper.

"Hello," said Richard. She stood beside him and
twined her small fingers into his right hand, the
hand that was holding the sports bag. "Where are
we?" he asked.

"On the awesome and terrible island of Westminster," she told him. It sounded as if she were quoting
from somewhere, but he did not believe he had ever
heard that phrase before. They began to walk together over the long grass, wet and white with melt-
ing frost. Their footprints left a dark green trail in
the grass behind them, showing where they had
come from.

"Look," said Door. "With the angel gone, there's a lot of sorting out to do in London Below. And there's only me to do it. My father wanted to unite London Below . . . I suppose I ought to try to finish what he started." They were walking north, away from the Thames, hand in hand. White seagulls wheeled and called in the sky above them. "Richard, you heard what Islington said to us about keeping my sister alive, just in case. I may not be the only one of my family left. And you've saved my life. More than once." She paused, and then, all in a rush, blurted, "You've been a really good friend to me, Richard. And I've sort of got to like having you around. Please don't go."

He squeezed her hand in his, gently. "Well," he said, "I've sort of got to like having you around, too. But I don't belong in this world. In my London . . . well, the most dangerous thing you ever have to watch out for is a taxi in a bit of a hurry. I like you, too. I like you an awful lot. But I have to go home."

She looked up at him with her odd-colored eyes, green and blue and flame. "Then we won't ever see each other again," she said.

"I suppose we won't."

"Thanks for everything you did," she said, seriously. Then she threw her arms around him, and she squeezed him tightly enough that the bruises on his ribs hurt, and he hugged her back, just as tightly, making all of his bruises complain violently, and he simply didn't care.

"Well," he said, eventually. "It was very nice knowing you." She was blinking hard. He wondered if she were going to tell him again that she had something in her eye. Instead she said, "Are you ready?"

He nodded.

"Have you got the key?"

He put down his bag and rummaged in his back pocket with his good hand. He took out the key and handed it to her. She held it out in front of her, as if it were being inserted in an imaginary door. "Okay," she said. "Just walk. Don't look back."

He began walking down a small hill, away from the blue waters of the Thames. A gray gull swooped past. At the bottom of the hill, he looked back. She stood at the top of the hill, silhouetted by the rising sun. Her cheeks were glistening. The orange sunlight gleamed on the key.

Door turned it, with one decisive motion.

The world went dark, and a low roar filled Richard's head, like the maddened growling of a thousand enraged beasts.

TWENTY

THE WORLD WENT DARK, AND A LOW ROAR filled Richard's head, like the maddened growling of a thousand enraged beasts. He blinked at the darkness, held tight to his bag. He wondered if he had been foolish, putting the knife away. Some people brushed past him in the dark. Richard started away from them. There were steps in front of him; Richard began to ascend, and, as he did so, the world began to resolve, to take shape and to re-form.

The growling was the roar of traffic, and he was coming out of an underpass in Trafalgar Square. The sky was the perfect untroubled blue of a television screen, tuned to a dead channel.

It was midmorning, on a warm October day, and he stood in the square holding his bag and blinking at the sunlight. Black taxis and red buses and multicolored cars roared and careered about the square, while tourists threw handfuls of pigeon feed down for the legions of tubby pigeons and took their snapshots of Nelson's Column and the huge Landseer lions that flanked it. He walked through the square, wondering if he was real or not. The Japanese tourists ignored him. He tried talking to a pretty fair-haired girl, who laughed, and shook her head, and said something in a language Richard thought might have been Italian, but was actually Finnish.

There was a small child of indeterminate sex, staring at some pigeons while orally demolishing a chocolate bar. He crouched down next to it. "Um. Hello, kiddie," said Richard. The child sucked its chocolate bar intently and gave no indication of recognizing Richard as another human being. "Hello," repeated Richard, a slight note of desperation creeping into his voice. "Can you see me? Kiddie? Hello?"

Two small eyes glared at him from a chocolate-covered face. And then its lower lip began to tremble, and the child fled, throwing its arms around the legs of the nearest adult female, and wailing, "Mommy? This man's bothering me. He's bothering me."

The child's mother turned on Richard with a formidable scowl. "What are you doing," she demanded, "bothering our Leslie? There are places for people like you."

Richard began to smile. It was a huge and happy smile. "I really am most frightfully sorry," he said, grinning like a Cheshire cat. And then, clutching his bag, he ran through Trafalgar Square, accompanied by bursts of sudden pigeons, who took to the air in astonishment.

He took his cashcard out of his wallet, and he put it into the cash machine. It recognized his four-digit pin number, advised him to keep it a secret and not disclose it to anyone, and asked what kind of service he would like. He asked for cash, and it gave him cash in abundance. He punched the air in delight, and then, embarrassed, pretended that he had been hailing a cab.

A cab stopped for him—it stopped!—for him!—and he climbed in, and sat in the back, and beamed. He asked the driver to take him to his office. And when the cab driver pointed out that it would almost be quicker to walk, Richard grinned even wider, and said he did not care. And as soon as they were underway he asked—practically begged—the cab driver to regale him, Richard, with his opinions on Inner-City Traffic Problems, How Best to Deal with Crime, and Thorny Political Issues of the Day. The cab driver accused Richard of "taking the Mickey," and sulked for all of the five-minute journey up the Strand. Richard did not care. He tipped the man ridiculously anyway. And then he walked into his office.

As he entered the building, he felt the smile begin to leave his face. Each step he took left him more anxious, more uneasy. What if he still had no job? What did it matter if small, chocolate-covered children and cab drivers could see him, if it turned out that, by some apalling mischance, he remained invisible to his colleagues?

Mr. Figgis, the security guard, looked up from a copy of *Naughty Teenage Nymphets*, which he had hidden inside his copy of the *Sun*, and he sniffed. "Morning Mister Mayhew," he said. It was not a welcoming "morning." It was the kind of "morning" that implied that the speaker really did not care if the recipient lived or died—nor indeed, for that matter, if it was even morning.

"Figgis!" exclaimed Richard, in delight. "And hello to you too, Mister Figgis, you exceptional security guard!"

Nobody had ever said anything remotely like that to Mr. Figgis before, not even naked ladies in his imagination; Figgis stared suspiciously at Richard until he got into the elevator and vanished from sight, then he returned his attention to the naughty teenage nymphets, none of whom, he was beginning to suspect, was ever likely to see twenty-nine again, lollipops or no lollipops.

Richard got out of the elevator and walked, slightly hesitantly, down the corridor. *Everything will be all right,* he told himself, *if only my desk is there. If my desk is there, everything will be fine.* He walked into the large room full of cubicles he had worked in for three years. People were working at desks, talking on telephones, rummaging through filing cabinets, drinking bad tea and worse coffee. It was his office.

And there was the place by the window, where his desk had once been, which was now occupied by a gray cluster of filing cabinets and a yucca plant. He was about to turn and run when someone handed him a cup of tea in a Styrofoam cup.

"The return of the prodigal, eh?" said Gary. "Here you go."

"Hello Gary," said Richard. "Where's my desk?"

"This way," said Gary. "How was Majorca?"

"Majorca?"

"Don't you always go to Majorca?" asked Gary. They were walking up the back stairs that led to the fourth floor.

"Not this time," said Richard.

"I was going to say," said Gary. "Not much of a tan."

"No," agreed Richard. "Well. You know. I needed a change."

Gary nodded. He pointed to a door that had, for

as long as Richard had been there, been the door to the executive files and supplies room. "A change? Well, you've certainly got one now. And may I be the first to congratulate you?"

The plaque on the door said:

R. O. MAYHEW
JUNIOR PARTNER

"Lucky bastard," said Gary, affectionately.

He wandered off, and Richard went through the door, utterly bemused. The room was no longer an executive supplies and file room: it had been emptied of files and supplies, and painted in gray and black and white, and recarpeted. In the center of the office was a large desk. He examined it: it was, unmistakably, his very own desk. His trolls had all been neatly put away in one of the desk drawers, and he took them all out, and arranged them around the office. He had his own window, with a nice view of the sludge-brown river and the South Bank of the Thames, beyond. There was even a large green plant, with huge waxy leaves, of the kind that looks artificial but isn't. His old, dusty, cream-colored computer terminal had been replaced with a much sleeker, cleaner black computer terminal, which took up less desk space.

He walked over to the window and sipped his tea, staring out at the dirty brown river.

"You've found everything all right, then?" He looked up. Crisp and efficient, Sylvia, the MD's PA, was standing in the doorway. She smiled when she saw him.

"Um. Yes. Look, there are things I have to take

care of at home . . . d'you think it'd be all right if I took the rest of the day off and—"

"Suit yourself. You aren't meant to be back in till tomorrow anyway."

"I'm not?" he asked. "Right."

Sylvia frowned. "What happened to your finger?"

"I broke it," he told her.

She looked at his hand with concern. "You weren't in a fight, were you?"

"Me?"

She grinned. "Just teasing. I suppose you shut it in a door. That's what my sister did."

"No," Richard began to admit, "I *was* in a fi . . ." Sylvia raised an eyebrow. "A door," he finished lamely.

He went to the building he had once lived in by taxi. He was not sure that he trusted himself to travel by the Underground. Not yet. Having no door key, he knocked at the door of his flat and was more than disappointed when it was opened by the woman Richard last remembered meeting, or rather, failing to meet, in his bathroom. He introduced himself as the previous tenant, and quickly established that a) he, Richard, no longer lived there, and b) she, Mrs. Buchanan, had no idea what had happened to any of his personal possessions. Richard took some notes, and then he said good-bye very nicely, and took another black taxi to go and see a man in a camel-hair coat.

The smooth man in the camel-hair coat was not wearing his camel-hair coat, and was, in fact, a good deal less smooth than the last time Richard had encountered him. They were sitting in his office, and he had listened to Richard's list of complaints with the expression of someone who has recently and accidentally swallowed whole a live spider and has just begun to feel it squirm.

"Well, yes," he admitted, after looking at the files. "There does seem to have been some kind of problem, now you mention it. I can't quite see how it could have happened."

"I don't think it matters how it happened," said Richard, reasonably. "The fact of the matter is that while I was away for a few weeks, you rented my apartment to," he consulted his notes, "George and Adele Buchanan. Who have no intention of leaving."

The man closed the file. "Well," he said. "Mistakes do happen. Human error. I'm afraid there's nothing we can do about it."

The old Richard, the one who had lived in what was now the Buchanans' home, would have crumbled at this point, apologized for being a nuisance, and gone away. Instead, Richard said, "Really? Nothing you can do about it? You rented a property I was legally renting from your company to someone else, and in the process lost all my personal possessions, and there's nothing you can do about it? Now, I happen to think, and I'm sure my lawyer will also think, that there is a great deal you can do about it."

The man without the camel-hair coat looked as if the spider was beginning to crawl back up his throat. "But we don't have any other vacant apartments like yours in the building," he said. "There's only the penthouse suite."

"That," Richard told the man, coldly, "would be fine . . ." The man relaxed. ". . . for living accommodation. Now," said Richard, "let's talk about compensation for my lost possessions."

*   *   *

The new apartment was much nicer than the one he had left behind. It had more windows, and a balcony, a spacious lounge, and a proper spare bedroom. Richard prowled it, dissatisfied. The man-without-a-camel-hair-coat had, extremely grudgingly, had the apartment furnished with a bed, a sofa, several chairs, and a television set.

Richard put Hunter's knife on the mantelpiece.

He bought a take-away curry from the Indian restaurant across the road, sat on the carpeted floor of his new apartment, and ate it, wondering if he had ever really eaten curry late at night in a street-market held on the deck of a gunship moored by Tower Bridge. It did not seem very likely, now that he thought about it.

The doorbell rang. He got up and answered the door. "We found a lot of your stuff, Mr. Mayhew," said the man who was once more wearing his camel-hair coat. "Turned out it'd been put into storage. Right, bring the stuff in, lads."

A couple of burly men hauled in several large wooden packing cases, filled with Richard's stuff, and deposited them on the carpet in the middle of the living room.

"Thanks," said Richard. He reached into the first box, unwrapped the first paper-covered object, which turned out to be a framed photograph of Jessica. He stared at it for some moments, and then he put it down again in the case. He found the box with his clothes in it, removed them, and put them away in his bedroom, but the other boxes sat, untouched, in the middle of the living room floor. As the days went on, he felt increasingly guilty about not unpacking them. But he did not unpack them.

* * *

He was in his office, sitting at his desk, staring out of the window, when the intercom buzzed. "Richard?" said Sylvia. "The MD wants a meeting in his office in twenty minutes to discuss the Wandsworth report."

"I'll be there," he said. Then, because he had nothing else to do for the next ten minutes, he picked up an orange troll and menaced a slightly smaller green-haired troll with it. "I am the greatest warrior of London Below. Prepare to die," he said, in a dangerous trollish voice, waggling the orange troll. Then he picked up the green-haired troll, and said, in a smaller trollish voice, "Aha! But first you shall drink the nice cup of tea . . ."

Someone knocked on the door, and, guiltily, he put down the trolls. "Come in." The door opened, and Jessica came in, and stood in the doorway. She looked nervous. He had forgotten quite how beautiful she was. "Hello Richard," she said.

"Hello Jess," said Richard, and then he corrected himself. "Sorry—Jessica."

She smiled, and tossed her hair. "Oh, Jess is fine," she said, and looked as if she almost meant it. "Jessica—Jess. Nobody's called me Jess for ages. I rather miss it."

"So," said Richard, "what brings, do I have the honor, you, um."

"Just wanted to see you, really."

He was not sure what he ought to say. "That's nice," he said.

She closed the door to his office and took a few steps toward him. "Richard. You know something strange? I remember calling the engagement off. But I hardly remember what we were arguing about."

"No?"

"It's not important, though. Is it?" She looked around the office. "You got a promotion?"

"Yes."

"I'm happy for you." She put a hand into the pocket of her coat and pulled out a small brown box. She put it down on Richard's desk. He opened the box, although he knew what was inside it. "It's our engagement ring. I thought that, well, maybe, I'd give it back to you, and then, well, if things worked out, well, perhaps one day you'd give it back to me."

It glittered in the sunlight: the most money he had ever spent on anything. He closed the box, and gave it back to her. "You keep it, Jessica," he said. And then, "I'm sorry."

She bit her lower lip. "Did you meet someone?"

He hesitated. He thought of Lamia, and Hunter, and Anaesthesia, and even Door, but none of them were someones in the way that she meant. "No. No one else," he said. And then, realizing it was true as he said it, "I've just changed, that's all."

His intercom buzzed. "Richard? We're waiting for you." He pressed the button. "Be right down, Sylvia."

He looked at Jessica. She said nothing. Perhaps there was nothing she could trust herself to say. She walked away, and she closed the door quietly behind her.

Richard picked up the papers he would need, with one hand. He ran the other hand across his face, as if he were wiping something away: sorrow, perhaps, or tears, or Jessica.

He started taking the Tube again, to and from work, although he soon found that he had stopped buying newspapers to read on his journey in the morning and the evening, and instead of reading he would scan the faces of the other people on the train, faces of every kind and color, and wonder if they were all from London Above, wonder what went on behind their eyes.

During the evening rush hour, a few days after his encounter with Jessica, he thought he saw Lamia across the carriage, with her back to him, her dark hair piled high on her head and her dress long and black. His heart began to pound in his chest. He pushed his way toward her through the crowded compartment. As he got closer, the train pulled into a station, the doors hissed open, and she stepped off. But it was not Lamia. Just another young London goth-girl, he realized, disappointed, off for a night on the town.

One Saturday afternoon he saw a large brown rat, sitting on top of the plastic garbage cans at the back of Newton Mansions, cleaning its whiskers and looking as if it owned the world. At Richard's approach it leapt down onto the pavement and waited in the shadow of the garbage cans, staring up at him with wary bead-black eyes.

Richard crouched down. "Hello," he said, gently. "Do we know each other?" The rat made no kind of response that Richard was able to perceive, but it did not run away. "My name is Richard Mayhew," he continued, in a low voice. "I'm not actually a rat-speaker, but I, um, know a few rats, well, I've met some, and I wondered if you were familiar with the Lady Door . . ."

He heard a shoe scrape behind him, and he turned to see the Buchanans looking at him curiously. "Have you . . . lost something?" asked Mrs. Buchanan. Richard heard, but ignored, her husband's gruff whisper of "Just his marbles."

"No," said Richard, honestly, "I was, um, saying hello to a . . ." The rat scurried off and away.

"Was that a rat?" barked George Buchanan. "I'll complain to the council. It's a disgrace. But that's London for you, isn't it?"

Yes, agreed Richard. It was. It really was.

Richard's posessions continued to sit untouched in the wooden packing cases in the middle of the living room floor.

He had not yet turned on the television. He would come home at night, and eat, then he would stand at the window, looking out over London, at the cars and the rooftops and the lights, as the late autumn twilight turned into night, and the lights came on all over the city. He would watch, standing alone in his darkened flat, until the city's lights began to be turned off. Eventually, reluctantly, he would undress, and climb into bed, and go to sleep.

Sylvia came into his office one Friday afternoon. He was opening envelopes, using his knife—Hunter's knife—as a letter-opener. "Richard?" she said. "I was wondering. Are you getting out much, these days?" He shook his head. "Well, a bunch of us are going out this evening. Do you fancy coming along?"

"Um. Sure," he said. "Yes. I'd love it."

He hated it.

There were eight of them: Sylvia and her young man, who had something to do with vintage cars, Gary from Corporate Accounts, who had recently broken up with his girlfriend, due to what Gary per-

sisted in describing as a slight misunderstanding (he
had thought she would be rather more understand-
ing about his sleeping with her best friend than she
had in fact turned out to be), several perfectly nice
people and friends of nice people, and the new girl
from Computer Services.

First they saw a film on the huge screen of the
Odeon, Leicester Square. The good guy won in the
end, and there were plenty of explosions and flying
objects on the way. Sylvia decided that Richard
should sit next to the girl from Computer Services,
as, she explained, she was new to the company and
did not know many people.

They walked down to Old Compton Street, on the
edge of Soho, where the tawdry and the chic sit side
by side to the benefit of both, and they ate at La
Reache, filling up on couscous and dozens of marvelous plates of exotic food, which covered their table and spilled over onto an unused table nearby,
and they walked from there to a small pub Sylvia
liked in nearby Berwick Street, and they had a few
drinks, and they chatted.

The new girl from Computer Services smiled at
Richard a lot, as the evening went on, and he had
nothing at all to say to her. He bought a round of
drinks for the party, and the girl from Computer
Services helped him carry them from the bar back
to their table. Gary went off to the men's room, and
the girl from Computer Services came and sat next
to Richard, taking his place. Richard's head was
filled with the clink of glasses, and the blare of the
jukebox, and the sharp smell of beer and spilt Ba-
cardi and cigarette smoke. He tried to listen to the
conversations going on at the table, and he found
that he could no longer concentrate on what anyone

was saying, and, which was worse, that he was not interested in any of what he was able to hear.

And it came to him then, as clearly and as certainly as if he had been watching it on the big screen at the Odeon, Leicester Square: the rest of his life. He would go home tonight with the girl from Computer Services, and they would make gentle love, and tomorrow, it being Saturday, they would spend the morning in bed. And then they would get up, and together they would remove his possessions from the packing cases, and put them away. In a year, or a little less, he would marry the girl from Computer Services, and get another promotion, and they would have two children, a boy and a girl, and they would move out to the suburbs, to Harrow or Croydon or Hampstead or even as far away as distant Reading.

And it would not be a bad life. He knew that, too. Sometimes there is nothing you can do.

When Gary came back from the toilet, he looked around in puzzlement. Everyone was there except . . . "Dick?" he asked "Has anyone seen Richard?"

The girl from Computer Services shrugged.

Gary went outside, to Berwick Street. The cold of the night air was like a splash of water to his face. He could taste winter in the air. He called, "Dick? Hey? Richard?"

"Over here."

Richard was leaning against a wall, in the shadows. "Just getting a breath of fresh air."

"Are you all right?" asked Gary.

"Yes," said Richard. "No. I don't know."

"Well," said Gary, "that covers your options. Do you want to talk about it?"

Richard looked at him seriously. "You'll laugh at me."

"I'll do that anyway."

Richard looked at Gary. Then Gary was relieved to see him smile, and he knew that they were still friends. Gary looked back at the pub. Then he put his hands into his coat pockets. "Come on," he said. "Let's walk. You can get it off your chest. *Then* I'll laugh at you."

"Bastard," said Richard, sounding a lot more like Richard than he had in recent weeks.

"It's what friends are for."

They began to amble off, under the streetlights. "Look, Gary," Richard began. "Do you ever wonder if this is all there is?"

"What?"

Richard gestured vaguely, taking in everything. "Work. Home. The pub. Meeting girls. Living in the city. Life. Is that all there is?"

"I think that sums it up, yes," said Gary.

Richard sighed. "Well," he said, "for a start, I didn't go to Majorca. I mean, I *really* didn't go to Majorca."

Richard talked as they walked up and down the warren of tiny Soho back streets between Regent Street and the Charing Cross Road. He talked, and talked, beginning with finding a girl bleeding on the pavement, and trying to help, because he couldn't just leave her there, and what happened next. And when they got too cold to walk they went into an all-night greasy spoon café. It was a proper one, the kind that cooked everything in lard, and served cups of serious tea in large chipped white mugs shiny with bacon grease. Richard and Gary sat and Richard talked while Gary listened, and then they ordered fried eggs and baked beans and toast and sat and ate them, while Richard continued to talk, and Gary continued to listen. They mopped up the last of their egg yolks with the toast. They drank more tea, until eventually Richard said, ". . . and then Door did something with the key, and I was back again. In London Above. Well, the real London. And, well, you know the rest."

There was a silence. "That's all," said Richard. He finished his tea.

Gary scratched his head. "Look," he said, at length. "Is this real? Not some kind of horrible joke? I mean, somebody with a camera isn't about to leap out from behind a screen or something and tell me I'm on *Candid Camera*?"

"I sincerely hope not," said Richard. "You . . . do you believe me?"

Gary looked at the bill on their table, counted out pound coins, and dropped them onto the Formica, where they sat beside a plastic tomato ketchup container in the shape of an oversized tomato, old ketchup caked black about its nozzle. "I believe that, well, *something* happened to you, obviously . . . Look, more to the point, do *you* believe it?"

Richard stared up at him. There were dark circles beneath Richard's eyes. "Do I believe it? I don't know anymore. I did. I was there. There was a part in there when you turned up, you know."

"You didn't mention that before."

"It was a pretty horrid part. You told me that I'd gone mad and I was just wandering around London hallucinating."

They walked out of the café and walked south, toward Piccadilly. "Well," said Gary. "you must admit, it sounds more likely than your magical London underneath, where the people who fall through the cracks go. I've passed the people who fall through the cracks, Richard: they sleep in shop doorways all down the Strand. They don't go to a special London. They freeze to death in the winter."

Richard said nothing.

Gary continued. "I think maybe you got some kind of blow on the head. Or maybe some kind of shock when Jessica chucked you. For a while you went a little crazy. Then you got better."

Richard shivered. "You know what scares me? I think you could be right."

"So life isn't exciting?" continued Gary. "Great. Give me boredom. At least I know where I'm going to eat and sleep tonight. I'll still have a job on Monday. Yeah?" He turned and looked at Richard.

Richard nodded, hesitantly. "Yeah."

Gary looked at his watch. "Bloody hell," he exclaimed. "It's after two o'clock. Let's hope there are still a few taxis about." They walked into Brewer Street, at the Piccadilly end of Soho, wandering past the lights of the peep shows and the strip clubs. Gary was talking about taxis. He was not saying anything original, or even interesting. He was simply fulfilling his obligation as a Londoner to grumble about taxis. ". . . Had his light on and everything," he was saying, "I told him where I wanted to go, he said, sorry, I'm on my way home, I said, where do all you taxi drivers live anyway? And why don't any of you live near me? The trick is to get in first, then tell them you live south of the river, I mean, what was he trying to tell me? The way he was carrying on, Battersea might as well have been in bloody Katmandu. . . ."

Richard had tuned him out. When they reached Windmill Street, Richard crossed the road and stared into the window of the Vintage Magazine Shop, examining the cartoonish models of forgotten film stars and the old posters and comics and magazines on display. It had been a glimpse into a world of adventure and imagination. And it was not true. He told himself that.

"So, what do you think?" Gary asked.

Richard jerked back to the present. "Of what?"

Gary realized Richard had not heard a word he had said. He said it again. "If there aren't any taxis we could get night buses."

"Yeah," said Richard. "Great. Fine."

Gary grimaced. "You worry me."

"Sorry."

They walked down Windmill Street, toward Piccadilly. Richard thrust his hands deep into his pockets. He looked puzzled for a moment, and pulled out a rather crumpled black crow's feather, with red thread tied around the quill.

"What's that?" asked Gary.

"It's a—" He stopped. "It's just a feather. You're right. It's only rubbish." He dropped the feather in the gutter at the curb, and did not look back.

Gary hesitated. Then he said, picking his words with care, "Have you thought about seeing somebody?"

"See somebody? Look, I'm not crazy, Gary."

"Are you sure about that?" A taxi came toward them, yellow for-hire light burning.

"No," said Richard, honestly. "Here's a taxi. You take it. I'll take the next one."

"Thanks." Gary waved down the taxi and climbed into the back before telling the driver that he wished to go to Battersea. He pulled down the window, and, as the taxi pulled out, he said, "Richard—this is reality. Get used to it. It's all there is. See you on Monday."

Richard waved at him and watched the taxi drive away. Then he turned around and walked slowly away from the lights of Piccadilly, back up toward Brewer Street. There was no longer a feather by the curb. Richard paused beside an old woman, fast asleep in a shop doorway. She was covered with a ripped old blanket, and her few possessions—two small junk-filled cardboard boxes and a dirty, once-white umbrella—were tied together with string beside her, and the string was tied around her wrist, to keep anyone from stealing them while she slept. She wore a wool hat, of no particular color.

He pulled out his wallet, found a ten-pound note, and bent down to slide the folded note into the woman's hand. Her eyes opened, and she jerked awake. She blinked at the money with old eyes. "What's this?" she said, sleepily, displeased at having been woken.

"Keep it," said Richard.

She unfolded the money, then pushed it up her sleeve. "Whatchyouwant?" she asked Richard, suspiciously.

"Nothing," said Richard. "I really don't want anything. Nothing at all." And then he realized how true that was; and how dreadful a thing it had become. "Have you ever got everything you ever wanted? And then realized it wasn't what you wanted at all?"

"Can't say that I have," she said, picking the sleep from the corner of her eyes.

"I thought I wanted this," said Richard. "I

thought I wanted a nice, normal life. I mean, maybe I am crazy. I mean, maybe. But if this is all there is, then I don't want to be sane. You know?" She shook her head. He reached into his inside pocket. "You see this?" he said. He held up the knife. "Hunter gave this to me as she died," he told her.

"Don't hurt me," said the old lady. "I ain't done nuffing."

He heard a strange intensity in his own voice. "I wiped her blood from the blade. A hunter looks after her weapons. The earl knighted me with it. He gave me the freedom of the Underside."

"I don't know anyfing about that," she said. "Please. Put it away. That's a good lad."

Richard hefted the knife. Then he lunged toward the brick wall, next to the doorway in which the woman had been sleeping. He slashed three times, once horizontally, twice vertically. "What you doin'?" asked the woman, warily.

"Making a door," he told her.

She sniffed. "You ought to put that thing away. If the police see you they'll run you in for offensive weapons."

Richard looked at the outline of a doorway he had scratched on the wall. He put his knife back into his pocket, and he began to hammer on the wall with his fists. "Hey! Is there anyone there? Can you hear me? It's me—Richard. Door? Someone?" He hurt his hands, but he kept banging and flailing at the brick-work.

And then the madness left him, and he stopped.

"Sorry," he said to the old lady.

She did not answer. She had either gone back to sleep or, more probably, pretended to go back to sleep. Elderly snores, real or feigned, came from the doorway. Richard sat down on the pavement, and wondered how someone could make such a mess of their life as he had made of his. Then he looked back at the doorway he had scratched on the wall.

There was a door-shaped hole in the wall, where he had scratched his outline. There was a man standing in the doorway, with his arms folded theatrically. He stood there until he was certain that Richard had seen him. And then he yawned hugely, covering his mouth with a dark hand.

The marquis de Carabas raised an eyebrow. "Well?" he said, irritably. "Are you coming?"

Richard stared at him for a heartbeat.

Then Richard nodded, without trusting himself to speak, and stood up. And they walked away together through the hole in the wall, back into the darkness, leaving nothing behind them; not even the doorway.

ACKNOWLEDGMENTS

MY THANKS TO ALL THE READERS OF THIS book in its various drafts and versions for their input, suggestions, and feedback—particularly to Steve Brust, Martha Soukup, Dave Langford, Gene Wolfe, Cindy Wall, Amy Horsting, Lorraine Garland, and Kelli Bickman; to Doug Young and Sheila Ableman at BBC Books for their help and support, and to Jennifer Hershey and Lou Aronica at Avon Books. I would also like to thank all the people who came to my rescue whenever chunks of this novel devolved to their component electrons, and Norton Utilities.

—Neil Gaiman

Here is an excerpt from

ANANSI BOYS

the much-anticipated new novel from
New York Times bestselling author Neil Gaiman—
a magnificent work of literary magic that is at
once exciting, scary, and deeply funny . . .

AVAILABLE SEPTEMBER 20, 2005 IN HARDCOVER
from William Morrow

I t begins, as most things begin, with a song.
In the beginning, after all, were the words, and they came
with a tune. That was how the world was made, how the
void was divided, how the lands and the stars and the
dreams and the little gods and the animals, how all of them
came into the world.

They were sung.

The great beasts were sung into existence, after the Singer
had done with the planets and the hills and the trees and the
oceans and the lesser beasts. The cliffs that bound existence
were sung, and the hunting grounds, and the dark.

Songs remain. They last. The right song can turn an
emperor into a laughingstock, can bring down dynasties. A
song can last long after the events and the people in it are
dust and dreams and gone. That's the power of songs.

There are other things you can do with songs. They do not
only make worlds or recreate existence. Fat Charlie Nancy's
father, for example, was simply using them to have what he
hoped and expected would be a marvelous night out.

Before Fat Charlie's father had come into the bar, the
barman had been of the opinion that the whole karaoke

evening was going to be an utter bust. But then the little old man had sashayed into the room, walked past the table of several blonde women, with the fresh sunburns and smiles of tourists, who were sitting by the little makeshift stage in the corner. He had tipped his hat to them, for he wore a hat, a spotless white fedora, and lemon-yellow gloves, and then he walked over to their table. They giggled.

"Are you enjoyin' yourselves, ladies?" he asked.

They continued to giggle and told him they were having a good time, thank you, and that they were here on vacation. He said to them, it gets better, just you wait.

He was older than they were, much, much older, but he was charm itself, like something from a bygone age when fine manners and courtly gestures were worth something. The barman relaxed. With someone like this in the bar, it was going to be a good evening.

There was karaoke. There was dancing. The old man got up to sing, on the makeshift stage, not once, that evening, but twice. He had a fine voice, and an excellent smile, and feet that twinkled when he danced. The first time he got up to sing, he sang "What's New Pussycat?" The second time he got up to sing, he ruined Fat Charlie's life.

Fat Charlie was only ever fat for a handful of years, from shortly before the age of nine, when his mother announced to the world that if there was one thing she was over and done with and if he had any argument with it he could just stick it you know where it was her marriage to that elderly goat that she had made the unfortunate mistake of marrying and she would be leaving in the morning for somewhere a long way away and he had better not try to follow, to the age of fourteen, when Fat Charlie grew a little and exercised a little more. He was not fat. Truth to tell, he was not really even chubby, simply a little soft-looking around the edges. But the name Fat Charlie clung to him, like chewing gum to the sole of a tennis shoe. He would introduce himself as

Charles, or, in his early twenties, Chaz, or, in writing, as C. Nancy, but it was no use: the name would creep in, infiltrating the new part of his life just as cockroaches invade the cracks and the world behind the fridge in a brand new kitchen, and like it or not—and he didn't—he would be Fat Charlie again.

It was, he knew, irrationally, because his father had given him the nickname, and when his father gave things names, they stuck.

There was a dog who had lived in the house across the way, in the street on which Fat Charlie had grown up. It was a chestnut-colored boxer, long-legged and pointy-eared with a face that looked like the beast had, as a puppy, run face-first into a wall. Its head was raised, its tail-nub erect. It was, unmistakably, an aristocrat amongst canines. It had entered dog shows. It had rosettes for Best of Breed, and for Best in Class, and even one Rosette marked Best in Show. This dog rejoiced in the name of Campbell's Macinrory Arbuthnot the Seventh, and its owners, when they were feeling familiar, called it Kai. This lasted until the day that Fat Charlie's father, sitting out on their dilapidated porch swing, sipping his beer, noticed the dog as it ambled back and forth across the neighbor's yard, on a leash that ran from a palm tree to a fence post.

"Hell of a goofy dog," said Fat Charlie's father. "Like that friend of Donald Duck's. Hey Goofy."

And what once had been Best In Show suddenly slipped and shifted. For Fat Charlie, it was as if he saw the dog through his father's eyes, and darned if he *wasn't* a pretty goofy dog, all things considered. Almost rubbery.

It didn't take long for the name to spread up and down the street. Campbell's Macinrory Arbuthnot the Seventh's owners struggled with it, but they might as well have stood their ground and argued with a hurricane. Total strangers would pat the once-proud boxer's head, and say "Hello Goofy. How's a boy?" The dog's owner's stopped entering him in dog shows soon after that. They didn't have the heart.

"Goofy looking dog," said the judges.

Fat Charlie's father's names for things stuck. That was just how it was.

That was far from the worst thing about Fat Charlie's father.

There had been, during the years that he was growing up, a number of candidates for the worst thing about Fat Charlie's father: his roving eye and equally as adventurous fingers, at least according to the young ladies of the area, who would complain to Fat Charlie's mother, and then there would be trouble; the little black cigarillos, which he called cheroots, which he smoked, the smell of which clung to everything he touched; his fondness for a peculiar shuffling form of tap-dancing, fashionable, Fat Charlie suspected, for half an hour in Harlem in the 1920s; his total and invincible ignorance about current world affairs, combined with his apparent conviction that sitcoms were half-hour long insights into the lives and struggles of real people. These, individually, as far as Fat Charlie was concerned, were none of them the worst thing about Fat Charlie's father, although each of them had contributed to the worst thing.

The worst thing about Fat Charlie's father was simply this: he was embarrassing.

Of course, everyone's parents are embarrassing. It goes with the territory. The nature of parents is to embarrass merely by existing, just as it is the nature of children of a certain age to cringe with embarrassment, shame and mortification should their parents so much as speak to them on the street.

Fat Charlie's father, of course, had elevated this to an art form, and he rejoiced in it, just as he rejoiced in practical jokes, from the simple—Fat Charlie would never forget the first time he had climbed into an apple-pie bed—to the unimaginably complex.

"Like what?" asked Rosie, Fat Charlie's fiancée, one evening, when Fat Charlie, who normally did not talk about his father had attempted, stumblingly, to explain why he believed that simply inviting his father to their upcoming wedding would be a horrendously bad idea. They were in a wine bar in South London at the time. Fat Charlie had long been of the opinion that four thousand miles and the Atlantic Ocean were both good things to keep between himself and his father.

"Well . . ." said Fat Charlie, and he remembered a parade of indignities, each one of which made his toes curl involuntarily. He settled upon one of them. "Well, when I moved from the local junior school to the middle school, my Dad made a point of telling me how much he had always looked forward to Presidents' Day, when he was a boy, because it's the law that on Presidents' Day, the kids who go to school dressed as their favorite presidents get a big bag of candy."

"Oh. That's a nice law," said Rosie. "I wish we had something like that here." Rosie had never been out of England, if you didn't count a Club 18-30 holiday to an island in, she was fairly certain, the Mediterranean. She had warm brown eyes and a good heart, even if geography was not her strongest suit.

"It's not a nice law," said Fat Charlie. "It's not a law at all. He made it up. There is no tradition of going to school on Presidents' Day dressed as your favorite president. Kids dressed as presidents do not get big bags of candy by an Act of Congress, nor is your popularity in the years ahead, all through middle school and high school, decided entirely by which president you decided to dress as—the average kids dress as the obvious presidents, the Lincolns and Washingtons and Jeffersons, but the ones who would become popular, they dressed as John Quincy Adams or Warren Gamaliel Harding, or someone like that. And it's bad luck to talk about it before the day. Or rather it isn't, but he said it was."

"Boys *and* girls dress up as presidents?"

"Oh yes. Boys and girls. So I spent the week before Presidents' Day reading everything there was to read about Presidents in the World Book Encyclopedia, trying to choose the right one."

"Didn't you ever suspect that he was pulling your leg?"

Fat Charlie shook his head. "It's not something you think about, when my dad starts to work you over. He's the finest liar you'll ever meet. He's convincing."

Rosie took a sip of her Chardonnay. "So which President did you go to school as?"

"Taft. He was the 27th president. I wore a brown suit my father had found somewhere, with the legs all rolled up and a pillow stuffed down the front. I had a painted-on moustache. My dad took me to school himself that day. I walked in so proudly. The other kids just screamed and pointed, and somewhere in there I locked myself in a cubicle in the boys' room and cried. They wouldn't let me go home to change. I went through the day like that. It was Hell."

"You should have made something up," said Rosie. "You were going to a costume party afterwards or something. Or just told them the truth."

"Yeah," said Fat Charlie meaningfully and gloomily, remembering.

"What did your dad say, when you got home?"

"Oh, he hooted with laughter. Chuckled and chortled and, and chittered and all that. Then he told me that maybe they didn't do that Presidents' Day stuff any more. Now, why didn't we go down to the beach together and look for mermaids?"

"Look for . . . mermaids?"

"We'd go down to the beach, and walk along it, and he'd be as embarrassing as any human being on the face of this planet has ever been—he'd start singing, and he'd start doing a shuffling sort of sand-dance on the sand, and he'd just talk to people as he went—white people—people he didn't even know, people he'd never met, and I hated it, except he told me there were mermaids out there in the Atlantic, and if I looked fast enough and sharp enough, I'd see one.

"'There!' he'd say. 'Did you see her? She was a big ol' redhead, with a green tail.' And I looked, and I looked, but I never did."

He shook his head. Then he took a handful of mixed nuts from the bowl on the table and began to toss them into his mouth, chomping down on them as if each nut was a twenty-year old indignity that could never be erased.

"Well," said Rosie, brightly, "I think he sounds lovely, a real character! We have to get him to come over for the wedding. He'd be the life and soul of the party."

Which, Fat Charlie explained, after briefly choking on a brazil nut, was really the last thing you wanted at your wedding, after all, wasn't it, your father turning up and being the life and soul of the party. He said that his father was, he had no doubt, still the most embarrassing person on God's Green Earth. He added that he was perfectly happy not to have seen the old goat for several years, and that the best thing his mother ever did was to leave his father and come to England to stay with her Aunt Alanna. He buttressed this by stating categorically that he was damned, double-damned and quite possibly even thrice-damned if he was going to invite his father to their wedding. In fact, said Fat Charlie in closing, the best thing about getting married was not having to invite his dad to the reception.

And then Fat Charlie saw the expression on Rosie's face and the icy glint in her normally friendly eyes, and he corrected himself hurriedly, explaining that he meant the second-best, but it was already much too late.

"You'll just have to get used to the idea," said Rosie. "After all, a wedding is a marvelous opportunity for mending fences and building bridges. It's your opportunity to show him that there are no hard feelings."

"But there *are* hard feelings," said Fat Charlie. "Lots."

"Do you have an address for him?" asked Rosie. "Or a phone number? You probably ought to phone him. A letter's a bit impersonal when your only son is getting married . . .

you are his only son, aren't you? Does he have e-mail?"

"Yes. I'm his only son. I have no idea if he has e-mail or not. Probably not," said Fat Charlie. Letters were good things, he thought. They could get lost in the post for a start.

"Well, you must have an address or a phone number."

"I don't," said Fat Charlie, honestly. Maybe his father had moved away. He could have left Florida and gone somewhere they didn't have telephones. Or addresses.

"Well," said Rosie, sharply, "who does?"

"Mrs. Higgler," said Fat Charlie, and all the fight went out of him.

Rosie smiled sweetly. "And who is Mrs. Higgler?" she asked.

"Friend of the family," said Fat Charlie. "When I was growing up, she used to live next door."

He had spoken to Mrs. Higgler several years before this, when his mother was dying. He had, at his mother's request, telephoned Mrs. Higgler to pass on the message to Fat Charlie's father, and to tell him to get in touch. And several days later there had been a message on Fat Charlie's ansaphone, left while he was at work, in a voice that was unmistakably his father's, even if it did sound rather older, and a little drunk.

His father said that it was not a good time, and that business affairs would be keeping him in America. And then he added that, for everything, Fat Charlie's mother was a damn fine woman. Several days later a vase of flowers had been delivered to the ward. Fat Charlie's mother had snorted, when she read the card.

"Thinks he can get around me that easily?" she said. "He's got another think coming, I can tell you that." But she had had the nurse put the flowers in a place of honor by her bed, and, several times since, had asked Fat Charlie if he had heard anything about his father coming and visiting her, before it was all over.

Fat Charlie said he hadn't. He grew to hate the question, and his answer, and the expression on her face when he told her that, no, his father wasn't coming.

The worst day, in Fat Charlie's opinion, was the day that the Doctor, a gruff little man, had taken Fat Charlie aside and told him that it would not be long now, that his mother was fading fast, and it was a matter of keeping her comfortable until the end.

Fat Charlie had nodded, and gone in to his mother. She had held his hand, and was asking him whether or not he had remembered to pay her gas bill, when the noise began in the corridor—a clashing, parping, stomping, rattling, brass and bass and drum sort of noise, of the kind that tends not to be heard in hospitals, where signs in the stairwells request quiet and the icy glares of the nursing staff enforce it.

The noise was getting louder.

For one moment Fat Charlie thought it might be terrorists. His mother, though, smiled weakly at the cacophony. "Yellow bird," she whispered.

"What?" said Fat Charlie, scared that she had stopped making sense.

"'Yellow Bird,'" she said, louder and more firmly. "It's what they're playing."

Fat Charlie went to the door, and looked out.

Coming down the hospital corridor, ignoring the protests of nurses, the stares of patients in pajamas and of their families, was what appeared to be a very small New Orleans jazz band. There was a saxophone, and a sousaphone and a trumpet. There was an enormous man with what appeared to be a double bass strung around his neck. There was a man with a bass drum, which he banged. And at the head of the pack, in a smart checked suit, with a porkpie hat and lemon-yellow gloves, came Fat Charlie's father. He played no instrument, but was doing a soft-shoe-shuffle along the polished linoleum of the hospital floor, lifting his hat to each of the medical staff in turn, shaking hands with anyone who got close enough to talk or to attempt to complain.

Fat Charlie bit his lip, and prayed to anyone who might be

listening that the Earth would open and swallow him up, or failing that, that he might suffer a brief, merciful and entirely fatal heart attack. No such luck. He remained among the living, the brass band kept coming, his father kept dancing, and shaking hands, and smiling.

If there is any justice in the world, thought Fat Charlie, my father will keep going down the corridor and he'll go straight past us and into the genito-urinary department; but there was no justice, and his father reached the door of the oncology ward and stopped.

"Fat Charlie," he said, loudly enough that everyone in the ward—on that floor—in the hospital—was able to comprehend that this was someone who knew Fat Charlie. "Fat Charlie, get out of the way. Your father is here."

Fat Charlie got out of the way.

The band, led by Fat Charlie's father, snaked their way through the ward to Fat Charlie's mother's bed. She looked up at them as they approached, and she smiled.

"'Yellow bird,'" she said, weakly. "It's my favorite song."

"And what kind of man would I be if I forgot that?" asked Fat Charlie's father.

She shook her head slowly, and she reached out her hand and squeezed his hand in its lemon-yellow glove.

"Excuse me," said a woman with a clipboard, "are these people with you?"

"No," said Fat Charlie, his cheeks heating up. "They're not. Not really."

"But that is your mother, isn't it?" said the woman, with a basilisk glance. "I must ask you to make these people vacate the ward momentarily, and without incurring any further disturbance."

Fat Charlie muttered.

"What was that?"

"I said, I'm pretty sure I can't make them do anything," said Fat Charlie. He consoled himself that things could not possibly get any worse, when his father took a plastic carrier bag from the drummer, and began producing cans of brown ale and handing them out, to his band, to the nursing staff, to the patients. Then he lit a cheroot.

"Excuse me," said the woman with the clipboard, when she saw the smoke, and she launched herself across the room at Fat Charlie's father like a SCUD missile with its watch on upside down.

Fat Charlie took that moment to slip away. It seemed the wisest course of action.

He sat at home that night, waiting for the phone to ring or for a knock on the door, in much the same spirit that a man kneeling at the guillotine might wait for the blade to kiss his neck; but the doorbell did not ring.

He barely slept, and slunk in to the hospital the following afternoon, prepared for the worst.

His mother, in her bed, looked happier than she had looked in months. "He's gone back," she told Fat Charlie, when he came in. "He couldn't stay. I have to say, Charlie, I wish you hadn't just gone like that. We wound up having a party here. We had a fine old time."

Fat Charlie could think of nothing worse than having to attend a party in a cancer ward, thrown by his father with a jazz band. He didn't say anything.

"He's not a bad man," said Fat Charlie's mother, with a twinkle in her eye. Then she frowned. "Well, that's not exactly true. He's certainly not a good man. But he did me a power of good last night," and she smiled, a real smile and, for a moment, looked young again.

The woman with the clipboard was standing in the doorway, and she crooked her finger at him. Fat Charlie beetled down the ward toward her, apologizing before she was even properly within earshot. Her look, he realized, as he got closer to her, was no longer that of a basilisk with stomach cramps. Now she looked positively kittenish. "Your father," she said.

"I'm sorry," said Fat Charlie. It was what he always said, growing up, when his father was mentioned.

"No, no, no," said the former basilisk. "Nothing to apologize for. I was just wondering. Your father. In case we need to get in touch with him—we don't have a telephone number or an address on file. I should have asked him last night, but it completely got away from me."

"I don't think he has a phone number," said Fat Charlie. "And the best way to find him is to go to Miami, and to drive up Highway A1A—that's the coast road that runs up the east of Florida. In the afternoon you may find him fishing off a bridge. In the evening he'll be in a bar."

"Such a charming man," she said, wistfully. "What does he do?"

"I told you. He says it's the miracle of the loafs and the fishes."

She stared at him blankly, and he felt stupid. When his father said it, people would laugh. "Um. Like in the bible. The miracle of the loaves and the fishes. Dad used to say that he loafs and fishes, and it's a miracle that he still makes money. It was a sort of joke."

A misty look. "Yes. He told the funniest jokes." She clucked her tongue, and once more was all business. "Now, I need you back here at 5:30."

"Why?"

"To pick up your mother. And her belongings. Didn't Dr. Johnson tell you we were discharging her?"

"You're sending her home?"

"Yes, Mr. Nancy."

"What about the, about the cancer?"

"It seems to have been a false alarm."

Fat Charlie couldn't understand how it could have been a false alarm. Last week they'd been talking about sending his mother to a hospice. The doctor had been using phrases like "weeks not months" and "making her as comfortable as possible while we wait for the inevitable."

Still, Fat Charlie came back at 5:30 and picked up his mother, who seemed quite unsurprised to learn that she was no longer dying. On the way home she told Fat Charlie that she would be using her life savings to travel around the world.

"The doctors were saying I had three months," she said. "And I remember I thought, if I get out of this hospital bed then I'm going to see Paris and Rome and places. I'm going back to Dominica. I may go to Africa. And China. I like Chinese food."

Fat Charlie wasn't sure what was going on, but whatever it was, he blamed his father. He accompanied his mother and a serious suitcase to Heathrow airport, and waved her good-bye at the International Departures gate. She was smiling hugely as she went through, clutching her passport and tick-ets, and she looked younger than he remembered her looking in many years.

She sent him postcards from Paris, and from Rome and from Athens, and from Lagos and Cape Town. Her postcard from Nanking told him that she didn't like the Chinese food in China, and that she couldn't wait to come back to London and eat *proper* Chinese food.

She died in her sleep, in a hotel in Roseau, on the island of Dominica.

At the funeral, at a South London Crematorium, Fat Charlie kept expecting to see his father: perhaps his father would make an entrance at the head of a jazz band, or followed down the aisle by a clown troupe or a half-dozen tricycle-riding cigar-puffing chimpanzees; and even during the service Fat Charlie kept glancing back, over his shoulder, toward the chapel door. But Fat Charlie's father was not there, only his mother's friends and relations, mostly big women in black hats, blowing their noses and dabbing at their eyes and shaking their heads.

It was during the final hymn, after the button had been pressed and Fat Charlie's mother had trundled off down the conveyor belt to her final reward, that Fat Charlie noticed a man of about his own age standing at the back of the chapel. It was not his father, obviously. It was someone he did not know, someone he might not even have noticed, at the back, in the shadows, had he not been darting troubled glances back . . . and then there was the stranger, in an elegant black suit, his eyes lowered, his hands folded.

Fat Charlie let his glance linger a moment too long, and the stranger looked at Fat Charlie and a he flashed him a joy-less smile, of the kind that suggested that they were both in this together. It was not the kind of expression you see on the faces of strangers, but Fat Charlie could not place the man. He turned his face back to the front of the chapel. They sang "Swing Low, Sweet Chariot," a song Fat Charlie was pretty sure his mother had always disliked, and the Rev-erend Wright invited them back to Fat Charlie's Great-Aunt Alanna's for something to eat.

There was nobody at his Great-Aunt Alanna's that he did not know. In the years since his mother had died, he some-times wondered about that man: who he was, why he was there. Whether Fat Charlie had simply imagined him . . .

"So," said Rosie, draining her Chardonnay, "you'll call your Mrs. Higgler, and give her my mobile number. Tell her about the wedding and the date . . . that's a thought: do you think we should invite her?"

"We can if we like," said Fat Charlie. "I don't think she'll come. She gets scared of flying. She's an old family friend. She knew my dad back in the dark ages."

"Well, sound her out. See if we should be sending her an invitation."

Rosie was a good person. There was in Rosie a little of the essence of Frances of Assisi, of Robin Hood, of Buddha and of Glinda the Good: the knowledge that she was about to bring together her true love and his estranged father gave her forthcoming wedding an extra dimension, she decided. It was not simply a wedding: it was practically a humanitarian mis-sion, and Fat Charlie had known Rosie long enough to know never to stand between his fiancée and her need to do good.

"I'll call Mrs. Higgler tomorrow," he said.

"Tell you what," said Rosie, with an endearing wrinkle of her nose. "Call her tonight. It's not late in America, after all."

Fat Charlie nodded. They walked out of the wine bar together, Rosie with a spring in her step, Fat Charlie like a man going to the gallows. He told himself not to be silly: After all, perhaps Mrs. Higgler had moved, or had her phone disconnected. It was possible. Anything was possible. He came up with a plan.

They went up to Fat Charlie's place, the upstairs half of a smallish house off the Brixton Road.

"What time is it in Florida?" Rosie asked.

"Late afternoon," said Fat Charlie.

"Well. Go on then."

"Maybe we should wait a bit. In case she's out."

"And maybe we should call now, before she has her dinner."

Fat Charlie found his old paper address book, and under H was a scrap of an envelope, in his mother's handwriting, with a telephone number on it, and beneath that, Callyanne Higgler.

The phone rang and rang.

"She's not there," he said to Rosie, but at that moment the phone at the other end was answered, and a female voice said "Yes? Who is this?"

"Um. Is that Mrs. Higgler?"

"Who is this?" said Mrs. Higgler. "If you're one of the damn telemarketers, you take me off your list right now or I sue. I know my rights."

"No. It's me. Charles Nancy. I used to live next door to you."

"Fat Charlie? If that don't beat all. I was looking for your number all this morning. I turned this place upside down, looking for it, and do you think I could find it? What I think happened was I had it written in my old accounts book, and it got thrown out by mistake. Upside down I turned the place. And I said to myself, Callyanne, this is a good time to just pray and hope the Lord hears you and sees you right, and I went down on my knees, well, my knees aren't what they were so I just put my hands together, but anyway, I still don't find your number, but I get you phoning me up, and that's even better from some points of view, particularly because I ain't made of money and I can't afford to go phoning no foreign countries even for something like this, although I was going to phone you, don't you worry, given the circumstances—"

And she stopped, suddenly, either to take a breath, or to take a sip from the huge mug of too-hot coffee she always carried in her hand, and during the brief quietus Fat Charlie said "I want to ask my dad to come to my wedding. Getting married." There was silence at the end of the line. "It's not till the end of the year, though," he said. Still silence. "Her name's Rosie," he added, helpfully. He was starting to wonder if they had been cut off; conversations with Mrs. Higgler were normally somewhere one-sided affairs, often with her doing your lines for you, and here she was, letting him say three whole things uninterrupted. He decided to go for a fourth. "You can come too if you want," he said.

"Lord, lord, lord," said Mrs. Higgler. "Nobody told you, did they?"

"Told me what?"

So she told him, at length and in detail, while he stood there and said nothing at all, and when she was done he said "Thank you, Mrs. Higgler." He wrote something down on a scrap of paper, then he said "Thanks. No, really, thanks," again, and he put down the phone.

"Well?" asked Rosie. "Have you got his number?"

Fat Charlie said "Dad won't be coming to the wedding." Then he said "I have to go to Florida." His voice was flat, and without emotion. He might have been saying "I have to order a new checkbook."

"When?"

"Tomorrow."

"Why?"

"Funeral. My dad's. He's dead."